In this series:

The Reluctant Fundamentalist, How to be Good, And the Ass Saw the Angel, Then We Came to the End, Americana, Lights Out for the Territory, The Believers, What a Carve Up!, Hawksmoor, Armadillo.

PENGUIN STREET ART

PENGUIN STREET ART

AND THE ASS SAW THE ANGEL

And the Ass Saw the Angel

NICK CAVE

PENGUIN BOOKS

PENGUIN BOOKS

Published by the Penguin Group
Penguin Books Ltd, 80 Strand, London WC2R ORL, England
Penguin Group (USA) Inc., 375 Hudson Street, New York, New York 10014, USA
Penguin Group (Canada), 90 Eglinton Avenue East, Suite 700, Toronto, Ontario, Canada M4P 2Y3
(a division of Pearson Penguin Canada Inc.)
Penguin Ireland, 25 St Stephen's Green, Dublin 2, Ireland (a division of Penguin Books Ltd)
Penguin Group (Australia), 707 Collins Street, Melbourne, Victoria 3008, Australia
(a division of Pearson Australia Group Pty Ltd)
Penguin Books India Pvt Ltd, 11 Community Centre, Panchsheel Park, New Delhi – 110 017, India
Penguin Group (NZ), 67 Apollo Drive, Rosedale, Auckland 0632, New Zealand
(a division of Pearson New Zealand Ltd)
Penguin Books (South Africa) (Pty) Ltd, Block D, Rosebank Office Park,
181 Jan Smuts Avenue, Parktown North, Gauteng 2193, South Africa

Penguin Books Ltd, Registered Offices: 80 Strand, London WC2R ORL, England

www.penguin.com

Original edition first published by Black Spring Press Ltd 1989
Published in Penguin Books 1990
Revised edition published in Penguin Books 2009
Reissued in this edition 2013
001

ISBN: 978-0-241-96479-8

www.greenpenguin.co.uk

ALWAYS LEARNING   **PEARSON**

For Anita

Prologue

Three greasy brother crows wheel, beak to heel, cutting a circle into the bruised and troubled sky, making fast, dark rings through the thicksome bloats of smoke.

For so long the lid of the valley was clear and blue but now, by God, it *roars*. From where ah lie the clouds look prehistorical, belching forth great faceless beasts that curl 'n' die, like that, above.

These sly corbies are birds of death. They've shadowed me all mah life. It's only now that ah can reel them in. With mah eyes.

Sucked by the gums of this toothless grave, ah go – into this fen, this pit, though ah fear to get mah kill-hand wet. In truth and as ah speak, the two crows have staked out mah eyes – like a couple of bad pennies they wheel and wait, while the rolling smoke curls and dies above, and ah see that it turns darker now and ah am but one full quarter unner, or nearly and gaining.

O little valley!

Two shattered knees of land rise and open to make a crease between. Down the bitten inner flank we go, where trees laden with thick vines grow upon the trembling slopes.

Travelling the length of the valley, south to north, as the crow flies, we follow its main road as it weaves its way along the flat of the valley's belly. From up here it could be a ribbon, as we pass over the first of many hundreds of acres of smouldering cane.

Tonight is the first night of the seasonal 'burn-off', an occasion of great importance and high festivity for Ukulore Valley, when the townsfolk all take to the tall fields to watch the wall of fire sweep the cane of its useless foliage, its 'trash'. Yet this night sees all strangely quiet here on the out-fields: wet sacks and snake-beaters carelessly abandoned, sparks and grey ash borne silently through the air on a low wind.

The sugar refinery sprawls out by the east flank, a mile from the town. We can hear the steady chugging of its engines. Trolleys – some empty, some part loaded – sit forgotten on the tracks.

Wing on and past, over the town itself, where the rusty corrugated roofs grow denser and we can see the playground and the Courthouse and Memorial Square.

In the centre of the Square, erected at the very heart of the valley, the marble sepulchre containing the relics of the prophet crumbles and splits beneath the slogging of three down-borne mallets.

A group of black-clad mourners, mostly women, watch on as the monument is destroyed. And see the great marble angel, its face carved in saintly composure, one arm held high, a gilded sickle in its fist; will they bring that down as well?

And on, through the commotion, through the town's stormy heart, where women mourn as at a wake, bullying their grief with breasts bruised black and knuckles bleeding. Watch how they fan the streets with their wild, black gestures, twisting the sackcloth of their robes with pleading seizures and dark spasms.

From up here they look like ground-birds.

Circle once these creatures of grief, and then onward across the stricken town, over the clusters of trailers where the cane-cutters live, at the heel of the rhythm of the crops. Here, at this dark hour, only their women and frightened children remain. Standing at their windows, the ghosts of their breath coming and going on the glass, they listen to the motors of their men roar northward then fade amongst the hiss and crackle of the fields.

Pursue Maine Road till the cane ends abruptly against bare wire fences, four miles from town, two miles from the northern valley entrance.

A lone shack on a junk-heap burns and burns, belching purple smoke into the restless air. Beyond the shack the land grows sodden, and from the marsh rises a wheel of vegetation – tall trees borne into bondage, rising from the cooch and crabbing dog-weed, carrying a canopy of knitted vine upon their wooden shoulders.

Here we dip and dive, for this is the swampland.

As we pass above, we see a line of torches winking beneath the dark canopy, moving inward and toward the centre of the circle.

Torn from the very centre of the swampland is a clearing, round like a plate, and within this clearing, like a wheel within a wheel, is a circle of quickmud, black and steaming, large enough to digest a cow. It glistens darkly at our passing. But stop. Look who lies on the surface of the mud, all curled up like a new-born! See how his bones cleave to his skin. How his ribs fan softly each time he draws breath. See how he is nearly naked. And look how very still he is.

But for that eye.

It rolls in its orbit, and, fish-like, fixes us.

I

It was his brother who tore the caul on that, the morning of their birth, and as if that sole act of assertion was to set an inverted precedent for inertia in his life to come, Euchrid, then unnamed, clutched ahold of his brother's heels and slopped into the world with all the glory of an uninvited guest.

The noon-day sun spun in the sky like a molten bolt and hammered down on the tin roof and tarred plank sides of the shack. Inside sat Pa, at his table, surrounded by his ingenious contraptions of springs and steel, greasing his traps and trying, in vain, to closet his ears from the drunken ravings of his wife, who lay sprawled and caterwauling in the back seat of the old burnt-out Chevy. Pride of the junk-pile, that car, sitting on bricks out back of the shack, like a great shell shed in disgust by some outsized crawler.

There, in the squirms of labour, his bibulous spouse shrieked against the miracle that swelled and kicked inside her as she sucked on a bottle of her own White Jesus, rocking the Chevy on its stilts and moaning and screaming, screaming and a-moaning, 'Pa! Pa-a! Pa-a-a!', until she heard the shack door open and then the shack door shut, whereupon she took leave of the morning and passed into unconsciousness.

'Too pissed to push,' Pa would tell Euchrid later.

Prising the liquor bottle free of her grubby clutch, Pa broke the bottle carefully on the car's rusted tail-fin.

Taking intuition as his midwife and a large shard of glass as his cutter, he spread his prostrate wife-with-child and dowsed her private parts in peel liquor. And with a chain of oaths spilling from his mouth, and with all the summer insects humming, with the sun in the sky and not a cloud in sight, with a hellish shriek and a gush of gleet, two slobbering bundles came tumbling out.

'Jesus! Two!' cried Pa, but one died soon.

Inside the shack, two fruit-crates lined with newspaper sat side by side on the table. The animal traps had been moved and hung around the walls.

Two boxes and in each a babe.

Neither made a sound and both lay quite still upon their backs, naked as the day and with eyes wide and wandering. Pa drew the nibbled stub of a pencil from his trouser pocket and, squinting, leaned toward the little ones, writing on the foot-end of the first-born's crib '#1', then, licking the tip, '#2' upon the crib in which Euchrid lay.

The babes had strange almond eyes, with slightly swollen upper lids and next to no lashes, blue but so pale as almost to verge on pink; intent, eager, never still, not for a moment – rather they seemed to hover, these weird chattering eyes, hover and tremble in their browless sockets.

Little Euchrid coughed, short and sharp, his tiny pink tongue lapping at his lower lip then curling back inside. And, as if waiting for a signal and recognizing it in Euchrid's timid hack, the brave little first-born closed his eyes and fell into a slumber from which he would never wake.

'Goodbye, brother,' ah said to mahself as he slipped away, and for a full minute ah thought that ah too was going unner, so fucken cold was his dying.

Then sailing through the still night came the raucous fray of her bitchship, mah mother, Ma, screeching in hoarse malediction through the very anus of obscenity whilst banging on the side of the Chevy and going, 'Wha-ars mah boddle!'

'Wha-a-ars ma-ah boddle!!'

Pa had fitted two improvised restrainers across mah ankles and chest, forcing me to maintain a horizontal attitude there in mah crate, but, consumed by an overwhelming need to observe what mah brother was up to now that he had launched so impulsively

8

into Eternity, ah endeavoured to raise mah head in the hope of catching a brief craning glimpse of him.

Having been hauled into Life without warning, jettisoned from the boozy curds of gestation – oh that snuggery where we would float and float! – and left now still reeling from the trauma of birth, mah conception of that final Enigma was, as you may well imagine, shamefully uninformed. Ah mean, how could ah have known just how bloody deathlike Death was?

In any case, much as ah thrashed and craned, there was just no give in the restrainers – nope, no give at all, and eventually ah abandoned all hope. Toil-worn and winded, ah just lay there thinking, thinking about mah sainted brother in the fruit-crate beside me, thinking how the hell was he gunna get to Heaven if he was having half the trouble that ah was in slipping his bonds?

But ah had managed to wrench one tiny arm free during that first, great, futile and ultimately portentous struggle – and with one grub-sized knuckle ah knocked out a message, using a system of coded raps, taps and gaps that mah brother and ah had devised while adrift in the purling fremitus of the womb.

Do – Not – Forget – Your – Brother – Reply

But mah brother did not. Ah tapped out a second time, adding a *Please* to the end, but again he did not. *Please*. Undaunted, ah told him what Life was like, and inquired about any special powers he may have developed in Death. Mah signals became urgent and disjointed. The futile raps sounded hollow and lonely as they hung unanswered above mah crate.

Life – Is – Bad – Is – Hell – Can – You – Fly – Hel – Hell – Help

Finally ah took control, and with mah knuckle barked and weeping ah tapped out one last message upon the inside of mah crate.

Night descended – but as ah lay in harness, supine in mah lonesomeness, and watched with increasing dread as the aching light of day grew subfusc and fraught with the freakish music of the darktime – hoots, incessant shrills, scuttles, blood-curdling howls – ah thought that the end of the world had come.

9

The Day of Judgement had arrived and all ah could do was lie there – yes, and ah guess that's precisely what ah did – lie there and let the dead of dark swaller me up, while ah waited for the Ark of His Testament and the lightning and voices, thunderings, earthquakes and great hails.

Slowly mah world was smothered in shrouds of fear and black shadow, and when ah could no longer see anything but the very pitchest murk ah heard ominous footsteps, leaden and uneven, cross the porch and come to a halt outside the door.

Ah cowered in mah crate.

There was a hideous skreek as the screen door swung back, a fumbling with the door catch, a resounding 'Fuck door', an explosion of white light, a door crash-bang-slamming, a terrible belch – and mah mother bowled headlong into the room, lolloped blindly past, and disappeared out the other side.

A single naked bulb hung from the ceiling directly over mah crib. The bulb throbbed hotly, brazen and hypnotic, as ah lay upon mah back and observed, with increasing annoyance, a growing number of night-insects serried around the humming cynosure. Ah watched helplessly as every minute or so an over-zealous moth or gnat or fly would collide with the deathly bulb, frying to ash its little wings and hair-like appendages. Thus its futile business would end in a screaming descent, invariably coming to ground within the fruit-crate in which ah lay. Spinning insectile amputees littered mah crib – died ghastly deaths, their last agonies performed in all their screaming luridness right before mah eyes, to bring them at last to the end of their days, bereft of life.

Ah knew then why mah late lamented brother seemed so subdued. There was no Life left in him.

Then the day returned. An erumpent sun bellowed shouts of buttery light over the eastern flank, waking the entire valley with its aureate noise.

Two crows chortled and cackled in the sky. A wild dog howled somewhere in the hills. Ah could hear the chirruping of hungry chicks. Close by, a mule brayed in despair. Ah heard the idiot twitterings of a lark. Bees hummed earnestly.

All about me the world seemed in need of attention.

Bells rang from the valley's belly. A cane-toad croaked. A fly buzzed. A car horn blared as it plunged down Maine.

All about me the world demanded that it be attended to. It was time all the fledglings and chicklings, weaners and catlings, lambs, piglets and babies were attended to.

Ah was in woeful need of attention. Ah was. Ah was in terrible need of nourishment. Mah body longed for sustenance. How long would ah have to wait? Do you know? Did ah tell you that ah was *very fucking hungry*?

Ah had contemplated eating one or two of the fried insects that sprawled across mah stomach.

Rather ah decided to make a bit of a ruckus – stir the attention of mah custodians in the manner of all hungry neglected children. So ah filled mah lungs with air and howled and howled and screamed and raged and gnashed and yelled out things like '*Feed me!*' and '*Food!*' and '*Tit!*' and all the while ah thrashed and kicked beneath mah ungiving restrainers, so ingeniously devised by Pa – a veritable master of the trap – that each kick and thrash of mah infantile body served only to draw the bonds that little bit tighter, frustrating mah movements all the more, so that within the space of a minute mah little fracas was restricted to a bit of buttock clenching, some pretty ferocious rolling of the eyes, lolling of the tongue, and, of course, mah embranglement of words – O how they rolled off mah tongue – O how they gushed from mah mouth – great bloody words torn from the very pit of mah belly – '*Feed me!*' '*O Death! Must ah starve?*' and '*Fucking feed me now!*' – and, you know – ah mean, *do you know what?* – in spite of all mah whoop and holler – all mah howling and yowling – all mah bull-like bawling and shit-storming and caterwauling, all – in spite of it *all* – do you know *what*?

Not a peep of sound did ah make – not from mah crate, not from mah cot.

No, not a peep of sound did ah make.

Ah felt bewildered by mah discovery. Cheated. Duped.

Ah felt lonely.

With mah one free hand ah tore at the newspaper that lined the walls of mah crate. Rolling it into small balls, ah sucked the paper to a soft pap and swallered it.

In time ah managed to sate mah hunger with that frugal supper and, belly full, ah yawned deeply and turned mah thoughts again to mah brother, who lay in the buzzing crate beside me. And yawning again, more deeply this time, ah closed mah eyes, wondering as ah fell away – was mah brother a mute too?

'Guess ah'll never really know for sure,' ah remember thinking, as sleep wound itself about me, 'ah guess ah'll never really know.'

Ah dreamed mah brother and ah were united in Heaven, incumbent on warm cotton clouds. He stroked his golden harp and a shower of silvery tones broke over mah body. We smiled.

Mah brother stopped playing and rose into the air. His wings were black and veinous and oozed a viscid phlegm. He rubbed two hairy legs and put the harp which was now a crown upon his head. Ah tried to fly but ah had no wings yet, just a white hairless wigging maggot's body – helpless on mah back – on mah back. Mah brother pointed at me and shouted *'Pirate!! Leave me!! Leave me!! Leave me-e-e!!!'* Then ah saw that Heaven had turned red and soupy and ah was floating slow and turning and all the time a double beat sounded *'Boom-boom . . . Boom-boom . . . Boom-boom . . . Boom-boom . . .'* like a heart.

Ah awoke.

Mah father loomed over me like a crooked stick. From out of his grizzled face two small, pale eyes hovered in their sockets.

So Pa sat, a bowl and a loaf in his hands.

Ah sucked a piece of milk-sopped bread that was offered to me and it was warm and sweet.

Pa's fingers smelt of pitch or grease.

Mah hunger quelled, ah closed mah mouth and turned mah head. No longer could ah tolerate the acrid chemical smell.

Pa stood.

His stool was a fruit-crate turned on its end!

Ah sought mah brother. Mah brother was gone! So was the crate! Beside me in its place was a metal animal trap, coated in black grease. Jaws yawning! Spring coiled! Teeth howling for blood!

Ah looked away, mah brains bloody.

Pa was walking to the door. Over his left shoulder was a long-handled spade. It was then that ah noticed the grizzled nob, the tufted cleft. His missing ear.

In his hands he held a shoebox bound in string. On its lid was written '#I'.

II

THE PROPHET
The voice of the Valley No. 38 Aug. 1932
!!Harken ye CHILDREN OF THE LORD!!
The SECOND FRIDAY of AUGUST in the year of our Lord 1932
marks the 70th YEAR of the
'MARTYRDOM OF THE PROPHET AND SAINT,
JONAS UKULORE.'
On the afternoon of the anniversary of this most blessed and
bloody day
our valley will mourn her Prophet and Patriarch,
JONAS UKULORE.
His earthly remains and his relics will be taken from their current
resting place in UKULORE VALLEY TABERNACLE
and enshrined within the town square which
from this day forth will be known as MEMORIAL SQUARE.
To mark this most holy day,
a monument befitting THE PROPHET
will be unveiled.
Faithful Ukulites
at 3.00 pm on this day, Friday, 12th August 1932,
the Children of Israel, ye Faithful Ukulites!
shall march from the Tabernacle on to Memorial Square,
where the body of the Prophet and Martyr will be laid
to rest for all time.
Prayers conducted by **Sardus Swift**.
Simon Bolsom, historian and biographer,
will read from his forthcoming biography
Jonas Ukulore: Prophet and Revelator, Man and Martyr
in the **Big Hall**.
Eliza Snow shall sing, accompanied by **Alice Pritchard**.
Supper will be held after the service in the **Little Hall**.
No plates necessary, ladies. Catering handled by **Valley Functions**.
– ALL SHALL ATTEND –

The monument was shrouded in a massive canvas tarp, with a rope threaded through brass eye-holes girding it at its foot. The tarp cover made it look like a great, grey Sphinx, eroded by the sands of time into faceless obscurity.

A huge truck had rolled into town the previous morning, with the monument standing draped and grey there in the back, looking just as it did now. Sardus Swift, who had left the valley at five o'clock that morning and taken a cane-trolley to Davenport and a train up to Orkney, insisted he ride with the contractors the 380-odd miles back to the valley 'in case of complications'.

Both of the memorial contractors, a fat Mr Godbelly and a fatter Mr Pry, looked exhausted but jolly. It had taken a dozen men to swing the monument, lowered by chain from the truck, into its allotted position in the Square.

Even some of the cane-men had lent a hand, though those not strictly of the faith were forbidden to participate in the celebration of what was, for the Ukulites, a Holy Day: the day commemorating 'The Martyrdom of the Prophet'. The valley's residents tolerated and had tolerated for many years the unorthodox practices of the Ukulites, who, though they comprised no more than one fifth of the valley's two thousand or so denizens, owned the refinery, most of the cane acreage, and the vast majority of the business and residential space. This, of course, was the chief reason why the small sectarian colony was suffered to operate in (and in fact control) the valley; but it was a precarious ascendancy, and the Ukulites had borne their share of adversity in the ongoing battle to retain their enviable, but not unassailable, position.

Since the time when, in the last days of winter 1862, Jonas Ukulore had led his small band of adherents into what was then an unfarmed, virtually uninhabited valley, the Ukulites had fought for, defended, and embraced their beliefs with uncompromising rigour. It was this steadfast adherence to a strict dogma, set down in a testament written by their prophet in 1861, coupled with the keen and aggressive business methods employed by Joseph Ukulore, brother of Jonas, which had assured the

Ukulite colony its longevity. Indeed, if Jonas was the prophet, Joseph was the profiteer.

It was in 1859 that Jonas Ukulore, a Welsh convert to the Baptist faith, began to have revelations, and in due course he had announced to the Baptist authorities his revelation that he was the 'Seventh Angel' predicted in the Book of Daniel, and that destiny would see him as 'a mighty man, yea a prophet in Israel'.

The following year Jonas and a few of his followers were excommunicated by the Church authorities, his revelations having begun to conflict with orthodox dogma.

On two occasions he had narrowly escaped death at the hands of orthodox vigilante committees, and observing the growing hostility toward all Baptists and other sectarian bodies Jonas and his band of adherents fled the trouble in search of a suitable spot to establish 'the new Fold'. Finding the secluded valley in 'a state of divine pendency', the group pooled all possessions and set up residence.

The Prophet spent much of his time in secluded prayer, as he prepared himself for 'the second coming', which had been revealed to him in one of his three hundred or so revelations, all of which he documented meticulously. Meanwhile his brother Joseph, former agriculturist and business man, took control of the valley's monetary interests and planted sugar-cane.

The cane flourished in the humid valley; soon the excess bulk of each crop was being sold, at a healthy profit, to the Davenport Mills.

The valley flourished. The crops burgeoned. The profits rose. It seemed that God had indeed been a generous overseer to the valley's growth, and the colony's future prosperity seemed secure.

Early in August 1872 the Prophet, wearing a white robe and golden crown and holding a gilded sceptre, announced to his disciples that 'the hour was nigh' – the second coming was at hand and all must prepare for the imminent crusade out of the valley.

One week later, as fifty or so men and women marched behind their white-garbed leader, shouting hosannas and singing his praises, Jonas Ukulore was shot through the head by an unknown sniper, the single bullet killing him instantly. The assassin was never discovered, but was naturally assumed to have come from the outside. Taking this as yet further evidence of the treachery of the Gentiles beyond, the Ukulites abandoned their projected crusade and remained inside the valley; and as this course brought rich rewards, they came in time to read into the tragedy a dramatic justification of their faith.

Under the guidance of the ever resourceful Joseph Ukulore the valley continued to prosper, the townsfolk eventually building trolley-rails to Davenport and little by little recruiting 'outsiders' to work the cane-fields.

In the year 1904 Joseph undertook the gargantuan task of organizing the building of the sugar refinery, fully aware that at the age of eighty-three he would not live to see its completion, let alone to share in the overwhelming rewards that his industry would certainly bring. The following year, the foundations of the refinery having only just been laid, Joseph Ukulore died, leaving the valley a legacy of ensured future prosperity.

From *Vargus, A Regional History* (Vargustone Municipal Offices, 1922)

And so it was that on this day the Ukulites mourned their prophet.

> 'Hail the Prophet, ascended to Heaven
> Traitors and tyrants now fight him in vain
> With God he's on high, watching over his brethren
> Death cannot conquer the hero again'

sang Eliza Snow.

And Sardus Swift pulled back the tarp.

III

Ah never cried as a baby. That is to say, throughout mah baby-hood never once did ah cry – no, not a peep. Nor did ah bawl away mah childhood either, and during mah youthhood ah resolved to contain all mah emotions within and never to allow one sob without – for to do otherwise surely laid one open to all manner of abuse. And now, as ah count away the final seconds of mah manhood – as ah don the death-hood – ah will not crack. No. In all mah lifehood ah have never once cried. Not out loud.

And as a tottering infant ah always tried mah best to stay out from unner Mummy's feet. Ah did. Nor did ah pester mah father when he was working – asking him a whole lot of dumb questions that he couldn't answer.

Yes, when all is said and done, no matter which way you view it, ah was, by anybody's standards, a model child.

Ah was also the loneliest baby boy in the history of the whole world. And that's no idle speculation. It's a fact. God told me so.

Mummy was a swine: a scum-cunted, likkered-up, brain-sick swine. She was lazy and slothful and dirty and belligerent and altogether evil. Ma was a soak – a drunk – a piss-eyed hell-bag with a taste for the homebrew.

Ma's drunks worked in cycles, consciousness following uncon-sciousness like two enormous hogs each eating the other's tail – one black, fat and unbelievably obscene, the other hoary, loud, with two crimson eyes, mean and small and close together – and these cycles she rigorously adhered to.

When Ma was conscious our little shack on the hill would cringe in horror at the prospect of the inevitable frenzy of destruction – usually occurring on the fourth day – which would immediately precede her term of unconsciousness.

Once awake, Ma would make increasingly frequent and

protracted visits to her stone bottle – the vessel that she always drank her likker from – until she was off and sailing, stumbling around the shack or the junk-pile, or sprawled out in her armchair, the stone bottle clutched to her vast bosom. Here she would rant and swaller and rave, recalling the days of her youth, before she had been sullied by the squalid hands of booze and men. And days would become nights and nights, days.

Then, having put away enough of her rotgut to floor an army, she would – and it gives me the screaming leaks just to think of it – she would – this very fucking sick, sick bitch – would begin to sing a version of 'Ten Green Bottles' in an increasingly furious bark. When she reached the part that goes '. . . and if one green bottle should accidentally fall, there'd be *no* green bottles . . .', she would simply run amok – yes, launch into a fit of such unbridled violence that it simply wasn't safe to be within bat-swinging range of her.

As soon as he heard the opening strains of 'Ten Green Bottles', Pa would drop whatever it was that he was doing and belt out the screen door, me toddling after him. Ah would seek refuge in an overturned pickle-barrel out back of the shack. It was such a secure feeling to be crouched in there with mah knees up against mah chest, the smell of vinegar still trapped in the wood, the cosiness of its size – you know, sometimes ah would crawl into that barrel just to feel safe for a while. In the barrel ah heard some very strange, garbled things – not from without but from within.

To this day ah am struck with wonder as to just how ah managed to stay alive through mah crate-bound days. For to say ah was a bashed baby would be more than a little correct – *it would be absolutely correct! Yes! Ah was one very fucking bashed baby!*

IV

In early 1940 a meeting was held in the Town Hall at which two bodies were required to convene: Ukulore Valley Sugar Board and the Ukulite leaders.

The authorities representing the cane-workers and their families had lodged a request proposing, amongst other things, that a Unitarian house of worship be built to cater to the needs of valley residents not of the Ukulite faith, pointing out that of the valley's population of approximately 2,100 a full eighty per cent were being denied spiritual gratification. Therefore it was suggested that in the interests of 'equity' and 'inter-relation' and as 'a gesture of continued concord' between the two factions, the meeting parties would, without question, find to accept the proposal. Though a foregone conclusion, the outcome had nevertheless been a triumph for the workers.

Sardus Swift, knowing full well that his hand was being forced, had agreed to the proposal and, in a gesture as inescapable as it was magnanimous, had then added that 'in accordance with my belief that a prosperous spirit is always manifest in the spirit of prosperity, and as leader of the Ukulite colony and representative of the landowners, I hereby accept the responsibility of allocating a suitable plot of land, and in addition, I personally will meet all construction costs.'

The Sugar Board (or UVSB) offered to take charge of arrangements for the erection, making mention of the fact that several building contractors in Vargustone were currently subject to their inspection. It duly requisitioned, for a fraction of the costs it had quoted to the penny-wise but pound-foolish Ukulites, the services of an infamous building firm which had been forced by a string of law suits coupled with a succession of lashings from the local press to change its promotional slant from 'creative architecture' to 'cut-price contracting'.

In late 1937, on a four-acre rise (which became known, ironically, as Glory Flats), the Vargus building contractors and a handful of labourers laid the foundations of what, they promised, was destined to be a heaven-bound leap in the history of the systemization of worship.

But heaven-bound the church on Glory Flats was not. Destiny would not allow herself to be so readily predicted.

For the church on Glory Flats would never be completed and the years of misadventure drew closer.

Sardus Swift had emerged from the Town Hall weary and taciturn, besieged by feelings of guilt and disgust at his own impotence; for he had known as surely as if there had been a war that he was surrendering his kingdom to the conquerors. And though his people received his announcement in silence and not a man or woman amongst them reviled or even blamed him, Sardus knew that he had betrayed his God, his prophet and his people, and that only an act of contrition could stifle the shame which he felt at having surrendered up, in a moment of unpardonable negligence, the Promised Land to the first idolatrous creed that had had half an urge to stake a claim.

V

A few words concerning Euchrid's ancestral stock. Euchrid's father Ezra was born in 1890 in the thick hills of Black Morton Range, a notorious yet largely uncharted region of densely vegetated hollows and hills.

A perilous dirt road winds about the region's eastern extremity. At the turn of the century this twisted trail had earned a certain infamy, due to the unexplained disappearance of some twenty-odd travellers who had sought to cross the range in quest of the promised prosperity that lay for the taking in the East.

Investigation into the disappearance of the Black Range travellers (the 'Morton' was added to the name officially in 1902) led to the discovery and subsequent disposal of one Toad Morton, or, as the press-gang tagged him, Black Morton. A low-minded, wart-worried giant, Toad had been driven from the Morton clan by his own kin, after they had found the family hog dead in its pen, covered in flies and human teeth marks – its back leg had been bitten clean off. Finding Toad covered in pig-shit and sucking a trotter, they had chased him out of the Mortons' valley to roam the gullies and gulches of the out-hills, a sore Goliath shunned by his own blood, without friend or companion save the league of demons that rubbed and itched amongst the crags and sunless cracks of his bad, mad and unholy brain.

Crouched in ambush on that tricky eastern road, Toad plucked at his pleasure lone-riders befitting his own infernal usage.

Found in a small stone cave bitten from the roadside, stitchless save for his great outsized boots and a plague of flies, fat on the human scrappage of dinners long past, Toad squatted in the slitted stomach of a warm child, eating loudly the face of her hapless, headless father, who sat a good foot off the ground impaled up the ass on a pointed post.

Looking up at the search-party silhouetted in the glare at the mouth of the cave, the great lonely oversized Toad said, gesturing at the carnage, 'Brothers, ah am found! You have come to bring me home! Pull up thy stool!' Then a hot tear broke upon each cheek and he smiled warmly up at them, his green teeth filed to wicked points.

The search-party had ridden up from Salem led by Deputy Sheriff Cogburne, who shot Toad Morton like a dog on the spot.

On the road running the eastern extremity of Black Morton Range is a large stone slab upon which is written in white paint:

BEWARE! MORTON'S MURDER MILE
O world-weery Pilgryms, unburden thy lode
Nowither a Doome mor horrid I know
Than that wich awaits Thee down bluddy roade
Prey! Bewar ol Black Morton. The murdress Toad!

Toad Morton was the eldest in a family of fifteen. Then there was Luther. Then there was Er. Nun came next, named after his father, and in the same year Gad was born. Ezra was soon to follow. Then came the three little girls: Lee, Mary Lee, and Mary. Then Ezekiel. Blind Dan. Little Fan, who died aged three and a half. Angel, who had three children of her own by the age of fourteen. Next came Batho, followed by Ben, who was quick to die.

So Euchrid's father, Ezra, was sixth in what seemed to be an endless stream of puling, snot-nosed offspring. He changed his name from Morton to Eucrow in 1925 after fleeing the merciless bounty-squads that terrorized the hills as part of Sheriff Cogburne's infamous clean-up campaign.

Since his early teens Ezra had suffered beneath the yoke of his kinfolk's incestuous practices. His family tree was as twisted and tangled as the briars that tortured the hills. Eye-blinding headaches, catatonia, seizures, trances and frequent outbursts of violence were the order of the day. Whether or not this was due to the consanguineous union of his ancestors, he knew not.

The question of heredity weighed heavily upon the God-fearing Ezra, who was capable of reciting great slabs of scripture by heart – the Bible being the only book his mother would allow inside the house, and Ezra being the only member of her brood that she had successfully taught to read. Yet, if Ezra was burdened with bad blood, his burden remained hidden.

Back then, ol Ma Morton had the run of things. The eldest two, Luther and Er, could still be controlled and wore the welts of correction to prove it. Ma ruled the brood as mercifully as Moses, pacing back and forth across the porch in her boots, the wicked nettle scourge in one hand, the jar of red pepper in the other, pacing and sometimes stopping, then hollering into the bush, 'Lu-u-ther!' or 'E-e-e-er!' . . . back then, before the Applejack, before the shotgun, before the bloody Morton Range Round-Ups.

Crazed with the effects of mountain liquor and pilfered petrol sniffed from jam tins, the older brothers, Luther and Er, were reduced to drooling lunatics. Nagged by toothache, hill-pox and the mad itch of scabies – the epizoon that would hound the Morton family to its various lousy graves – they would howl in duet like dying dogs. Plunging from utter despondency into displays of the most heinous violence, the brothers would seek relief from their discomfiture by brutalizing their dull and drivelling sisters, raping them at gunpoint into mulish motherhood.

The day before Sheriff Cogburne and twenty men rounded up the whole Morton clan, Luther and Er beat each other to death in a fist-fight. That day Ezra slipped from the house, taking the mule, the Bible, Er's shotgun and a pocketful of cartridges, feeling in his bones that catastrophe was close at hand.

Having milked a full quart of liquor from the still, he stole into the tall timbers and, with the mule in tow, gun resting over his shoulder, he descended into the valley.

The year was 1925.

And Ezra, son of Nun, went down into the valley and a cloud descended over the valley.

And for six nights and six days Ezra made his headlong way and for the first day he kept to his left side the sun that he might surely be making distance away from his home, for the valleys grew thickly.

And Ezra knew not that to which his flight would bring him.

And on the first night of the first day Ezra slugged long on his bottle and felt the taste of mountain madness for the first time, yea, and passed along a river-bed that was dry and rock-full.

And he knew not its name and still he had the gun over his left shoulder like a black bone.

He took for his resting place a high smooth stone and drank of his bottle till it was empty and laughing he threw the bottle over and it broke and the noise it made seemed to pierce in his ears and rush with a cold rod of sound and he saw the stones were white and there were many skulls beneath the moon that rose to his rear and sat upon the tip of black bone by his cold rushing ear and smooth for he spun in roaring white skulls and fell backward upon the footstones and hid the ear within the greatest blood-blown bang and smoking bone in a bed of blood-speck he got up and laughing for his ear he fell across his mule which bore Ezra away and stitched the hills with drips of blood.

'Swall this,' said the widow.

Ezra woke and gagged on White Jesus.

He convulsed and retched, lurching his upper body over the side of the bed, and disgorged a ribbon of mustard bile on to the foot-worn sod. He hung there, half on, half off the bed, letting the prickling blood rush to his head.

A blind bolt of pain hammered into his left ear. He groaned and pulled himself up and flopped on to his back again, his eyes screwed up and him spiralling down and down and down.

'Swall.'

Again Ezra's gullet filled with the foul White Jesus and he roared and again spat his stomach on to the sod.

He lay in the bed of the widow they called Crow Jane. In her shack. In Ukulore Valley. On the outer reaches of Ukulore town. And Ezra saw her and wondered.

'Ya ear shot off. Ya mule is hitched,' said the widow. 'Ah waited twelve years but ah knew ya'd come on back.'

Ezra fell into a sleep and dreamed he stood at the bow of a great ark that was shaped like an ear, and that he took a crow and sent it out across the water that stretched to every horizon and that on the sixth day the crow returned and in its beak was a black bone.

And that's how Ezra, Euchrid's father, came to Ukulore Valley, and that's how he met Euchrid's mother, and he lived there, tucked beneath the sour and flabby wing of his spouse, till they were both dead.

Euchrid's mother was almost thirty when Ezra's mule, soaked in the blood of his earless and delirious master, entered the yard of the little clap-and-tar shack. Though the woman had not been seen in the township since the day of her marriage in the winter of 1913, the memory of her was still firmly locked in the stocks of public ridicule. The cane-men had given her the cognomen 'Crow Jane', taken from a song that old Noah, the coloured barber, would sing in his low rich voice as he clipped and shaved and swept in his little shop on Maine.

Jane Crowley was infamous in Ukulore Valley on account of the fact that her day of matrimony in the winter of 1913 had provided the valley with its one and only shotgun wedding. A virago through and through even then, at the age of seventeen she had accused – in a torrent of tears and flump-footed tantrums – a dim-witted and wholly innocent cane-worker named Ecker Abelon of having taken advantage of her on the understanding that they would marry within the month. All was done in alliance with her unruly kin, who went so far as to denounce the fornicator and publicly demand that he make good the family name of Crowley which he had so readily sullied.

In the sight of God and under the unblinking eye of a Winchester rifle, Ecker had delivered the sacred pledge and tied the nuptial knot till death do they part.

Two weeks later, Ecker crossed the valley to the cabin of his new-found kin on the pretext of borrowing Old Man Crowley's notorious shotgun, saying simply, 'Cats are breedin fastern ah can hit em with a bat.' And with a slap on the back from his father-in-law, Ecker Abelon walked into one of the south fields and pulling both triggers blew his face away.

Old man Crowley solved the mystery of the body in the field when he recognized the Winchester as his own. Buried in the graveyard at the foot of Hooper's Hill, box and marker courtesy of the Workers' Fund, Ecker slipped the nuptial knot for ever.

Though Ecker lay dead in the ground, no member of the community had been willing to shoulder the responsibility of informing the wife of the deceased.

Crow Jane took to sitting on the front porch day after day, awaiting the arrival of her new spouse, passing the long hours slugging liberally from an unlabelled bottle containing one of her home-brewed liquors, which she made and bottled out behind the junk-pile under the old disused water tower. Though it was barely drinkable, even to the most seasoned sot, Crow Jane managed nevertheless to palm off the occasional pint to one of the hobos that haunted the outer regions of the valley or to a pick-up full of drunken cane-cutters who were too shit-faced to care about such minor hurdles along the road of intemperance as drinkability.

Casually, the widow would ask each visitor: 'Have ye spied Ecker Crowley today?' and the men would shuffle and reel as she tapped off a pint and awaited their answer. 'No mam, not this day,' each would reply from behind a trembling hand, 'Not today, mam.' And as they clambered back on to the pick-up and roared off toward Maine they would burst into fits of laughter, rolling around the back and knocking back slog upon gagging slog of the widow's gut-rot.

For twelve years Jane awaited the return of her husband, drinking herself day upon night into madness.

The image of her truant partner began, in time, to fade into obscurity, becoming eventually a vague and abstract notion that hung like a shroud over the ever increasing be-shitment of her rationale.

So when the mule carried Ezra – earless by one and in a state of acute delirium, a river of dried blood caking the mule's belly and hind legs – into the widow's yard, the vagaries and obscurities of the past decade began to solidify once more, and, as if hearing a great golden bell tolling in the stillest of nights, she knew her man had found her.

Ma Crow has three stills. These are the brews: White Jesus, Apple Jack, Stew. The hobos call White Jesus – which she makes from potato peelings – White Lightning, but the cane-men call it Ecker's Tears. Ma Crow's choice is White Jesus. The Apple Jack is Jack to the hobos, Widow's Piss or Widow Water to the cane-men. Apple Jack is the most popular brew as it is nearly drinkable. Unlike White Jesus, Apple Jack will solidify when frozen. The hobos call Stew Stew mostly, though some of the older ones mix it up with Ma Crow's choice and call it wrongly Stewed Jesus. The cane-men call it Stiff, Piss, Swill, Bilge, Shit, and it is made from any fermentable scraps. This brew is often touch and go and is sold cheaper than the rest.

VI

Ah want to explain about Pa and his traps. He collected metal scraps from the junk-heap – pieces of car body, hub-caps and bumper bars, wires and metal brackets, springs and coils, rusty nails, paint tins, petrol canisters, steel cylinders, copper piping, lead piping, nuts and bolts, old pans, cutlery, metal panels, steel barrels, chains and ball-bearings – and by subjecting them to bulk-cutters, metal-shears, files, pliers, tin-snips, fire and icy water, hammer and anvil and lead-headed mallets, he would heat and bend and bash them into monstrous shapes or file and shave them to sinister points, weld and wire tin teeth and fangs of shaved nails into heavy black jaws, cut and moulded from hardened plates of steel or bits of track or bumper bars weighted with bolts and rocks. Then he'd also fashion a spring, a catch, a lock and a trigger. Coating the whole contraption in a black, acrid grease that glistened darkly on the cruel and ragged teeth, he would wrench the slippery jaws apart and lock in the catch so that the greasy fangs yawned wide, grinning and salivating with skunk-oil in an obscene leer that begged to be fed.

Pa would then trigger the trap with a piece of broom-handle, and watch as the black jaws crunched the wood in a splintering fracture.

There was no single design. Or, rather, if there was – that is to say if there was a single homogeneous trait – it lay in the fact that they were all unnecessarily cruel and all cruelly ingenious. Even the small traps, the ones for rats and scorpions, were ferocious in design.

A characteristic, certainly, of all the traps was that they were built to detain and to maim but not to kill. Pa had no use for dead animals.

Each morning Pa would load Mule with as many of the

29

chattering black traps as the beast could carry and, having decided beforehand where he would set them, click his tongue against his palate and mumble, 'Gitch, Mule,' as he led the beast away.

Set, the traps would all cry like babies.

By the time they returned home from checking the traps, with the sun just falling behind the hills, Mule would invariably be loaded with six or seven hessian sacks, some of which squirmed and whipped and kicked, some of which growled and hissed. Pa would hitch the mule to one of the stilts that supported the old disused water-tank and then begin to climb the rickety ladder, carrying one by one the squirming sacks and emptying them into the tank that sat on the wooden platform at the very top. When all the sacks were emptied, having first checked that the chicken-wire top was secure, he would climb on to a high stool which he had erected on the platform and gaze over the side of the tank.

Like some mad imperator Pa would perch on the edge of his rickety throne, twenny feet in the air, and, peering into the rusty arena, gloat upon the massacre within.

But, if one were a looker like me, one could see his hard little hands screwed white into fists, resting on the rim of the corrugated tank, and a tortured vein worming across his forehead, his keen little eyes bugged and popping and fluttering from side to side.

VII

Her name was Cosey Mo.

She stood upon the threshold of the caravan doorway, slumped slightly.

She was twenty-six.

Dressed in a faded pink slip she shimmered, pinkly and damply glistening, and yonder a dragonfly alighted on Euchrid's knee.

Her toenails, painted thick with countless coats of red lacquer, were badly chipped. Her thin white arms hung limply by her sides, swinging slightly as she rocked upon her heels.

Sitting at her feet, on one of the caravan steps, was an open vanity box. In it, on a bed of coloured cotton-balls, stood four minikin vials of Prussian-blue glass, each one containing a measure of scented water.

Euchrid was deathly still, breathing low and long the lavender air as Cosey pulled the crystal stopper from one of the vials and splashed her cheeks with the essence. She dabbed at her nape with a yellow cotton-ball.

The skin of her arms was faultless, save for where she stuck in needles to wilt those brittle bones and make her limbs hang weakly, to make her heavenly body rock, to and fro, inside her shivering silk skin. Her thin garment strained against all the languid life contained within.

There were ten pearl buttons down her front. Two at the top and two at the bottom were undone. Her hem flapped with each summer gust and her breathing was deep and deeply rose her breasts.

Her hair was long and yellow and worn loosely back, held with a bunch of coloured pins, and her upper lids hung heavy and her slack mouth moved around the words to some half-remembered song:

31

'I'll fear not the darkness
When my flame shall dim . . .'

As the sun slowly sank, a snatch or two of her song floated behind the bush and reached Euchrid, and he listened to the music of her breathing, caught back in little gasps, all to the rhythm of her sultry rocking.

Then, with a little push of her body, she moved down the steps and, hand shading her eyes, looked down the hillside road. Pursued by a coil of dust a pick-up roared up the slope toward her. Euchrid leaned back. His heart groaned.

Cosey Mo spun around on her heels and darted back into the caravan.

Euchrid watched the open doorway as the motor grew louder.

Positioned back in the doorway, Cosey resumed her rocking, like before, only this time a little firmer, a little more deliberate, heel to toe, heel to toe, and Euchrid, frozen by her pulchritude, observed with the finnicky eye of the voyeur that there were three buttons undone up top.

He saw her mouth. Messy now, with a thick red slick of lipstick.

'You will be ever there beside me . . .'

Euchrid slipped off, back down the way he had come, crouching behind a stump as the pick-up hurtled past him.

VIII

The whole town, especially the Ukulites, considered the swampland to be an abomination. No one ever went there. Ah cannot, in all honesty, state the exact age ah was when ah first entered the swampland. What's more ah cannot pinpoint any one day and say – this day was the day on which ah first ventured into the swampland. No, ah can't.

But me, well, ah was drawn to this grim and murky place where ordinary souls would not dare to venture: where the mist lifts off the compost that lines the floor and hangs amongst the woven ceiling of vine and branch like an artificial sky – where the tall, thin trees all seem to bend toward me in attitudes of worship – where a million lumping shadows collide and circle, collide and circle, trunk to scrub – all, in secret, shifting through dim manoeuvres betrayed by jets of nostril steam. At the time it seemed to me – being little more than a decade old – that ah had spent a lifetime in this place, that ah had always walked upon sodden uncertain ground, breathed heavy air and pushed mah bare hand into the crawling hearts of a thousand rotten stumps, that ah had always worn a black web for a veil. So the urge to slip across the marsh flats that separated the circle of swampland from the shack where ah lived seemed natural enough. Not that ah bounded in! O no! Not bounded in!

The first few times ah believe ah only ventured a number of yards inside the damp spissitude of the swampland. Ah found the heavy scented air exhausting and confounding and it spooked me a little that mah nervous footfall faltered on the strange layered substratum of mushed leaf and soft, wet wood.

Skeleton-webs like sticky shrouds clung to mah skin.

Marsh-toads as big as fists swelled and croaked lowly in the gloom. The air hung upon me like an unwanted skin. Mah head swam and mah boots filled.

Yet ah returned to this forbidden place again and again, each sojourn finding me a little deeper within its warm wet heart.

And just as the swampland became, day by day, mah sanctuary and mah comfort, so too the angel did ease herself into mah world.

First there was just a whispered word. Then a flutter overhead. A day or two later, mah name was uttered, sounding strange to me – unrecognizable – for no one had ever called me by mah name. Next, a flapping shape, darting up amongst the trees, stirred the fog a fraction.

Then, the wing and the silver floating feather – time by time, bit by bit – until at last ah sat upon a slimy log in a tiny clearing, the drugged air draining mah body, mah head in mah hands and mah eyes weary and sore; and ah perceived the air to fan slightly as if it were being beaten gently and ah lifted up mah head, ah think, and the breeze that she stirred was cool and of a heavenly hue.

From the soft forbidden movements of this umbrage she came, only for a moment – a moment too brief – thief of mah heart.

Immersed in a cobalt light, she hovered before me. And this visitation, she spoke sweetly to me. She did. 'I love you, Euchrid,' she said. 'Fear not, for I am delivered unto you as your keeper.'

And ah sat back down on the slimy log in the tiny clearing and put mah head back in mah hands feeling weary, aching, drugged. Looking up again, ah saw the clearing was like it had been before – dark and murky – and what looked like a falling knife, spinning down from above, came toward mah heart. A silver feather pierced the damp fabric of mah shirt.

BOOK ONE

THE RAIN

I

Harvest time in the year of 1941 and the sun ached in the sky and all around me the swollen air throbbed, holding me warmly as ah, in turn, damply warmed unto it, our sullen summer pulses humming as one.

Sitting on the porch steps with mah elbows propped on mah knees and mah chin resting in the palms of mah hands, ah let mah eyelids go lazy as the heat doped me like a drug.

Ah lobbed a bead of spittle over the crackling nettles that twisted up between the steps and watched the frothy pearl land in the dust and roll an inch or so, collecting a fine russet skin upon its outer surface, leaving in its wake a tiny furrow.

The red bead blocked the path of a bull ant which nudged at the boulder and, unable to budge it, spun in an angry circle and charged past it, feelers groping wildly. On its back it freighted a crumb. Weaving a little, the intrepid ant mounted its hill, and no sooner had it disappeared down the hole at the hill's crest than ah noticed a second bull ant, shouldering yet another crumb and similarly in a mad scramble to get to its nest. With increasing concern ah watched its progress across the block of shadow cast by the lower step, as it too hiked the face of the anthill, drumming the air wildly with its antennae in the same spastic flurry as its brother.

Ah yawned, rubbed mah face and looked again. Mah eyes had become accustomed to the crafty camouflage of these creatures, red as the earth upon which they scrambled, betrayed only by the bright speck of their burden. Ah saw that the hot dust swarmed with ants carrying a cargo of crumbs, in frantic flight, jockeying their way to the tip of the hill and piling into the hole that led to the mother-nest. The air was haywire with their giddy radar.

37

Ah know ants. Ah know them well. Well enough, that is, to know that something was gravely amiss – for in all mah years of studying ants ah have never known them to begin hoarding food so early in the summer months, never!

Hoping mah footfall would spare the majority of mah wise and busy friends, ah leaped across the anthill and bolted into the yard. Ah looked toward the ancient dead tree that stood at the foot of the booming crop, its two arms raised heavenward.

In the numb gesture of this ever-dead, a pair of pinguid crows hopped, foot to foot, along one pleading limb, like two conspiring nuns, cackling and pecking and squawking at the foot of the murmurous crop. Like the ants, the rogue crows seemed unquiet, fidgeting and flapping blackly up there in the arms of that hollow gallows-tree. Ah watched the birds take wing at last and, cawing a rude warning across the valley, circle up and over the west versant to disappear behind the valley ridge.

The air had turned tactile and tinted red – it stuffed the valley thickly and there was an electricness about it that crackled inside mah head like paper. It kinda oozed – this air – oozed into mah lungs, soupy and reeking of evilness. And ah could see it – ah could see it rolling across every crag and crack, every knurl and knoll, every ridge, each ditch, every hill and hole, through groves of cottonwoods, each knotted chine, the knitted boles of the killing vine, each impressed dent and darksome hollow, over glen, gully, gulch, gorge, gill, glade, gallow – *even this very fen*, and ah expect this bog – yes, this suck, this darkling quag. There in the very blood of the air ah could sense the most hell-born forecast, hear the murky rhymes beneath its breath-bombinations, hexes and muttered spells – hear the beat of its breath – the first tremors, distant and faint, but coming, coming – feel its plodding pulse, now fuller still, its pounding! This special evil – Coming! Drumming! – and this special air tensed to receive it.

From the backyard came the freakish bray of Mule, joining the driving drums of air, rising now with every quaking count, so that together air and mule raged horribly.

Keeping close to the wall, ah bolted down the side of the shack. Always suspicious of commotion, ah rolled one quick eye around the corner, just in case Pa was reprimanding Mule by way of a 'damn good smote'. He was not.

Something had spooked Mule – it had – and he was madder than ah'd ever seen him – braying and bucking and hurling his rump skyward – wrenching at the chain that held him to the hitching post. More often than not he would slam a baleful hoof into the face of a sooty frying-pan that dangled on a wire hook suspended from the roof.

The sky, like mah scalp, tightened. It had taken on the look of a vast membrane that stretched itself, like peeled skin, across the valley to form a roof, sealing in the stuffed light. It teemed with a network of intumescent red vessels, tested to capacity by their booming blood.

The frying-pan made a final crashing protest and flew off the hook and into the roaring air, landing at mah feet and spinning like a top on the spot, describing with its long, bent handle a near-perfect circle in the dust around its pan, as if it were claiming the territory within as its own. Its face stared darkly into mine.

Suddenly Mule stiffed and fell silent, as though ossified. The clouds of red dust engulfed the beast, then fell away and settled in veils at his feet. We stared at each other. Mule, it seemed, was cast in lead and draped in falling red veils. His lips curled back to reveal huge yellow teeth. He frothed. He foamed. His demented eyes egged in their orbits as if they were being laid. And all the while he goggled horribly, over mah shoulder, at *it* coming.

The throb had stopped. The pulse. There was not a sound to be heard, as if the entire valley now held its breath beneath the spreading penumbra.

Ma and Pa stood together on the porch, speechless, eyes cast south. Ma held her bottle limply at her side, sobered by the sight of *it*. Pa just stood there beside her, dumbfounded – the two of them bound, at long last, by a common bond, one to the other in the fetters of terror. Stuck by the unerring horror of *its* coming, they stood petrified like two filthy pillars of salt.

And ah will tell you this: if ah were standing as ah was then, but with a pole-axe raised at mah hind, ah could not have felt more vulnerable than ah did on that day. And if ah were on bended knee in the very lion's den, or if mah skull was rested between the hammer and the steely anvil ah could not have felt more intensely threatened than ah did at that moment, mah back turned on *it* – gravely coming – this cold, breathing beast.

Ah have met with fear before, but believe me, on this day, the first day of the summer of 1941, ah felt – well – let's just say, sir, that ah was one very fucking shit-scared mute.

Ah felt ah could not look upon *it*. Ah'm not sure why now, yet even with mah eyes inclined toward the ground, ah knew exactly the nature of the thing that loomed at mah hind. And ah knew – for all along mah bones this knowing blew – that the bounded duty of this abomination was part of something that only He can comprehend, all working as part of His massive scheme, moving us in ways we often cannot unnerstand. And keeping mah eyes downcast, ah watched mah squat black shadow melt into the treacherous umbra that engulfed us all, spreading over the valley like dark, gelid lava.

And the silence could not have held its breath a moment longer.

At mah feet there broke a faint but firm sound. Three slow-metred drops – themselves a prophecy, ah would realize in the years to come – leaked into the very centre of the frying-pan, trespassing within the bounders of its claim, with a ring some-where between a ping and a plunk – an ictus, solemn and even, upon its punished face. That trio of cold, tin chimes broke the tumid silence like distant curfew bells carried on the new night air. And it seemed to me at that time that this trinity of tears – like the curt taps of the maestro's baton or the three commands barked at the fusilade – struck the fetters from the cataclysm.

It thundered. *It did*. The skin of the sky ripped open, spewing forth its burden into the valley's basin. Corrupt and putrid and unrecanting, it came in slashes of bilge and sheets of swill – vile and poisonous waters, as if all the welkin bile had been pumped

40

from the sewers of Hell then vomited in a black and furious torrent down upon the shack and the cane, soaking me through to the bone before ah even thought to run, before ah even thought to raise mah head. Ah watched the raddled dust pock, then turn to running mud around mah boots. Ah let the rain bite at mah nape and naked arms, figgering shelter to be a waste of time, and in any case ah could not stand to hear the bloody fracas inside – for ah had seen Ma, still on the porch, raise one porky fist at the rain and engage in a brief but stormy exchange, to be cut short as the rusted guttering above her head buckled unner its sudden, muddy load and pissed a soup of leaf and possum crap down her thrashing tit.

So ah just stood there like that, in the rain, feeling mah skin go numb – a little from the pelt of its hard waters, ah guess, a little from the cold.

Above the wrath, above the din, above all the angels' barking thunder, ah heard Mule making a wheezing 'Hee', then release a long and heavy 'Haaaw', and ah looked up and ah saw Mule, and Mule it seemed looked straight at me – and we stood that way for a numb, wet moment, pondering the folly of each other's lot: the mute and the mule, the mule and the mute.

II

Inside the tabernacle the congregation sat atrophied on pine-board pews, all eyes fixed upon the vestry door. There was a stench of wet rags and a sneaping clamminess in the air. No one spoke. Only the rain could be heard, slamming down on the old iron roof.

For this glum assembly the catharsis was over. For five fevered days and nights, the streets of Ukulore had reflected, in a hundred puddling eyes, the shapes of sackcloth reeling, in morbid genu-flection, like the fast shadows of bats and birds, as the Ukulites petitioned their God for mercy.

The Ukulite women found, it seemed, in times of death or high catastrophe such as this, an irresistible vehicle for dramatic expression.

There in the night, hidden beneath veils of rain, they had wailed and weltered in the mud, punishing themselves with frightening abandon in an orgy of self-abuse. Shoeless, their sackcloth robes torn and sodden, each wearing over her face a black veil – as often as not discarded in the throes of penance – the Ukulite women tore at their hair, beat their breasts with stones, crawled through the streets on bleeding knees and purged their bodies with nettle wands, disinfectants and irritants.

Into the early hours of the morning they had performed their weird piacular rites, each in deep and delirious potation with her own pain, each a single hump of convulsions unto herself and each in a self-effacement as determined as the tempest, inflicting brutal rebuke upon her own person, for these were the dues exacted by a collective shame.

But the downpour did not abate, despite every morbid bid for atonement. The air hung heavy, reboant with spent oblations and worming acts of contrition, all tossed back by the rumbling nimbus, like undersized fish.

And all the time the rain still fell, spreading puddles into each other to form pools so dark – even in the half-light of the new day – that they looked like pockets of ink, and every so often the eye would be deceived by a discarded veil lying lost upon the ground like a pool.

The vestry door opened and Sardus Swift entered the chapel. Thin and stooped, he had eyes that stared fish-cold from their orbits.

The congregation's mood seemed to darken further still as he moved into the glow of the candles, and the people saw, in the buckled figure that bid genuflection to the altar, all the vile doubts so apparent in each one's heart.

Sardus walked a broken line to the mahogany pulpit. The rain punished the tabernacle with a roar and a crash. He raised his voice and petitioned his Lord, but his words were lost in the relentless drumming of the rain.

Water dripped upon them, there, within.

III

These figures tell the story of sugar production in Ukulore Valley in the early 1940s.

Season	Area Harvested (acres)	Total Yield of Cane (tons)	Yield of Cane per Acre (tons)	Yield of Raw Sugar per Acre (tons)	Tons of Cane needed to produce 1 ton of Raw Sugar	Total Yield of Raw Sugar (tons)
1940	530	13,250	25	3.7	7.07	2,120
1941	nil	nil	nil	nil	–	nil
1942	nil	nil	nil	nil	–	nil
1943	nil	nil	nil	nil	–	nil

IV

Below is a page.
  Ah took it from a book – part inventory, part diary.
  And it belonged to Pa and it was a secret.
  It spanned the years from 1937 to 1940.

FIRST DAY IN JUNE 1940

Main 'BURN-OFF' CATCH ... NTH-EASTROW

Baggers
50 Rats (approx)
6 Toads (all dead)

Wire nets
15 Rats
40 Toads (approx) (10 dead)
2 Vargus Fan Lizards (1 dead, 1 part eaten)
3 Grass Snakes (2 large, 1 small) (1 dead)
1 Horned Lizard
1 Blue-tunged Lizard (dead and eaten)

Trip-traps + Teeth-snares
1 Barking Wolf (med) (bitch) (b. legs gone but live)
2 Razorback Hogs
3 Feral Cats (1 w/litter (8) everyone dead)
1 Lizard (type unrecognizable but dead)
1 Possum (burnt but live) (maimed)
1 Black Snake (poisoners)
1 Toad (d)
7 Rats (all dead)
1 Crow (trippt snare while scabbing on cat)
        (first bird catched in land-snare) (dead)

Pit-trap
35 Rats (approx) (6 dead)
1 Black Snake (5 ft) (dead. part eaten.)
1 Feral Cat (dead. eaten.)

Loops + Coils
0 Zero (all trigged)

Spike-slap
0 Zero (not trigged)

Drop-beam + Tangle-beam
0 Zero (all trigged but one)

Grab-sacks
7 Toads (all dead + eaten + part eaten)
1 Feral Cat (dead + part eaten)
  Rat shite + big holes gnored in hessian

Ah found it, this diary, this inventory, in the very same tin trunk in which ah was to discover the jacket, the telescope and the compass, each wrapped up in newspaper. Only the Great One, in all his omnipotence, could have foreseen just how crucial it was that ah, His Servant, His cog, should break the lock and lift the lid of that forbidden tin trunk and remove, one by one, each parcel wrapped in yellowing newspaper and, like a fruit, peel away the pith of mah predestination – and in God's measured time, expose the core of mah calling.

The trunk was kept covered by a hessian potato sack in mah parents' room. The heavy lock bulged beneath the coarse cloth. Pa kept the book a secret, for it was wrapped in newspaper when ah found it. Even though ah had fashioned a spy-hole in the west wall of their room, ah never once saw Pa make one solitary entry in the little battered book. Yet it was printed in Pa's slow hand, in Indian ink, which, kept in a tiny bottle, was also wrapped carefully in newspaper, stored in the trunk that stayed always in their chamber, until they were dead and both long gone.

Ah was absolutely forbidden to enter mah parents' room.

When ah was just four mah Ma grabbed ahold of mah ear and, twisting it viciously, hissed into mah eyes, 'To enter me an ya Pa's room, baw, keep ya spyin eye peeled for *the VIXO*! Beware! *The Vixo* will ask ya for the password and if ya cain't say it out loud, baw, it will jump up and jam a tin-stick square ups ya lil ass and all his screamin *wogs* and *hog-dogs* will hunt ya down and eat ya brains for supper. Unnerstan?'

Ah was scared – yes, ah was. Ah could feel mah innards become bundles of livid rope from which swung a chattering sabbat of hunchbacked bell-ringers – the dread gnashing *wogs* – vile misshapen gnomes shinning up mah spine for a brain-bake – and ah could feel *the Vixo*'s bloody butcher's knife punched up mah flue – oh yes – and the gush of guts running down the insides of mah legs – oh and listen – here come the *hog-dogs* grunting and snarling in the distance, hungry and drawing near and so on and so forth.

Ah can only add at this point, that at four years of age mah mind was but a thirsty sponge. It was absorbing all the wonders of life without prejudice, drinking at every fount and spring, drawing no conclusions, no correlations, making no order of mah observations, accepting the long with the short, the good with the bad, without question and without query.

In mah infant years and so through to mah teens – even as a young man ah sat not in judgement of mah fellow man. But hear this. Even as ah dangled from one pinched empurpled ear, a wincing woeborn puppet surrendered up to the paedophagic freak show which mah mother would so sadistically invoke – even then, no more than a mite, not even a lustrum of life's waters passed – ah, Euchrid Eucrow, harboured such a hate for that sick fucken bitch that ah felt mah glands fill with a deadly venom that polluted mah bodily secretions – it did. Ah emitted a lethal catarrh – black spit, foul and deadly.

Ah was corrupted by hate. Ah was monstrous. Ah was diabolical, deadlier than a rattlesnake, and while the sow slept, the snake – it struck! Listen. Once, while Her Slutness lay sprawled in her armchair, ah slid up to her and deposited whole mouthfuls of warm, morbid sputum into her bottle. Then ah left the house, making sure ah woke Her Bitchship with a slam of the door. Ah slipped around to the south wall, pulled the spigot from the spy-hole, and put mah eye up to the hole – mah black little heart romping in its cage, happy as hell.

Ah watched her down the killer elixir in one long swig. Mah eye went cold. She belched ominously and shut her eyes like before. She began to snore. A minute passed and ah fell into a sickly sweat. Mah mouth filled with foul and acrid rheum.

Ah slammed the spigot back in its hole and hissed.

The hog was immune.

Utterly shitted, ah gobbed at mah shadow and watched an onion-weed curl and die on mah left shoulder.

Needless to say, ah never entered the room until Ma and Pa were both dead and gone. Even so, *the Vixo* reigned long in mah brains, butchering the passing years.

V

Sometimes ah would sit unner the dubious shelter of the
porch and watch as the parade of vehicles climbed and descended Hooper's Hill – unner the curtain of the rain, deep
into the night.

Sometimes ah would single out one vehicle and watch it crawl
down the harlot's hill and ah would follow with mah eyes the
bright fanning of its beams all the way to the faceless driver's
nuptial nest.

Often ah could see, like the glowing doodles left hanging by a
firefly upon the face of the night, the car beam's after-light, like
a golden chain binding together whoredom and wifedom – like
two massive lead balls – and shackling them to the shins of the
false-hearted fornicator who could never again feel the presence
of one without suffering the weight of the other.

But as the rain persisted and the months passed and the
seasonal and permanent workers alike began to abandon the
ruined valley, the parade to and from Hooper's Hill gradually
thinned.

Even so, the little pink caravan remained upon the hill like
a valentine.

For a time.

VI

When the malignant year 1941 finally abdicated, it left as its successor a black and monstrous spawn. A sullen year was 1942, stewing in the pits of constipation but nevertheless pissing a dark and gravelly stream down into the valley as if it were a pot.

The deluge had lost its former wrath and roar, but the bane of the valley was far from lifted. To the townsfolk, God seemed as a mule who would not budge: a dog in the manger of mercies. The grey and bitter swill of the Second Year steeped the valley and its denizens in a bog of glum torpor.

The streets lay all but empty, the streetlights in permanent use; for the days were dim and pitch-dark were the nights.

The town slumped. Things rotted. Others swelled. Some got bogged while others sunk. There were things that withered and things that shrunk.

The Second Year saw the funk and fear thicken as apathy closed up the eyes and ears and grew upon tongues like a mould. Able-bodied men succumbed to an inertia that saw them spend more and more days on their backs, in their beds. Women sat at windows, lost in other worlds. Some bore the scars of rejection in their hearts, others upon their faces. There were those big with favours given, and those wasted by favours taken.

Intemperance. Self-abuse. Gluttony. Sloth.

There were some homes that took in Madness as a tenant.

It was on one wet and eldritch eve that Rebecca Swift, Sardus' young but abstracted wife, heard a knocking in her head – too loud this time to ignore – and with trembling heart and tiny, trembling hands, drew back the big, black bolt a crack, and let the tenant in.

Rebecca was slave to a crushing melancholia that plundered at will her frail person and lay upon her like a spent lover. As these attacks grew longer and more funest, so too her moods, deep and blue as bruises, grew more deeply fumid, and Sardus paid agonized witness to his beloved's slow but steady estrangement, seeing himself in his long-practised, self-abasing mind's eye as an odious mockery of manhood – a wretched travesty, cuckolded by an incubus, by a circus of blue devils.

But it was in the nature of these fits to shun the afflicted with as little warning as they possessed her. Even under the head of the storm she would perk up, her blue mood suffusing with silvery light.

Like a laughing lark in a fountain of mirth, Rebecca would hop and chirp, her chatter kittenish and fanciful, flapping about her heart-sore husband as she gushed forth her eidetic vision like a child.

Sardus would listen, battling to keep a smile upon his lips, indulging her in her monomaniacal chatter as if he had not heard it all before. With tiny hands dancing about her in a succession of fluttering gestures, the childless Rebecca Swift would gaily evoke a world of frosted pink and baby blue, of booties and bonnets and bunny-rugs, of rattles and rubber teething rings.

Cooing and clucking over her ecstatic imaginings, her eyes filling with tears and cooling her flushed cheeks with her own shivering fingers, Rebecca would squeeze shut the real world and behind closed lids create around her the same crystal palace that she always built: a palace of frosted spires and arches of glass, cloud-capped towers and mirrored floors and staircases, white and winding, crystal walls and porcelain doors, the clear peal of vesper bells like the laughter of children – all spilling with warm light beneath a spinning silver sun.

And there she would stay for a day or so, until the sun spun white and melted her babies and the palace of glass all down around her. And there in the heavy folds of melancholia she would brood, drowned beneath her own little rain that would wash across her heart, but could not bring to bud one shooted seed, to swell and to split inside her. No. Not a solitary one to breach the grief of Rebecca.

On the afternoon of 12 August 1942 – that is, the Second Year of The Rain – Doc Morrow had the unenviable duty as the Swifts' family doctor of informing the couple of what he had ascertained: that although Sardus was as potent as a goat, his wife was unfortunately as barren as a stone, and that all the love and the seed furiously spent in the name of procreation was thus issued in vain. The doctor knew it would not be necessary to add that, in the light of such knowledge, the act of love (which, as crucial to the process of multiplication, was tolerated) would become, if continued, downright fornication, which the Church could not condone.

Dropping in on the Swifts on his way to vespers, the doctor found only Rebecca at home, Sardus having already gone on to church to prepare for the service alone. Rebecca Swift's bad attendance record was becoming a point of concern for many of the elders; of this both Rebecca and the doctor were fully aware.

Rebecca stood before the cold mouth of the hearth and warmed herself in imaginary flames. She asked two questions and the doctor replied with two words.

'Can we have a child?'

'No.'

'Who?'

'You.'

Nothing more was said. Doc Morrow left her to make his way to church. Rebecca Swift had had but one lone crutch upon which to prop her tormented world, and with two words the crutch had shattered beneath her.

Shortly after Sardus had returned home and – depressed, exhausted and appalled at the doctor's news – had fallen into a worried sleep, Rebecca slipped out. Through the back door, wearing only a nightdress and carrying before her a spirit lamp, she crept like a bird into the night. She stopped only to collect a length of rope from the tool-shed that stood at the rear of the rain-battered yard. With the rope coiled over one shoulder she left the garden by the back gate, her cotton nightdress glued to her body like a shrivelled skin, soon to be dispatched.

No sign remained of her garden – yet it had once been envied widely throughout the region. Before the rain had beaten the spring blossoms to rotten pulp, the little garden had literally burst with clusters of sunflowers, gold and sun-gorged, tropical vines, and a prize-winning vegetable patch which had swollen with giant beets, titanic pumpkins and bounties of large beans that had cleaned up in their respective fields in three different fairs in three different counties. It had once been a glorious garden indeed, one of the finest in the valley.

'Have you ever seen so many awards? Look at these ribbons! Green thumbs! By Heavens, there's nothing my wife can't grow!' Sardus had once boasted. He would remember this alone at home, in days to come.

Lamp outstretched, Rebecca walked the length of her street, then turned left up Dundass and made her way across the courtyard of Wiggam's General Store. There she approached the old disused well. Painted in faded letters on its little tin roof were the words:

'WIGGAM'S WISHING WELL'
– make a wish come true –

There upon its little slab wall she rested the spirit lamp. Then she tied one end of the rope she had brought to the central crankshaft of the hoist, and composed a crude hangman's knot at the other. She disrobed. Her hands flickered about her like white flames as she incanted a last prayer into the cheering downpour. Black ribbons of rain broke upon her pale arms, her tiny breasts, her futile belly, and a system of dark, ropey veins coiled and crawled down the sheer slopes of her body like a plague of shimmering snakes. From the pocket of her discarded nightdress she took the plastic bag which contained her suicide note – this she stuffed between two of the piled slabs of the wall, up on to which she duly climbed. Lifting the halter, she clapped on the noose and pulled it over her head, tugging the rope till it fitted snugly about her throat.

Tottering a little beneath the great knotted growth that sat grotesquely upon her right shoulder, she wavered a brief moment upon the brink of the well, then leapt naked into the dark hole.

Wondering why he still bothered to look out his window of a morning, a certain early riser and creature of habit, Baker Wiggam, did just that and was greeted by the lamp's last waning light calling from the well. Baker Wiggam grabbed his coat and pocketed a large torch.

Thirty minutes later, Wiggam's fat and evil son Fitzgerald – known to one and all as 'Fists' – bowled through Sardus Swift's open back door and, without so much as a knock, burst into his bedroom. Grabbing hold of the foot of the four-poster, he bullied its brass rail violently. A shaken Sardus awoke to the sight of Fists Wiggam grinning and rolling on the spot like a bad penny, the terrible news a trembling bubble on the top of the boy's fat tongue.

The boy chuckled as Sardus rubbed his face with one hand and explored the empty space beside him with the other. Both hands fell still as it dawned upon him that there was no wife in his bed; he lay there with the one frozen upon his face, the other outstretched to where the barren belly of his woman should have been.

The boy drew breath and spoke:

'Not dere, Brudder Sawdus. Wife not dere. Tain't cookin neither. Tain't moppin. Tain't scrubbin. Tain't even in da house, Brudder! Nope! But *ah* know where dat woman is, Brudder Sawdus! Know where?!! *Ya wife done backa our well wit not a stitch on!! Ha! Ha! Stark naked assa babe!!*'

Later, as he stood between the murmurous circle of public outrage and the dark shape of the well, Sardus Swift bent visibly beneath his grief and shame. Hunched over, he stared hopelessly at the dogged and beaten face in the puddle between his feet, unable to recognize it.

His ears rang with a string of the most wicked expletives and curses, to which the town's citizenry also was subjected as it huddled around the well, clucking and gasping as the stream of filth spewed from its nether-regions.

Baker Wiggam and Doc Morrow fished the mad woman out of the well, naked save a few livid leeches fatted to the size of thumbs. Beneath the collar of rope, a rubescent wound oozed pink water. Her delicate little hands were worn raw, flayed by the coarse fibre of the rope, the rough rope that she had clung to all through the late spring night as she bobbed in the near-brimming well, her 'long drop' a mere two feet down.

Over the following days, the faces of the townsfolk began to look to Sardus like a gallery of crude portraits which, framed in their window squares, gazed vacantly down upon him as he doggedly awaited the specially equipped ambulance to drive the four hundred miles from Marilyn Cottages, Delaware, on Cape le Winn.

When, after much delay, they had finished signing the final committal papers, Sardus and Doc Morrow watched the grey windowless Maria plunge into the hyaline midnight sky and disappear behind its starless screen to become yet another puddle of no-colour, its wriggling cargo jacketed in soft grey pads and grey leather straps, seized in a convulsion of grey insanity, borne off to Marilyn Cottages, off to Marilyn Cottages, off to Marilyn Cottages.

Sardus Swift retired to his home, which was to become his fortress, as the rain beat out a constant recital of his loss upon the tin roof.

And so it was without a leader that the Ukulites entered a new circle of depression and of apathy and of torpor. And each day was steeped and further steeped in numb uggr. And the rain came down and washed each last shred of hope away.

It was clear that the Ukulites needed a new leader. Yet although those suggested were adequate candidates to take the wheel of their community, each one found an equally adequate argument to disqualify him from the position. Not a man among them would accept.

The regular prayer meets gradually dissolved. Some of the faithful even attended the hymn-singing fiascos that were organized each Saturday night in the Unitarian Church which stood, abandoned by the contractors, ghastly and unfinished, up on Glory Hill.

Along with their apostasy came the moral downfall of some of the men, who took to frequenting the saloons, crap-shoots, poker games and the whorehouse.

Many of these men traded off pieces of the valley in order to pay back gambling debts.

Midnight calls were made on the balkers. Ugly scenes. Ugly scenes.

Ugly scenes to which Sardus Swift was oblivious as he lurked in the shuttered bounds of his house, all the angles of his face locked in bitter grimace and lost in time beneath a long unruly beard.

VII

As ah get called unner, flesh by little flesh, with the comely boggery swaddling mah loins in its warm and sulphurous issue, tugging meatus unner, unner, to its nether-lands, its no-whither-lands, ah make the space about me open up its wounds. Ah squeeze shut mah eyes and let the colours come. The night holds out a dark lantern and springs its shutter open, so that in the pitch of mah blindness, behind mah lids, mah scotoma is blasted into a battle sphere of wild meteors, blood-blown moons, suns and molten planets, butchered asteroids, berserk comets, lum-inary clusters, gaudy wreaths of stellar motion, green nebulae, gaseous nebulae, white and spiral nebulae, hairy-stars and fire-balls, shimmering sun-spots and solar flares, blinding faculae, flocculi, and day-stars, new moons, red planets, and stars of blue and tinsel, trinket-yellow and white stars, harlequin showers, spectral moons and mock moons, Sol, Helios, Phoebus. Mars, Saturn, Dipper, Saucepan, Big Bear and Little Bear, in collision, in colour, here, in the guttles, of the sump, alone and at war with the macrocosm, unner-borne, eyes squeezed shut and rolling-squeezing, squeezing out the last drips of the spectrum behind mah lids, till ah open mah eyes again and feel them adjust back to grey, for everything is forever grey and the pressure unner mah ribs is hurting me, breathing is getting harder, lungs will cleave apart, only just on one half swallered and the pressure . . . the pressure . . . the planets of pain . . .

Mah life in review as ah go down. Listen to this.

It was the Second Year of The Rain and ah was hidden in the womb of the old Chevy – mah obstetrical glory hole, if you remember, the stripped and gutted crate into which ah was dispatched along with mah martyred brother – low-slumped in the black seat ah was, nursing a shoebox marked 'Cicada Cicada Cicada'. It contained nineteen cicada shells – all in perfect condition. Ah had plucked them from the trunks of trees up on the thickly wooded eastern versant, before the rain had come and smashed the shedded paper pods and finally driven the cicadas from the valley. How hollow seem the hills without their shrillance.

A sleepy kind of calm had infected me as ah pondered upon the awesome mysteries bound up in the brittle pods, and safe inside the crate ah let mahself drift away, drift away, only to be wrenched awake by a freakish noise coming from the corral. Placing the shells carefully on the cotton-wool pads that lined the bottom of the shoebox, ah peered out the car window, keeping low.

Mule flung himself about the corral, bucking, kicking and beating his hooves in a bid to wrench himself free from the hitching post, slipping and skidding in the mud and emitting a queer 'Hawnk-neee! Hawnk-neee!', blowing through his lips and slamming his hooves against the side of the shack. 'Hawnk-neee, hawnk-neee!' For a second ah wondered what the fuck had flung Mule into such a funk.

And then ah saw it – through the leaden folds of rain it came – a flurry of canine limbs cannonballing up the slope toward the corral – a wild dog – a blood-bent beast – a hill-hound driven down from the hills in search of living food. And ah will tell you this. Ah have seen a lot of these hill-dogs, or 'barking wolves' as they are known locally, but ah swear this slavering brute had to be the meanest, hungriest, ugliest, most desperate-looking inbort ah had ever laid eyes on – great green fangs and drooling flews, blood-shotty eyes, flattened brow and massive shaggy shoulders that tapered away to a ratty sawn-off rear-end, tailless and hairless and covered in crap. Ah watched the dog leap up the corral fence with a liquid snarl and attach itself to Mule's flying rump.

'Haaawnk! Haaawnk!'

Blood ran red down Mule's rump, as the dog, high upon his

back, spun and whipped and kicked and bit. The panicking ass floundered and tottered beneath the onslaught until finally, with mouth agape and tongue lolling, Mule buckled, and with a splash and a drub fell flat on his side.

The vicious cur held on fast, and only at the sounding of Pa's shotgun did it unlock its jaws and bolt back down the slope. Pa came marching along the back of the shack, shotgun up at his shoulder, and, with aim wild and myopic, he emptied the other barrel just as the dog bounded into the sodden cane-trash.

Cussing obscenely, Pa entered the corral.

Mule lay upon his side, unmoving, a rain-soiled puddle of blood growing at his hind. And ah watched as Pa removed his hat and crouched by Mule, poking at the beast with his finger. Mule did not respond and the rain pissed down, and after a time Pa rose and walked to the apple barrels, where he unhooked a spade. Then, head lowered, hat back on, spade across his shoulder like a grey bone, he crossed the yard to the old water-tower.

There, a few feet from the rickety support upon which the tower stood, he began to dig.

Leaving the shoebox wrapped in an old shirt in the glove compartment – thoroughly checking first, of course, for roaches or rats – ah crept from the Chevy and footed it over to the corral.

Ah saw mah romping body on the pocking faces of the puddles. Splashed a few too.

Mule lay ossified in a petticoat of scarlet lace. His toothy rictus made it look like he was laughing.

Ah drew mah hand in a soft stroke across Mule's neck. His wet grey coat was warm. Ah uttered the beast's name softly, 'Mule,' and Mule rolled one spooked eye open and upward into mine – and the ass saw the angel, eye to rolling white eye, and long-locked was the looking. Slowly, and yes, miraculously, Mule climbed to his feet. Blood ran in rivulets down his hind legs. Ah looked for Pa and found him bent waist-deep in the grave, cussing and furiously digging.

So, me and Mule, we exchanged a second glance, but it was me this time who broke the spell.

Ah returned to the Chevy, and found mah cicadas still secure as ah had prayed they would be. And ah sat rapt in mah box of little bleached cast-offs, one of which ah held gently up between thumb and fore to the grey light that oozed through the windows. So engrossed was ah that ah barely registered Pa's whoop of joy when he returned to the corral to find Mule – lolloping a little but alive. Eye right close up to the weightless shell, ah pored over the wing's tessellated arterial skeleton, and mused upon the myriad bifurcations and forks, the branches and anabranches revealed against the murky light.

Suddenly the person of Ma lumbered on to this field – entered it drunk and reeling, with the last wobbling circumgyrations of a clipped skittle. Clad only in a lurid floral dress she came, having donned neither stocking nor slipper, nor any coat against the rain – her stone bottle clutched in her paw. As she rolled the length of the cicada wing, I trapped her, there in that awesome network of subdivision.

Then, still looking through the cicada's wing, ah thought this: 'Ma is gonna fall in Mule's open grave.' And d'you know, that is precisely what she did – slipped mah fetters, disappeared off the face of mah cicada's wing without a trace. Mah heart pinked and ah exploded into a dumbshow of laughter. Absently ah crushed the wing and shell in mah hand, unaware that ah did so. Such was mah elation!

Pa had disappeared around the side of the shack, so ah felt it safe enough to climb on to the roof of the car. Below me, like a giant turtle upon its back, thrashed mah phocine Mama, working herself ever deeper into the sucking mucilage that threatened to engulf her and overwhelm her and drown her for ever.

Pa returned, with Mule in tow, led by his chain.

Ah made mahself scarce. Low. Unner the Chevy.

On mah belly, the ground beneath me felt damp and cold, but ah suffered in silence – having no other choice. Ah looked toward the corral and could just see, through the thrashing torrent, Mule's four blood-stained shanks and the huge muddy boots of Pa, all straining away from the grave-hole, and the chain leaping from the great puddle like a silver snake, alive and hissing. Then Mule let forth a cracking bray – at least ah think it was Mule. Slowly a giant mud-coloured gastropod – a black and flapping slug the size of a baby whale – rose horribly from the brimming slough and sprawled out, to merge with the mud beside the trench – amorphous, atramental and viscid. The thing wore a heavy chain girdle about its middle.

Pa's boots marched toward the lumpen mass, his stride heavy with badness, and ah watched Pa prepare to kick this writhing shit-hill all over the valley. But no, to mah amazement he didn't even lift a leg to stomp on it – *he just stood there*, shuffling a little, pointing in one direction and then another, like he was looking for something.

In time, a pink gash opened at one end, and from this bright hole the steaming zoophyte appeared to breathe, as the rain rinsed away the mud. Its lower region split to form a mammoth set of legs, and above these grew two pink flailing arms, one of which clung to a bottle made of stone. Her two hunkering pins kicked and crossed and folded as the gaping cavern in her face – for it was Ma – hollered and barked:

'Pa-a! Paaaa! Git off dis chain!'

As ah lay on mah back beneath the Chevy, mah eyes met with a wondrous discovery. A vast web hung above mah face, stretching right the way across the chassis, spun – judging from its great span – by an uncommonly enterprising arachnid. Ah swear ah had not seen a spider's web spun outdoors since the rain had started two years before. And so damn big! And such a goddamn handsome specimen!

It swam before mah eyes. It did. Everything seemed suddenly geocentric to the axis of this knitted floss – this hypnotical net – as, spinning around its spectral convolutions, whorl by tightening whorl, the spiral drew me to its darksome core, which loomed there above mah head. Darkness whelmed about me and mah eyes began to see nothing but deepening shades of night . . . drawing me down . . . unner . . . into its hexing heart . . .

Ah wrenched mahself back and flipped on to mah belly again, breaking free of the trance that would have digested me like a fly, had ah not turned away.

VIII

All mah life ah have lurked about the periphery and watched –
kept tabs on the hapless concatenations, the contretemps and
the downright calamities of the people within mah dominion –
Ukulore Valley.

Ah was, you might say, a Voyeur to the Lord. All mah days
ah have served as an informer, gleaning what ah could from what
ah happened to see or hear or sniff out. Yes, now that ah am well
on the way to Paradise – mah rightful dominion – it gives me a
certain pleasure to reveal this lifelong secret. By divine appointment ah was God's snitch. Ah mean, no one can keep a secret
better than a mute.

Though God has told me Himself that mah work on earth was
of an incomparable standard, not all mah missions were free of
misadventure. In fact, like Ezekiel, Daniel or Jonah, the very
essence of mah success was rooted in great personal catastrophe
– priceless information gleaned as from the pit, or the den, or the
whale's belly.

One instance of this was a mission that found me forced
to look into the dealings of Cosey Mo, the harlot of Hooper's
Hill.

It was early evening and pissing rain, and as ah reached the
crest of the hill ah came across a pick-up, its front lights on full
beam, parked outside the little pink caravan.

'Cosey has company,' ah thought, making a mental note of
the fact.

It was safer to watch Cosey Mo at night, for, as she was wont
to burn the midnight oil inside her caravan, ah could climb up
on the wheel-guard and watch through the little round window
without being seen from inside.

Inside ah could now see a man's muscular back and hind-quarters – an inky menagerie tattooed upon it – punishing the harlot, or the little that ah could see of her – a shogging thigh, an aureate splash of hair, a crooked and clipping arm and an arm outflung. As ah watched mah heart quopped longingly, for, even with the tumultuous downpour crashing all around me, ah could hear her trembling bleats – short and rhythmic – her cry in the night – O Cosey . . .

Ah must have lost sense of things for a while, hypnotized by the gruesome menagerie that roamed the glistening contours of his body – a cobra with a rat caught between its fangs, a pouncing panther, wolves fighting, a unicorn etched upon his huge shoulders, a nuchal eagle passing judgement on the restless brood.

So resolutely was ah conducting mah mission that ah did not hear the footsteps coming up behind me.

'Okay, sickboy, the show's over,' came a voice, thick with likker, and as ah swung round a six-inch steel blade pinned me to the wall. Ah could feel the blade pricking me lightly, nervously.

'Climb down, sickboy,' sneered a lean, unshaven cane-man, with a gold tooth and the letters H-A-T-E tattooed across the knuckles of his right hand, and across his left, similarly, H-A-T-E.

'Don't touch anything – leave 'em as they are. Ah want mah very mean friend to see you as ah found you. We'll just wait around in the shelter here for him to finish . . .'

Ah stood there shivering, suddenly cold, very cold.

'This is a very unlucky day for you, sickboy. Mah friend Jock Snow,' he continued, 'why, mah friend Jock Snow is gunna tear your head off and shit in your neck.' And we waited for what must have been ten minutes, every muscle in mah body shitting and a-shaking, and him with the gold tooth whispering, over and over again: 'This sure ain't yer lucky day,' and every time ah tried to adjust mahself, he'd hiss, 'Ah said leave them alone, sickboy.'

Eventually Jock Snow climbed down the stairs, his shirt thrown over his shoulder. He had a great fucken grin on his face.

Then he saw me. Then he looked incredibly mean. And very low.

The last thing ah remember seeing was the face of Christ, a configuration of blues and greens, come floating toward me, his forehead studded with red pearls of blood, and ah remember thinking what overwhelming compassion resided in His eyes. Then something like a mule kicked me.

Ah awoke to the aroma of lavender.

Ah tried to open mah eyes but mah left eye felt like it had two angry leeches for lids, leaving me the merest slit to see through. Mah right eye simply would not open at all. Everything ah could see was bathed in a scarlet light and ah wondered where the fuck ah was. Was ah still in the land of the living? Had ah died and gone to Hell?

Then a cool hand descended and touched mah brow lightly. It was attached to a pale, draped arm and the arm was part of the sweetly scented body of Cosey Mo.

Ah was helpless. There was nothing ah could do to defend mahself. Ah tried to stand but mah body protested with a thousand aches and algos, great and small. Ah watched her as best ah could – bathed in red – dabbing and stroking and patting me, and ah tried to figure out what she was up to – touching me like that all the time. Was she hexing me? Casting some terrible spell?

Ah needed water and ah lifted mah head slightly and was about to at least mouth the word 'war-tah', when she said: 'Drink this. It's water.'

'Don't try to speak. Just lie back. It's all right, I saw what happened. If it weren't for me calling off those dogs they would have . . . Here, lie still – he's one mean brute, that Jock Snow – ssshhh, don't speak,' she whispered, and, pointing one fire-crowned finger, she gently pressed it to mah lips.

Cosey Mo's face was tinted in scarlet light, pinking her chrysal curls that tumbled down each breast as she leaned across me to dab at mah battered face, and despite the protestations of mah sorry body ah could feel the multitude of her locks brush lightly across mah trembling thigh.

'Sooo, you're the peep . . . so, you're the watcher,' she said with a peculiar smile upon her lips. 'That ain't the first time, is it, sweetheart? You've been here before.' Then lowering her voice she said, more to herself than to me, '. . . those chicken-shit sons of bitches . . .'

Her smooth white breasts swelled and shifted beneath the slippery satin fabric of her nightgown. Ah inhaled a sweet axillary sourness. With those two honey-hued orbs filling mah mind and her hushed voice saying, 'Ssshhh, close your eyes now, sugar,' ah guess ah fell away . . .

IX

Listen, ah don't wanna speak ill of the dead but have ah told you that mah mother was a great whopping whale of a cunt? Well she was precisely that – a great whopping whale of a hog's cunt with a dry black maggot for a brain.

The slobstress was wont to play pedagogue when she'd hit the piss just enough to be able to stand and to speak. It was a woeful thing to see.

One particular evening when Pa had retired early, Ma decided she wanted to teach me about mah heritage, mah ancestry, mah family tree and so forth. Ah was sitting in the hardback chair and we were playing this sort of game she used to enjoy.

Ma roared, for she rarely spoke. 'Your family tree, baw, on y'Pa's side, is one very shady tree, and ah don't mean it's gotta lotta leaves growin on it neither. Ya Pa's side is just one big fucken black twisty knot planted in the backest backwoods – I'm talking hill-stock, baw, and there ain't no lower ass-ended inborn breed than that. That's why ya Pa's a half-wit – that's why you're not all there either, not countin ya dumbness. Ya know ya name ain't Eu-crow? Ya Pa changed it when he left the hills. Ever hear of the Morton Clan? Well it weren't healthy having Morton as ya tag forty years ago. Forty years ago they were hangin Mortons by the dozen. Hills were fulla them. Rounded most of 'em up, but a few got away – like ya Pa. Blew his own ear off doing it. Them Mortons were the lowest inbred animals t'ever pleasure a pig! Their blood was *black*! Same's yours. *Sick black blood!* Look at ya eyes. There's some troubled blood in there. I seen it from the first. Troubled blood . . .'

And so on and so forth, her monologue turning with the time and with the moonshine *bad* in her brains – *bad* talk, *bad* time, *bad* shine – right there before mah eyes – yes, right there before mah very troubled eyes. And ah would wait, sitting in the hardback chair, bent double at the waist and bound by the wrists to its wooden legs, like a witch on a ducking stool awaiting the inevitable 'trial' – mah test – awaiting the stings and stripes of that fat fairy's wand, awaiting the eventual spilling of mah sick, of mah black, of mah sick, black blood.

'Just as ah remembered,' ah thought, with genuine relief, 'red.' Ah dug a fresh hole with mah good hand and returned the scissors to the ground at the foot of the gallows-tree. Ah mean, if this rain is washing up coffins and tombstones, then a pair of scissors was not gunna last too long in the ground unless it was anchored with something solid. Ah stomped on the sloppy grave as best ah could, knowing full well that this mud was not the burying kind.

Perching on a root that rose like a blanched knuckle from the eroded soil at the base of the gallows-tree, ah took a large handkerchief and ah daubed at the dark pool of blood that swelled and slowly filled mah cupped hand. Holding the bloody rag up to the dim afternoon light the blood looked even redder.

Convinced, ah rinsed both hand and handkerchief. Ah laid the latter over the scarlet bead that sprang from the hole in mah palm and knotted it back.

'Ah will look again tomorrow,' ah thought, knowing full well ah would pick the sick, black scab away tonight.

X

And then came the preacher, Abie Poe.

The crack of his blue steel pistols shattered the massy scab of despond that had spread across the Ukulite community like some alien excrescence. All along Maine musty curtains fluttered and parted and the haunted faces of the once faithful hovered like so many blaked and unhappy moons. Apprehensively each one looked toward the commotion in the town square, surprised to see that one lone man on a horse was responsible for such a formidable alarum. Their murine faces twitched and cringed with each bullet spent as they strained to comprehend the nature of his business above the roar of his guns and the ceaseless, pounding rain into which he fired.

Emptying his six-shooters in a wild salute, Abie Poe bade welcome to Ukulore Valley. He spun his guns like propellers. He shot holes in Noah's barber-shop sign, and Noah's dark habitude darkened still more. Two pot plants exploded into clouds of terracotta dust and blew a russet blanket over the windows of Joy Flockley's haberdashery. He shot at Wiggam's Wishing Well, and an ounce of lead wedged itself between two piled slabs of the wall, inches above a plastic bag containing a note that a pale and trembling hand had deposited there, in that ashlar surround, months before. The wall splashed a puff of dust. Stuffed into a window, the Wiggam family huffed. Abie Poe fired blindly into the sky. Drips sizzled on his rods' hot barrels. Smoke curled in blue arabesques.

Abie Poe sat astride an absurd pine-wood mount, under which his ancient horse swayed and strained. Poe reeled extravagantly, pivoting from the saddle, describing with his wiry torso a series of deep and sweeping arcs to the left and right, back and forth, wild and thrashing, and though it is true that the nag made no motion to move, it must be said that, in all his perilous reeling, Poe never once left the seat of his mount.

The mount upon which Poe pivoted was a makeshift contraption invented by Poe himself and patented in Salem, under the name 'Poe's Throne'. Although ostensibly a deluxe sedan, it was in reality two overweight 'A' frames with a home-made saddle of leather and possum pelts slung between, a built-up back-support, canvas side-flaps and a standard under-brace. Apart from the hide seat, the whole structure was built out of pine lumber and weighed close to twice the amount of any more conventional equivalent.

But really, the crowning feature of this invention was a contrivance that Poe added a year or so after the patenting. It was a safety harness that secured the rider in the saddle at all times and which was indeed the very device that enabled the drunken, gun-slinging Poe simultaneously to weave his wild way, sound both irons, and remain cleaved to his throne.

If it had not been for 'The Throne', Abie Poe would not have been in this God-forgotten valley at all, for it was under the pretext of finding someone to manufacture the mount that he had up and left the lonely prairies of the west and headed south. Figuring that westerners knew too much about horses and had too little cash to be spending it on fancy saddles, Abie Poe took his design to where everybody was 'stinken rich or fucken stupid'. Or so he thought.

But the south had proved no more sympathetic than anywhere else he'd wandered. No one was interested in buying the patent on a pine-beam mount, saddle and safety harness.

Poe had found employment as a truck driver, tobacco picker, dish washer, poacher, rustler and housebreaker, none of which lasted further than the first pay packet.

Hired as a salesman selling silver cutlery sets door to door, and utilizing his innate powers of persuasion, Poe would insinuate his way into the lives of the young wives who formed the bulk of his clientele, bullying them with soft nothings, flirting through a sham of oily compliments and guiding their trembling hands toward the dotted line which bound them lock, stock and barrel to contracts which they had no chance of upholding. Poe generously took their sexual favours in lieu of the instalments, and in doing so seated himself in a position of absolute control, whereupon he proceeded to extravasate them mercilessly for their all. Those years had seen Abie Poe slip his tongue into the most sordid pies.

Seven years passed and Poe had found himself serving a term of four years for two counts of extortion and three counts of fraud in the scandalously over-populated Binbridge State Penitentiary. The last six months of his term he served in the prison infirmary, owing to a severely advanced infestation of *Trichuris trichiura*, more commonly known as whip worm.

The figure that had entered Binbridge Penitentiary in the winter of 1935 returned to the free world a changed man. He was thoroughly emaciated, his once baby face now drawn and bloodless. A thin purple cicatrix emerged from one bushy eyebrow and hooked around his right eye, terminating at a small, latent mole sprouting short, clipped hairs – like a fish hook baited with a little black beetle. His small teeth had grown flavid and troublesome, and his most profitable asset – his large, seemingly veridical eyes – seemed to have lost their directness, grown icy and prone toward gazing at the middle space, the area between things.

His rangy gait had stiffened and affected a rolling limp, the parasites responsible for his atrophy having spread from the enteric region and infested his right thigh, and his posture had become stooped and broken.

Depressed and taciturn, Abie Poe took a train and moved one town further down the line.

He found lodgings the same evening, renting a room from a Swiss spinster named Heidi Hoch, becoming her sole boarder. Heidi was a devout Anabaptist and at the age of eighty-three still walked the quarter-mile to her church each week.

The white-haired spinster nursed her sickly lodger back to health. But later, Heidi Hoch was stricken by a severe case of Black Measles.

At her deathbed, Abie Poe had barely been able to bring his eyes to look upon the haemorrhagic rash that blistered upon her face and scalp. So chronic was the pemphigus that her scalp seemed to be crawling with black ants. Then, opening her eyes and lifting a scarlet hand to her face, Heidi had said: 'Look what is upon me, Abie. Your sin. Your sin which I have gladly rooted from you. I will take it with me when I go. You are clean, Abie. I have made you clean!'

Abie Poe filled a tea-chest with Heidi's tiny carved dolls, wrapping them in her hand-painted linen and embroidery and laying a white pearl crucifix on top. He carried the box to the Parish Welfare Centre and traded the lot for a severe black suit and tall wide-brimmed hat, made of felt and also black. Looking in the mirror, Abie Poe saw a man lean and hungry-looking, his face grave and stern and deeply carved by the unremitting tools of remorse: a man imbued with a mission, a calling.

'There does God reside, stamped like a brand upon my face,' thought Abie Poe by way of initiation into his new-found ministration.

Back at the little house, Abie took Heidi's Bible and then left for the last time.

From that day on, the evangelist pounded his Bible at every opportunity, be it on street corners or at makeshift tabernacle citizen meets, in saloons, or down the lost beats of whoredom, in squares and parks and in schools and gaols, up the elm-lined streets of the rich and throughout Salem's infamous slums – echoing the words of his dead landlady, and infusing them with thespian thunder as he shouted, 'Sin! Sin is everywhere, Sir! It is upon everything! Madam! Are you so steeped in muck you cannot see it?'

Yet Poe's true calling was yet to be found.

It was not until he began hearing reports concerning the sordid activities of certain families living in the mountain areas

– xenophobic 'clans' involved in blood feuds, murder, rape, infanticide, incest and so on – that Poe the sin-seeker felt his life-mission had truly commenced.

Abie Poe bought a horse and rode to the range. At the ridge that marks the official gateway to the mountains, he met a young girl of eight or so years. She was sitting by the road amongst a massive pile of bedding.

'Come here, child. Direct me to the nearest house of worship in these parts,' said Poe.

The girl stood. The skin on her cheeks was cracked and raw. She held a small green grass snake in her grubby hand. Observing in her eyes the first clots of blindness forming like a skin, Poe asked a second time.

'Your chapel? Where is it? Point the way.'

The child lifted a sheet from the bedding. A woman lay beneath it, her skin alive with the parasites of the long dead. Said the little girl with difficulty, 'The worms git Ely . . . git Maw now . . .'

Abie Poe covered up the woman, leaning her against a stone-slab sign that had been made illegible by the passing of the years.

The girl turned and walked off into the mountains, the evangelist following closely. He looked at every shrub and stone for sinners.

It would be seven months before Abie Poe rode his nag back out of the Black Morton Range. A pint of moonshine in his saddle-bag. A six-gun on each hip.

Though his guns remained holstered, the measure of his inclemency tempered not; rather Preacher Poe stormed the church in a rampant state of crazed malediction, raving prophecy, revelation and inflated promises – echoes of his black-clad gestures – and winning the occasionally renitent but generally beseeching trust of those in attendance, Ukulite and non-Ukulite alike.

One or two of the elder Ukulites made token attempts to quiz the preacher, but Poe danced through their snares, skipping deftly through their jaws. Even the ill-tempered Wilma Eldridge, always ready with a crow to pluck, had her affront turned upon her when she questioned Poe's insistence that he was invested with the spirit of Elijah, and had been sent to the valley under divine instruction. Wheeling her squealing chair toward the preacher, she cut him off in mid-sentence with her bitter croak: 'Forgive my not standing, Prophet Poe, but I wish to know just what sign has the Lord given you to prove that you are what you profess to be?'

'They who are not blind see it,' answered Poe and took a pace forward, refusing to be intimidated by the cripple.

'Surely the Almighty makes His signs more evident?' she replied, rubbing her numb legs till her knuckles showed white.

'Blinder than he who has lost his eyes is he who closes them tight and refuses to see the light of day.'

Then the preacher stretched forth one accusatory finger and moved his hand in a slow semicircle until it had pointed to everyone present. Proffering not a word, Poe allowed the slow, pained squeal of the wheelchair to speak for him. A weary Wilma Eldridge made her retreat, retracing her muddy tracks.

'And ye,' said Poe, finger pointing at one and all, after the chair had at last stopped its terrible puling and the attention of the congregation was his again, 'ye cocks of the dunghill, ye strutters on the muckheap of the world, ye who have kissed the devil beneath the tail, pray to the Lord God Almighty that He have mercy upon you! For His hunter has his arrows drawn, and, like the way to the kingdom, his aim is straight and clean. Pray, wallowers, for His hunter's heels are raised! Wicked hearts shall be lanced, and their carcasses swallowed into the earth!'

'Who is the hunter?' called a trembling voice.

'He is before you, even now,' said Abie Poe.

Ah listened to the preacher's first sermon from unner the church that tottered upon two feet of pine-wood stilt. Ah could hear his words plainly from that crawlspace, his limping footfall, the murmurous throng uttering hallelujahs in solemn communion, the cry of the cripple's wheels, and ah knew from the force of his

74

thunderings that they were as much a self-delusion as they were a public deceit.

'Who is the hunter?'

'He is before you, even now!'

Ha! The irony of it all! Poor deluded Poe! The mad preacher's prophecy was almost correct! O, the torment of saints and would-be saints. Ha! Never to bask in the glory of his forecast affirmed! Had he only known that the hunter of whom they inquired was, in fact, *me*!

Poe wasted no time in putting to the test the boundaries of his sanity. Three days after arriving in Ukulore, on a wet Sunday, the maniacal preacher embarked on one of his most farcical exploits. It began at the church.

Satisfied that all the townsfolk were present, Poe began.

'Sinners! Look not to your neighbours' hands, but to your own. Not a soul among you is clean. You are all steeped in filth. Muck is upon you and your neighbour. But behold, backsliders. The wicked are known from the womb and they are sullied as such till death spits them into the abyss. They stand amongst you now. Before we can know the truly corrupt, we must first ourselves be cleansed. Harken to my word, sinners. *Ah speak of the conversion of the spirit through the mystery of baptism! Too long have you wallowed in the muck and mire. Forward! Follow! The healing-pool of the spirit is pure! Come, sinners! His waters await your apotheosis of faith.*'

If it had not been for the bolt blasting the left arm clean off the gallows-tree, ah might never have let up playing with mah blood at all. As it was, mah anxiety in regard to the uncertain nature of mah delinquent blood saw me digging up the shears from beneath the gallows-tree and smuggling them into mah room. Ah had already gouged a sizeable hole in each palm with a fang of ragged tin, prised from the grinning jaw of a trap that hung rusted and redundant on the shack wall – one of a vast gallery of ghastly steel goblins. As it turned out – though things turn a little murky here – ah did not use the shears upon mah person, though ah do remember snipping mah bed sheets into strips that ah used, one by one, wound upon wound, as bandages. Later, when ah had taken control of mahself, ah folded the used and crusty bandages and put them in a shoebox. Ah labelled the box 'Strips'.

After three days and three sleepless nights, with the corked and sordid air of mah cell sticky and damp and the rain outside showing signs of a fucken *monster* thunderstorm – ragged pitchforks of blue fire, deafening tonitruation, thrashing rain – ah sat in mah unnerwear, oozing grey sweat, corpse-like and ashen-faced through lack of sleep and food and quite possibly blood. The initial inspection of mah claret's complexion having taken a murky turn, ah picked at the evil, black crusts that capped each wound with a dead and ghastly crown. New blood would bubble in each one's place, bright and red at first but darking blackly at the heart to a grim crimson curd, finally to clot and to harden, sick and black. Yes, *sick and black*. Ah put the scabs in a tobacco tin that ah lined first with cotton-wool, and put the tin in the shoebox with the hair and nail clippings, the shoebox labelled 'Clippings'.

Ah rose weakly and stumbled from the shack, across the front porch and into the yard, mah hands bandaged into two filthy gauze mittens. Ah felt the heavens' cold emission upon mah upturned face, on mah tight-shut lids, rinsing the muck from mah gaping mouth, from mah scalp, from the slum of mah body. The storm thundered and crashed, the air crackling with electricity. Rain thrashed about me. The atmosphere swelled with God's brawling legions – butting bull clouds grew tusks of fire, renting the leaden bellies of other welkin beasts of war.

'Cleanse me,' ah thought. 'Cleanse me,' and the heavens whelmed me with their ablution.

Ah opened mah eyes and looked to the smitten gallows-tree, and ah thought for a moment that the thunderbolt had struck the long-dead tree to life, for in silhouette *both* its arms seemed lifted again, heaven-raised and thrashing wildly, its thin fingers raking the sky and its trunk reeling on its spindly roots. And then it was magically given voice, and in that second a flash of white light burst upon the horizon and exposed the enchanted gallows-tree for the madman it was – Abie Poe.

Standing there in mah nakedness ah watched the horse-borne preacher ride toward me, and all of a sudden ah was overwhelmed with dread – the horror of imminent doom. Ah heard a voice inside mah head intone: 'Death wore black and came by horse and many thronged behind him,' then repeat it, and in that instant mah palms began to itch madly and ah inspected the blushing holes and the itch and the rain and the bellyache of the clouds, and the voice inside mah head – which seemed to me like many voices now – and the man that came toward me shouting, always shouting.

Darkness drenched the valley as men and women slipped and skidded down the muddy slope in the wake of Poe, who, gesticulating wildly, led them in a wide half-circle around mah shack, to stop at the brink of the murky and bloated waters that surrounded the swampland – a vast moat, a circular girdle of black, poisoned water.

Through the milling crowd that teetered upon the moat's uncertain edge, ah glimpsed Poe wading fearlessly through the atramental waters, clad in white unnerwear, his sinister black jacket and shirt and his ridiculous black hat – ah hate hats – doffed and left with his horse back on terra firma somewhere. By the way he took to the water, it is mah belief that as the raving wompster waded deeper and deeper into the drowning-pool of his swollen religious mania, he saw himself not as one in a long line of disciples re-enacting the sacred ritual of Baptism, but rather this cachectic and beardless huckster, who was now bellowing at his followers to join him, believed he was the great hairy hydrophiliac himself, and that his sodden and shapeless longjohns were no less than camel skins.

One or two of the throng had stepped gingerly into the water, frightened by Poe's tirade and the grim vision he proffered for any who did not partake of his exoteric ablution. Bulrushes rocked and reeled in the low waters. People swarmed about me, closing in on all sides, bumping me on.

The thin shadows of bulrushes, backlit by spirit lamps, reached across the tar-black waters, so that gilded fingers of light raked the swelling dominion of the wild-eyed baptist with their eerie fidgetings.

'Praise the Lord!' bellowed Hilda Baxter, who, judging by her busty anhelations, had clearly pushed Wilma Eldridge on her two cranky, mud-packed wheels from the church to the lip of the baptismus, quite probably unaided. But now, her sanity temporarily unhinged through sheer exhaustion – or so it seemed – she ignored the frantic objections of the crippled crone and, abandoning her place behind the wheelchair, leaped monstrously into the raven drink and thundered toward the evangelist.

'I am vile! I am foul! My spirit stinketh!' she roared, as ah squatted in her spot behind the chair and watched through the wheels.

'Wash me! Wash me!' she cried, and ah noticed the wheelchair, packed with black muck, sink an inch into the muddy bank. The cripple stiffed, hovering as she was on the threshold of ablution.

'Elijah! Baptize us!' burst forth Carp Boone and, hand in hand with his wife Sadie, he pressed past me and plunged into the sinister water. The throng inched forward.

'I want to be clean! Renew my spirit, Baptist!' piped pink-eyed Sadie, and a thunderbolt rent the heavens with a spike of blue light.

'And I, Baptist! Wash away my sin!' cried another who had braved the floodlands. Ah turned around and attempted to push back through the crowd, but people were clambering from the rear ranks to the front, pushing and shoving their way to redemption, and ah found mahself, after considerable struggling, precisely where ah had started – pressed against the back of the wheelchair.

Wilma Eldridge had a front-row seat and she sat facing the soup, frozen stiff and speechless with fear, her two bony hands gripping the sides of her contraption, her bare wet head sitting erect on her scrawny neck – and, well, ah was kind of sandwiched between this twisty old gimp and the roiled throng – and, well, all the time the pushing and the shoving and the jabbing was getting more intolerable – yes, it was – and the cloacal sump that they were rejoicing in was filling more and more with candidates ready to be purified – and, well, a lot of things were working their way through mah mind – like, well, first off, ah didn't belong here with these people, and, secondly, ah was going to be up to mah eyeballs in sewerage if ah didn't do something fast, and ah was thinking about some kind of diversionary tactic, and how, if something fairly drastic happened to Poe or one of the faithful – and someone elbowed me again and ah thought 'Dear Wilma Wheelchair, why is it that we unfortunates, the lame and the dumb – why must we forever be the ones who catch all the crap? Why?' and as ah leaned over and yanked back her safety brake, ah believe ah almost heard her draw breath in order to answer me – ah did – as ah squeezed to one side and let the surge of the mass do its ugly business.

The chair rolled forward with a groan of vulcanized rubber against steel, a flurry of futile fingers furiously back-braking, raking the mud-caked spokes, hammering the handbrake. It leaned, toppled forward and loomed out over the water's grim catoptric surface that stretched before her, and then completing a half-somersault plunged headlong into the shallows of the abysmal, baptismal bilge.

A minute or two passed in the watching where all the madness was just a distant murmur in mah ear, as if infected by mah sense of quietude, and then ah saw the left foot twitch and almost immediately ah saw it twitch a second time – this dead foot – trying to gain someone's attention, ah expect – and after much floccillating she was remembered, and the stronger men of the concourse were upon her, hoisting the wheelchair and the gagging woman out of the turbid, reeking shallows and into the rain. Wilma Eldridge wore a hood of tar-black sewage that stretched down over the tops of her shoulders, the rest of her body being coated in a lamina of surface scum – dead leaves, rotten reeds, bulrush seeds. She was lifted, rigid and blue, back into the chair by the Schultz twins, all three ignoring the ferret-like fussings of her husband. Baker Wiggam dropped his massive grey great-coat over her shivering body as the cripple lifted her face to the inclement heavens and let the hood of filth be washed away.

Somewhat sobered by the incident, the crowd, with the intention of deferring its baptism for a short time, gathered around the bank, whilst Abie Poe, who had himself climbed from the waters, stood behind the decrepit wheelchair, gripping it by the handles. Conducting a long, drawn-out scan of his congregation, staring into silence each of those that still talked, he took one deep nasal intake of air, then cried out, 'Can you smell the sulphur? Breathe it, everyone. Learn that stench! *Sulphur! The stink of Satan!*' He leaned over Wilma Eldridge and spoke softly to the stunned crone – to her, yes, yet to all – the way only Poe knew how, his tirades being full of sinister whispers and poison hisses, though never a word escaped unheard.

'Praise be to God, Wilma Eldridge,' he whispered. 'Satan, thy name is Calamity. The Devil's is the hand that pusheth us forth into the abyss! But it is the hand of the Lord that pulleth us out!'

'Hallelujah!' bleated the crowd sequaciously.

Then, from only a few feet away, came the sing-song tauntings of a child, pealing out above the din of the rain, above the mob's dumbfusion, above the tumid throb throb throb of mah heart's condition.

'There's ya Deevil! There's ya arm that done the pushing! Him, there! Ah seen him do it! Threw the safety catch and let her roll! Kerspla-a-ash!! See? In the reeds yonder, chicken-scared 'cause he knows he done it!'

Fists Wiggam stood, legs astride, puffed up with spite, one pudgy arm pointed at me as he yelled, 'Idjit threw her in the sewer! Idjit threw her in the sewer!' with screwed-up nose and sour mouth. 'There's ya stinker! There's ya stinker!'

Suddenly everybody seemed to have taken a step in mah direction! Then another!

In no time at all Poe had loomed out of the mob, rolling one soppy sleeve of his unnerwear way up above the elbow. He plunged his arm into the rushes and hauled me out, one huge, black hand clamped vice-like about the back of mah neck.

The whole damn mob crowded around, all staring and craning and looking disgusted – all nodding and going 'Uh-huh' and 'Ye-e-s' and 'That's the one', and suddenly there were two hundred witnesses all crying, 'Sabotage!' Ah just stared at the ground, Poe's steely fingers still clamped around mah neck.

'Who are ya, baw?' snarled Poe, and then to the crowd, 'Who owns this child?'

Fists Wiggam piped up. 'This kid's trash, Preacher! Lives in the shack yonder.' And again his little fat hand did its bit of pointing.

'What's your name?' said Poe, grabbing me by the chin and jerking mah face upward so he could better see me. *I asked you your name, baw.*

'Ain't got one! Couldn't speak it if he had'n! He's a idjit! His daddy's got hill in him! He's schoopid dumb, Preacher!' squealed Fists. Ah looked up into Poe's terrible face. The intensity with which he stared at me was becoming almost embarrassing. And then, before mah eyes, ah saw his face dramatically change. The cruel crimson scar blanched and became a pale violet, and his vulturous eyes glazed, turned hyalescent – but strangely smoky too, as if the hell-fire that had raged behind them had burnt itself out, but still smouldered steadily. His tone of voice became suddenly hollow, and when he spoke to me it was as if he was addressing someone inside of me. The crowd moved closer, mouths agape, infected by the preacher's turn of mood.

'Behold, a child which hath a dumb spirit. How long hath this futile spirit been within? I say life-long! I say possibly ten years or longer hath his spirit lain dumb. O faithless generation, how long must I suffer thee?' cried Poe.

'How long must I suffer *thee*?!' cried ah, inside.

'I am the spirit of Elijah,' continued Poe, weirdly, 'a little cleansing, a little healing, a little crying in the wilderness.'

The crowd moved in and ah sought desperately for an opening in its ranks.

'If thou canst believe, then anything is possible. Dost thou truly believe?' asked the preacher, abstractly, and a few said 'Ye' and 'Ah do' – uncertain of who the preacher was talking to.

'Then, dumb spirit, I charge thee! Come out of this child and enter no more!' Poe cried out.

And, well, ah felt a squirming of mah entrails and suddenly ah knew – ah just *knew* that ah was going to speak – yes, ah did – and the squirming tore into mah chest and roiled up mah glottis into mah mouth, and ah spat with all mah heart. A great glob of sputum hit Abie Poe on the right knee, dangling greenly there, then dripped and slid obscenely down his foot and between his toes.

XI

A wholly joyous moment burst upon Fists Wiggam's mean-spirited horizons.

With the intention of selling Abie Poe's spent bullets to the Ukulites as souvenirs, the Wiggam boy had furiously searched the slate-slab wall that encircled the wishing well. He found instead a note, folded inside a plastic bag, that had been stuffed between two slabs. His eyes narrowed and he chuckled as he read.

Dear Sardus,

I am struck barren and deemed unworthy to mother your child. I will remain your wife through all eternity. We will be united in a kinder world, for we have both known another so bitter and terrible. I await your hand and in the Kingdom stand, for here in my heart be your seated place.

     Your advent embrace,
     Rebecca

By mid-afternoon, Fists had pinned the suicide letter to the public notice-board outside the Courthouse. By six o'clock, there was barely a soul in the whole valley who had not visited the Courthouse to read it, except perhaps Sardus Swift himself, who had not been seen since retiring to his lonely fortress nearly a year before.

XII

This period of perpetual rain became known amongst the Ukulites as The Three Years of the Malediction and was synonymous with death, catastrophe, divine vengeance and destruction. As the figures show, by the end of the second year, 1942, the mortality rate had risen to over double the tally of 1940. In 1943, more than three times as many deaths occurred as did in the year before the rain. Observe these figures:

1940	5 deaths
1941	9 deaths
1942	12 deaths
1943	16 deaths

But if we are attempting somehow to come to terms with the extent, or rather the depth, of the Ukulites' tragedy, we should also note that at the end of 1943 there were four *more* Ukulite adherents than there had been before the rain. The reason for this is simple: the pluvial downfall was responsible for a mad escalation in the number of births over that same triennial. Here are the figures:

1940	3 births
1941	4 births
1942	18 births
1943	17 births
1944	16 births

Thus, if one considers only the statistics given above, the years of catastrophe could just as easily have been tagged 'The Three Years of Fecundity'. The children conceived in this triennium became known as 'Rain Babies' or, later, 'Rain Children'.

XIII

'What shall we do with this day? *What?* Now that we have cleansed our souls in the sacred waters, what shall we do? *What?!*' demanded Poe from the pulpit.

A dark murmur travelled through the congregation, each looking one to the other. But most eyes rested finally on Philo Holfe, eldest and tallest of the Holfe brothers, who had been unofficially elected spokesman for the Ukulite community. One-time curator of the small Natural History Museum located in the annexe of the Courthouse – now sadly neglected and rarely opened – Philo Holfe was a simple but well-meaning man, commanding respect if not for his brains, then for his brawn.

Philo's considerable bulk rose from his pew, afloat in a galaxy of lobbying looks. Eloquence was a word Philo did not know. After some time he reluctantly spoke. 'If you please, Preacher Poe, perhaps that question is best left up to you? What shall we do this day, now that we have been cleaned?'

'Perhaps we should lay right down in the same stinking cesspit that first sullied us? Is that what you want?! Shall we sit on our goddamn laurels and bemoan our accursed misfortune?! Shall we just bide our time and wait for heaven to run dry?! *Shall we wait?! Brothers and sisters! No, I say, and again I say no!* Today is a day of reckoning. God watcheth this day and judgeth all. In most the seed of the Lord will flourish, rich and green – but lo! There are yet those who grow, even now, black and twisted amongst us. It is they who have corrupted the valley, have infested its soul, and have brought the wrath of God down upon you!'

The rain seemed to hammer a little harder in support of the preacher. Wetly, Philo asked, 'How shall we know, Preacher Poe? How shall we spot the black 'n' twisty plant?'

The congregation approved the question with a low murmur.

'I, Abie Poe, am a specialist in weeds! I am the hand that roots them out! They shall no longer say "I am the Branch of Life" – they who are the Stalk of Death!'

Poe raised his hands to the rafters and curled them into fists. 'I am the sickle that hovereth poised at the foot of the Stalk of Death!'

Poe slammed down both fists simultaneously, thumping the leather-bound Bible that rested upon the pulpit.

'But who, Preacher Poe? Who?' asked Carl Holfe, standing suddenly, his urgent question echoed by the entire congregation as it rose to its feet in a rowdy clamour. With fingers outstretched, Abie Poe raised his hands a second time. He stood there for some minutes, head lowered, hands extended. Finally the din quelled and Poe lifted his head.

'I think we have one brave soul here willing to cast the first stone. Mrs Eldridge, would you like to come forward?'

From the congregation came forth six women, led by the cripple. A platoon of hags with ruckled faces disfigured by the bitter bile of their days and eyes small and yellow and mean with spite. Six wives like six hooded lizards, blowing lethal breath. The mussitation of the crowd dropped instantly. All that could be heard was the squeal and scrape of the battered wheelchair as it drew up before the pulpit and slowly turned to face the congregation. Hilda Baxter, the cripple's constant companion, stood behind her tightly gripping the handles of the chair. Eliza Williamson and Bess Snow stood either side of her like a pair of matching suitcases, and behind them, to the left and right of the pulpit, tiny Hulga Vanders and giant Kate Byrun gave the stone sorority a lopsided look. Each woman gave Poe a nod of recognition then turned to the congregation, now seated, and silently challenged any dissentient. Wilma Eldridge fingered her crucifix, massaging the silver Christ to warmth.

'Clearly, brothers and sisters, Satan has planted a thistle in God's very soil.'

'A-men,' said the women around her in unison, the claque echoing them a moment later.

86

'And clearly we must locate that thistle and tear it from the earth.'

'A-men!'

'Brothers and sisters of the prophet Jonas Ukulore, I know where it grows! That thistle! That weed! I know!'

'A-men!'

'That evil weed, perverting and corrupting! *I know!* That evil weed, whose solicitating arms reach down into the very hearts of our homes!'

'*A-men! A-men!*' the men and women of the congregation blattered with growing momentum, though there were few amongst them who knew whom it was they prosecuted.

'The weed grows deep, and black are its roots. Scarlet is its demon flower!'

'A-men!!'

'*Yea! Ukulites! Yea! Soldiers of the Lord!*'

'A-men!!'

'*That weed grows deep on Hooper's Hill! Together we must find the strength to cast it out! A-men!!*'

'A-men!'

The women all rose to their feet, thin hard hands clasped to rising chests. Those who had them looked to their husbands, and the transgressors amongst these men were the first to stand in support. Gloating smiles slid into the mouths of the women. Wilma Eldridge drubbed the arms of her chair and Poe thumped at his Bible till all four fists were beating the same grave and direful metre. Soon the valley sounded with the manifold thump! thump! thump! of fist against leather or polished oak. Thump! Thump! Thump! pounded the heart of the House of the Lord, up on Glory Hill.

XIV

Cosey Mo lay slumped in the kick and prickle of morphine, the bloody syringe hanging, spent, between thumb and fore. She tied off. The crashing rain retreated, becoming a distant murmur to her ears. Her heart's heavy beat lay like a wonderful egg, warm in its wet and crimson nest.

Naked on the bench seat, she curled toward the window that overlooked the valley and peeled back its curtain. Drawing up, she forced her eyes to focus. Catching sight of a set of headlights moving up Hooper's Hill, her eyes drifted to the clock on the wall. It was twelve noon. Sunday. In the past few weeks, Sunday afternoon had become one of her busiest periods; even so, twelve o'clock seemed very early.

Naked still, and perched on the end of her bed, Cosey applied her make-up, her limbs' former languor lost in a series of well-practised movements – a blackened stroke, a blushing smudge, a smear of scented cherry, a lavender dab – until her heavy lids and sullen pout were brought magically alive. She pulled on a pair of stockings, hitching them to nothing, and, lastly, the pink robe. Buttoning it down the front, Cosey Mo seemed oblivious to the number of vehicles that had pulled up outside her caravan.

Glancing first in the mirror and then at the clock, she took a deep breath and opened the door, her breasts swelling and shifting inside her scant robe. 'Well now, who's the early bird, then?' she teased to the drumming rain. There, leaning and rocking on her heels, as she was, back and forth, in the doorway of the caravan.

From amidst the teeming folds of the rain-drenched noon, Abie Poe's chill skull loomed forth a carping bone of accusation, hissing:

'Behold, brethren! Behold the scarlet sloven! Discovered! Hear this, whore! *Dirtiness is next to anti-Godliness!* Yea! Painted seductress, your den is upturned! *Temptress! Whore!* Speak not, for your tongue is cloven! *As is your gender! Cloven as the viper's tongue! Cloven as the hoof of Satan!* Your words know only the alleyways of trickery and deceit! Speak not, for our ears are warned against you! *Bloody lily of the muck-heap! Begone! Yea! Get thee behind me, Satan! You have riddled this pious acre with sin and sloth! But your day has come! Out! Out! Get thee from our ground!'*

The sisterhood of screaming heads hovered around the preacher, forming a grotesque gloriole about him. They barked like wounded bitches, Wilma Eldridge leading the pack.

'*Out!* Fornicatrix! *Begone!* While we still have a mind to let you! Base baggage! Minx! Or is it better we *burn* you out? *Wicked temptator! Witch! Out – or burn you we shall!'*

Bobbing about the periphery of Cosey's comprehension like smaller dogs, the menfolk, in sheepish support, finally echoed the bitter maledictions of their wives. Those who wore the leg-irons both of wifedom and of whoredom rattled their chains the loudest.

Framed in the doorway, Cosey had a tired quality to her appearance that served only to enhance her vigorous sensuality. The muscles that lay beneath her thin robe tightened as her body locked into a stance of defiant outrage. Her top lip curled back, baring strong white teeth, and she hissed and seethed and glared at her castigators. Trembling with rage, Cosey thrust one damning finger forward and the men cowered and dodged its accusatory line as if it were a hexing wand that she pointed, or a witch-doctor's terrible bone.

The crowd fell silent, the rain hammering at its hind. Only Poe's burlesque banter and the hawking squawks of the cripple, writhing and thrashing in her chair, rose above the rain's interminable din.

Cosey pointed at Franklin Eldridge, who stood behind his wife, but it was the jaundiced eyes of the cripple into which she stared. Cosey's lips rose in a cruel, mocking smile.

'Why, Franklin! For shame! You know your day is Friday and here you are again and it's only Sunday! O such is the lure of a good, strong set of legs!' Cosey's robe parted for one taunting thigh.

'Fra-a-a-anklin!' roared Wilma Eldridge. 'Shut her up!'

Franklin, a small sad man, hiked the steps of the caravan and, wheezing like a distant dying siren, delivered a blow to the harlot's mouth. He stood back, mouth agape, shocked at the measure of his deed, shocked by the violence and drawing of blood.

Dabbing at her lip and again extending her finger, Cosey saw more damage to be done. She singled out a bigger, badder target.

'Oh it's Doggy-Dawes! Down on all four . . .'

And with fists the size of Cosey's face, Douglas Dawes pushed Franklin Eldridge to one side and, barking once, batted the harlot's skull first left, then right, back and forth, spinning her this way and that, and wrapping her in the beaded curtain that hung in the doorway. There she dangled like a limp marionette, then collapsed in a heap at his feet as though discarded by some reckless puppeteer.

Douglas Dawes descended the steps and was swallowed up by the slow-closing crowd. No sooner had he disappeared than the body of Cosey Mo stirred, as if driven on by the numbing narcotic. She raised herself to her knees, lifting her right hand a fraction and speaking through a mouthful of blood and pieces of teeth; she gurgled, she blithered, stupid. But the crowd was upon her before her utterance could take form, drowning her in a hail of fists and feet. The storm raged unabated, quelling only when her body lay, naked and limp, in the blood-coloured mud at the bottom of the steps.

Tilting her head toward the battered harlot and straining at her clogged wheels in an attempt to motivate herself, Wilma Eldridge cast her stupefied spouse a sly, conspiratorial glance.

'Wheel me, Franklin,' she barked, her voice set a-tremble by the violence she had witnessed. 'Closer!'

Franklin Eldridge dutifully complied, the mud sucking noisily at the chair's wheels as he pushed his wife alongside Cosey's motionless body.

'Lepers and harlots should be marked! Your shame shall not go unrecognized, Mystery!' said the cripple, and proffering her hand palm up she added impatiently, 'Franklin! The shears!'

Franklin reached into his jacket, produced a large pair of scissors and pressed them into his wife's hand.

'May your sin be upon you, whore!' she said, leaning out over the side of her chair. And the enraged woman set about hacking off to the scalp Cosey Mo's bountiful locks.

She sat back in her chair with the long muddied locks of hair in her hand, and the cruel smile that had formed upon her lips as she attended to 'the marking' turned suddenly into a sneer of disgust. She flung the fistful of hair on to the churned-up ground.

'Whore hair!' she said, each word spat out like it was too foul for the mouth.

Philo Holfe broke up the crowd and Doc Morrow knelt by Cosey, lifting one arm by the wrist.

'She'll live, I think,' said the doctor bitterly, and laid her arm down again.

The mob dispersed without a word. Franklin Eldridge took the handles of his wife's chair. Wilma looked at him, her mouth twisted into a rebarbative smile of contempt. She nodded toward the outstretched arm of the battered whore and, wet-lipped and gloating, was borne away. Cosey's brittle fingers cracked like candy beneath the wheels of the chair.

Philo Holfe shuddered and for a moment shut tight his eyes. Then he said, 'We'll take her. Carl and me, we'll take her out.'

The two brothers lifted the broken woman gently into the front seat of their pick-up. The doctor covered her with her sopping robe, brown and bloody.

Carl Holfe drove, making a wide turn atop Hooper's Hill before plunging down the drive toward Maine.

Abie Poe backed his nag into the little caravan and, with some added encouragement from his wicked spurs, the animal sent Cosey Mo's tiny pink parlour tumbling down the side of Hooper's Hill like a runaway toy.

Alone atop the hill, Abie Poe dropped to his knees and,

stretching his arms heavenward, he wept. A thunderbolt leapt from a cloud's blackened belly.

'Thank you, Lord, thank you!' cried the preacher into the crackling thunderama. 'O thank you, and again I say, O Lord, *I thank you!*'

Ah saw the little caravan come careering down Hooper's Hill and explode in a splinter of wet pink wood. From where ah sat the caravan was exactly the same size as mah thumbnail and ah watched the crowd as it followed it down the hill, led by the raving priest. With the wreckage at the bottom they managed to build a blazing fire, despite the rain. Poe flapped up blackly against an infernal backdrop of flame, framed in dark clouds as the kerosene smoked thickly. The windows exploded with four loud cracks. Showers of yellow sparks burst like constellations of new stars.

Ah saw all of Cosey Mo's sexy red unnerwear hanging across the bushes like devilish fruit, and on the ground too in sheery pools of scarlet lace and bloody silk.

In mah mind's eye, ah saw the hill all covered with naked, writhing whore-wraiths that moaned and romped in the mud, all humping ghosts in the mad grapple of copulation.

The following day ah sifted through the pile of ash and cinder that lay at the foot of Hooper's Hill, and found amongst the charred remains a blackened beauty case. It contained the blue-glass bottles of scented water. Coloured cotton-balls and bottles were both undamaged. In the case was also a hypodermic syringe and three attachable needles that were very sharp. A bubble of blood sprung upon mah thumb. Also a photograph of Cosey Mo, upon the back of which was scribbled a short poem, signed and dated June 1930; two tiny brown vials, the seals of which were as yet unbroken; a packet of three pink balloons that needed stronger lungs than mine to fill; and a gold locket containing a kindergraph of a little girl that was unmistakably Cosey Mo. Ah treasured these things in a shoebox that ah lined with strips of newsprint and filed under 'Cosey Mo, 1943'. Ah also took a white nightgown ah found snagged on a shrub. When wrung out and dried it looked fresh and crisp.

That day, if mah memory serves me well, mah scalp was a battlefield of tuft and bloody clump, of scab and gash. Later, in mah room, ah dabbed at the six or so crusts that dotted mah skull with a ball of cotton-wool soaked in the essence of lavender. Mah skull stung as the scab grew soft and lifted from the slitted scissor wounds. Those fucken scissors! *That fucken bitch!* Ah could hear mah mother cackling with glee up at the shack at the freakish mess she had made. Rage throbbed through mah brains, humiliation burned mah ears.

If it were not for the fact that ah shine victorious over the whole lot of them here in mah dying time, then humiliation and rage would, ah have no doubt, consume me still. As it stands, mah countenance has been soured only marginally by the memory, and certainly her massive personage would shrink to that of a gnat if she were here, now, in these grander, greater days.

Mah butchered scalp was fragrant with Cosey's waters. Lavender. Rose. Musk.

Ah kept the sorry clumps of hair that littered the shack floor in with mah other clippings – finger and toe nails, dead skin, teeth, eyelashes, scabs, that sort of thing.

Kept beneath mah bed ah had twenty-two shoeboxes full of mah things. Ah visited Cosey Mo's box without restraint. Each time ah took a drop or two of the waters. Heaven scented these growing years.

Yes, but up on Hooper's Hill . . .

Up on Hooper's Hill ah scoured the ground for traces of her – some blood, maybe, or her body print still held in the mud. But whatever secrets belonged to this hill the cryptic rain had erased from its memory, or else the hill simply wasn't telling – or so it seemed.

Disappointed and not looking forward to mah slippery descent, ah made to leave, pitching the empty pickling jar ah had brought along in case of a lucky find down the hill.

It was then ah discovered two curious parallel furrows about three feet apart, each rain-filled stripe about two inches wide and twice as deep – evil, mean-looking furrows they were, and ah followed them to a place where the terra gumbo had been all churned up.

There, floating in a large pool of muddy water, ah found the harlot's hair.

The flaxen locks shone like a reef of pure gold as ah fished them from the dingy rain-pocked puddle, and as ah did this ah couldn't help but be struck by the uncanny duality of the incident – the coincident shearing of our crowning glory. And as ah stood there with the rain pissing down on mah ravaged scalp ah experienced an overwhelming sensation of incomparable shame – *her* shame – and for a moment in time the signals of mah heart and those of the harlot crossed paths, and ah knew that at that very moment, wherever she might be, Cosey Mo was experiencing a hell fully different to what she had known before – *mah* hell, just as ah was living hers.

The lock of hair which ah carefully wrapped in a handkerchief was the link. Yes, it was. The lock was the link. Yes, it was.

As ah slipped and lunged and skidded and rolled homeward, mah mind turned each word – the lock was the key. The lock was the key. The lock was the key. The lock was –

XV

At around eleven o'clock that Sunday evening, the rusty red pick-up belonging to the brothers Holfe could be seen approaching the valley.

Now, as they passed through its northern entrance, the pitch firmament issued what seemed at this late hour to be a torrent of gushing oil, pissing down upon the windshield and coiling about the windshield wipers like asps, black and alive.

'It isn't stopped, brother,' said Philo.

Carl shook his head and flicked the lights on to full beam. Pressing his face right up to the windshield so that his body curved in a hunch over the wheel, he squinted into the rain. 'No, it isn't.' Then a little farther down Maine, he added, 'Brother Philo, I think that if there is one thing clear in this whole valley, then it is . . . that it isn't . . . stopped.'

To be sure, the heavy drizzle of early afternoon had swelled to a fully drenching deluge. Nothing had stopped. Nor in the days to come did it stop, nor quell, or even temper. Not a single ray of sunlight broke the black and brawling firmament. God, it would seem, was blind to their acts of contrition. Their despair was all-consuming. There was nothing left to do but remain in the valley and suffer, or pack up and leave for more sunny climes and so live in guilt and shame for ever.

Poe, the self-appointed Messiah, became almost overnight the living embodiment of a township's private shame, a manifestation of their wretchedness and the focus of insuperable hatred. He refrained from entering the township itself again.

The church on Glory Flats grew ever more derelict – eventually leaning, as the months drew on, a little askew on its stilts, attended by no one except an increasingly drunken Abie Poe. His black apparel ragged and soiled, his harried face bitten by deep crevices of shadow and his eyes lost in the dark pools of their orbits, the deranged preacher would skulk around the chambers of the church, muttering half-remembered prayers, sometimes climbing into the pulpit to deliver lunatic sermons to the ever-faithful – the rats, the toads and the rain. The roof leaked. Windows got broken. Never rung, the vespers bell rusted in its frame. The once refulgent interior grew squalid and foul.

Thus another year passed. And the rain pissed down.

XVI

A wind whistled through the valley and blew on through the town. Ah sat in the rain, by the petrol station, listening to the Texaco billboard knock above the pumps on the count of three each time the wind hit it – the first always the loudest, the last you could barely hear. *'Knock!!* Knock! knock.' *'Knock!!* Knock! knock.'

The string of red and white canvas flags tied on to the cornerpost of Noah's Barber Shop would flutter and flap, flutter and flap with each new gust. Just as the last knock of the sign sounded, the little canvas flags, hanging limply, would perk up as the same bluster of wind hit the barber shop, and all red and white they would gaily flutter and flap, flutter and flap, until the gust passed onward down Maine, and then they hung silent again, awaiting the sign's next signal.

If the wind did not whistle then nor would the sign knock, and if the sign did not knock, up there above the pumps, then the canvas flags would hang, limply strung, never to flap, never to flag and never to flutter.

And if the wind did not come waltzing through the valley on this wet and windy summer night of 1943, then the township of Ukulore Valley would in windless silence be – bar the fremitus of the rain, of course, its incessant racket like the endless clamour of the blood, long since gone unnoticed by the ear.

And if the wind did not waltz, then not a flap, knock or whistle, not a single pump or rustle, would break the solemn silence of those wind-worried things.

Did ah tell you how we did not hear the rain anymore?

Not a soul could ah see in town, for not a one could be found – not a solitary one nor a strolling pair. It was customary for the Ukulite elders to walk in pairs – in pairs that is – though many

97

often strolled alone, as is the custom of the aged all around the world – that is to say all around the world, strolling for the old is quite the custom – paired or alone, till the ends of their hearts, or their legs, or their days – alone or in pairs and into their graves.

But not here in town – not a strolling, whistling, waltzing soul – not in a house, up a hall, on a stair – not along Maine nor in Motherwells nor in Memorial Square.

And thusways ah allowed mah mind to ruminate on this rainy day, so much so that ah almost did not register a thin, hunched figure hobble past, dressed from head to toe in a filthy dun-coloured blanket. This enigma walked as if its shoes were filled with sharp stones. From the coarse cloth in which it was clad a deep cowl had been fashioned, and as it hobbled down Maine the stranger looked to me like a rogue leper right off the pages of Leviticus and ah imagined the quick raw flesh hidden in the folds of the sopping sackcloth.

With the veils of grey rain obscuring mah pursuit – both sound- and vision-wise – ah found ah could tail the shambling wretch at close range. Occasionally the mysterious figure would buckle at the waist as if gripped by a nagging colic, then hitch the ragged blanket at the shoulders, cough thinly and continue the painful trek down the centre of Maine.

Leaving the road at the gardens, the figure paused beneath a wrought-iron arch – the main gateway into Memorial Gardens. Framed in a romping embranglement of iron filigree, crimson roses and rusting cherubs, the hooded blanket remained un-moving. A yellow bulb throbbed and crackled overhead. Ah stood about ten feet away, the pluvial curtain mah only form of concealment.

Ah searched for an exposed hand, a peeping toe, a slice of face caught in the humming light – proof that a being of flesh and blood existed within – but ah found none. And the more ah considered the enigma before me, the more ah thought how like a phantom or enshrouded wraith the figure seemed to be.

Ah was reminded of an illustration ah had torn from a book ah had found buried unner some mutilated girlie magazines on the junk-pile out back of the shack. It was called *Go Ask the Angel* or *O the Ass on that Angel* or some such smut. Anyway, if it had ever had any pictures then they had all been torn out – all except one, on the very first page.

It showed a little girl, feverish and wasted and terribly sick, lying in her little bed. All around her were bunches of red and yellow and pink flowers, and standing at the end of the bed was a macabre figure – dressed in a long, hooded robe and looking all the more ghastly because of its gaping, faceless hood and empty sleeves, one of which was raised and pointed at the little hollow-eyed sickling. Along the bottom of the picture it read thus:

'. . . and it being time, Death called Angel home, saying slowly and resonantly, "Angel . . . Angel . . . Angel . . ."'

Ah had cut the picture from the book and put it in a large paper envelope labelled 'Pics. Cut-outs. Signs. Omens'.

Examining the figure huddled in the gateway to the Square ah was left aghast at its similarity to the picture of Death. Ah was. A formicating horror spread across mah person and mah mind jabbered doggerel, chilling and terror-riven.

Then the grim phantom stepped slowly into the Square – at least, ah guess that's what happened – ah mean, well – what ah mean is that ah mahself had been temporarily arrested by the increasingly swollen tides of terror, and, well, ah don't know exactly, but ah lost some minutes to deadtime – have ah told you about *deadtime*? Yes? No? Well ah *did* lose some time to mah other sel– . . . shit, forget it – suddenly ah took control of mah consciousness again, alerted by the smashing of glass, and ah found mahself crouching behind the drinking fountain with Death, the wraith in the dirty blanket, still in mah sight.

And, well – Hell's pale agent – that is, Death, the king of terrors – yes, that frightful, formless, faceless phantom, Death – yes, Death – why, Death had entered the circle of yellow light that flooded the sepulchre and the monument – but not only that – Death, Life's hooded hangman and time's earnest executioner – yes, pale, pale Death had grown two flesh-and-blood, skin-and-bone hands. And what is more, those two mortal hands nursed a curious bundle the shape and size of a large loaf of bread. Wrapped around the bundle was the dry but rotting robe of the prophet, Jonas Ukulore. Ah could see from where ah squatted that the glass display case of the sepulchre that housed the crown, sceptre and robe worn by the prophet had been broken into – ah remembered the sound of breaking glass which awoke me – and, having compared the size of the hole in the glass to that of the rocks that lined the side of the sepulchre, it was clear to me that whoever or whatever it was that busied itself so openly in that circle of spilled light was no cat burglar or professional thief – no – nor was it Death – o no sir – o madam ah say no – it weren't the Grim Ripper – it sure weren't Death.

Ah watched this fraud – this wretch masquerading as the final Enigma, its face still hidden in the shelter of the hood – place the bundle on the second step of the monument. And, with hands now free of their burden, the impostor began to execrate the heavens. And ah noticed that one hand seemed to be bent out of shape, deformed. Ah could not help but wonder what freakish deformities could be concealed within the hood and the sackcloth, to allow so readily the display of such a hideous appendage.

And suddenly the hill of sackcloth and the two mismatched hands were joined by a voice – and it was a *boy's* voice – *and it was a boy's voice* – a terrible screeching soprano.

And though ah could not make out a single word of his tirade, muffled as it was by the drumming rain, ah could tell by the furious pace of its delivery and the mad raking gestures of his hands that this boy was something of a kindred spirit – a fellow outcast, a brother in pain. And – well, you can imagine the excitement that ah experienced at having found someone to share the strafes and stripes of public rebuke – a companion to cling to through the long dark night and through the longer, darker day – someone ah could plough mah lonely furrow beside – a companion through the laughter and the tears – in short, a *friend* – and ah awaited an opportunity to present mahself without him becoming scared and taking flight.

But at that very moment, the light in Doc Morrow's surgery window lit up, followed by the porch light spilling on to the street.

The stranger, having ceased his ranting, leaned back against the monument, thoroughly drained. And it was only when the doctor emerged from his surgery and stood on the edge of the porch, probing the rain with a flashlight, that the boy in the dun-coloured blanket began to limp painfully down the steps. As one crabbed claw pulled back the hood and he cast a furtive glance in the direction of the doctor, a strip of tell-tale light betrayed a woefully disfigured countenance.

It took me a full minute before ah could put a name to that savaged face.

'That ain't no goddamn boy!' ah thought, as ah watched the figure move away. 'That ain't no goddamn little *boy*!'

Doc Morrow crossed the street and entered the park, so ah was forced to remain crouched behind the water fountain, while . . . while . . . while Death left by the side-entrance.

Dressed in a big blue rubber mac and matching hat, the doctor walked toward the monument, picking up his pace a little more with each approaching step. He was running by the time he reached it.

Stooping, he scooped up the bundle wrapped in the prophet's robe that had been dumped on the steps. Then, hunching over the bundle, he urgently retraced his steps back to the surgery.

By the time ah stumbled on to Maine, it was pitch black and pissing down, and though ah searched the northern end of Maine ah could not find her again . . .

Ah returned to the shack alone, where ah passed the night in restless pursuit of her memory – of when her face was more beautiful than anything ah had ever seen.

And ah cursed mahself for having lost her.

And ah cursed mahself for having lost her again.

XVII

Euchrid sat in the cold cloisters of solitude, eyes screwed shut. Cut adrift in a plethora of sensation, he surrendered wholly and completely to the murk of his chosen sanctum: The Swampland.

He heard the shrinking corset of kudzu bruise the mighty main-stem of the cedar tree. He listened and heard the tree's ancient limbs groan as it surrendered to the killing woven vine. He heard, too, the harping song of the tarantula, crouched in a corner, plucking each dew-dipped string of his web. Nor did the crackle of leaves in a stump's hollow heart go unnoticed. Or the bones and beaks of dead birds. The mad scrabble of a trapped wing. Eggs opening. Nests burning. A tumbling clump of fur. A dislodged feather. A squall. A trickle. A shrill.

He listened now to the sound of his own body in bondage, his spine and costal crumbling, his tested plexus straining, his innards' hissance and the business of his skin and bones all moaning, all collared, all grounded upon the grim pin of existence.

Then he asked for his angel and henceforth an effluence of ultramarine light spilled across every log and knoll, each stump and knot and knurl, the blue luminary swamping the nook and the crack, the crack and the burrow, every dark and squalid hollow, each and every bog or mire or wallow, from that which is deep to that which is shallow; Euchrid's world, all echo and rhyme, all touched by shivers of hyacinth light.

The angel, now at his fingers' trembling tips, hovered on coral pinions, and her pinking robe of slippery silk billowed with upfanned air. Her dark tresses tumbled down her breasts, swollen now and heaving to his touch. Her lips just slightly parted as she came bending forward to plant a dizzying kiss upon his mouth, and to fill his hands with her warm breasts – fondled and gripped through the spasms and curds of love.

Euchrid put his face into the empty cups of his hands, and rolled on his side to face the wall, plunging deeper and deeper still into the bathos of the spent.

A blustered branch scratched at his window. Euchrid sighed and fell asleep.

XVIII

That night ah found little sleep. Torrid bloodings, spontaneous emissions, deaths-heads sweated into mah bedding . . .

Ah rose early to find Pa hitching Mule and setting off down the mudded track to Maine, head bent low, swiping the folds of rain with his stick. Mule shuddered and twitched neurotically, as numb to the old man's rod as he was to the rain. Ah was consumed by an urge to follow – drawn on, you might say – and, unnercover of the grey rain, ah did so.

Turning off the track and on to firmer ground, ah saw mah father stop suddenly by the side of the road and bark at Mule – and even from where ah stood ah could detect a certain urgency in his voice. And after beating the brute to a standstill, ah saw him throw down his stick and squat by a ditch at the roadside, transfixed by whatever it was before him.

Ah scrambled forward, climbed through the wire fence and peered through the wall of rotten cane-trash a few feet in front of him. In a ditch filled with water by the side of the track, one thin white arm floated like a blaked eel upon a blanket full of holes. Ah watched him fish the blanket out, lift her livid body from its watery grave and lay it down – stiffed already, ah think, from the ungainly attitude of her limbs. Taking a box of matches from Mule's saddle bag, he set about burning off the leeches that fed upon her body. He wiped her hair from her eyes and looked down at her ravaged face. Even from mah coign of vantage ah recognized the fine-boned nose – broken, her top teeth gone, her eyes puffy and dark and her skin broken in parts by a raging pemphigus. Her once luxurious body was wasted to death and the water had left her skin blanched and wrinkled.

With the help of Mule, Pa carted the body of Cosey Mo over to the cottonwoods. He did not look up and ah was undiscovered

– nor did ah care, so thoroughly numbed did ah feel. Ah looked on as Pa dug a hole and lifted her in, first making sure that she was covered by the blanket. The hole was off the track, a little closer to the swamplands but still on firm ground. He dug it deep, covered her over, and then patted the mud down with the back of the shovel. Then he took his whittling knife and a little chunk of wood about the size of a deck of cards, and, sitting on a rock which he had rolled over the grave, he set about carving something into the chunk, then wedged it unner the rock. After he had gone I rolled off the stone.

C. MO
R. I. P.
1943

Ah had never seen Pa do anything with such tenderness and feeling as when he buried the harlot of Hooper's Hill.

Ah got the urge to return to town. All mah bones were knocking up a notion that something was brewing.

XIX

By the early afternoon of 19 May 1943, just about every soul in Ukulore Valley knew of Doc Morrow's discovery. Most of the denizens were uninterested; others, namely a number of the womenfolk, changed that day from the nightdresses which had become their habitual garb into habiliments of coarse black flax and smocks of white, each one plaiting and coiling her long, loose locks and covering them with a strip of white lace.

By three o'clock around fifteen or so women huddled under the shelter of Doc Morrow's porch, their heavy shoes clopping upon the bare boards. This huddle of women included, among others, the invalid Wilma Eldridge, with her truckling companion Hilda Baxter rubbing constantly the handles of the wheelchair; Hulga Vanders – a wooden-head ogress, deep disgruntled furrows carved upon her face, great arms folded across her vast bosom; Nena Holfe and Olga Holfe, precious wives of the brothers; and, clinging to the arm of Nena, Edith Lamb, a shivering miniature porcelain antique of ninety, bent and blind and bloodless.

Three years had come and gone and not a day had passed that was not infused with God's drumming displeasure. The soot-and-ash sky, the rain, its incessant racket, the absence of sun and light and warmth, the damage to property and land, the ruined crops, the dwindling numbers, the flagging assets – all the calamities resultant from His wrath had ceased to be questioned by the band of believers who remained in the valley. The rain simply endured, stolidly suffered by the long-suffering Ukulites; but not without its toll.

One could see, in the group of womenfolk serried together on the porch, that something had indeed changed, or rather had gone missing. In the prolonged hibernal existence of the rain years, something had been worn from their once hard-lined faces

– washed away with the waiting. Something that had been rooted deep in the hearts of these pious souls, that had shone through their eyes, had now vanished. Certainly, the redolence of calm was gone, as was the look of inner confidence, of exclusiveness; and no longer now did the quiet belief in their own supernal destiny colour their expression.

Gone was the God in them.

Instead there was a look of resignation, of defeat, of shame – a flabbiness about their faces that reflected a flabbiness of the soul.

As they awaited the doctor, they spoke amongst themselves and their voices, flat and world-weary, were swallowed up by the drumming downpour and by their own muzzy dumfusion.

'. . . swathed in a swaddle and blue as a plum!' said one.

'It vill be a miracle zat it should live . . .' intoned Olga Holfe, and Nena Holfe, cupping her monstrous man's hands to her great brawling black-clad breasts, added, 'And such a tiny zing.'

'And wearing our prophet's very robe! Unthinkable!' fumed Wilma Eldridge.

'And wearing the prophet's sacred crown upon its little head,' elaborated Hilda Baxter, a chronic fabulist by nature.

'Rubbish!' spat the crippled Eldridge. 'Utter rubbish! Sacred crown indeed . . .'

Then, as if struck dumb, the women hushed, each drawing breath as the door to Doc Morrow's surgery swung open.

Across the road, perched on a public bench, sat Euchrid. He removed one water-filled boot and emptied it. He removed his other boot and did likewise. Bare-footed, his boots beside him on the bench, he peered through the inky precipitation at the black-clad sorority that milled about the doctor's office.

Euchrid watched as the surgery door swung open and the women, unanimous in their sudden breathless silence, formed a neat half-circle about the doctor. In his arms he cradled a bundle swathed in a clean white blanket, and smiling broadly he appeared to address his audience, though his words never reached Euchrid, drowned as they were in the fremitus of the rain.

Euchrid slid back into his boots and, unable to contain his curiosity, began to walk cautiously across the road. He heard a cheer rise from the onlookers, and as he reached the porch, he caught the last of the doctor's speech rising from the huddle.

'. . . it's a God-given miracle that she is even alive . . .' And then the doctor's words were lost in the coos and clucks of admiration, the squeals of delight that issued from the gathering.

Hesitantly, Euchrid climbed the steps, craning to glimpse that which inspired so much attention. He heard the doctor's voice booming again. '. . . gently with her . . . try not to wake her . . .' Then, her eyes fixed on the little pink face that peeked from the swaddle, Nena Holfe took the bundle from the woman next to her, rocked it gently, hummed a little, turned, cooed and, without looking up, pressed the babe into the arms of Euchrid the mute.

Euchrid looked at the babe and the babe looked at Euchrid.

A second or two passed in deathly silence.

Then a consentaneous cry of alarm leapt from the lips of the women as they comprehended the situation. Euchrid stood, overcome with panic, juggling the tot in his arms, unable to run.

Then the babe reached from her woollen swaddle and dug her tiny fingernail into Euchrid's neck.

Hulga Vanders retrieved the child with one massive paw, while beating Euchrid across the head with her umbrella. Nena and Olga Holfe followed suit, striking him repeatedly about the head, and soon the entire platoon, armed with umbrellas and walking sticks, had fallen upon Euchrid with a rain of blows served across his hunched and bucking body.

Eventually Euchrid was able to see clear of his attackers and take flight, tumbling down the steps into a deep and muddy puddle, and lurching off like a beaten dog into the rain and all down Maine, while his assailants remained in the shelter of the balcony, waving their umbrellas at the retreating figure.

Head down and hunched, Euchrid made his way through the thrashing rain, his paces reckless and irregular as he skidded and stumbled and slipped down the treacherous roadway.

Watching the ground for potholes and puddles, he became

aware of the faint but frantic stain of his shadow pooling about his feet, and was overcome by a curious sense of having found something that he thought he had lost for ever. As he ran and jumped and barrelled homeward, he saw, with increasing rapture, his long-lost companion grip ahold of his heels, and, passing the city limits sign, he slowed down – the reason for his mad flight forgotten in the light of his recent reunion – and with eyes glued to the ground drew to a halt, half expecting his shadow to keep on going or fade away again just as it had come. But it did neither, and he marvelled at the dark shape as it steadily deepened in intensity, hunched and squat about his feet.

Overcome by a thousand conflicting emotions, Euchrid bit his bottom lip and choked back a sob. So consumed was he by matters of the heart that when he tasted blood, the source of the flow did not register in his mind until he noticed a drop of it break the still surface of a puddle of muddy rainwater.

'Hey, shadow, ah've got a bloody nose,' thought Euchrid, as he pinched his nostrils and tilted back his head. His eyes closed, he felt his face glow warmly. He opened them to a dazzling light that was almost blinding, and, squinting, he saw that the sky above him was of infinite blue, cloudless and warm. The sun spun aloft, an erumpent orb of balling glory thrilling the blue sky with its brilliance.

Face lifted to meet the sun, Euchrid felt the hotness, heard the silence, breathed the new air, sensed his new-found shadow cringing at his feet.

'Well what do you know, the rain has stopped. The sun is out and the rain has stopped. What do you know?' said Euchrid to his shadow.

Then he heard the cries of jubilation coming from the town, but he was running now. Away. Away.

XX

So the infant came and the rain stopped, and the vast black cloud parted across the firmament like a leaden curtain and all the people of the valley beheld the glory of the blue and saw the great sun in the sky. And they raised the babe heavenward so that she might be the first to feel the warm breath of atonement and so that their God would see that the incarnate token deposited upon the monument steps had not passed unnoticed and that the dual miracle was indeed fully understood, one to one and never to be forgotten. And, falling to their knees, wailing and weeping, it was God and the babe whom they praised and praised – this frail bundle juggled, hand to hand, so brightly glowing, bound in its swaddling cloth, this miracle, this reward of faith – upheld and jostled, thus, aloft.

BOOK TWO

BETH

(Six Years On)

I

Six years passed. Six young gunfighters down on their luck. Six pine boxes to carry them in. Six crooked miles walked. Six broken stiles crossed. Six passing bells swinging but making no sound. Six widows weeping. Six plots of cold ground. Six blackbirds throwing six crooked shadows. Six sinking moons. Six wounds. Six notches. Six muddy crutches broken in two.

So rolled the years of mah springtime.

Six wicker baskets.

Into these did the years of mah youthhead roll.

II

They had christened her Beth, this little one.

Shoeless, she crouched upon the bottom step of the monument, arms wrapped around her knees, the form of her slender body lost in the folds of her white cotton smock. She rested her chin in the crooks of her arms, looking neither here nor there, wriggling her toes in the dusty gravel of the path leading up to the monument steps and shining white in the glow of the lights, like a spectral companion to the great marble angel that towered behind her. Her little black pumps sat, side by side, next to her. Her blonde plaited locks shone golden as the pall of night descended all about.

As she sat, she sang, soft and slowly chiming,

'There is a sleepy river I know . . .'

until the slam of Doc Morrow's door and the sound of her father's voice cut short her song.

'Beth! Time to go home!' called Sardus Swift from the doctor's porch, and the child was already buckling her pumps and tramping down the path to the road.

Sardus lifted his daughter into his arms and kissed her lightly upon the forehead. Beth smiled at some secret thought of her own, showing her new teeth, small and white.

'Home,' she sighed, putting her arms around his neck, her blonde bangs bright and strangely out of place against the coarse black bush of Sardus' beard.

Humming softly with the child asleep in his arms, Sardus Swift looked to the winking stars and saw the moon – a smirk on the face of heaven – as he made his way home.

*

In the golden days of reprieve that followed the end of the rain, when sheets of mudded water rose in veils from field and road and valley floor, and the Ukulites rejoiced at each bright day that passed, and thanked in prayer their God most merciful, a certain doctor by the name of Morrow had stolen from the heart of jubilation to visit one still unlit corner that he might chase the chilly spirit from its last, dark hiding place.

At first Sardus Swift would neither answer nor unbolt his door and the doctor would return to his office further down Maine with the then unnamed foundling cradled in his arms. But on the fourth visit, the doctor knocked and the old plank door gave, unlatched, and swung slowly open.

Doc Morrow entered, stepping over a pile of mail that lay unopened upon the floor. Such was the arrant squalor of his friend's hermitary that the doctor recoiled at the sight before him. A surge of anger rose in his throat, but the more he plumbed the depths of self-loathing written in the very swinishness of his surrounds, the more the feelings of anger gave way to a sadness of heart toward the impossible lot of his brother.

He walked down the hall, coming to a halt upon the threshold of the old living quarters, once so bright and so fair, of the mad and barren Mrs Swift.

Midst the debris of his undoing, rotten and morbific – the sordid amassment of the sorrow-worn – sat a terrible Sardus Swift, unwashed, jaundiced, gaunt, his face besieged by a black matted beard and obscured by long greasy hair. His hands were folded in his lap. He sat in an armchair cluttered with newspaper. Balls of screwed-up paper, grimy clothing and rotten food surrounded him, and he looked upward, toward the door, where Doc Morrow stood speechless, bundle in arms.

Barely allowing his blistered lips to part, Sardus spoke in a hoarse whisper, his voice drifting off at times to become little more than a hiss. He did not move his hands from his lap, but sat, neck craned toward the door, eyes fixed upon the doctor. Doc Morrow rocked the baby nervously, unable to call to mind a single word of his proposal, and the seconds crawled by as the wretched recluse whispered word upon bitter word.

'The noise of the rain . . . has stopped. Are we entering the days of reprieve, Doctor? I gather the Almighty has . . . granted us clemency. Praise the Lord.'

He broke off, looked at the palms of his hands loosely clasped in his lap, and then continued, returning his attention to the doctor, with a look of anguish in his face.

'So grave our misdeeds, good Doctor, yet see,' Sardus gestured with a flourish to the azure sky beyond the window, 'the world is resplendent with His infinite Mercy! O Lord! Shower me! Shower me with your tender mercies!'

His whisper was nothing but a croak now and Doc Morrow was already shuffling down the hall. Sardus sat and did not rise, waiting for the slam of the kitchen door, and upon hearing it he remained seated, just so, there midst the sea of garbage.

Doc Morrow visited the next day and the next day and for many days after that, each time bringing with him the tiny foundling.

The third and mostly silent party in their daily colloquy lay cradled in the doctor's arms throughout, and the doctor made no move to mention it. It was not until late into the fourth week that Sardus asked about the child.

In the days that followed, the doctor unfolded the story of the miraculous infant, and gave the foundling at last to the shabby recluse to hold.

The moment that Sardus peered into the bundle and beheld the beauty of the child's face, felt her tiny body, warm and coddled in his own thin limbs, both he and the doctor could see, it seemed, the light of Truth begin to shine, stretching its hand a little further into the bramble of their mystification.

The man who had once been the proud leader of the Ukulites handed the girl-child back to the doctor, and, leading him through the kitchen to the front door, said with solemn intonation: 'Doctor Morrow, I must ask you to bring neither the child nor yourself to my household for one full week. Promise me that.

Come Tuesday next, at the usual time, and bring the little girl with you. I will be ready, then, to receive you both.'

In the week that followed, Sardus slaved within his house. With the aid of some of the womenfolk he swept the floors clean of trash, scrubbed the kitchen tiles and skirting boards, and all the ledges and mantels. Assisted by the brothers Holfe, he scraped and painted the walls, inside and out, while his new neighbour Jude Bracken repaired the porch and replaced the broken stove-pipe. He polished up the brass on the beds. He washed the windows and hung new blinds.

As news travelled through the valley that Sardus Swift was to take the blessed infant as his own, donations from his brethren came flooding in. New sheets and blankets; tables and chairs; lightshades, toys and books; foodstuffs; ornaments and vases; an old pianola that had belonged to the late Elisa Snow; clothing by the boxful, including three handmade cotton smocks.

The smocks had been made by Edith Lamb, whose hooded vision was so impaired that she could not leave her house across Maine to deliver her labour of faith, but was forced to send another with the gifts.

By Tuesday, the house was again a home. And just as it shone glorious from its reparation, so too it was a new and grinning Sardus who met his two guests at the door.

And so the little girl found a bright new home.

III

Ma spent an increasing amount of time in her bed, but she continued to tyrannize the household, bawling orders from her room. Pa obeyed her without complaint, as did Euchrid, but as the years passed and the matriarch persisted in testing to the limit her husband's resilience, his body could be seen to shudder some, his hands begin to shake, and Euchrid, watching through one of the peep-holes, could not help but notice the way Pa's jaw would clench and his eyes narrow at each barked command, and a white ring of suppressed rage appear around his mouth.

Often Euchrid was sent to the still to tap a pint or two of liquor, and this he would do, though the punishing stench of rotted carcass that wafted from his father's chamber of death made him gag as he squatted beneath it, waiting the two minutes or so that it took for the crude distilling device to piss out its pint of poison.

Pa would often be seated on his throne above, gnashing and muttering as he watched the crippled menagerie do battle inside the old water tank, the air alive with its freakish hullabaloo. Euchrid would peg off the hose and hammer the bung into the neck of the bottle, his face bluing with kept breath, and after dashing across the junk-pile to the shack he would slump in the doorway, sucking and blowing the new air, hearing now not the song of the dying beasts but that of the deranged despot within, bawling like a babe without its bottle. He would leave the pint, with a clunk, at her bedroom door, barely registering the door's groan or the grapple of the fetching paw as he entered his own room, his mind a mire of murder.

One day, Pa brought to the house a near dead wolf-dog he had found crippled in a trap. Instead of hurling it into the tank with the rest of the day's catch, he covered the windows of the old wreck with chicken wire – double-ply – and emptied the snarling mongrel into the car, slamming the door shut behind it.

The dog had triggered one of the larger hog-snares, and the massive jaws had sunk high into its left thigh – snapping the bone like a twig, but being too blunt to take the leg clean off.

Curious, Euchrid had watched his father with the mad dog, but only after the old man had caged the beast and wandered inside did Euchrid come out from the tin drums behind the corral and approach the huge iron cage.

Inside, the dog growled and spat, turning a tortured circle with its three good legs, great shoulders buffaloing and bristling, the skin of its brow drawn down over bloodshot eyes and its flews, in contraposition, curled upward in a mean snarl.

Euchrid rested the animal with his presence, much the same as a priest would one possessed by demons, and once it was thus chased of its madness, Euchrid tended the dog, swathing the stump in gauze and pulling over it a thick woollen sock, black with yellow diamonds around the ankle.

Euchrid mused over a name for the beast, deciding after long and serious consideration to call it 'Yellow'. Later that afternoon he changed its name to 'Diamond' and then to 'Yellow Diamond', but after further consideration he abandoned the idea altogether, reluctantly accepting the pointlessness of it all.

He fed the dog on rats and toads mostly, and water, until it regained its strength and Euchrid let it go.

The dog hobbled down the hillside and into the cane by the gallows-tree. Standing upon the crest, Euchrid watched it go. He counted the crows that circled overhead.

Three days later Euchrid observed a small cluster of school-children running along the main road, and he wondered, as he hopped down the porch steps, what they were doing so far out of town. He took another look before bounding down the slope – they appeared to be waving their arms above their heads, but from that distance it was hard to tell.

He dived into the cane and hurried down his runway toward them. Every minute or so he would stop and listen to their

119

chiming, becoming louder and louder as he drew closer. Finally he spotted a huddle of colour on the side of the road, about twenty feet away. The shouts of the children were manic now, piercing the balmy afternoon with shrieks and squeals of delight. They no longer ran.

Suddenly there was silence.

Euchrid crept as far as the boundary, obscured from view by the cane-trash that hung from the wire fence. He watched as the children turned tail and took off down Maine, heading back to town. He climbed through the fence and watched the retreating group, his eyes slits of rage. Some waved sticks, others were tossing them into the cane. One knock-kneed boy chased a shrieking, bandy-legged girl, a grubby hood pulled over his head – black with yellow diamonds around the throat.

'Look!' cried the girl, who had stopped running and stood looking down the road, her arm outstretched with one derisive finger pointed straight at Euchrid. The other children ground to a halt and turned. The child in the mask collided with another boy and was sent sprawling on to the road, skinning his knees and the palms of his hands.

A fearful silence ensued, broken only by the muffled moans of the raw-kneed boy. For a moment or two Euchrid was alone with the double thud of his heartbeat. He saw red.

Scooping up a rock from the ground, he stepped forward and took aim. The children had turned tail and were fleeing down the road before he had a chance to throw it.

The rock in his fist was sticky with blood.

At his feet lay the three-legged dog, its naked stump cocked obscenely. Its head had been bashed in and its brains squeezed through a split in the top of its skull like a cock's comb. Its tongue lolled from its mouth, coated in dust, looking twice as long as it should have. A splinter of fractured bone had pierced the meat of its good thigh, poking through the red fur like a jellied finger. A thin trickle of blood seeped from its anus, soaking into the piss-wet soil at its hind.

'That's how they got him,' observed Euchrid. 'Knocked out his other leg.'

'Yep,' he thought, his suspicions confirmed by a swept trail of wet dust; which began ten yards away and ended at the dog's smashed hindquarters.

Euchrid dragged the carcass off the road and slung it into a ditch.

Then he walked down Maine and retrieved the sock, slapping it for dust as he slipped back into the cane.

The Lamentations of Euchrid the Mute, No. 1

Ah am one luckless bastard. God knows. Dumber than a hat full of earholes. A vile thing. Unworthy. Worthless. O yes! Grotesque in form. Misshapen. Yes! Misshapen and vile of mind. *O hideous deed*.

IV

After the great rain, a task force was organized by the Ukulites to reconstruct the cemetery at Hooper's Hill. Their job was to gather up the human scrappage, the split and swollen caskets and the crude plank boxes made of pine, the rubble, the roods, the stones and urns and markers, and so on. For the most part they succeeded in piecing together the old graveyard, although whose bones went in which box went in which hole was anybody's guess, and for many years after the rain's end and the graveyard's reparation it was not uncommon to stumble upon the odd knuckle or kneecap or rib, buried or half buried in the downgrade.

Few of the original cane-men stuck out the storm years, and the reconstructed graveyard was rarely visited, let alone tended to. What had been a morbid mud-pit became, in a few short years, a sea of weed and creeper. Bald white headstones like the domes of drowning men sank beneath the mat and tangle of ivy and vine.

The vine was unique to Ukulore Valley, and grew only on and around the plot occupied by Hooper's Hill Cemetery. Sprouting in the wake of the rain, and seeming to flourish in the rain-ruined soil, this freakish flora known as 'Tolley's Trumpet Creeper' was the only trumpet creeper on record to boast a navy blue bloom. Little is known about Frank Owen Tolley, upon whose stone the plant first bloomed blue. His stone and its inscription offer no clue. The creeper's secret must remain with poor Tolley and God – and no doubt the Devil. Only they could tell from what poisonous sump this creeper drank to deepen its velvet bell's complexion to such a deathly midnight hue.

V

Mah sanctum – mah cave of vine and moss – is to mah right about ten paces into the thicket that surrounds me now. So dense grows the swampland that sometimes it would take me up to thirty minutes to find the little hideaway ah had fashioned, though ah had been there hundreds and hundreds of times. Ah would look for the strips of white sheet, bright like bush ghosts, that hung along the woven walls – they would tell me where.

All about me were mah treasures. The stained bandages like flags. Boxes of nails and tacks. A crate of electrical cord. Mah hammer. Candles and plastic bags full of matches and tapers from the church. Mah Bibles. Twine. Animal bones and feathers and bird skulls. Shells and nests. Some of mah shoeboxes – about ten. Pictures ah had cut from magazines and threaded through the walls. The tiny blue-glass bottles of scented water.

And with these ah kept mah Life-trophies, mah God-tokens – the parts of her left behind – blood mementoes. The whore's hair. Her nightdress. The portrait of Cosey that ah had delivered from the hands of those who rose up against her, sheared her, cast her out. The kindergraph and the instructions she had written, in verse, aback of it. The painting of Beth – of *her* – fastened to the walls and ceiling of the grotto, angled so that it hovered above me as ah lay in mah shell.

On a carpet of pink silk and frill – yes, and the ten pearl buttons leaving their evanescent impression down mah back or belly – the stroke of hair – a ruby bead sailing down a yellow strand – a trembling scarlet drop – the bitter-sweet sip – O the lifetimes lost in queer congress, holed up in that dark retreat – holed up in that dark retreat –

A felled tree trunk, carved down the middle by a cleaver of lightning – during the rain days, ah guess – made a kind of a pallet where ah would lie, stretched out between the two halves that ah had padded with cardboard and moss, encapsulated by two walls of umbrage that twisted about a few clapboards nailed to the trunks as supports, the vines intertwining overhead to form a low ceiling. Ah could sit up with a full foot's grace – room enough for mah angel too, who would, in mah later years, appear on the tree stump at the foot of mah cocoon, then come inside and lie with me.

Sometimes ah heard thousands of voices, for God is many-tongued, whispering things to me as ah lay there all alone. All mah feelings of fear and of anger and of despair that ah ate daily like bread would depart from me, and ah would feel most powerful. Most powerful.

They tol– . . . *He* told me things that ah know were special knowledge. Of mahself at first. Then of others.

Without really realizing it, the Ukulites had begun to prime Beth for sainthood the moment the sun had first reached through the cover of cloud and kissed the curl on the foundling's forehead. Never did the flesh of one seem so precious as did the earthly body of Beth. Nor was a child ever so pampered, preened and downright spoiled as this unwitting deceiver.

Having no mother and an adoptive, inexperienced father, Beth became in her infant years part-daughter to a hundred doting sometime-mothers – or would-be sometime-mothers, each determined to tend to the needs of the Heaven-sent in a manner that befitted the blessed fruit of such miraculous circumstance. Women took turns in cooking for Sardus Swift and little Beth, proud when the infant ate their pap, despairing when she refused it.

The attentions of this many-breasted, multi-voiced, preening, pinching mater seemed but a boon to the tot as a babe in swaddling clothes. Beth's first five years passed without incident, in health and abounding good temperament, and, as a quiet and self-possessed child, she remained good-natured toward the ever-fussing string of women, finding in time a way of smiling, coy and dimpled, that would guarantee a coo or a cluck from the sternest matron – warm reward for their efforts.

And each year on the anniversary of her coming, the Ukulites would take Beth – a pearly white bundle, her head wreathed in a chaplet of violets – into the town square. Beneath the august monument strewn with garlands of inky blooms cut from the burial grounds of Hooper's Hill, Sardus Swift, holding the babe heavenward, would deliver a prayer of thanksgiving – his eyes, two wells that once had sprung with the bitter vinegar of grief, now clear and blue, flowing with the deep, sweet waters of joy. And all about him his sobbing flock mustering a bigger rain.

Then, one by one, the members of the congregation would fall to the ground to kiss the sun-warmed step upon which the foundling had been discovered, the summer air full of hallelujahs and hosannas and the sickly scent of trumpet blooms.

During the child's sixth year, the eye-batting spinster Molly Barlow would return Beth's queer little smile and say, 'This child is surely of more saintly stuff than me or thee, Sardus,' her hawking remark wet with innuendo and tuberculosis.

'Let us hope so, Sister,' Sardus would reply coldly, secretly tired of the do-gooders who plagued his home to coddle the child and fatten the man, tired in particular of the Molly Barlows who saw him not as Sardus the father but as Sardus the eligible.

But these feelings were never allowed to surface, for Sardus only needed to look to his daughter to know that he would continue to eat whatever the women dished in front of him, would listen to their incessant chatter and return their oily compliments, for it was all a small price to pay for the continued health and well-being of his child, Beth, his single and superlative joy.

Beth yawned and arched her little body back; for a blissful moment all her young muscles stretched over her soft, growing bones. Infecting the room with her yawn, she watched as both Sardus and Molly Barlow moved to their own deep, sleepy breath.

'Thank you for dinner, Miss Barlow. May I go to my room, Daddy?' asked Beth, beaming at them both.

They beamed back in reply, and even as Beth entered her room and pulled the door gently closed behind her, the two adults sat there still smiling silently – happy victims of the child's contagious device.

In the solitude of her room, Beth's smile slipped from her mouth like an unwanted thing. Fat dolls with fat wax heads and hands sat, fifty-fold, in two fussy rows along the wall opposite her.

She fumbled in the pocket of her smock, her green eyes wide and turning inward to set another world in motion, a world unsullied by bigger hands. Humming to a tune she alone could hear, Beth pulled from her pocket a wooden clothes-pin and held it tightly in her fist.

'Don't cry, Peg. Mother is home.'

The Lamentations of Euchrid the Mute, No. 2

Another time, ah watched two young men from the refinery fuck a girl at the bottom of Hooper's Hill Cemetery. Seth and Billy were their names, and when they had finished, instead of following the trolley tracks down along the back of the fields, these young men walked straight up and through the graveyard – right in the direction of where ah was crouched. They grabbed me and pulled me down on top of a stone slab, winding me. Seth straddled mah chest, pinning mah arms down with his knees. When the girl finally caught up with them and saw me, she threw her arms over her face and began cussing and bawling. 'Kill him! Seth! O Billy! Kill him! He'll tell on us! He'll tell – O kill him!!'

Seth gave mah face a slap. 'Calm down. Who's gunna believe a goddamn crazy baw? Look!' The girl, still sobbing, sort of edged over, her hands masking her face, teary eyes peering through her fingers. 'Hold him, Seth. Tight!' she gasped and came close, looking down at me, her breasts rising and falling. She reeked with the smell of sex. A shriek leaped from her lips and she was laughing and laughing and did not stop laughing even as Seth set about whupping the shit out of me, and, dismounting, let Billy sit and slog at the slops. Laughing to the last. The bitch.

But not every down-borne hand that sought to chastise me was crooked. O no! The godly, the meek, the righteous – they too were party to mah persecution. For mah tormentor, he was many-masked. Surrounded as ah was by his apparatus of deception, there was no limit to his atrocious device. The workers, the faithful, the children, the homeless, the drunken, even mah own flesh and blood were but limbs of the persecutor – puppets! The rack, rod and stake, the block and the blade, the pillory, the stocks, the switch and the stones and the witch's stool, the whip and the wheel, the crank, the plank, the boot and the fist and all the rest, the endless list – hidden and waiting, regardless of the path ah chose.

More than once did the God-fearing Ukulites chase me from the town. Still ah am baffled by an incident that occurred when ah was maybe fourteen. Listen.

Ah was sitting on the step of the marble monument, squeezing the dark sap from a trumpet creeper that ah had found there, when ah noticed a group of maybe seven or eight Ukulite menfolk, one brandishing a hay-rake, crossing the Square. Ah watched as they marched toward me, wondering at the reason for the commotion. Slowly it dawned upon me, the crazed mob only yards away, that ah, Euchrid Eucrow, was the object of their gall! Such was mah innocence! Ah leaped to mah feet, tangling mahself in a gilded rope – tasselled and low-slung – that surrounded the steps, escaping the madded throng by inches, by seconds, though they chased me through the town, puffing and panting and shaking their fists, till ah was but a scorned and skulking speck upon the horizon.

It was by no means the first time that the good folk of Ukulore Valley had retched and heaved and sicked me up on the town's outboundary. O no, nor would it be the last! Even now as ah inch unner, something rushes at me. Something of hellish reason – evangelists hooded scarlet come, turned vigilante with bloody deed done! O wicked little Beth! What havoc we have wrought!

VI

'The Martyrdom of the Prophet' by Gaston Georges had hung on the south wall of the Ukulite tabernacle since the year 1935, when the respected academic portrait painter had taken up residence in the booming vale, having been struck by the 'utter uncomplicity and tireless dedication' of the Ukulites to the memory of their prophet.

'Your greatest treasure is your unswerving faith, a gift more precious than I will ever know,' remarked Gaston as he presented the commissioned portrait, refusing any payment but the permission to make his home in the valley.

'You have made me very happy. I will continue to serve you, in the hope that I will one day find peace through your example,' he continued, trembling with emotion but plagued by prickling doubts that he was never to resolve, though he would remain in the valley for the rest of his life.

His right foot buried beneath the hem of his frothing raiments – a fierce drama of gleaming ripples and deep, dark folds – and his other foot, his left, slung in a gilded sliver of moon, the prophet ascended heavenward on a cloud of romping cherubim. A great spilling robe stained scarlet at the heart, a dazzling sceptre and crown, dewy blue eyes – all pulled the eye upward to the darts of light that sprang from the crack in the clouds parting to receive him.

Gaston Georges dedicated the remainder of his life to documenting through his portraiture the history of the Ukulites. The stark fundamentalist principles practised by the pioneer Ukulites came to stiffen the painter's brush somewhat and bridle the boisterous voice of his imagination; so much so that the series of eight portraits, oval in shape, that flanked the chill interior of the Town Hall bore no resemblance to their predecessor at all.

These were lean, haggard, pious faces, scowling behind beards and beneath stiff, black bonnets. Eight grim sitters – cold and unadorned pillars of the community – the product of a cramped and shackled hand.

But Georges was yet to paint his unrivalled masterpiece. This he would do some six years after the rain had stopped.

'Beth' hung opposite the spiralling afflatus of 'The Martyrdom' in the Ukulite tabernacle, on the north wall. It was despised by some, lauded by others. Others it simply baffled. Sardus Swift made the decision to have it hung in the tabernacle. It was of Beth aged six.

VII

She was seated in a simple hard-wood high-backed chair, surrounded by a deep sepia void. She wore the same white cotton
smock as always, but not stiffly as before. Instead the skirts were
hitched a little to reveal her knees, the blouse thin and loose. Her
limbs had been elongated a little, ah think, and though she was
sitting formally, for a portrait, there was a certain ease of poise
that made her appear totally unselfconscious, as if ah were
watching her and she didn't know it.

Maybe the beam of the torch was responsible for deepening
the murky surrounds and accentuating the ghostly brilliance of
her smock and the loosely tossed locks of gold that fell across her
shoulders, but – and this is near impossible to explain – reaching
from the pale shores of her face, like two hexing hands twirling
and dancing their witching device, came her eyes. Drowning-
pools, emerald green and mesmerizing like winter webs or the
circles on a devil-moth's wings, hexing and hexing, peering from
unner two heavy lids, kinda outward but kinda inward too, filling
mah mind with jabbered mutterings – weird, dark murmurings
– mah blood pounding in mah head – sucking me unner – down
and down and unner . . .

How long ah stood there, spellbound in the dark of the
tabernacle, ah could not, in truth, say, but it must have been a
long time because the image of her face began to fade, like a
dying moon, until ah could barely see it any more, and this is
what eventually broke the spell, the batteries in mah flashlight
flatting. That, and the voice.

'Is it that I have depicted the saintly in a human, or could it be
that I have shown there to be humanity in a saint?'

Ah spun around, pointing the flashlight at the voice. Lit by the
dying beam, a dark figure stood in the doorway. Ah pointed the

flashlight in every direction searching for an escape. There was none to be found.

'Do not fear. I am honoured that one of you has returned to view my picture in private. I have not come to hurt you. You have committed no sin in being here. Tell me, why have you come back to look on 'Beth'? What is it about the pictures that has brought you here?'

Ah tasted blood, for mah nose had started. Ah could feel the punishing sticks and stones of public rebuke even then, as ah spun round and around, searching for a way out.

'You may go if you want. I wish you no harm.' He moved forward, clearing the entrance of the tabernacle.

'Sure you fucken don't,' ah thought. 'Sure you fucken don't.'

Ah bolted down the hall, thundering across the bare boards of the tabernacle. Ah waved mah arms, windmilling them in furious circles as ah lunged toward the interloper. Ah tried to scream, and ah guess ah must have looked pretty menacing coming at him like that, because he had second thoughts about jumping me and just held back as ah flung mahself out the door and down the steps, not stopping running until ah had reached the turn-off that led up to the shack.

Ah dabbed at mah nose with a handkerchief, mah heart pounding, too fucken scared and cold and breathless to see the significance in it. Mah blood nose.

Ah lay upon mah back beneath the cover of the hedgerow. The moon was new and in the sky ah saw it become one thousand things – a slice of lemon rind – a sinister fin menacing the welkin water's royal pool – a pellet from the golden fleece – the Reaper's tool – a golden bow released – a single slipper made of glass – a lamp cast in gold – a fold – a gilded horn within a maiden's gown – a lick – a tongue – an angry thorn – a manger's roof – a crib or a cradle – a ladle – a tooth – all up there, above me and beyond mah touch. Removed.

Ah rolled on to mah belly, keeping an eye on the matter at hand.

Beth was unbuckling her pumps and still she murmured a song:

> '. . . O field of mustard, field of clover
> Bird with crooked wing flew over . . .'

But the fucken cicadas blasted again upon the night with their shrill-splitting alarum and ah could not make out another word. So ah simply watched the child clutching her knees beneath her crisp cotton dress, loose and very white, and if it had not been for the fact that her toes were curling and flexing and moving in the dust, her shiny pumps discarded by her side, ah could have mistaken her for a lesser work, chiselled by the same deft hand that had created the marble angel – sickle and blonde bangs bright as the moon that loomed aloft, and deadly still.

Beth of stone.

Spawn of sin.

Spawn of sin.

See Pa sit, his brow knitted in deep concentration, his hand sure, steely, nerveless. See the towering edifice made entirely of playing cards, stacked one on one, upon the table before him. See how slow and with what excruciating patience it climbs? See the picture of calm – Pa with his quiet cards. Floor upon floor.

Yet, not even thirty minutes beforehand, ah had watched Pa, through a spy-hole in the outside wall, standing, legs astride and with an old knotty walking stick, hammering Mule again and again. Whack! Whack! Whack! See the wet welted stripes that blister across the poor creature's back and rump. See how Pa viciously beats his beast until he is literally too weak to raise another stroke of the stick. Hear Mule's sick bray. Hee-haw! Hee-haw! Hee-haw! Half on his haunches and half off.

See how, even as Mule brays, Pa is rolling up the sleeves of his shirt to begin on the first floor of cards?

See Mule churning a hopeless circle in the corral as he tries, in vain, to lick the bloody wounds that cut across his rump.

See Mule infected with Pa's sickness. And Pa – his madness gone! Passed on! Working calmly. Painlessly. Forever upward. See?

It was past midnight by the time ah entered the Ukulite tabernacle, the shears tucked unner mah belt, flashlight in hand. It was near one o'clock when ah left, the great roll of canvas unner mah arm.

Ah hung it in mah grotto the next day – a kind of figurehead that watched over mah dim retreat. With the kindergraph of the whore in mah hand, ah would marvel at the likeness – the yellow curls, the same sullen attitude, the sense of glum abandon that rested in the bold swivel of puerile hips and the idle bunching of angled bones, the curious tilt of the head and the booty of spilled gold that fell across each shoulder. Ah would lose mahself for hours in the witching pools of their eyes – of her eyes – *her* eyes – of *her* witching, pooling eyes.

VIII

Beth was afraid of the other children.

Having spent her early years smothered beneath a scrum of fussing mothers, she had never known the companionship of other children, and when Sardus Swift entered his daughter at Ukulore Valley School fears that had previously lain hidden became manifest in the child. Beth was simply unable to feel at ease with children of her own age. Nor did time serve as a poultice; as the weeks passed by and the first term drew to an end, Mr Carl Cullen, headmaster of U.V.S., suggested to Sardus Swift that his daughter be removed from the school and placed under private tutelage.

In a gesture that was more than a mere courtesy, for the decision could not be made alone, Sardus met with a handful of the foremost amongst the adherents, and together they discussed Beth's future. Her welfare was, said Sardus, 'as much a community concern as a parental one'. It was decided that, as things stood, more harm than good was being done in keeping the child at school, and that a Mr Henry Mendleson of Davenport, cousin to Wilma Eldridge, be approached for the position of private tutor.

Beth secretly grew to despise Mr Henry Mendleson – dreading the daily advent of his shiny, pink pate, which bounced nervously on to her horizon at eight o'clock sharp each morn. She shrank at the sound of his tiny, polished shoes as they squeaked across the linoleum and stopped outside her door. She hated the little 'ahem' that would follow, and the pursy, one-knuckled knock. But what really boiled Beth's blood was the way he called her 'Beeth', with a near-inaudible tremor in his intonation: 'Morning, Be-ee-th.'

Yet, despite her loathing for Mr Mendleson, Beth thanked God that her sentence at Ukulore Valley School had been terminated. No longer need she feel the terrible enmity that she had faced during the three cold months she had spent as a pupil there. No longer need she face the children who hated her. No longer need she feel their jealous, appraising eyes, hear the scornful whispers and laughs, the cruel taunting rhymes.

Such had been Beth's fear of the other children that she had taken to spending her recess and lunch-break on the far side of the peach grove at the back of the school, squatting in the wind-whispering cloisters of the orchard. Her eyes would gaze at the space before her, still and wide and somehow vacant. What worlds so absorbed her as she squatted in the pink and white peach blossom we can only guess.

IX

The day: 6 October 1952.

Mule lays down and dies. Euchrid buries both the beast and the stick that killed him. A mound of soft earth at the foot of the water-tower marks the place.

Euchrid's father builds a house of cards – fifteen storeys high.

Sits all night in front of his master-work, until the morning sun turns the paper palace into gold. Head bent.

Pa beat Mule to death in autumn, for copper and gold were the leaves. Ah remember because it was the fallen leaves, slippery with morning dew, that made it possible to drag Mule's carcass over to the old water-tower. His back had been brutally beaten. Ah suspected a broken spine.

Ah took the long-handled shovel and began digging, mah attention being diverted at times from the business of burial by Mule's cold stare. He was dead and the dead must be buried, everyone knows that, yet his eyes seemed to beg for mercy as if it were ah who had beaten the life out of the poor brute and not Pa.

Mah spade upturned darker earth and, without any other warning, there upon the blade of mah shovel lay what looked like the skeleton of a small dog.

Squatting aside the grave and loosing the rust-coloured earth from the fanning bones, ah discovered a child's tiny skull. Next, a rotting radius and ulna connected to a brittle little hand – and by the time ah had exhumed mah brother's earthly remains, lifting out all his bones intact and laying them out on a soft floor of fallen, golden foliage, ah was sobbing noiselessly, mah eyes streaming.

Ah buried Mule's carcass and laid mah brother's skeleton out in an old cutlery drawer ah found on the heap. Ah built a simple sliding lid for it, and, taking the box with me into the swampland, ah propped it against the inside back wall of mah sanctum.

He remained there – mah treasured companion – for a good three months, that is, until the day that *she* spooked the Turk's nag into the swamp and the townsfolk found mah haven and destroyed it.

But that all comes later.

Ah love you, little brother! And ah'm coming home!

All fear did subside.

Mah body was seized by a delicious trembling. Shudders of glory. Mah whole being surged with power – with *the* power. Mah blood smoked in mah veins and kept coming – humming. Singing. Mah blood sang. Pounding through me. Mah heart pulsing, drumming up the blood. The pumps of pleasure berserk and sounding. Mah flesh like warm mud.

All fear did subside.

Ah felt as ah had in the church, the day ah found the crippled hobo, when ah stood over him, hacking the air with the shears, looking down at him looking up at me. Watching him whimper. Ah remember his filthy bearded face twisted with terror, his pavid hands trembling, his pathetic sobbing, and how even the purple scar hooked unner one streaming eye was blanched with fear.

Together We did weed him out. Him and his kind, Kike.

All fear did subside.

Ah sat there and watched the billowing smoke come rolling from the blazing church as the fire consumed it – as the Devil reclaimed it. A black hood covered Glory Flats as the fires of Hell raged brightly.

Ah had proved mah worthiness to Him, and so He pleasured me, that ah should know mah task had been counted and that He was content. That He was content – that was mah ecstasy.

Ah did not walk alone. He held mah hand.

And all fear did subside.

The Ukulites, armed with torches and hay-rakes, looked like ants from where ah was poised, on the rise, near the shack. They barked and chanted and fanned the flames. Ah wondered how they must look to Him, these ants, these frantic specks down below. Ah held out mah hand. They were no bigger than mah thumb. Stretching wide the fingers of mah hand, ah saw that it spanned the width of Glory Flats and ah slowly folded mah fingers in, crushing them all, fire and all, in mah fist.

Ah laughed and the valley trembled, ringing with it.

X

Most of the peep-holes had corks for bungs, but the plug in mah bedroom wall was moulded from a paper-mash. Ah could find no cork to fit it. The spit-ball that ah made for it was as fat as mah thumb and took all week to dry. Even then it shrunk. Still, it served its purpose and the spy-hole was never discovered.

Ah plucked the stopper from the wall and a spear of trembling yellow light pierced the darkness of mah room. The air was like dog's breath on this sleepless summer night. Ah held out mah hand, fingers splayed, and let the play of light hammer at mah palm. The circle of light, heavy and gold in mah hand, shone bright as a new ducat. And ah lay there upon mah back, eyes drawn toward the golden shaft, and just watched as motes of silver dust, curled and serene as sea-horses, floated, rudderless and alone, in and out of the beam. A midsummer-night sadness descended and ah fell victim to it, stifled by its murk and sticky sombre.

Ah sat up and the beam splashed across mah face, and squinting into the light ah brought mah eye up to the hole. Ah scanned the front room, from wall to wall.

The door was open for air. A spirit lamp hung in the doorway, throwing a ragged blanket of copper light about the room and spilling the remainder out on to the porch. Every winged bug in a night's flight clamoured in the doorway in a frenzy of death – stupid gnats knocking their brains out to enter the bright eye. The floor beneath was littered with their singed corpses. The room droned with their madness.

Pa sat at the table, repairing a huge spring trap with a jaw-span of over five feet. It was his favourite. The Black Bastard. Beside him was a tin of grease.

Pa looked twisted, like he was being whipped with thistles. A roping blue vein embroidered his beaded brow. His eyes were little slits. His jaw set, Pa ground his cud. Every minute or so, for no apparent reason, an obscenity would leap from his lips as he sat, racked with agitation, testing the trap with a new and heavier spring. Ever since Mule had died, Pa had seemed consumed by a festering rage that he was unable to suppress. Like fighting a needle with a raw nerve.

Ah changed eyes, mah left cold and stinging, aggravated by the light's chilly finger.

Comatose, Pa's wife, the slobstress, buried an armchair beneath her bulk. Mutinous springs wormed their way out from unner her. She snored.

Pa wrenched apart Black Bastard's massive jaws and set the trigger. The spring groaned. Pa painted it carefully with axle grease.

Ah saw Pa lean back in his chair, his eyes fixed upon the yawning jaws. He folded his arms across his chest. The vein throbbed upon his temple. Ah looked at Ma. To the colliding gnats. Back to Pa. He ground his teeth. Minutes passed. The bugs hummed on. Ah changed back to mah left eye. Sleep came merciful.

When ah awoke, still ah clutched the paper-mash bung. Sitting up, ah felt mah eye drawn toward the peep-hole. Ah tried to fight it.

At last, ah peered in.

XI

She spooked the nag. That ah know. Ah saw it all. And she saw me.

Ah was in town on account of it being the night before the 'burn-off', when cane-workers and Ukulites alike celebrate the beginning of the harvest, and people, on the whole, are too busy eating and drinking and flirting with the neighbour's wife to make an example of me. But that doesn't mean that you can go and do a rain-dance in the middle of Memorial Square either.

Ah sat on a painted rock beside the old pump and trough, and, looking between mah knees, ah read the little copper plaque that had been embedded in it.

> 'Ho, every one that thirsteth,
> Come ye to the waters.' *Isaiah 55:1*
> Donated by U.V.S.B. 1921

Ah listened to a four-man jug band that stomped about on a low trailer, to which the goddamn sorriest-looking nag ah had ever seen was hitched. How a horse could get that bowed, ah'll never know. In an attempt to brighten up the festivities in his own little way, the Turk had crowned his horse in a flame-red fez, complete with black tassel and black elastic chin-strap.

It was while ah sat there, minding nobody's affairs but mah own, that mah hair began to bristle and mah hands grew raw and itchy and ah felt this peculiar sensation that ah was being watched. Ah began to sweat, grow short of breath, wheeze. Mah hands burned and pulsed and ah blew on them but that did no good at all, so ah plunged them up to the elbows in the cool water of the trough. Ah held them unner for a full minute – then, when ah felt mah blood seem to level up, ah lifted them out. Ah shook mah arms around until they were almost dry, too afraid to look up and hoping to hell that this feeling – that ah was the object of someone's scrutiny – would pass. It did not.

Ah looked up and our eyes locked. Just like in the painting! She was standing beside the nag, patting his neck but staring straight at me. Through me.

Ah wrenched free and tumbled off the rock. It was only the size of a pumpkin, but ah sprawled on mah side in the gravel, grazing mah hip in the process. It stung like shit. Ah heard some people laugh.

Ah sat back on the rock, bent low, head between mah knees, wincing in pain, her eyes tearing into me. When ah looked up again she was smiling at me – an evil, gloating grin that showed her small white teeth. She mocked me. A mere child.

Leaning closer to the nag and patting his nose with her little pale hands, she raised herself up on tippy-toes and whispered something in the horse's ear. Witch's words. A hex. She smiled again, and again she showed her teeth. A moment or two later, ah saw one white eye roll wild in the horse's head, then he reared and kicked and reared again. With a freakish neigh, the spooked beast bolted free, crashing through the hedgerow and raising a trail of red dust all down Maine.

A cheer went up. The men, drunk as lords, piled into their pick-ups and utilities and charged off after it, bottles and ropes and whoops all going. Impulsively ah jumped in the back of one pick-up with about ten other men, but a quarter of a mile up Maine they tossed me out, hardly even slowing down to do it.

Ah saw in the distance the crazed beast veer off Maine and hoof it part-way up the track that leads to mah place, then veer again and, splashing through the marshes, disappear into the swampland. Ah tasted blood and fished for a handkerchief, holding back mah head.

Ah limped down Maine, hardly able to see a foot in front of mah face for fucken dust. By the time ah reached mah shack, ah could see men filtering out of the swampland, mah sanctuary, somewhat sobered by whatever had taken place within.

The following day ah entered the swampland. It was cool and

dark and, as ah drew closer to mah sanctum, ah detected a sweetness to the air that was foreign to these hidden gardens, these dank and fusty regions – as if a woman had slept the night nearby and then departed. Ah breathed the perfumed air once more and ah remembered . . . the lavender sweetness of her body . . . Cosey Mo.

Something flashed at mah feet and ah thought for a moment that it was simply a tear spent in memory of her, but it was not. It was a piece of bottle – a minikin Prussian vial that had once held the essence of lavender.

Mah brains roared and bit by bit ah absorbed the horror of it all. A shoebox lid caught in a sling of vine – a bird skull and a Bible illustration all trodden into the mud – a bloodied rag draped across a tree trunk – clumps of hair trapped in a web – empty liquor bottles – the busted skull of mah brother – all scattered helter-skelter in the creeping greenness of the umbra.

Ah lay down because ah could no longer stand, and ah closed mah eyes on all the ivy and vine and ah opened mah mouth wide, in utter desolation.

Sorrow was his name. He would answer to no other.

Fireworks hissed and spat aloft. Heaven's darkening vault was scoured by whistling jets of spark. Catherine wheels spun, gushing lurid sprays. Sky rockets, spewing fire, tore the night sky with their blazing egress. Wicks fizzed. Bangers exploded. Smoke and blue sparks filled the air. Children stood in mute wonderment, gazing at the circus of spectral showers above, their gawping faces reflecting, in shouts of colour, all the crackling mischief of the cope. It was the night before the 'burn-off' eighth harvest after the rain. It was a balmy summer evening in 1953.

The nag hid in his feedbag, unnerved by the explosions. All that was visible of his head was a pair of twitching ears, pricked and trembling on either side of a red fez. His owner, the Turk, drunk on home-made wine, slept in a wicker chair.

Behind Sorrow stood a hay float upon which a fiddler, a largophonist, a caller and a man hunched over a box bass gave

swing to the proceedings with a string of popular jigs, flings and
barn-stomps that had all the cane-workers and their women and
a handful of younger Ukulites up on their feet and dancing. Then
Ted 'the Red' Hanley replaced the caller for some sing-a-longs,
and was halfway through the final verse of 'Portland Town' –

> 'I was born in Portland Town
> I was born in Portland Town
> Yes I was, yes I was
> Yes I was, yes I w– . . .'

– when the now frantic nag suddenly reared, bucked and kicked
himself free of his clamorous burden, overturning the float and
dumping haybales and musicians in the dust.

The Turk said later that it was the fireworks that had spooked
his horse, but Wilma Eldridge, a confirmed music hater, said it
was the music that had caused it – especially Ted Hanley's
singing. Ted ignored the remark, more concerned with how he
was going to chop his season's quota of cane with a fractured
wrist. Mary Hanley, Ted's new wife, a tall, intelligent-looking
woman with dark eyes and a moustache – the children had been
quick to spot the aptness of her nominal spoonerism – stepped
forward and said icily: 'Must we all partake of your sour grapes,
Mrs Eldridge? Surely you could peddle your miserable opinions
elsewhere,' causing a titter to ripple through both sectors of the
community.

The spooked nag galloped northward, an ancient bow-backed
beast, a thick trail of dust rising at his heel. Then, glimpsing the
open marshlands to the north-east, stained yellow with the dying
sun, he broke away from the main road and bolted up a largely
unused track toward those magical waters.

The sounds of twenty or so pick-ups coming up the rear, horns
blaring and engines roaring, drove the sorry beast galloping
onward through the marsh and into the strange circle of vegetation at its centre. The swampland. The spooked horse headed
for its heart.

The drunken followers abandoned their pick-ups as close to the swampland as the marshy sod would allow and, leaving their lights on high beam so that they pointed into the dark arena, the reeling, jeering band – armed with ropes and torches, machetes and bottles – ventured in. They hacked through the woven jungle of vine and creeper, machetes and low-curved sickles swinging.

When the mob broke through the thick tyre of growth that encircled the bleak domain of the swamp, they found Sorrow beating wildly at the air with his front legs – his rump and hinds already claimed by the black circle of mud – working himself deeper with each thrusting movement as he made to escape. Bloody foam covered his face as he bit the maddened air, making no sound other than the hollow chopping of his jaws. His eyes bulged and rolled in their sockets as he gulped air and regorged jets of nostril steam. The fire-red fez remained precariously perched on his head.

Looped ropes lashed out at the animal, slapping the black face of the quag as they missed their mark. The flailing mob of forty-fold took turns at throwing, each trying to lasso the sinking beast as he grabbled the air in blind terror in an attempt to keep his forelegs above the surface. The gamblers took the opportunity to place bets on the outcome. Bottles changed hands.

Finally, someone succeeded in slipping the gin about his neck and a team of seven or eight men manned the rope and heaved, while those who had placed cash on 'the swamp' chanted 'Sink! Sink! Sink!'

Sorrow sank.

What vile sight greeted the eye beneath the tarred curtain of the pit? What horror lurked below? What hell has Hell?

The pitch skin of the bog closed over the old horse like a secret door and the cheers and hoots of the riff-raff ended sickly, as if the evil eye of the bog had robbed them of laughter. In the awkward silence that ensued, the milling circle gazed at the sinister expanse of quickmud, shuffling and fidgeting, all eyes fixed upon the terrible nothingness. Not a word was spoken. Nor did the sullen bog offer one solitary belch in memory of its meal.

Then in one mighty purge, the horse crashed up through the blackened mirror, his massive head flung back, wrapped in a hood of black mud. And with the warm soup of death oozing into his open mouth Sorrow did at last surrender. And the mud took him under.

Silently the men headed back toward the beams of their pick-ups, until two or three of them halted in their tracks, their torches shining on a weird grotto-like edifice built from planks of wood and small sheets of corrugated iron bound together with string, electrical wire and vine: a strange one-man shelter, more like an animal's lair or a thief's hideaway filled with booty.

Bloody bandages had been threaded through the walls and a selection of tools had been hung from little looped strings inside: a hammer, a huge pair of scissors, a fretsaw, a screwdriver or two, some knives, nails, syringes.

Hanging on little strings from the ceiling were seven or eight bird wings. From a stack in the corner, one of the men kicked over a shoebox and fifteen or so birdskulls rolled out, glowing yellow in the torchlight.

'Jesus Christ. This is hobo ground,' said one.

'Goddamn animals,' said another.

And as if some great weight had been lifted from their shoulders the cane-workers set to chopping the grotto down, united at last in an act of arrant destruction, scattering the boxes, stealing the tools and smashing the bottles.

They set little fires.

Meanwhile, the owner of the hideaway limped down Maine, his head held back, a rag held to his nose, covered from head to toe in red dust.

Meanwhile, the carcass of an old nag floated deeper and deeper, bumping the slow-moving corpses of other things – some thousands of years old, preserved by the weird mud and suspended, in limbo, silently drifting and descending.

A week prior to the 'burn-off' Fists Wiggam lost both hands playing 'chicken' with the cane-trolleys. His friends fled, leaving the belligerent youth to stagger two hundred yards down Maine unaided, before collapsing outside his father's general store.

His hands, were they more graceful, could have been those of a pianist sitting at his instrument, the way they lay side by side, twitching there on the tracks – two bloodless bundles of slow-dying nerves.

Coming out of hospital and answering only to his given name, Fitzgerald, the young man seemed to have aged somewhat, mellowed out.

And in this lavender hell ah lay, upon a bed of tangled vine, and all the spinning webs did leave a sticky grey veil about mah face. And when she did appear, floating above all the desecration, her pinions fanned the scattered offerings up into a pile of hair and skin and bone, of paper and ash, of feather, tooth and nail, of blood and rags and fractured glass, and consumed them all in sudden fire that leaped and licked the tips of her wings and crackled unnerfoot. And though the hood of web masked mah eyes, ah could see the sad and sultry aspect of her face, and her hair worn loose, and her damp, swelling breasts, her painted lips and nails and her heavy-lidded eyes – and though mah ears were wrapped in web, ah could hear her slow breathing and the lazy turn of her words as she told me that ah must know mah enemy.

Exhausted, ah sought to leave the swampland, and as ah trekked through the thickery, tramping the damp and spongy unnergrowth beneath mah feet, ah felt that ah was leaving this dark haven for the last time, never to return. Fear and doubt now knew this place. Never again could ah lose mahself within these sacred climes. For how could ah ever now be certain that within the menagerie of shadows that shifted all about me, there was not one that was the shadow of man? Never again could ah trust this umbrage, now that it had been laid open by others.

As ah neared the perimeter mah foot caught on something hard, and ah sprawled in the tangled growth. And as ah lay there something cold bit mah ankle. Ah climbed to mah knees and found at mah foot fierce evidence of mah sanctum's violation –

a grinning sickle. That sickle, it felt heavy in mah hand. Ah slashed the air.

Gone was mah faith in the absence of man.

'Is there no place they would not follow me?' ah asked mahself.

'Slash, slash, slash,' ah dumbly replied.

XII

God is not gushy. You won't catch Him expelling a lot of heavenly gas on pleasantries and idle confabulation. Nor does He go in for a hell of a lot of preachifying, either. Gone is the hard sell of the old days – the old fire and brimstone pitch. These days God deals in a specialized commodity – people now are less inclined to part with their precious creature comforts and earthly pleasures for the promise of a celestial kingdom after death. God's clientele is small and select. The Devil has a shovel.

God has matured. He is not the impulsive, bowelless being of the Testaments – the vehement glorymonger, with His bag of cheap carny tricks and His booming voice – the fiery huckster with His burning bushes and wonder-wands. Nowadays God knows what He wants and He knows *who* He wants. If in His majesty He has seen fit to select you as an instrument in His Greater Plan, then, ah tell you, you must be ready to receive, comprehend and act upon His instructions, without question or debate.

Ah was His sword, sharp and keen and poised to strike. Ah glinted in the sun.

Ah sat alone on the crest of the slope that ran from the back of the shack down to the cane. Ah had mah arms folded over mah knees, which were drawn up to mah chest, and the lower part of mah face was sort of lost in the crooks of mah arms. Huddled up like this, ah watched the valley.

Ah did some thinking as ah looked down.

Ah watched the valley and saw the black fields and tall, charred sugar-cane, stripped of its trash and no longer whispering – hushed and waiting now, as death closed in. Ah saw the groups of cutters, sweating and smeared with soot, slamming low at the stalks with their machetes. The cutters swung and the cane fell.

Ah watched mah runway systematically destroyed by these men – the very same swine that had penetrated mah swampland and razed mah grotto to the ground. The same scum that had smashed and scattered mah treasures – all the mysteries ah had amassed – dark pockets of accumulated wonders – ancient shells – shivering feathered collectibles – boxes and boxes of rare and terrible secrets – brittle bones and beaks – captured noises – frail prizes – waters and glutens – specimens scraped from a lifetime of being – all that ah had ever thought or done or was, kept corked or lidded or unner glass – all that was *ah* – the skeleton upon which mah pale and paltry skin hung – gone. Mah fucken home, mah very bones – *gone*. In that wanton violation of mah self, these vandals of the soul had taken with them mah very past – mah history – and left, in its place, a shadow. A shell.

As ah sat there upon the scrap, watching and thinking, ah felt something hard and thorned, thistle-like, grow within me, filling me, replacing all that had been destroyed, smashed and ground to dust beneath boot and down-borne fist. Ah squatted and hissed and mah hands pulsed and swelled, feeling as though ah had thrust them to the wrists in a wasp nest. Ah blew on them, but mah breath burned. All the tiny welts and the larger, older scars made maps of mah hands and wrists, like smarting purple brands.

Similarly mah brains seemed gorged with blood, for stirring and squirming awake in the slumberous subcaverns of mah mind poisonous thoughts crawled forth, as if from some age-long hibernation – pit asps craving red meat. Ah sweated. Ah wheezed.

Ah looked back to the fields in the hope of lifting mah mood. Ah tried to extract some pleasure from the sight before me – dog-weary workers engaged in the punishing, back-breaking labour of field work – but the thistle of hate flourished all the more.

'Cunts,' ah thought.

Ah found mahself wishing – praying – that the noon-day sun, already hell-hot, would spin itself still hotter, until the vast acres of uncut cane would begin to smoulder and smoke, and the skin of the workers would bubble and blister, and as the sun beat down and the crops burst into flames, the roasted flesh would peel away from their arms and legs and backs and screaming faces in wet, red strips, layer upon layer, until their black-baked bones pierced the thin tissue of skin, shredding the webbery of veins and the last tattered rags of hide to a bucket of gore, then crumbling down, these eaten skeletons, to ash . . . to a thimble of cinders . . . to screaming dust . . . to dead fucken death.

Fearing that ah would be the one to burst into flames if ah continued to entertain such incendiary thoughts, ah cast mah eyes elsewhere.

Ah looked across the fields to the main road, where a party of thirty or so schoolchildren milled about the perimeter of the crop, receiving first-hand a lesson on the valley's sugar industry.

With them was a handful of adults and ah instantly recognized Miss Annapearl Wells, assistant headmistress at Ukulore Valley School, by her dazzling bonnet – not unlike a nun's coif – covering her ears and neck but with a ludicrous upsweeping peak at the front, like a giant duck's bill, mid quack.

Though quite a distance away, ah could also easily make out Mary Hanley, towering a good head and shoulders above her husband, who ah recognized by the blaze of red hair and the new and brightly glowing surgical sling. Mary Hanley stood by – a Goliath amongst the first-graders – while Miss Annapearl Wells, her peek-a-boo face red as a raspberry against her starched bonnet, worried and fussed at the heels of her flock, shepherding them this way and that.

A fat man in a hat with a clipboard in his hand – doubtless a mill man – appeared to be answering questions put to him by the children. So utterly black was mah mood that day, that the thought of creeping through the long grass on the other side of the road and spying on them failed to send even the slightest tremor of excitement through me. Ah just sat and looked and after a while ah was looking but kinda not looking as well, unable to bridle mah fugitive thoughts.

Sometime, somehow, mah attention drifted to the two tin

holding sheds that had been erected up on Hooper's Hill a year or two earlier for the purpose of storing sugar, raw and refined, pending delivery to Patterson.

Ah thought about the tubs of molasses that lined the inside walls of the sheds and ah thought of the dark, heavy syrup, so sweet and sticky. In mah mind's eye ah recalled the little sugar-pink caravan that once had sat upon that self-same hill, and in the treacle of mah day's dreaming, sweeter than a sorghum spring, ah conjured the image of *her*, honey-skinned and candy-boned, and for a time ah floated in ambrosial molasses and visions of Cosey Mo, climbing her honeycomb hill to her little pink honeypot – and with mah heart beating bliss-time ah plunged mah hands in – but the buzzing was not of bees, no, but of flies, for now she floated front up in a ditch, her face covered with the stigmata of the beat whore, black eyes and broken nose and not a tooth in her head, her body spotted with the scabbed badges of harlotry, her arms martyred by the pricks of addiction, her breasts bruised and her hair thin – a dirty dead whore in a ditch – because once you've got one scar on your face or your heart, it's only a matter of time before someone gives you another – and another – until a day doesn't go by when you aren't being bashed senseless, nor a town that you haven't been run out of, and you get to be such a goddamn mess that finally it doesn't feel right unless you're getting the Christ beaten out of you – and within a year of that first damning fall, those first down-borne fists, your first run-out, you wind up with flies buzzing around your eyes, back at the same place, the same town, deader than when you left, bobbing around in the swill – a dirty deadbeat whore in a roadside ditch. But a little part of you doesn't die. A little part of you lives on. And you make an orphan of that corrupt and contemptible part, dumping it right smack in the lap of the ones who first robbed you of your sweetness, for it is the wicked fruit of their crimes, it is their blood, their sin, it belongs there, this child of blood, this spawn of sin . . .

Ah drew mah attention to the road again. Beth dazzled in the dust, unner the blinding sun. By her side a little hairless man in a dark suit struggled to open a huge scarlet sun umbrella.

She stood straight and still. Her snow-white smock and crown of golden curls shone with a shameless brilliance that burned mah eyes. Ah screwed them shut. Her glare trembled in the darkness like a silver tongue of flame, dipped in gold – a luminary in mah moment of blindness. Her serpent-like locks rolled and curled over her shoulders and issued some kind of aura, almost like a gloriole – a quiet brightening of the air surrounding her silken crown. And ah'll say this – if ah had not been chosen as sole witness to the child's inception in the valley, to harbour alone this single nub of knowledge – ah could well have fallen prey to her outrageous deception.

O radiant impostor! O fiendish deceptor!

Ah scanned the road again. The schoolchildren were gone – shuffled off to their classrooms, ah expect – and the road was empty but for the two tiny figures, the dark speck and the bright speck and the stubborn, scarlet umbrella, and ah watched them watch the cane-men, on this, the first day of the seasonal ingathering.

Ah recalled the words of the prophet Isaiah:

But draw near hither, ye child of the sorceress,
the seed of the adulterer and the whore.
Against whom do ye sport yourself?
Against whom make ye a wide mouth, and draw out the tongue?
Are ye not a child of transgression, a seed of falsehood?

And this is where the Lord who called me from the womb spoke to me with instructions clear and simple, in a voice more beautiful than ah could bear.

'Euchrid,' he began, 'Euchrid . . .'

And ah sat and listened in mute wonderment as He spoke.

'Euchrid . . .' he began.

XIII

Beth was perched on the edge of her bed. She wore a pair of cotton underpants and one white ankle sock. With one knee brought up under her chin, she wriggled her tiny foot into the other sock, expelling a little grunt as she did so. Dropping one bright young leg back down to dangle aside the other over the edge of the bed, she peered up through sleep-swollen lids at Sardus, who stood before her, immaculate in his black Sunday suit and brushed black beard. He fanned his face with his hat and smiled down at Beth.

'It's Sunday,' said Beth, quietly but firmly, as if disclosing the answer to some long-awaited question.

'That's right,' said Sardus, 'and you've got to be ready for Mrs Shelley.'

Beth's brow furrowed beneath a nest of golden locks.

'Father, does God breathe funny?'

Sardus sat down beside her. Clasping her naked shoulders in his large man's hands, he turned her gently around to face him.

'What's happened, child?' His dark eyes penetrated hers.

'I think I heard God last night, at my window. Kind of breathing and whistling when he breathed. And He . . . I mean . . . His shadow, it was there. I s-saw it, just waiting and whistle-breathing . . . there at the window . . . a-a-and then it floated past. I went to the window, trying not to be afraid, but God was gone . . .'

'Why do you think it was God?' asked Sardus, unable to suppress a tremor of rage in his voice, for he knew well the reason why.

'Well, because God is coming to visit me. That's what Mrs Baxter says, and Miss Sarah Blume. And I know I musn't be afraid. Did I scare God away? Will He be angry and punish us again?'

Sardus wrapped his long thin arms around his daughter and held her suddenly very frail little body to his.

'No, baby, that wasn't God,' said Sardus.

XIV

Ah visited the graveyard now and then, and spent a bit of time walking around the crops, but there was little point in that as new crops had been planted after the harvest and were too low to actually set foot in without being seen. Ah began to explore the hills, having to walk several miles to get to them, but up in the rocky parts ah found the lairs of wild dogs and climbed out on the tall timbers there. Ah would kill evil sleeping snakes that baked on the hot rocks by snatching them by the tail and spinning them around mah head, and then cracking them like a whip, in the air, or simply dashing them against a rock or tree trunk. Hanging their carcasses from a tree, ah would feel powerful – like a machine. Other times ah would just sit up there and do nothing, just looking down at the valley and thinking. Ah even slept out, unner the stars, once or twice. But most of the time ah passed away in the comparative safety of mah room.

Occasionally ah would pop the cork on mah peep-hole and watch Ma and Pa battle it out, and wonder to mahself just how much longer it would be until Pa finally cracked and tore the bitch to pieces. Ah thought of the baking snakes and just how goddamn easy it was.

It had to be soon. Ah could feel it.

Well, it was.

Autumn. September 1953. Ah peered in.

Ah could see them both. Pa sat at the table, a churning nest of nerves. He was building up a house of cards. Already it towered so high that ah could see his face only when he peered around to check if the sides of the construction were straight. It was then ah could see his eyes, squinted mean and yellow with bile.

Ma, her back to Pa, stood across the room in deep potations

with a stone bottle of shine, scrutinizing a photograph of herself framed and hung on the living-room wall.

She cackled and ranted on about what a little flower she had been before she had been plucked and left to wither and die, her jaws stopping only to suck on the bottle.

Ah could see Pa's hands shake as she spoke. The house of cards trembled in front of him.

Ma bemoaned her life, tipping the whole can of worms on to Pa's plate, as though if it hadn't been for him she would still be that little flower in the picture. She carried on about what a lazy old bastard Pa was and how he was going insane.

The house of cards leaned, hung in the air for a moment, then collapsed, and so did the frail edifice of Pa's mind.

Pa leaped from his chair and threw himself across the room, picking up all the speed he could muster, while his wife drew long and intimate upon her bottle. He slammed his body into hers, hammering her head face first against the wall. Glass splintered as the bottom of the stone bottle, still in her mouth, smashed the glass in the wedding picture, and a strange sick gurgle accompanied it. With a fistful of hair Pa wrenched back her head and pounded her face into the wall again. The bottle sank deeper and even from where ah was ah could hear her jaws cleave apart with a clear 'cra-a-ack', so that the third time the bottle slipped into her throat, splitting her grin's skin from ear to ear.

Pa swung her around and let her slide down the wall, so that she sat, legs outstretched, arms hanging at her sides, with her head standing up like some mad fat puppet grinning, her neck stretched out like a cane toad's.

Pa picked up two bricks from off the top of the old pot-belly stove, and one in each hand he swung them out-a-ways – then brought them in together like a pair of cymbals crashing, clapping his wife about the ears and smashing the bottle inside her.

Blood.

Her head dropped forward into her chins and the busted neck of the bottle pierced the back of her neck, forming a neat little funnel that jutted out, parting the greasy slab of hair at the back like a spout, the size of mah thumb, and gushing steamy blood and peel liquor.

Pa let the bricks drop from his hands. They made a dull, wet clunk as they hit the blood-mudded sod. He breathed, shallow and sharp. A high-noted moan bubbled on his lips in a series of queer, short-lived expulsions. In his right fist was a clump of grey hair. He stood there, doing and saying nothing, until his boots were two islands adrift in a sea of steam and scarlet.

Ah punched the nog back in the hole, slid off mah bed and entered the living room. Ah waded over and stood by mah father.

Pa slowly inclined his head, so that eventually his eyes stared into mine. He shivered like a pup, his eyes clear and alive.

'Git the sheet offa your bed. And bring some strong rope.'

Ah returned with mah dirty bed linen, handed him the bundle, then went back to mah room to sort through mah stuff, saying in mah head, 'Rope rope rope rope . . .'

In the talcum light of dusk, as the fleeting sun retrieved its bright spears and the fine black hem of night veiled its brow, Ezra and Euchrid made their way across the marshlands. Each wore across his shoulders a simple pine-board halter from which ran about fifteen feet of thick rope hitched to either side of a giant pallet of corrugated tin. Freighted upon the pallet's considerable circular expanse was a vast and ghastly carcass, enshrouded in muddy white cloth and trussed in coloured electrical cord. Both figures strained against the lumbering deadweight that they hauled behind them, their bodies angled forward, a knotted walking-prop clenched in each fist, their faces strangely void of grimace, of effort. Each solemnly bore his burden as if some shred of dignity was to be retrieved in the trappings of ceremony – hence the grim grey hoods, the sombre masks. Hence the crying, straining muscle beneath.

The marshlands were cast in gold, the syrupy waters silent and still. The funeral party of father and son slowly approached the floodwaters that encompassed the infernal black island, two slanted posts roped to their bloody burden – that hill of death dragged across the sloblands now raked by the futile, gilded fingers of the dying sun.

When they reached the uncertain edge of the water, Ezra and Euchrid removed the pine-board halters and, without pausing for a second's rest, began to haul in the ropes, lugging the cow-big corpse the final few feet until it was flush with the lip of the land. And without a word or a glance or a nod, without a prayer or a song or a sprinkling of clay, the old man and the boy, with a firm push of their feet, rolled the huge white slab from the pallet into the water.

She sank beneath the surface, the scoriac waters not splashing, not leaping up, but opening to take her. And for a moment she was no more. Father and son stood silently on the bank looking down at the inscrutable waters, and watched as the enshrouded cadaver bobbed obscenely to the top and revolved there upon its side.

Then slowly, helplessly, and not without some prodding from their sticks, it fell to the tug of the swampland's fetching waters. Bound in its bloody trousseau, the vast mass of death sailed toward the dark wheel of vegetation, as if reeled into its evil black heart. The two grim figures on the bank, mere shadows now, looked on as varlet crows dipped and swooped aloft and marsh rats swam to claim this new slow-moving ground, and the great floating isle died in a double darkness of swamp and night.

XV

Strange days followed the death and disposal of Ma Crowley.

The old man seemed to float around the shack with the same kind of weightless euphoria that is felt after the laying down of some carking burden at the end of a long and arduous journey. He did not smile or sing or do a little jig; rather Pa seemed to be infused with a quiet pleasure, a contentment, a deep appreciation of the absence of his spouse.

Stranger still was the bond that formed between Euchrid and his father in the wake of his mother's death, grafting them together as fast as the most enduring Siamese ligature. Ma had been as a vast and poisonous sea separating a father and his son, and in one monstrous catharsis Pa had parted the waters and fallen into a kindred embrace.

But the bond that tied them together was of a manifold weave, and this served to strengthen their strange friendship all the more. Euchrid became the perfect foil for Pa, for the invisible ties that bind a father and his son, a murderer and his accomplice, a confessor and priest, and a raconteur to his rapt listener – all meshed to create a steadfast and oddly devoted union.

Each evening, at the living-room table, Pa would embark on long reminiscences, recalling the lawless days of his youth, the wild escapades of his deranged kin, the ill-fated journey into the valley, the bottle of mountain madness that had cost him an ear – all imparted to a spellbound audience of one. Other nights, Pa's muttered discourses took on a distinctly confessional air and Euchrid would sit, spooning down hash and boiled cabbage, listening intently as the mad old man unburdened himself. Some evenings he would speak of Ma, and the scourge of his words was enough to flay her in her grave. Yet, despite the conviction with which he denounced 'the queen of the trollops', or 'the potted hog', as Pa repeatedly called her, something rang untrue – like a cracked bell – and the more Euchrid listened to his father's harangue the more vulnerable Pa seemed to become, as if there were other emotions at play that perhaps even the old man himself was unable to acknowledge and hence repressed, instinctively swamping them in bitterness and bloody-mindedness. Euchrid saw, to his increasing bewilderment, that the tirades on which Pa embarked were in fact diligent disguises, worn like fast armour over a shabby skeleton of regret and guilt and a deepening sense of loss. As difficult as it was to accept, Euchrid was forced to conclude that behind the old man's brag there trembled a glum heart that swelled with remorse at the measure of his deed.

'Guilt?' Pa said, one evening, laughing sick. 'Do ah feel guilt at what ah done? Haw haw! That's a goddamn cracker if ever ah heard one! Did George feel guilt when he slewed the dragon?! Was David regrettin when he pole-axed Goliath?! No sirree! And King Jehu – did he rue the day he stomped Jezebel and fed her to the dawgs?! You're damn right he didn't! And you're goddamn right ah don't neither!'

A blowfly crawled across the table and Pa snatched it up with one nimble swipe. The insect screamed in his fist as he held it to his good ear.

'Why, that piss-eyed hell-bag had more monster in her than a pack o' dragons and was a damn sight more ornery than any Philistine ogre and twice as ugly. And furthermore – an here ah'll swear on a stack – ya could drag all the sewers in whoredom 'n' still ya wouldn't land a sloppier, more downright low-livin scum-monger than the hog that bore you.'

Euchrid swallowed.

The blowfly had ceased its long spinning frenzy and lay mostly silent in Pa's closed fist, buzzing briefly in fits and starts that became less frequent and less urgent.

'She was the original Whore of Babylon – and now she is no more . . .' Pa said, opening his hand and flicking the fly corpse out the door. 'And now she is no more,' he repeated quietly.

And Euchrid sat and Euchrid saw and Euchrid said nothing at all.

Yet, mumchance as he was, Euchrid the mute wished more than he had ever wished before that his tongue would stir and wag awake and burst the shackles of the million unspoken secrets that lay incarcerated in the dungeons of his heart. He petitioned God in silent prayer that He might grant His humble servant an evening's tongue-time. Or even an hour's. But Heaven handed out no miracles on this day.

Such was his need to speak that Euchrid put aside his faith for an instant and questioned the sanity of the Lord's 'greater scheme'. He thought of the dying blowfly and how even brute creation's lowliest and most putrid of creatures, the shit-eater, was capable of trumpeting its own petty demise, while a chosen soldier of the Lord, an earthly appendage of God Himself, His rod and His staff, was denied the gift of speech.

Euchrid wondered as he sat, his father's vitriol a far-away buzz, whether his muteness was a necessary provision in order for him to receive the word of God. He thought of Heaven and wondered if he would be dumb there too. He shuddered. He wondered whether God actually heard his silent prayers and petitions, and if He did, what did his voice sound like? Did he mumble like Pa? Or snarl and bark like Ma? He wondered, as a slumberous dark engulfed him.

He dreamed he was a ghost moving in slow motion through the dark convoluted alleyways of iniquity. He saw the moon marbled with blood and milk. He felt the heat hanging on him, hot as a brothel. He saw beat whores working the chippy shift and grinning pimps in doorways. Winos nursing bottles crawled like legless dogs, and urchins set fire to sleeping bums. Mugs in cars waved bundled cash, cruising through him as if he were not there. The streets grew crippled, convoluted, the cracks directing him. He passed an open window and discovered a sleeping child. Her head was facing the window. Reaching in, Euchrid seized her with his left hand and began to strangle her, roaring with laughter until the little naked child awoke. His prey struggled, twisting and stretching and beating the crib as she fell into unconsciousness. Euchrid took her head and held it hard down upon an embroidered satin pillow and stabbed her in the throat with a pair of mud-caked shears many times until an old whore behind him said, 'O bless thee, thou hast slain the bad queen! Her blood is spilt. Sisters of Whoredom! We are free! Free from the valley of the shadow of Beth Beth Beth Beth Beth . . .'

The dreamer's elbows slipped out from under him and his nodding head dropped with a sick crunch, his forehead cracking against the edge of the table at which he sat. Euchrid tasted blood, sour and salty. Rising from his chair, he stumbled across the room to the pot-belly stove upon which sat a metal tub of water. His head ached and he plunged it into the tub, holding it under and letting the cold water dissolve the webs of sleep and rinse away the blood that streamed from his nostrils. His whole head submerged, Euchrid listened to the roar of water in his ears, gradually discerning a dull thudding pulse that seemed with each passing second to quicken its pace, and with each deep beat to rise in intensity, like a kettle drum in crescendo, hammering, hammering, rocking his brains with its thud-thud thud-thud thud-thud . . .

Ah mean, what would *you* call it?

Ah call it an act of mercy – and for a short time following it, Pa was rewarded with a term of quiet pleasure, and the whole of our humble household seemed infected with it and for weeks we lived like that, content in each other's company, him talking and me listening, mah head brimming with all manner of things, brimming and spilling as if by proxy, so often did he seem to take the words right out of mah mouth – speaking wildly at times and exciting mah mind to wildness. So it was that mah brain shouted out thoughts of such unbridled brass – O such wild wild poetry – that the old man's tongue merely shaped and spoke them, the way the crow of the morning cock is really an echo – an echo of the tongueless eloquence of the new day's first and most glorious inspiration. Brimming with special blood, we were – of the *kept* kind, unnerstand, of the *confidential* kind – both of us, father and son – and on those long hearing-hollering nights, we had ourselves an association, the air fully bursting with our wild, wedded gas.

Pa called it an act of mercy as he mixed up a bucket of whiting, size and water and set about first scrubbing then whitewashing the bloody, tell-tale wall. Ah rinsed and painted the bricks and put them both out on the front porch to dry. The sun, ah remember, did battle with a pack of fat cotton clouds and the shadows came and went and came and went, until the hooded night did up and bag them all. Ah went indoors and fetched a spirit lamp. Pa had finished the wall and sat in his chair, staring at the great, white glistening expanse. Ah lit the lamp and returned to the porch, now hearing Pa blithely humming from within. Ah watched through the doorway. Ah saw him stand, get a hammer, go to the wall and drive three four-inch nails, in a row, about head-height, into the freshly painted planks. Then he walked to the other end of the room and out of view. Ah put the lamp beside the two wet bricks and cursed the order of Thysanoptera – both bricks were covered with a zillion fucken stuck thrips. Ah nudged the bricks off the edge of the porch and into the dust.

Inside, Pa had resumed his position, seated in his chair, staring proudly at the whitewashed wall. The Black Bastard, all thirty pounds of it, greased and hungry, hung on the nails, leering back at him like some giant prehistorical jawbone.

Ah stunned a winged thing with a sly swipe, thinking, 'That's one for the bricks,' and, thinking on, ah figgered it had been almost two weeks since we set Ma afloat. Two full weeks, sitting in the shack, swatting at a swarm of blood-hungry gnats, and ah wondered then, as ah still wonder now, here, stuck as ah am in this quickmud like a thrip on a sticky brick, why Pa waited so long before he coated the killing-wall.

But our term of simple contentment together as father and son drew closed like a leaden curtain, slammed shut like a door in mah face, and, ponder as ah may, the matter still baffles me. Listen.

It was the end of the second week of mah life-without-Ma. It had been a pleasant eve and Pa had retired to his bed, his spirits high and jaunty. Yet, come the next morn, a very different father did emerge. Grim and crooked, he was, as if some carking incubus or succubus or whatever had squatted on his chest through the night and sucked dry his happy heart and filled him full of dread and desolation. It was as though Pa knew he was walking his last mile. He moped around the yard like a sick dog. He dragged his chair on to the porch and spent hours at a stretch gazing across the marshes toward the swampland. He spoke not, but seemed muzzled by some awful sorrow-sick lowness that clung so fully that it defied cause or reason or . . . His heart was entombed in an unplumbable pit of black woe. There was no 'because' for there was no 'why'. Yet still ah wondered. Still ah wondered. And wonder still, ah do.

How often have ah cast mah mind back to the night before Pa's mysterious change of nature. It was the last evening that our home would know the spirit of contentment. Ah was helping Pa bundle together all of Ma's belongings – little more than a few armfuls of rancid rags – carting the sour garments around to the rear of the shack and shoving them in one of five forty-four-gallon drums that ah had rolled all the way from Glory Flats – the scorched and ashen church grounds now an unofficial dumping-ground for the valley's unwanted junk and, might ah say, a virtual goldmine. Pa deposited all the articles that belonged to his wife inside the oil drum, every last ugly memory. Included in the rejectamenta were a few sundry personals from her younger days that she had hoarded in a hat box trussed up with a now rotten satin ribbon. Under the ribbon had been slipped a small gilt-edged card, which stated in a neat girlish hand:

This box belongs to Jane Crowley
Keep out
1910

Pa read the words out loud, and with an indifferent grunt tossed the box, unopened, into the drum with the rest of the junk.

Before ah had a chance to retrieve the mysterious hat box and all the secrets that it contained, Pa emptied a half-gallon can of meths over the lot and was already striking a match on the bonnet of the Chevy. He flicked the match into the drum and ah watched mah chances of ever examining the contents of that wonderful hat box – emerald green with gold stripes it was, and on the lid was a gold embossed crown, nestling in a group of three crossed purple feathers and across the top a banner that said:

The House of Three Plumes

held either side by two slanting spears and around the bottom, in stately Gothic demi-bold face:

Hatters of Excellence for Over Fifty Years

– go boom.

And then Pa was gone, while ah kind of stood there, feeling the warmth of the incinerator pinking mah cheeks and inhaling the dizzy fumes, not really aware of much at all, mesmerized by the dancing flames that leaped over the lip of the drum, all yellow and white against the soot-black smoke that vomited forth, bullied this way and that by the late summer night's breeze.

And then Pa was back with his Bible in his hand and together we sat on the bonnet of the car, side by side, yes, father and son, and for a minute we remained that way, spellbound by the blaze. Then Pa opened the book and turned to the Psalms.

'Ah want you to concentrate. Ah want you to try and unnerstand. Can ya do that? Ah want you to listen with both ya ears and try and unnerstand,' said Pa at last, kneading the nob of his ear and spitting into the fire.

Ah nodded but did not take mah eyes off the fire, and Pa tilted his book a little toward the flames in order to read the dense black type. Ah listened intently to his grave and emphatic recital, even though ah knew the Psalm by heart and recognized it the minute he began. Psalm 58. How often had Pa read aloud Psalm 58 as ah sat crouched in hiding, a mere pup, low-breathing in the pickle-barrel, listening.

PSALM 58

1. Do ye indeed speak righteousness, O congregation?
Do ye judge up – rightly, O ye sons of men?

Ah answered not and a great belch of smoke lumbered over us for a dark moment, like a dirty grey ghost, before mercifully rolling and curling back upon itself –

2. Yea, in heart ye work wickedness;
ye weigh the violence of your hands in the earth.
3. The wicked are estranged from the womb:
they go astray as soon as they be born, speaking lies.

And an icy chill clutched mah heart and mah head swam, but not from the smoke, not from the fumes –

4. Their poison is like the poison of a serpent:
they are like the deaf adder that stoppeth her ear;
5. Which will not harken to the voice of charmers,
charming never so wisely.

– not from the poison fumes did mah hands grow hotter and hotter, raw and rubbed and throbbing horrible, mah snaking veins worming, throbbing and worming –

6. Break their teeth, O God, in their mouth:
break out the great teeth of the young lions, O LORD.
7. Let them melt away as waters which run continually:
when he bendeth his bow to shoot his arrows,
let them be as cut in pieces.

– mah teeth shooting up mah face and fucking mah ears, so that
Pa's words are melting, mah poisoned brains are boiling full –

    8. As a snail which melted,
  let every one of them pass away:
  like the untimely birth of a woman,
  that they may not see the sun.
    9. Before your pots can feel the thorns,
  he shall take them away as with a whirlwind,
  both living, and in his wrath.

– of other voices, angry voices –

    10. The righteous shall rejoice when he seeth the vengeance:
  he shall wash his feet in the blood of the wicked.

– righteous voices. O blood –

    11. So that a man shall say,
  Verily there is a reward for the righteous:
  verily he is a God that judgeth in the earth.

– O bloody reward –

Ashes glowed faintly in the drum but shed no light and the
starless night served as a veil, so that mah father could not see
the stream of tears that had wet mah fiery cheeks. We sat in
silence. Then Pa said, his voice sounding from the darkness,
suddenly old, choked and old, 'Boy . . . don't cry, boy . . . it's all
right . . . it's all right . . .'

Then Pa's hand reached out of the darkness, but ah was not
so upset that ah didn't see it coming and quick smart ah ducked,
keeping low, but – and it – *he touched me* – no, but gently, placing
his hand over mine, mah right one – just like that, *gently* and ah
could hardly hold mah hand still, trembling as it was – and
the feeling was so goddamn strange – so completely, goddamn
strange – his cool, rough human hand, over mah hot little

throbbers. Only for, say, about four seconds and then he gave it a little pat, sliding as he did it off the bonnet of the Chevy.

Ah remained seated there, in the humming darkness, mah whole being quaking, and ah listened as he trudged across the yard, hearing the clank of the pail and the slop-splash of the trough-water as he filled it, and again his footsteps, and finally a hisssss as he emptied the bucket into the drum.

'Even the ashes stink,' ah think ah heard him mutter, as the sound of his retreating footsteps died in the night.

After a while, when the tingling had stopped, ah too slid off the bonnet and crossed the yard to the incinerator. Ah took a deep sniff as ah peered in. Ah smelled nothing, or, rather, ah forgot to smell something, as the full face of the moon laughed at me from the bottom of the drum, mirrored in the dirty, ashen soup.

Exhausted, ah charged indoors.

XVI

The sun rose and waked the cock. The cock a-doodled and waked the wild dog. The dog gave a ho-o-o-owl and waked the crows, who took to the air, flying low, going 'caw-caw-caw' and not stopping till the whole fucken valley was woke. Little wonder every season is open season on crows.

Ah crawled from mah bed, mah mind a slaughterhouse. Plucked birds with big yellow beaks fell victim to the cleaver. Mah head throbbed with the 'caw-caw-chop', 'caw-caw-chop' of mah bloody morning thoughts. Ah dressed and entered the front room, creeping past Pa's room so as not to wake him, hoping like hell that his darksome mood of the last two days had lifted.

Mah conjunctivitis – something of a family thing, on Pa's side – could not have been worse than on this bugger of a morn. So raw and itchy and swollen were mah eyes that ah figured the sandman must have died and they'd called in the mustardman as a replacement. Ah picked at the mucus crusts as ah groped mah way toward the tub, feeling like ah had cat's tongues for eyelids. Ah dipped a handkerchief in the water and, holding back mah head, folded the soppy cloth across both eyes, dabbing and patting at the sockets, feeling the coolness seep through mah lids.

'If it ain't one thing, then it's a hundred others,' ah thought. 'Weighed in the balance and found wanting. Defect and Deformity. Blemish and Flaw. Handicap, Inadequacy and Malady. Will this shabby lot hobble for ever at mah heel, from now unto the grave, evermore to be the sorry dogs of mah days?' ah grieved, feeling downright sorry for mahself. 'How can ah launch a holy war' – ah beat at mah sunken chest with mah free hand – 'when mah battledress is more chink than fucken armour?' Ah shook one plaintive hand heavenward.

God, what a morning. Ah wiped away the eye-muck, made

soft by the soppy compress, and, squinting and blinking, ah looked for the first time at everything about me. All was as it should've been.

All was as it should've been, except . . .

On the table, only an arm's length or two away and towering a good foot taller than me – and ah'm scraping five and a half mahself – six, if ah could stand up straight – was a house made up of playing cards. Only this time Pa had excelled himself, for it was a colossus of truly awesome highness. Yet its base was only five cards square – lengthwise arranged, of course. Ah counted as ah stood there – frozen in mah tracks, breathing but not breathing, afraid to even *look* too hard at it – exactly twenty storeys, stacked one on top of the other, making the soaring monolith a full four feet high – that's a heaven-tickling seven feet, if you include the table, leaving a meagre twelve inches' grace between its topmost storey and the fucken goddamn ceiling! Can you imagine just how many cards it would take to construct an edifice of such lofty perpendicular proportion?

And can you imagine just how fragile, just how prone to collapse this structure was? Do you realize just how much this building *ached* to fall down?

'Ah sure as hell don't plan to be around when it does,' ah thought, as memories of mah mother, dead and pasted on the north wall, flooded mah mind. And just at that moment a giant green blow-beetle flew through the shack door and, chirruping loudly, ploughed straight into the middle of it.

Pa's masterwork collapsed in on itself like it was imploding, flatting floor by floor, with a sinister method to its undoing – a cold symmetry and a tragic inevitability that froze me stiff, even as it came crashing down. Ah watched in horror but what ah *heard*, ah heard in disbelief!

The tower of playing cards crumpled with a sound of splintering wood, followed closely by a god-almighty 'cra-a-a-ash' that literally shook the whole damn house as the paper cards fell into a pile on the table top. And then . . .

And then there was silence, complete and utter silence.

'Is it not enough that ah am voiceless? Is it not enough that mah eyes still burn-itch from this morning's clagging? Is it also necessary that mah ears go idiot on me, just now?' ah thought.

Ah stood like a wooden Indian, petrified, feeling like there was no one left alive in the world but me – alone – in fear – with all the voices coming now, rushing in, telling me, telling me . . . but ah knew – O God, ah knew . . .

Then Euchrid was hurtling across the front room, upturning the table and sending the paper ruins of the card-house spilling across the sod floor as he careered past. Crashing through the screen door and taking all three porch steps in one lunge, the terror-fraught mute threw himself along the front of the house, swung around the corner and headed down the side of the shack to the junk-pile.

As he grew closer his frenzied sprint suddenly slowed to urgent paces, like some berserk clockwork toy winding down, and those paces soon became faltering steps, until Euchrid was no longer moving but standing rigid, his back bent and shoulders stooped in such a way that his posture appeared even more crooked, even more comical than usual. He stood with his hands folded over his head, in the manner of chimpanzees seen at the zoo, his lower jaw slack, sucking and blowing deep lungfuls of the new air, his red-rimmed eyes quivering. He stared.

Euchrid remained riveted before the sight that confronted him. An unspeakable sadness crept over his face. *All his fears were founded*.

The rusted iron water-tank – Pa's gladiatorial arena and men-agerie of death – lay upon its side. The splintered stilts of its base jutted up behind like so many unearthed bones, brown and rotten, whilst the corrugated tank itself had flattened from the impact of its fall and was now oval in shape, the chicken-wire lid having sprung free so that the top or the mouth of the tank looked liked a monstrous maw spewing forth a gutful of death, a jumbled hecatomb of bleached and eaten bone, many-spined and many-limbed and many-skulled, skins and furs and feathers rotted from the pale remains, with skulls still spinning and rolling even as Euchrid watched.

And thrown beyond the spillage, lying on his side though still in a sitting position, his stool only inches away, lay Pa, a growing pool of black blood spreading about his smashed skull and a thin string of watery blood bubbling from the nob of his missing ear.

One eye, still and yellow, hung by its optic nerve from a blood-pooled orbit. Dead eye. Crow bait. On Pa's shoulder a wily black scavenger sidled back and forth, across his arm, fending off two smaller crows, taking sly pecks at the dangling morsel then flapping back along the arm to thrust its vicious beak at the squawking interlopers.

Euchrid spun on his heel, entered the shack and returned within seconds, the shotgun cradled in his arms. He aimed, fired and blew the head clean off the big crow. He fired again and blasted the second into oblivion. The third bird fled, flapping into the morning ether as, reloading and aiming again, Euchrid squeezed the trigger, winging it so that it flailed and squawked and plummeted earthward, landing a barrel's distance from Euchrid's foot. It flapped weakly in the blood-specked dust, one pleading black bead fixed on Euchrid.

Gun at his hip, Euchrid aimed at the crow, then lifted the gun again and, sobbing now, tears breaking down his face, brought his foot slowly down upon the bird's shivering head, hearing the skull give beneath his boot as he ground its head to pulp. He wiped his boot clean on a patch of onion-weed.

Euchrid pulled a handkerchief from his back pocket and shook it open. He walked over to his father and draped the white linen square across the old man's face. Then he walked over to the Chevy and climbed on to the bonnet, and with his legs dangling over the side he lay back beneath the shimmering sun.

He reached into his front pocket and retrieved a second handkerchief and, unfolding it slowly, he let the thin fabric float over his own face, until that too was enshrouded.

He let the gun down by his side.

The handkerchief was sea-green.

He lay just so, locked in silence, until mercifully he fell away; for he could go no other place than the dark retreat of sleep – to the poultice of his dreams where there was no cause to wonder, to comprehend . . .

The sun was hell and all the flies hummed and in a matter of seconds Pa's shroud turned a deep crimson, like a flag red and wet.

Euchrid buried all the corpse and carcass of that black morning right there, in the yard, where the tower had stood. His face was as impassive as the sun's was triumphant and he bent beneath the blistering flog of it all and dug and further dug and continued digging, while the sun rolled fulgent about the heavens, a haughty bully, filling the valley with all its brag and swollen business.

First he dug around the splintered stumps of the tower, which were still entrenched in the earth. Straining beneath the weight, he hauled them out, each rotten pylon anchored with a lump of concrete and wire.

Then he began to dig the hole.

He dug from noon until nightfall, smeared with sweat and grime, his face a blank page, like a dead man's; all through the hell of the day, until the dark earth rose, piled high about him, and the pit grew dim in the gloaming hours, dim and drowned in shadow, so that Euchrid could no longer see to dig.

He dragged his body from the grave and collapsed upon a hill of sweet clay, blistered and bloody palms turned upward.

The following day, each hand swathed in a grimy mitten of gauze and tape, Euchrid shovelled all the dead and rotten spillage back into the overturned tank, then, attaching a rope to one side of it, hoisted the tank around so that the mass of putrid hecatomb began to slide and spill, with a rattle of bones across tin, into the pit. Euchrid dragged his father's corpse by the feet over to the hole and dumped it in, having to get down on his knees and push with his hands in order to roll the stiff dead weight in.

'So much death . . .' he thought, and wished himself to die.

BOOK THREE

DOGHEAD

Time is pressing. Yes. Time . . . is . . . pressing. Strange that, for it has never pressed before. Not once, that ah recall. Not once in mah twenny-eight years of living. Not once that ah recall. Twenny-eight years – that's roughly ten thousand laps of a clock-face – Jesus! When ah think that ah've sat on mah dumb ass and listened through eighteen million ticks and eighteen million tocks of the idiot-faced clock with nothing to call mah own but a shit-load of time and now, at the hour of mah dying when ah could use a little room – what happens? It's 'Move along, chucklehead – wind her up, Jack.' It's *'Let's get fucken pressing!!'*

Not so easy, all this dying, nor so easy at all. O for a decent lungful of air. Trussed up in this mud's crush and suck, but floating too, awash in a galaxy of constricting atmosphere, mah innards tossed by waves of nausea as they do battle with the closing fingers of mah ribs, almost as if skin and bone had married to become a fiendish corset intent on seeing me sick up mah gizzards, mah heart, mah lungs, the lot. Bile is steadily rising in mah throat, apparently in accordance with mah descent. O mah descent! O mah descent! As in life, in death, all downward spent! Blades of pain from eye to brain. Ah gag on the effluvium. Poison vapours coil like serpentine wraiths about me. But they do not scare me any more. Not with their mutterings. Not with their fondling. Ah have survived the hauntings of more freakish beasts than these. Ah say fuck this phosphorous greensick gas! Let it roll upon me! Within me! Through me! Mah brain is a grimy sponge saturated with this piss-pond's poison vapours! What does it matter if mah deathtime reminiscences are coloured a little by the sulphurous miasma of this pit? Ah can brave it out. Ah mean, ah never asked for an easy exit.

No sir! Fuck! Who wants to go in their sleep? Not me! Not Euchrid Euchrow, son of God. Give me a death ah can remember for the re– . . . Shit! No! Ah say let me pop off with a *bang*! No bog, no bug-a-boos, no bounty hunters, no-bloody-nothing can rob me of this. Because ah know a better place awaits me. There below. O yes. There below this pit's skin. A bliss God lays His children in. Damn! Mah skull is polluted with sickly poetry. Poisoned with sing-song rhymes. There are days when every thought that passes through mah mind will bring another, in its step, in rhythm, stress and rhyme. Listen.

'It seems you're inching unner, sir, inching slowly unner
But what it is you're inching in, ah cannot help but wonder.'
O booming voice up in the clouds, to speak cuts like a knife
Ah'm simply inching into Death, while inching out of Life.
'You're wrong, you poor deluded boy, True Death's up here with
    Me
Hell's dungeons boil below you, child, Eternal Agony!'
'O climb down off your crap-hill, O fiend hid in the sky
You're Lucifer! The Great Deceiver! Your word is but a lie!
You will not fool me any more with your wrath and rolling thunder
'Tis God that stands behind mah wheel and inches me now unner.'
The bog it yawned and pulled me down, mah body trussed in chains
And Satan sighed and shook his head, played harp amongst the
    flames.
'It's Hell up there in Heaven too, for all that that is worth.
Heaven is just a lie of mine to make it Hell on Earth.'

As ah said, it ain't so easy dying – but ah'll tough it out.

Do you think ah'm hedging? Ah mean – *am* ah hedging? *Bullshit!*

Do you think that ah don't know what's running through your minds? Well let's straighten some simple truths that seem to be getting mighty twisted. Ah did *not* sabotage the water-tower. Ah mean, for Christ's sake, the goddamn stilts were riddled with woodrot. In any case, me and Pa were close. God rest his soul.

Perhaps they crept up from town and did it? Ah can't, in fairness, directly blame *them* but ah wouldn't put it past them. Would you?

Ah'm no killer, no. Well, yes ah am. OK – so ah killed a few hobos last year. But one thing at a time and each thing in its place.

Do you know that you will be a party to mah inevitable and irreversible demise? No? Well, oil your shotguns and grease your machetes and noose up a nice fat rope, for, know it or not, you are the ones that will hunt me down – yes! Hunt me down and kill me. Hunt me down and kill me. You hate me and you don't know why. But one thing at a time and each thing in its place. Now to return, to the grave where mah daddy lay for the rest of his days. For the rest of his days.

Ah lay and lay for days and days. The sweet and gravid earth, once flattened by the whack and the slap of mah spade's back, now bore across its length the crooked imprint of mah body. For ah lay like some forgotten unburied, unmoving there, atop of it all, so dead. And ah swear ah heard those there beneath me, mah cheek pillowed in the soil, through the days and through the nights. A little comfort, a little crying, a little eating of the clay.

Ah simply could not leave that grave – though ah did not lie in wait, for ah expected nothing, nothing at all. For you must unnerstand that ah was possessed by a torpor of inexpectation. Ah was unable to resist that sweet, cool place upon the mound – not just because of the weird music rising from within that seemed to sap mah life-blood, mah strongness, but – and this may have occurred to you – because ah was afraid. Afraid for mahself, now that Pa had left me all alone. The junk-pile, the backyard, the burnt-out Chevy, the porch, the goddamn shack and its three rooms, the front yard, the gallows-tree, the track leading into the town, the cane, those acres on rotation – ah can't go on. Ah can't go on. The animate and the inanimate appeared to me in sinister collusion, as if enjoying mah weeping and gnashing of teeth.

Ah had suffered for days and for nights and mah bones waxed

old and aching during mah erratic slumber. For a day and a night the rankling hand of the deviant was heavy upon me. Excruciating pain developed at mah heart, equal to kill me. And all the while that ah lay there, the hum-mutterances of the dead, the knoll's rowdy gestation rose through, with a hundred half-unnerstood, half-relevant utterances.

'The wicked have many sorrows.'

'The God of Glory thundereth.'

'We are counted as sheep from the slaughter.'

'Destroy me not with sinners and bloody men.'

And – and, well, from the clamour of those smaller, lesser voices came the voice of God – and it was – it was *awesome* – it was – it was like Psalm 29. You know, the one about His voice breaking the cedars and shaking the wilderness.

He called me servant. He said, 'Servant make for Me a wall.' He told me that they would come and that ah must keep them out. He said, 'Servant build it high, build it out of wood and wire.' He told me to build it round. He said within would be mah Kingdom and that ah would wear the crown. He told me to fill it with the faithful and make for it a name.

And ah took a bone – a skull – and called the Kingdom:
DOGHEAD.

Doghead. Mah fortress of refuge. Mah Kingdom by appointment.

Unner command by Him – The Great Preserver and Righter of Wrongs.

His many voices, sometimes whispered, sometimes shouted, spoke the most amazing things. Most amazing. Things mah head can barely contain. And things most terrible. Sworn secrets, so terrible, so amazing – truths of such ineffable trueness – whew! Ah say, too many, too mighty and too damn immaculate to be sullied by such a crooked ruck of cunts as you. You who will deny me more than thrice, by God. O yes, Mister! And you, Miss! You who pucker even now your traitor's lips, your Judas kiss!

Each and every deviant thought harboured in mah head was chased from mah brains by His holy choir – His chanters. All obscenity, all the degenerate heavy breathing that for so long had wheezed and whispered its ugly air inside of here – inside mah head – was drowned in the choofing stress and metre of His command. The sure choof of a train, it was, its ictus even-handed, almost hypnotic – a train on a straight, level track, neither speeding up nor slowing, no, just the piston's pumping fists – build-uppa-wall build-uppa-wall – on and on, in monostich again and again, then build-it-up-tall build-it-up-tall build-it-up-tall, over and over and on and on, they're-comin-to-call they're-comin-to-call, over and over and onward and onward.

The wall itself took a good six months to complete, ah figure – ah mean, winter followed autumn followed that bugger of a summer when the building all began. It was a big wall. It was an awesome wall. It reminded me of a saw-toothed serpent consuming its own tail or some quilled eel feigning sleep but ready, in a instant, to bite. In the winter, when the wind hit at the tin and the clappers, the great ringed beast would bark and gnash at each blusterous advance, as if the wind were not to be seen as any less of a threat than the others – the eradicators, the real intruders, the grim snuffers – *you*.

Standing in the turret that ah built upon the roof of mah clapboard castle, ah would turn a slow circle and run mah eyes along the great wall for clues – clues to be found in the planks and assorted timbers, the stacks of fruit-crates and tea-chests, the pickets and the odd piece of trellis, the great slabs of corrugated tin and steel sheets, paint-pot lids, boarded-over window frames, the doors of the Chevy, cyclone wire, chicken wire, barbed wire, posts and pillars, scaffold scraps, ropes and cables, bottles broken and unbroken and so on. Ah could always see, even after half a year of back-breaking toil, areas there in the wall that were clearly not as sturdy as they should have been – yes, clearly weak, and hence affording the chance of a trespass, whether by a flapping picket or a buckled tin sheet, a cross-beam come loose or the fraying of a piece of rope on which, God knows, the fortitude of the entire superstructure might depend.

In fact, and it is safe to tell you this now – safe for me, that is

– right up to the last few pre-terminal days the wall was not nearly as impenetrable as it appeared to be. It had a little more bark than bite, perhaps. In any case if the interlopers, or should ah say the failed interlopers, had possessed a little more pluck, they could have been triumphal in whatever it was they were up to.

Still, irregardless of the wall's specious aspect, it did its job. It drew a line between me and mah persecutors. Yes, although ah knew they lay in wait for me beyond the wall, the shambolic and unsteady bulwark with its crown of ragged tin fins and rusted nails – a pauper's crown, trussed in barbed wire, like Christ's, but studded with shards of green and amber glass – prevented the treachery that festered on the outside from poisoning mah King-dom. No! More! From poisoning their King!

It was a weird feeling that crept over me as ah looked down from mah lofty turret – a feeling of accomplishment, of pride, because first off it was a fucken mean-looking wall and that made me proud, of course. But ah guess what really brought a throb to the throat was that ah knew there was another King looking down from on high, just like me, only higher, kinglier, and He was seeing this – seeing me and nodding knowingly to himself and thinking, 'That boy has done me proud,' and lying back, lying back on His cloud and thinking, 'Yes, 'tis nearly time to send him out. 'Tis nearly time to send him out.'

Ah did other things in that time of building up. Other things, such as tearing down. After Pa left me alone, the shack's interior became insufferably repellent to me. The killing-walls of the living-room repulsed me. Nor could ah enter mah own wretched coop, the dying-room, the blooding-hutch. And the dread ah felt toward their room, the master-room, consumed me.

One brave day ah managed to open its door but an inch, only to recoil, mah mind swimming in hideousness, even though the despot, mah Ma, had been dethroned and done away with so very long ago. That piss-eyed sow, you know, she wasn't gone – not completely, not in total. No. Not at all. Her putridity remained. There in the rank and rot of her room. The trapped air, that was hers. You could taste it. You could smell it. You could feel it. There in that one quick whiff was enough sensory information to jog a shitload of ugly re-runs, flickering through mah head in all their posthumous repulsion – pictures of Ma – mind-sadists dealing brutal brain-slaps. Ah recoiled, like ah said, lurching through the front room and out the screen door, mah guts heaving as ah slumped across the rail to gurgle a thin rope of bile across the thistle, the sweet pea and the periwinkle.

That same afternoon ah bashed out all the plank walls of the shack's interior. By nightfall neither mah room nor their room existed and ah sat exhausted in the middle of a clapboard shell. Large now and different. Nothing remained of theirs – the bed, her armchair, the planks, all part of the outer wall now. Even the bad air had moved out, all fusty and fumid, moved out as good air moved in.

Only the trunk that belonged to Pa remained. Ah had dragged it into the middle of the shack and it sat at mah feet, heavy with its unknown quantity, mumchance of its inner mysteries, padlocked at the lip.

The key to the chest was not to be found amongst the rubble of the day's demolishing, ah knew that, for the key was with Pa, unnerground, deep in his pocket somewhere, lost for ever of its lock. Ah mused to mahself as ah took a crowbar to the chest's lock-plate. Where was mah key? In whose pocket did *it* sleep? Was it above ground, up here, or was it lying beneath the surface, down here? Am ah, at this moment, leaving it or joining it? Surely joining it, for ah have not come across it above ground, nor it me. What about *this* truant key, that could turn the mechanism of mah facility of speech? Where is *it*?

With a protracted groan the lock-plate gave way and the padlock dropped with a thud to the hard sod floor. O, if it were only that easy for me.

From the hills came the eerie bay of a wild dog and ah sat a minute, in silence, listening to it and staring into the chest.

A label on the inside of the lid told me that the chest had

originally belonged to a Captain Theodore Quickborn, and this chest, this old discarded junk-pile relic, judging by the hundred faded badges that it boasted, had travelled to ports east and west, north and south, far and wide, along raging latitudes and unending longitudes, to wind up its uncertain journey here, in a remote inland valley, on a mountain of trash so many miles from the sea.

Captain Quickborn's all seemed to be contained within this chest. Why its active life had ended here, a hundred miles from the sea and the sand, became clear to me the moment ah began sifting through his salty belongings. Ah gave thanks.

First ah removed the Captain's jacket, wrapped in flaky, age-stained paper. It was navy blue with gold buttons and heavy golden epaulettes, shaped like keyholes or fantastic padlocks, each fringed in a rim of gleaming tassels – two great, gilded chips squatting heavy on each shoulder. A weave of gold and silver braid adorned cuff, lapel and collar. It was spotless, as if it had been cleaned and pressed especially for the term of its redundancy. 'Why?' you ask. '*Exactly!*' ah reply. Because the jacket's *real* life had only just begun. It lay, in wait, for me! Me! ME! MEEEE!

A little roomy, perhaps, but with the cuffs rolled up and a leather belt pulled in tight to the waist, the bone of mah chest pushed out, cock-like, it fitted me fine, as God knew it would.

In the left-side pocket of the jacket was a small green velvet box. Inside it lay four medals, side by side, each snug in its own velvet dent. Brassy and embossed, they hung heavily from thin strips of coloured silk and ah pinned them to mah left breast, which was already studded with gold bars and bright, striped ribbons.

Using the treadle of an old sewing machine and a whetstone that ah probably stole from one of the cane store-sheds and a primitive system of axles, cogs and belts, ah had built a knife-grinder. Ah ground down the rusty sickle that ah had found in the swampland. Now the sickle shone a wicked silver, curled sinister like a witch's finger, slung through mah belt pirate-style.

In the mirror, mah hair now long, ah looked like a fucken prince. A *king*. King Euchrid the First. Monarch of Doghead. Don't fuck with the King, brother. Don't fuck with the King. And then ah looked again to Heaven and again ah gave Him thanks.

There was a hat, which ah tossed in the trash. Ah hate hats. There were maps and logs and official papers which ah searched for further orders. But ah found only a lot of figgers, equations, nautical jargon from which ah could glean no further instructions – nothing. The Captain's diaries were crammed with a dense, minuscule scrawl. It was clear that the tedious process of unravelling these knotted ramblings would not benefit me at all. God's word is plain. It is straight and true. This is no game that we are playing here.

As ah tossed the journals aside two photographs slipped from their pages on to the ground. One was of Captain Quickborn. He was bigger than me and much, much older and he had a heavy white beard and wore a cap, but, seeing his image and the reflection of mahself, there in the long mirror, ah was struck by the momentary likeness between him and me, me and him, caught there, inside the glass. Ah knew his eyes were blue and though his face seemed rugged, even swarthy in the sepia tones of the photograph, it was obvious that the sea and salt had been instrumental in darkening what was once a pale and bloodless complexion – like mine. Sure – coincidence. But, believe me and ah should know, coincidences stack up.

Reaching for the second photograph, mah hand froze mid-stretch as its content became clearer. It was a photograph of his ship – the bow of his ship. It was a photograph of the figurehead, there upon the bow of the ship. It was the head and torso of a girl-child, fashioned from wood and painted with a soft, round face framed in long golden curls. A chaplet of flowers sat upon her head and two angel wings spread backward along the starboard and port sides of the bow. Thin-shouldered with two small, budding breasts, the figurehead seemed the veritable image of *her*. Beth. But her name was not Beth. It was *NATASHA I*, as was carved in block letters on a plate beneath the tip of her port-side wing. *NATASHA I.* Ah saw the photograph reflected in the mirror and for a moment ah was transfixed by what ah saw – the image of Beth unner which was written *I AH SATAN! I AM SATAN!*

'So, what's new?' ah thought and tossed the pictures, maps and log books into a far corner of the shack with the rest of the junk.

Ah pulled from the chest a battered tubular case made of leather and wood and ah opened it at one end and out slid a black telescope. A telescope! In three slipping segments! A third sliding eye! An instant spy-hole that breached the grey vagaries of distance – that eradicated the possibility of detection. An unblinking optic on an extendable stalk!

A rush of pure blood-power coursed through mah veins, and mah heart, a clenched inner fist, punched me from mah seat, mah locomotive organs already racing. Ah bounded on to the porch, the telescope folded unner mah arm – mah right and mighty arm, with its gilded wrist and golden shoulder – and standing on the south end of the porch ah uncapped the saucer-sized lens and, working it up to its full magnificence, ah aimed the long, black rod at the town. Ah twisted the telescope's big eye in and out of focus, homing in on Memorial Square in search of the white marble angel wielding the sickle. But mah view was frustrated by the peaked façade of the Courthouse. There ah found the image of Justice, with her scales and blindfold, carved upon the façade above the front double doors. Seeking a better view, ah climbed upon the porch rail, and balancing there ah thought ah saw the glint of the angel's upraised sickle before ah lost mah footing and everything blurred in mah new eye, rushing at me, turning black and then exploding into a flash of blinding light. The big eye met the ground, the telescope mercifully truncating in a three-move invagination – avoiding any damage to itself, but bouncing mah right eyeball off the frontal lobe of mah brain. 'A good, strong telescope,' ah thought, testing it with mah good eye. 'But a better coign of vantage is required,' ah mused, before mah head was ambushed by a clamouring rabble of thought, all shouts upon shouts of big ideas – brain mayhem – and ah limped back inside, and sat back down, recognizing the symptoms and waiting patiently for the racket to abate – for the voice of God with its firm, cool system – its system of solution – to rise above all the head-din. And before ah even became aware of His choir – the chanters – ah found mahself surveying the ceiling with mah eyes and thinking that if ah took a saw and cut a circular . . . tunnel . . . tunnet . . . no . . . turret, yes – a turret, a *turret*! And ah envisaged the whole concept in its entirety right there and then – the sloping ladder steps, twelve in all – the heavy watertight trap-door – and the lookout itself, a one-man turret perched atop of the shack – the circular castellated parapet made of tin and thigh-high – the corrugated-iron roof, like a Chinaman's hat, supported by three metal poles and crowned by the official flag of Doghead. And ah saw the telescope clamped to its swivel-hipped tripod and – and ah had to smile at the wonder of it all. Yes. And ah turned mah attention to the mirror, or rather to the one reflected therein – that is to say He, the mad King of Doghead, clad in the bemedalled and outsized uniform of his sovereignty, armed with a wicked steel sickle, hair lank and greasy, his eyes wild as wheels and one, his right, spinning behind two fat purple lids, his arms clasped tight around his person, as he rocked in his chair, boots flying, gums gorged with green teeth, expelling with all his might a soundless belly-laugh – a laugh of shameless, unabashed insanity. And ah shuddered and darkened and sat with a scowl watching and hating that buggy bastard before me.

The most practical aspect of the turret was its vantage point. If ah manned the scope and screwed a tight circle in a clock-wise direction, this is what ah could see. The length of Maine. The doctor's home. The Tabernacle. The gas pumps. The eastern versant. The mess on Glory Flats. The northern pass. The marshes. The swampland. The west side versant. The sugar crops. The graveyard. The storage-sheds on Hooper's Hill. The refinery. More crops. The school. Memorial Square. The marble angel above the prophet's sepulchre. Wiggam's General Store, or at least the wishing well. And, completing the full circle, the house of Sardus Swift. The house of her. Beth. O and the playground in the Square and the swing.

Another practical purpose of the turret was that it allowed me to check the traps whenever ah got the notion and without leaving the Kingdom. This ensured that a snared animal would not have to wait till the end of the day before he was bagged and delivered of his crippling irons. Over the last two years, ah managed to catch eleven wild dogs in this fashion, without one of them dying in the trap itself. In their cages, maybe, but not in the traps.

Like the wall, the turret served as a deterrent for any would-be tormenters, because it gave the whole area an atmosphere of security-consciousness – a general feeling of 'Say the word, Mister, ah'm ready.' And me in mah uniform, mah uniform of war and all, saying, 'Try it, just fucken try it, friend!' The general air, the tone, like it was saying to the outsiders – to them – to all the people, *'Come on, kill me! Just try and fucken kill me! Kill me! Kill me! Kill me-e-e!'*

One day ah was asleep at mah post. Ah remember clearly it was the first day of spring, last year. Either that or the year before. It was certainly not the springtime of the year before that, to be sure, because at that time ah was not alone, nor did ah have a post or a turret to dream in.

Ah remember the dream. It was one of those atmospherical ones – a mere doodle of a dream, without a story or plot or narrative to speak of. Mah nap had been ambushed by a host of winged dolly-heads, golden-curled and cherry-lipped, with pale blue wings beneath their chins, swooping down at me and snapping and biting mah hair. And the more ah beat at them, the harder they came, chopping at mah poll and taking bloody locks of hair in their pearly teeth – off to their heavenly nest somewhere. Off to their heavenly nest somewhere. Off to their heavenly nest somewhere.

Ah awoke with mah arms flailing about mah head, beating off

those imaginary honey-haired harpies – the telescope spinning on its tripod like some berserk gatling gun and the whole turret rocking and shaking up there on the shack roof. The fact is ah was causing one hell of a hullabaloo for someone supposedly sleeping.

Slowly it dawned on me that there was a counter-commotion in progress, down by the still. Ah had shifted the stillage – the boiler, the tubes and beakers – a few feet closer to the shack when ah dug the initial post-holes and laid the supports for the wall, and now the whole apparatus sat a safe pace inside the confines of mah Kingdom. Or so ah had thought. Now, squirming through a small hole in the wall, ah could see the ratty rear-end and broken-booted legs of what was clearly a hobo. The tail of his mud-caked greatcoat had become snagged momentarily on a finger of tin, and in the mad flurry of flight he managed to kick out one of the legs to the boiler-cradle. The whole apparatus collapsed with a crash of glass and a glug and a hissssss of escaping liquid over fire, and as the boiler rolled down to the wall its coiled hose pissed undistilled sugar-water into the bum's beating boots. The puddle of inflammable hooch moved toward the burner as if inescapably drawn toward it and the flame, too, seemed like it was straining and stretching to touch the hooch. They met with a fierce roar and hot flames leaped into the air. Belching black smoke, the fire roared triumphantly for a minute or so, ran out of juice and died. By which time the hobo had wrenched himself through the wall in a fit of panic, leaving a scrap of dirty green felt, like a calling card, snagged in his wake.

Ah spun around in mah tower in search of the yard-dogs ah had posted on ground duty, only to find them on the other side of the shack, copulating. They had only six legs and a stump between them. The passive partner, the unnerdog, was sprawled out like a sack of dung upon the damp earth, while her smaller but more intrepid pedicator humped and fumbled at her hind. With his front legs hooked around her huge rump and his single back leg springing somewhere between a hop and a stagger, the lame beast pumped piston-quick convulsions upon her inert back-end, never missing a beat as it staggered and stabbed blindly, swinging right to left, left to right, on one shaky leg. 'Shit!' ah thought, looking from hole to dogs, dogs to hole, a dilemma forming in mah mind. 'Fix the hole or beat the dogs? Fix the hole or beat the dogs?'

Later, mah arm exhausted and mah head full of howling, ah crossed the yard to the wall and surveyed the damage. One of the stills had been destroyed – a brew lost, grass scorched – and a tin panel in the wall had been bent upward and out. That too would need beating. Such was the damage to mah property. But how does one measure the severity of the blow to mah confidence in the Kingdom's security? In strokes of the switch? In dog pain? Ah took up the hammer and, even as ah brought it down to flatten the tin and close the hole, mah mind became possessed by alternative thoughts and ah threw the hammer away, leaving the gaping cavity as it was. Hands in pockets, head inclined, ah sauntered over to the porch steps and sat down.

Ah looked at the ground. Ah looked at the sky. Ah looked to mah left, biting mah bottom lip, then looked to the right. Then, eyes welling, ah looked back at the sky and a deep sob broke upon that cloudless afternoon of the first day of spring, and ah cried there upon the porch steps – out of worry, out of lonesomeness.

The new season's insects hopped and burred and clicked, hovering over the purple bursts of thistle, over the periwinkle's tender new blooms and the runt pod of the sweet pea. Bees beat and bounded about the first pale bells of the comfrey. Spring had broken, yet still mah head resounded with the winter's wailing, and in mah mind a bitter wind began to blow as ah thought of the wretched interloper who had trespassed upon mah property with the intent to rob me, perhaps to kill me. Mah eyes slit and mah lips curled back off mah teeth as mah brain pickled in poison thoughts. In silence ah listened to the plotters and schemers that lurked in mah mind and to the low murmur of their treachery.

Ah turned mah attention to the olive-leafed nocturne that crawled loose and heavy up the corroded gutter-spout and along the porch rail. Every contour of that creeper spelled meanness, ah swear to God. Fleshy, split-clefted leaves like a colony of black felt tongues bobbed sullen and toxic on thin sinuous stalks, curling up and around pillar, post and spout. Being at eye-level with the railing around which the vine was wound – with the dying sun splashing across the black dancing leaves – ah remember thinking that the vine looked as though it had been dipped in a tub of dull gun grease, like it was a gigantic gun-metal serpent or a weapon of death. And indeed it was a weapon of death as the chanters slowly came.

Ah leapt to mah feet and began picking the creeper's fleshy, spade-shaped leaves, stuffing them into the pockets of mah captain's jacket. Ah juiced them the same evening by mashing them between two smooth river rocks. Ah pressed the soppy pith to a dry pulp, and with the aid of a tin funnel channelled the milky sap into a small green-glass bottle, three quarters filling it.

The new spring moon looked naked, almost brazen in its fullness. It was the colour of mah angel's skin, but with a hint of the mistreated in her unblinking majesty, her skin faintly darkened by pale grey bruises.

Ah twisted the tiny cork from the neck of the miniature bottle and lifted it to mah nostrils, deeply inhaling its toxic vapour. Ah glimpsed the moon from out the corner of mah eye, and saw in that fleeting glance the top of the orb open as would a wound in flesh and spill a scarlet veil down her great naked face. 'A whore-moon steeped in whore-blood,' ah thought, and ah squeezed the image from mah eyes and let a minute pass. Mah head clear, ah looked again and found the moon as it had been – a gleaming orb of angel's skin, glowing silver, punished.

Under the cope of night ah kneeled at the still closest the wall and emptied the bottle of poison into the beaker of hooch. Ah squatted and rocked on mah heels and ah laughed with the idiot-moon – moon and mute noiseless against the clicking evil of that treacherous night.

Two mornings later the beaker was gone. Ah checked the hole in the fence and found that it had been bent open even more. Ah wriggled through on hands and knees and found the hobo, sitting against the outer wall, quite dead. The tip of a pointed stick paired the wings of his chest, poking rudely through his blood-soaked shirt like a dripping dog's dick. The beaker that had contained the fatal dose was empty but upright, locked in his death-grip. Obviously the bum had downed the liquor the moment he was free of the wall, swooned to the call of the toxin and braced his bulk on the pointed stick. The fool.

'Well, look at you now!' ah thought, as ah took him by the lapels of his greatcoat and slipped him off the stick. Ah shouldered his stiffed weight face-down on the dew-covered grass, then, crawling backward, hauled him by the boots through the hole in the wall and into the confines of mah Kingdom. Ah returned to the outside and beat at the flattened grass with a leafy branch, slapping away his puke and his blood. Then ah removed the bloody stick and, after close scrutiny, when it seemed that no tell-tale evidence remained, crawled back through the wall, shaking the branch behind me as ah went. Ah hammered the bent corner of tin flat and nailed the whole panel down, lacing it with barbed wire.

The yard-dogs, their lesson well learned, hobbled over to the dun-coloured heap, strings of clear saliva bridging their bared teeth. 'Spare the rod and spoil the dog,' ah thought, as ah crossed the yard and entered the shed. Ah climbed up the steps, through the open trap-door, and took mah place in the turret. Pulling in the telescope for short range, ah systematically surveyed the land in a two-mile radius. Ah found no witnesses. None.

'Spare the rod and spoil the dog,' ah found mah head repeating, as ah focused down on mah side of the fence and screwed in the scope in order to get a close-up of the hobo. But the damn dogs were there now fucking up the view. Ah looked at the blue sky and a bird with a crooked wing passed darkly across mah vista, turning everything black, and ah slumped forward, asleep. Bums' heads on bloody sticks – No! – bums' heads with rutting dogs' dicks humped at mah day's dreaming.

*

These last two years, you know, they have been hard time spent. Not easy, flighty years, no, but hard time spent. You know what ah mean? O yes. Though not in sleep, no, but – ah guess, some kind of sleep. So these last two unsane years of mah life have been spent in tedious measurement of the minutes and the seconds and their ultimate passing. Or, rather, have been time spent in the attempt to account for such time past spent or served or lent . . .

These last two years, you know, have been hard time spent. Mah capacity for reminiscence – mah recall – well, these faculties, you know, once so sharp, so keen, have been – have been ruptured by yawning canyons of grey wool, like uncharted man-holes down Memory Lane. Whole clues gone lost from the riddle. Days of fog. Of fear. Of blood and terrible laughter from the dark.

Pray tell me. Is this news to you? Did ah tell – have ah told you? At some other moment? In some other mind? Have there been other occasions, ah ask you, now lost irretrievably in the webbed fabric of days gone by, in the sheer and spectral silks of yesterday? Tell me, ah want to know. Are these words ah speak now – are they already part of memory's cape draped across the shoulders of mah time spent? If ah could fill in all the deadtime, how beautiful would memory's cape really be? Would it lend a little razzmatazz to the shambolic passing of mah days remembered? Or would it be an unclean thing, this ragged uniform? Would it shed blood or skin like calendar leaves? Ah will ask you just one more time. So pay attention. *Have ah said all this before?*

Have ah told you about the hellish fright of *deadtime*? Do you know about the *bloodings*? The *chills*? Mere fragments of rushing life retained . . . like handfuls of wind. Time gone haywire. Night and day, the following and the followed, pitch their shining sky-globes from horizon to horizon. Sun serves, moon returns, searing time's cope with their mad flight, back and forth, to and fro, dark and light, like a hypnotist's watch swinging in the fob of heaven – O yes, like the pendular action of a naked bulb, hung and set aswing in an empty room. An hour! A day! Gone! Snuck past! Escaped unsullied, unsalvageable, never to be lived. All in the blinking of an eye. *Deadtime! Deadtime! Where do you go?! Who uses you, if not me?!* The killers and the killed. Murdering of mah lifetime – mah living-time. The agony-rack of mah day's passing and the slow method of its crank and shaft, the endless chatter of cogs ticking away the minutes, the bonecrack count and seconds of raw pain – the insufferable stretch of Time. Time lived. But what of all the *deadtime*, all the days unaccounted for? Where do they go?

Euchrid lay sprawled across a heap of strangled bedding. Unmoving in the moon-glow, he wore a singlet stained with rings of dark, leaked sweat and patches of gravy-coloured blood. His denims were stiff with grime and gore. His bed, a heap of sacks thrown in a pile on the floor, could barely be distinguished from the garbage and rubble and animal filth that surrounded it. Lit by both moon and lamp, the squalor seemed alive under the pale but stuttering light. The recumbent Euchrid appeared bereft of life. Crucified upon his rotting heap, his stick-thin arms were flung outways and peppered with many smarting punctures that blinked like bee-stings against his waxen flesh. The exposed skin on his arms, shoulders and belly gave him the appearance of a flagellator who had been recently engaged in a bout of self-correction. Hanks of greasy hair stuck to his sweat-streaked face. Flies fed on the crusted corners of his open mouth and danced about his wide liquid eyes, which were the only sign of life about this pale, listless creature; they shivered, shifting from left to right, up and down as if many things were present to Euchrid in the grainy yellowed nothingness. Fearful things, for they were pinned, those pupils, pinned and wild.

The room had an eerie absence of sound, as if spellbound. There could be heard only the shifting of straw, the creaking of undersized confines, the wind whistling through cavities in the wall. The tea-chest kennels each held captive a wild dog, most unable to stand in their crates. They lay like drought cows, unmoving, awaiting death. Others had been so grievously mutilated by the traps that to stand was no longer an option. So mostly the dogs just lay in the warm slimy straw, drunk on the liquor and water mix in which their oats or wheat grain floated, brown bandages hanging loose from their splints and stumps and clearly septic wounds.

Awaking from its stupor, a roan bitch inched forward on its two front stumps and butted the wire batch of its kennel with the flat of its low-sloping brow. A doped snarl rose from deep within its throat, and baring sulphur-coloured gums it bit at the wire, rocking its box and rousing a dozen other beasts to petition their Lord and Master. The Kingdom resounded with the anguished protests of its subjects, but the King made no motion to appease the rabble, allowing the hiss and snarl and bark and screech and howl to grow and grow until the whole shack vibrated with the protests of the beasts. It was only then that the King deemed it appropriate to stand. He rose, slow and pained, like a ghost, and threw the filthy naval jacket across his shoulders. He paced a slow, thoughtful circle around the room, as if to address each miserable beast personally, though he looked not at the cages but at the ground-filth through which he waded. He circled and circled and he seemed to be the focus of a thousand beaded eyes that closed or glazed or crossed, each according to its nature, as their King circumnavigated the room one final time. He drew to a halt and considered his surrounds. The animals, soothed, now slept. He sighed deeply. Then Euchrid, bending at the knees and wincing with pain, lay down again upon his back, arms outstretched on his sack heap – not to sleep, but to gaze, as before, into the porous, jaundiced darkness that engulfed him.

Ah had the entire Kingdom to run. Single-handedly. Ah had no advisers or counsellors, no brain-trust, no syndicates or professional consultants, no mentor, no nestor, not even a fucken scullery maid. Ah mean, there wasn't a flunkey to flog in the whole of Doghead, but you know – believe it or not – ah managed. Ah managed. Yes, despite the fact that it was the King who had to don the camouflage and creep into the outer world when stocks ran low, ah managed. And even though it was the King who had to prepare the food and feed his loyal subjects, ah got by. Yes. Ah got by. And though ah had a lot of plotting and planning to do, not to mention being self-appointed lookout, policeman, executioner, judge and jury, tutor to mah beasts, caretaker, maintenance man, trapper and trainer, nurse and nanny, head-shrinker and sawbones to the wounded, ah coped. Ah did. Yes. Through sheer power of will, ah managed.

But to think that ah spent all of mah time tucked away inside the confines of mah Kingdom, immersed in domestic duties, would be a great mistake. O no. Many times – countless times – ah trudged the east- and west-side slopes, setting traps or bagging catches or walking about the foothills, climbing the trees that grew on each side of the valley, or just sitting. Sitting up in those trees and thinking. Listening to the brag and bully of some of mah mind-preachers. And there were the night-stalks and the day-raids on the houses around the outer periphery – just to steal a couple of tins of peaches from the pantry or maybe a can of spirit oil from the shed. There were the storage-sheds on Hooper's Hill and three big tool-sheds over by the refinery, full of the most incredible things. The most incredible things. Ah think ah made innumerable visits to these, ah can't rightly remember. But, to be truthful, most of the time ah spent outside the fortress ah just lay low and watched other people live.

And *her*. Ah watched *her* a lot.

The foundling the townsfolk took to be their own. The child that the Ukulites have all but canonized. The one, they say, who soothed the wrath of Heaven. The girl-child who brought with her the sun. God's gift to the penitent. The miracle. Beth.

Ah watched Beth a lot. But did ah tell you about how other times ah would go stealing?

Was Beth delivered to the Ukulites merely as a sign of the end of their castigation? Or was there a greater purpose behind Beth's presence in the valley? As the child grew older, there were many women amongst the Ukulites who were wont to suggest another reason for Beth's existence, a purpose with great and far-reaching implications.

Ah would creep down into the valley, a hessian sack over mah shoulder.

*

As Beth's well-being was the most important factor in the Ukulites'
lives, and as the tending of the little girl was women's work, Sardus
watched his child drift further and further from his sphere of influence.
In fact, the entire Ukulite sect, whether they realized it or not, was
fast becoming an out-and-out gynaecocracy, controlled by a gaggle of
superstitious, gossip-guttling crones, spinsters and widows. They even
went as far as to hold clandestine meets, in the early afternoons, to
discuss the question of Beth. Then, later, to discuss the question of the
preparation of Beth. It was not long before the crones decided that Beth
herself should attend one or two of their meetings, for there were things
she should know, things she should learn. Scared sick, Beth swore on a
Bible never to tell Sardus of the meetings.

But most of all ah liked to watch *her.*

On one particular afternoon ah spied on a meeting of women.
It was late spring, ah think, and hot as all fuck. Beth was there.

Ah squatted in a geranium patch beneath the living-room
window. It was open an inch or two. Beth sat in a chair of black
leather, away from the circle of nutant, nattering heads. She had
slipped down in the chair, her hips jutting up and her young
nut-coloured legs pushed forward so as to allow the breeze from
the window to pass across their damp and downy brightness.
Her thin arms dangled carelessly either side of the chair. She had
her eyes closed and her head turned to one side feigning sleep,
but she was listening. O, she was listening.

On squeaking rubber soles, a small, compact woman in a white
uniform – not from Ukulore Valley, that was clear – marched up
the path without even seeing me. So starched and pursy was her
gait that she looked neither left nor right but straight ahead.
Judging by the red cross on the front of her white cardboard hat,
and the pale grey cape across her shoulders, ah figured her to be
some high-ranking canoness or Madam Superior of a neighbour-
ing sect, brought in for advice. Trotting up the steps to the front
door, she dealt a short, sharp rap upon the frosted-glass panel.
The door opened immediately and a voice from inside inquired,
'Nurse Dethridge?' 'Were you expecting someone else?' replied

Nurse Dethridge, as rudely, and without further ado she pushed inside, greeting the ladies en masse with a brisk nod.

Beth opened her eyes and her body tensed at the sight of the nurse. She pulled the hem of her smock down over her knees and continued to stare at the stranger.

Mrs Eldridge spoke from her worn-out wheelchair, in a manner that said, to me at least, 'This crippled witch has talked to many such nurses. She will not be intimidated. She knows from experience the exact matter-of-factness that she needs to employ. She has known many, many such nurses.'

Mrs Eldridge said, 'You're to take a look at Beth. See if she is still intact. She is. There can be no mistake there. Then we want a full medical testimony, signed by yourself, certifying explicitly that Beth was in full possession of her virginity at the time of your examination.'

Nurse Dethridge was already pulling on a pair of thin rubber gloves. No one had acknowledged the presence of Beth as far as ah could see. 'We shall see,' said the nurse, and Widow Roth, upon whose home this gathering of hags had converged, piped up, 'You can use this room,' making an unnecessary gesture toward a doorway which the nurse was already shepherding the child through. You could see it in her eyes – the crying getting ready to flow, getting ready to go. The rubber hand of the nurse pulled the door closed behind her.

Ten minutes later, rubber gloves gone and white gloves on, her buttocks clenched beneath her tight, bright uniform, Nurse Dethridge marched out of the front door and down the cobbled path, her shoes squeaking as she retreated off to a death in the west somewhere. Off to a death in the west somewhere. Off to a death in the west somewhere.

Ah saw all this from a crouch, bloom height, through a bank of pinking geraniums and bobbing bees. The heady, pollinated air was bitter to taste.

Inside, Mrs Eldridge held the medical certificate in her arthritic claws like a sea-bird with a scrap of beach trash. The black-clad sorority converged upon her, squinting and craning through spectacles, silent but for the odd expulsion of kept breath, the knowing coos and clucks and occasional whispered word of compliance. Then ah heard a pithy 'A-men' and the squeal of hard rubber tyres on the wood floor as the cripple pared the huddled group and wheeled herself toward the examination room. The gaggle obediently followed, saying flatly 'A-men' in response.

Beth already stood in the doorway. Her face was raw and stung with tears. She stared at the floor, then raised her head and looked to the women, a question riding the contours of her face. But she found no voice to express it. The women all nodded and smiled, grotesque in their cognition.

In the starker months, ah found mahself enthroned in mah shack, watching mah subjects in silence, or on guard duty in mah turret – but come springtime, ah found the . . . itch to leave the Kingdom too persistent to ignore, and the sport of night-stalking would take precedence over mah many other roles as ruler. As spring became summer, and mah insomnia drove me beyond the bounds of mah jurisdiction, it is possible that ah was wont to neglect some of mah kingly responsibilities, preferring the thrills down in the valley below. Perhaps mah Kingdom suffered a little from mah negligence – ah don't know. It is hard to gauge. Ah tried to feed mah subjects as often as ah remembered and most stayed alive – just looking a little crazier by the day. Ah mean, you should have seen the frenzy of gore if ah decided to reward one of the dogs with a piece of live meat! In a matter of seconds both kennel and dog would be strewn with blood and steaming bone, the bulk of the squeaking vermin indiscriminately gobbled up, skull and all. The bloody face of the carnivore, never satisfied, would tear at the wire frontage of the cage screaming for more.

Sometimes ah would wait in mah turret, the telescope directed at her house, dark and sleeping, below. *Ah would wait for her signal.* And sure enough, around the midnight hour, the lamp at her window would be turned up and its sticky yellow light would spill across the porch. It was then that ah would go down.

After ah saw a pattern emerge in her midnight vigils, ah would often find mahself staked out amongst the myriad shadows of Memorial Square – crouched in lidless agitation, mah heart bailing blood to a fury of palpitations as if driven by some ramping slave-drum that threatened to alert the sleeping township of mah forbidden emprise. Owl hoots, lunar moonings, cricket shrill, shadow scuttle and the crackle of bat radar – such were the meagre comforters left untended by the shut of day.

It took me some time before ah could summon the courage actually to stand at her window, but step by step, night by night, ah ventured closer. Eventually ah was able to creep bootless on to her porch and, hidden in the shadows of hedgerow or pressed against the weatherboard wall, ah would lurk by her window, prick-eared for the creak of bedsprings and the rustle of starched bedding prelusive to the flimmering lamplight. A block of sticky light would blink upon the porch and it was then that ah would peer in. She would be sitting in her white nightdress, legs slung over the edge of the bed in the quiet abandon, so reminiscent of her mother, that was inherent in her every action. Her head inclined as if in prayer, her back to the window. Always she kept her body turned away from the window. The room swelled with yolky light.

And there she would sit and there ah would stand, saying nothing, but locked, both of us, in a cocoon of expectant, anticipatory silence. She would sometimes release a weary sigh or stifle a yawn – and me, ah would be engaged in terrible battle with mah whining breaths and bloodbeats, mah braided arm sliced by the lamplight as ah stood there by the window, half in the light, half out.

It occurs to me now how similar was the thrill ah experienced in watching this child on her nightly vigils to that experienced over a decade ago, when ah would press mah face up to a certain window of a certain pink caravan parked up on Hooper's Hill, and watch the sweet and salacious rituals of harlotry in progress. How similar, yet how very different. Yet how very vital to His greater plan were they both.

And time passed. Mine in the watching. Hers in the waiting.

And then something strange happened. Something truly strange. Listen. One night a ring of white light flashed upon the wall above Beth's head and it seemed to hover there like a halo. Beth gasped when she saw it and seemed to become transfixed by its saltatory fulgence. Ah craned to take a better view of this mantic manifestation – this margarite conjuration – this uninvited third party. Ah loomed closer, and in that moment the light seemed to fall to the floor and disappear. Ah retreated and the apparition leaped back to its place on the wall, dancing there above her head. 'It knows of mah presence and it fears me,' ah thought, and again ah sought to take a closer look and again the magic circle fell away. Back and forth ah rocked, watching it come and go. Beth seemed confounded by this etherealization, erumpent yet agitated, and so was I, until ah discovered its nature. It was the lamplight beamed back on to itself by the dazzling arc of mah sickle, moving in and out of view with each body-shift. Mah whole body heaved and soundlessly, there on the porch, ah roared with laughter – at her stupidity. Ah manipulated the sickle so that the circle of silver light danced above her head. But mah mirth was short-lived, for suddenly she spoke. Weird words. And though they ran smooth and well practised from her lips, these words seemed, if not foreign to her mouth, then to her mind, as if not fully unnerstood, spoken with a trembling tongue, as if she were conscious of the magnitude of her monodrama but not of its content.

Ah stiffed outright. Ah suffered a full-on fucking blooding like ah had never known. Ah considered running. Hiding. Exploding. A trickle of blood ran from mah nose, splatting on the porch boards between mah feet. A tide of blood surged in mah face – mah head – and ah felt as though mah skull would split in half such was the pressure. Ah saw everything through a crimson film. New veins erupted beneath the skin. Mah brains ached horribly. Mah whistle-wheeze rose an octave, and across town ah thought ah heard a dog bark. But she did not stir – not Beth – she did not turn around. Instead she spoke, her strange words chiming softly.

'O Lord, how excellent is Thy name.
Give ear to my supplication when I cry unto Thee,
when I lift up mine hands to Thy holy temple.
With my whole heart I have sought Thee.
Thy word have I hid in my breast
that I may not sin against Thee.
My soul doth magnify the Lord.
I am Beth.
The affirmation of Your mercy.
Only Chastity and Purity have known me.
Regard me in the humble estate of handmaiden to the Lord.
I await the exacting of Thy Word.
I am prepared.
May the Holy Ghost come upon me
and the Highest overshadow me,
that I may bear blessed fruit
from which all generations shall spring.
Lord, I await the exacting of Thy Word
as revealed to the most blessed prophet Jonas Ukulore.
This is the day which the Lord hath made!
Thy righteousness endureth for ever.
Thy horn shall be exalted with honour.
With long life I will satisfy Thee
and shew Thee my salvation.
A-men.'

And then, as if it had been awaiting the end of her supplication, a light went on in the next room and ah saw the knife-like shadow of Sardus Swift rise into view and slide across the blind like a dark fin. Ah pinched mah nose and made mah escape, across Maine and into Memorial Square. Ah slipped into the shadows undetected. Ah kept low. Ah watched.

First there was a long silence. Then ah heard the muffled sobs of Beth. Then crying, but much louder. Sardus Swift flung wide the front door and marched around to the window where ah had been standing. Beth followed, crying, 'Don't scare him, Daddy!

Please! He has come for me!' Then Sardus was crouching and dipping his finger into the cluster of blood spots ah had leaked on to the porch. Next, the houses on either side of the Swift home blinked alive simultaneously, and a second later ah saw two bullocking matrons emerge, wrapping themselves in flannel nightcoats and converging upon the scene. Ah recognized them from the meets.

Ah barrelled across the Square and headed for the town limits, reaching relative safety as the commotion at the Swift house spread across the town. Ah could already hear the hawking exclamations of the two neighbours, brought to mah ears by a late summer breeze. Ah rocketed off, the lure and tug of mah Kingdom suddenly strong. Very strong.

Ah dug a pit inside the shack. Up against the west-side wall. Ah had bagged many snakes – too many to keep in separate cages. So ah dug a pit and finned the sides with pieces of down-sloping tin to prevent the snakes from crawling up.

The snake-pit became something of a fascination with me for a while. Ah used to spend time safe on its perimeter, watching the deadly trogle and keeping record – the ways of the squirm. Sometimes ah would lower a rat or a hamster down and watch the knotted pool rise and jump at the bobbing, squealing vermin. If the vermin did not squeal ah would do mah best to save him, committing him to mah ranks. Power ranks.

Menaced by cachinnations of the corvine kind, ah awoke one spring morning in mah turret. Instinctively ah loaded mah cata-pult and sent half a brick spinning toward the family of fucken hecklers. The brick slammed into the trunk of the gallows-tree and, with one final, choric screech, the four oily crows leaped into the air and chortled off. 'Fuckers' ah wanted to cry. Ah wanted to cry.

Ah sat back down, then carefully put mah eye up to the telescope. Beth's house. Beth's house. Beth's house. It was focused on Beth's house. Ah had fallen asleep waiting for her signal, as ah had done many times before. Ah felt the telescope being pulled toward Memorial Square – toward the playground in Memorial Square.

The playground, if you can call it that, consisted of a swing, a see-saw and a sandpit. Nothing more. It was erected the year before Pa passed on. A Ukulite had died and left a legacy and a pitiful penny it must have been too. Still, it bought her a brass plaque and the assurance that her name would be etched into the spilling pages of perpetuity, along with the million other Miss Bitches and Mister Bastards that willed a trust fund and bequeathed their petty savings, so that the beggary of their miserable lives could be enshrined in a park bench or a horse trough or a fence post. 'Lest We Forget', if ah recall correctly, 'The Miss Eartha Pylons Memorial Playground, South West Corner of the Jonas Ukulore Memorial Gardens, Maine Road, Death Valley, State of Mourning.' Ah mean, this playground – what is it? It's a goddamn scandal, that's what it is. Two bent poles, twenny feet of chain, a plank and a box of dirt. O thank you, thank you, Myrna! Hang your head in shame, Martha!

Ah mean, if it isn't a dog turd then it's a brass plaque. They'll get you every time. Mah blood shudders when ah think of all the skinned shins, scraped knees, split toes, nosebleeds – all the flying gravitations, leaping defluxions, forced landings, pratfalls, ground pounces – all the cannonballs, gravel rakes, land attacks, gutter bungles, pile-ups, prangs – the stinging tears of shame, of rage, of defeat – all the fucken jeers and all the fucken japes – encountered and again encountered through the existence of these sly ground plaques. *Lest we forget*. Ma'm, sir, mah brain squirts, glands leak and ah go cold. Wicked cold.

Far be it from me to thunder on unduly, but show me a free-standing structure and ah'll show you a brass plaque. Ah mean, for Christ's sake, you can't have an erection in this town without some clammy cadaver roping it off and slapping an 'In Memoriam' marker unner it. This town is owned by a bunch of stiffs. This town is built on graveyard charity – on a low-house legacy. Its very foundations are interred, bound in white linen, sunk six feet down and anchored in pineboard coffins. It gives me the creeping leaks just to think about it.

Windowless. Mah shack is windowless. Once there was a window – three, in fact – but ah sealed them up with planks. Ah cemented the ledges in broken bottles, just in case. With the trap-door in the ceiling shut and the front door closed and the padlocks, bolts and chains checked, ah could render the panting interior almost void of light, penetrated only by the steaming needles and fast fins, the guillotines and steak knives of leaked light – sun-silver lances, like ah was the bikini-clad assistant in some magician's trick gone horribly wrong. Yes! Sometimes ah would watch steely sunlight, ragged, serrated, saw me in half. Ah spent an afternoon plugging the major leaks with plaster but the minor clefts, pocks and crannies, the sly seeps and trickles, the countless chinks in mah castellated armour, ah left unhindered. Perforations. Air holes hammered in the lid of mah coop. Of mah coffin.

If the beasts were up to it we would talk. In this hushed, sepulchral stillness, with the air putrid, septic, heady and receptive, a lot of thought waves got moved around. Rat chat, crackling cat shriek, snake hissance and lizard fizz, chipping rabbit blather, hare air, bug thrum – beast din, muzzled, telepathic. O but the drooling dog thoughts – dull, belligerent, doped, full of mean transmission – blood, meat, sex and so on. Lame, cock-eyed hill-bitches, agitated into a perpetual state of oestrus, turning mean, nasty, as they frot and butt and rut and hump in the ordure and straw, gnash and grabble in their squatting capsules on the floor.

When their murgeoning got out of hand, ah would give them a goofball. A calmative. OK – a *comative*. One part water. One part White Jesus. Half to one powdered sedative. Never failed. A bowl or two of that – they lapped it up – and they'd be goo-gooing like sucklings, all pooped out. All the mad air slaked. The feral static, the hate waves abated. Ah would sit and nod and

nanny these lumpen fadges of incumbent dung. There were no
in-between moods. No slippers brought to the bedside. No hobble
around the block. Either those brutes were in a state of high
coma or they were coming at your face.

But that's the way they had to be. That's the way ah wanted
it. It's the way God had it organized. That pack of riggish bitches
and low bloods – O they will get their chance to make good.
Like me. They will have their moment of Glory too. And very
soon, ah think, and very soon. Let the sleeping dogs lie. But don't
believe a word they say. Ah am the Truth. Ah am the Light.
Every dog has its day.

Ah am having mine now. Mah time is nigh. You're too late,
Mister Hay-Rake, Mister Spade. Ah said, hey boss, take up that
cross and put on your walking shoes. Yes, you lose, Mister Noose.
Today belongs to me! Not thee! *Me!* Me! Me! This day is mine!
Into the ranks of the elite ah climb, saying, 'This is the last day!
This is the last day! The last day is mine!' There are plenny
others, brothers. Take your pick. Take your hoe. Take your
goddamn gallow. Leave this day alone. Sift through all your
yesterdays. Don't count on your tomorrows. Ah can see them
coming and it's not a pretty sight. The fear is here. The fright.
Here is the night.

At the centre of Doghead was a raw board palace with twelve plank
steps leading to a cylindrical, one-man, saw-toothed turret. Pitched on
eight poles, the turret sported an octagonal, pyramid-shaped roof. It
was from this roof that the flag of Doghead was hung.

The flag was a rag of once fluffy, once grey fur. The sun had seared
and hardened the pelt, so that unfurled it was approximately the
same shape and size as a man's opened hand. The furred side was
weather-beaten, the grey fluff soiled and clotted with umber muck. On
the other side the skin was withered and orange. The flag was secured
to the pole by means of a stocking threaded through a series of small
eye-holes poked through the skin at one end. Still attached to one corner
of the flag was a leg and a tiny paw the size of a lady's finger.

Hung either side of the main steel-gridded gates to the Kingdom were two more such flags, and three others – unprepared, unskinned, and in a state of advanced decay – hung on a nail on the back wall of the shack, out of reach of the yard-dogs and the ground-rats, though not of the million blowflies that teemed across them like a restless, gangrenous epidermis.

The wind moaned. The turret rocked. A sheet of greasy newspaper wrapped itself around a steel oil drum. The fortification shifted and strained. A sheet of tin flapped like a cranky lip. The kitten-skin flag upon the turret jerked around its pole. The wind abated and likewise its little havoc. But the wall continued to girn as it moved its weight around.

The King was neither in the yard nor in the shack. Nor was he sitting in his turret. In fact the King was not within the walls of Doghead at all, for the King was without, down in the town, making some calculations. Yes, ah was down there, in epaulette and in braid, ticking in the shadows as ah figgered things.

Then Beth started propositioning me by way of notes and weird little offerings left on the ledge of her bedroom window. The first time she did this ah suffered such an arrant blooding that ah almost keeled over, right there on the porch. She had never done anything but sit quietly on the edge of the bed and sometimes recite her petition – always the same words – so ah was taken unawares at the time, battling with the buttons on mah trousers as ah was. The light went on and by the time ah looked up she had slipped from her bed and was walking directly toward me. Boom, boom, boom went mah blood as ah stiffed and sucked in mah breath, praying to God that she would not look up – for her head was inclined, as she came walking shoeless across the boards. Head still bowed, she opened the window just enough to push the piece of folded paper through, then turned and without so much as a sound moved across the room to her bed. She sat there motionless for a moment, then reached with one golden arm and turned the lantern down. The glutinous light slipped from her thin form, and mine, as she slid between the cotton covers.

Ah unfolded the piece of paper and read the opening line – 'To God' – and ah silently drew a 'G' on the glass in nose-blood. Then, grabbing mah shoes and stuffing the note into mah open shirt, ah bounded off, homeward.

That first note was wrapped around a lock of her hair. The lock was tied at one end with a length of navy-blue velvet ribbon. The lock had a lavender perfume . . . a lavender perfume . . . a lavender perfume – like mah angel – like Cosey Mo.

DEAR GOD,

I know You are there at my window. I know You watch over me at night. I love You as You love each of Your children. The wise ladies say I am being tested and that I am part of Your big plan. I ask them what is the big plan and they say it is not for me to know. They say I am ready ever since the sign of the blood. Yours and mine. Your sign on the porch brought mine, as You know because You know all things, and that too is part of the big plan, as the wise ladies say. Please make it soon, because I love You.

    Your little doll,
    Beth

Wrapped inside the note was the lock of her lavender-scented hair. As bright as spun gold it was. Ah would hold the lock of hair in mah hand and read the note and a shiver of excitement – anticipatory, tearful – would run through me. Ah mean, good grief, even now, in the light of all that has transpired, there is a chilly portentousness to those words. 'The big plan', she called it. How right those ladies were. And 'the sign of the blood' – ah wonder, did she have bloodings too?

A few days later there was another note. This one was rolled into a kind of scroll and tied with a piece of embroidered lace from one of her nightdresses.

DEAR GOD, MY FATHER AND MY FRIEND FOR ALWAYS,

I am ready, God. I will not resist. No matter what. But please make it soon. Every day they look at me to see if it has happened. They ask me if I have been good and pure. Yesterday Mrs Barlow said that I must have been shaming the Prophet. I have kept Your sign a secret. The one You left by the window. The sickle of blood.

But please, come to me soon, I beg you,

Beth

Ah draw a 'G' and she sees a sickle of blood!

O the lace and the hair. Her neat hand. The glow of the lamp exposing her young body beneath the cotton smock.

Each time ah returned her message in the same way. Dipping mah finger in a stray spot of nose blood, ah would draw upon the window the letter 'G'. But once she had called it the 'sickle of blood', it was hard for it not to take on the shape of one.

Another letter, the third or fourth, said:

DEAREST GOD,

The wise old ladies scare me but You do not. They grow impatient I think. They say if I am not good the rain will come. But I know it will be soon when You are ready. I am not afraid of You, God, no matter what. But please make it soon. For them. Make it soon, no matter what.

I love You.

Beth

P.S. Why are You waiting? What is wrong? Have I done a wrong thing? Please tell me so I can stop.

The funny thing about it all was that she was right. It would be soon. Ah could feel it, too. And the voices – the chanters –

already they were throbbing, stirring, getting ready to go. O yes, it would be soon. It would be soon. No matter what.

Ah had found a brand-new tractor battery and a box of forty-watt light globes. The box was marked with a blue Crayola, so ah knew it had come from the tool-shed up by the refinery. How ah had secured them and the means by which ah had transported them back to the shack was a complete and utter mystery to me. Ah had no memory of it at all. Here was deadtime at its spookiest. Ah must have hauled the stuff back from the refinery mahself, ah concluded, figgering that a memory-wipe wasn't near as bad, on the sanity scale, as having an imaginary helper working the night-raids for me.

Ah had rigged up a cable making a line from the battery to one of the globes, and ah listened to the hum and crackle of the electricity as it coursed along the wire. A sickly yellow glow pulsed from the bulb and, spellbound, mah eyes focused on the droning bolus. Perched on mah bed, ah watched the bulb become a living, breathing thing, like some ghastly human appendage – a jaundiced, convulsing organ, pumping sticky gobs of wobbling light. Ah closed mah eyes, but already ah could feel the knot of nerves twisting its way up through mah body, forcing me to mah feet.

Mah legs felt weird – unsound – and by way of experiment ah took one misadventurous step forward and stumbled drunkenly into a kennel, turning the whole thing over and on to its wire-meshed front. Inside the cage something thumped, dull and heavy.

Suddenly ah was laughing as ah struggled to haul the kennel back over, humping and laughing with all mah might, hoping to exhaust mahself in the process, mah body thoroughly ravaged by a need to sleep as ah grunted and heaved and laughed at the stubborn kennel – at the caged beasts around me – mah Kingdom – the town – the valley – the whole stinking, shit-sucking planet – laughing and pushing until the kennel tore free of its chicken-wire frontage, leaving it anchored to the ground.

Ah flew backward into a pile of hessian grain sacks, the empty tea-chest still in mah hands. A stack of greasy kerosene tins collapsed and crashed about me as ah lay sprawled upon mah back, naked and helpless with laughter. Ah beat and thrashed at the dinning air with mah stick-thin limbs like a doomed insect awaiting the pin.

When ah had taken control of mah laughter ah crawled to mah feet, still sniggering behind mah hand but somewhat embarrassed by mah outburst, and found lumped on the wire face of the kennel the stiff and bloated corpse of a she-bitch. Lying on its side but with its legs angled straight out, the inflated bitch looked as if it had died on its feet, stiffed, and then been blown over. Drawing closer, ah could see the maggot nativity, wet and teeming, infesting the dog's teated unnerbelly. Ah chucked a grain sack across it and stumbled back to mah bed.

Ah swilled down another powder with a bottle of peel, then kind of crumpled into the bedding in a heap.

Muzzled in slumber, mah vassals squatted in their boxes, nodding unner, lesson over. Theirs was a well-earned rest, for ah had spent the best part of the day in pursuits of the pedagogic kind. They were as those *being perfected*. They were as those *being initiated into the great mysteries*. Yet it was not mere sleep that these beasts succumbed to, but a trance-like state – though it is true they needed a little help, sometimes, to get them there. But the fatigue engendered by the very closeness – the very coopedness of their confines – was, more often than not, enough. Anyway ah preferred not to waste the dwindling sedatives on mah bestial ranks, as sleep refused me entrance to its anodynic domain with increasing insistence. The fact is ah just did not get to sleep at all unless ah was barrelling through slumbertown's back door, stoked to the gills on poop-powder and peel juice.

Ah listened to the electric light but found no comfort there.

Ah laid the strip of lace from her nightdress across mah naked chest and ah threaded the lock of hair through the fingers of mah right hand.

And, in time, something did descend upon me. But was it sleep? A hex cast, perhaps? A spell? A petit mal? A waking dream? A sinister pall? An hallucination? A visitation? A fragrant passing of an angel's wing? A nothing?

No? Yes? A little of each perhaps. First, an adumbrate pleasure rising only to abate in a wince of pain. A release and a certain ensuing calm that allows an hour for dreaming. No more. No less. This little release that brings you down – takes you unner – but lo! Take heed. Beware! The Devil's hem, the burning hair – and the love. O, the love, sweet Beth, off in your heavenly rest up there. Off in your heavenly rest up there. Off in your heavenly rest up there.

On this day ah had gone down from Doghead, mah fortress, because *ah could not stand it any more*. The sun was setting over the western slope and the firmament was scarred with long sanguineous cirrus. The crops, heavy with harvest, were nudged by a warm breeze, rocking and rustling in a low sough.

Normally at this time of year ah would have taken extra precautionary measures against the riff-raff that had begun to filter into the valley in time for the impending harvest. Some of the trailers at the work-camp had already been occupied and in a week the valley would be swarming with these drifters, drunkards and low-livers, and it would be open season on male mutes, crap-catching time for soldiers of the Lord. But on this particular day in the year of 1959, the presence of these men was to take me completely unawares. Ah had other things on mah mind as ah moved down the slope to where the gallows-tree still writhed in rock-like supplication, its plea still pending review – for mercy – a little mercy – lest we all die of longing.

The cane was talking. Perhaps it was a warning. Maybe it said danger. Danger. But not to me it didn't.

Suffer. Said the cane. Sssssuuuuuffffffaaaaaggghhh. An asthmatic sibilation to its low-spoken sough. Sssssuuuuuffffffaaaaaggghhh. The gallows-tree groaned.

Ah sat upon a root. Ah gnashed. Ah stood. Ah was despairing and ah was suffering and ah was having a really bad time.

There's enough daylight for me to be able to take the short cut through the cane, ah thought absently, but ah wasn't thinking much about the daylight or the cane or being able, no – what with all the mind-murk, all the death up there – up *here* – all the ugly and all the sick, all the sin and all the woe – O God! How long must ah run on? And ah unslung mah sickle and threw it over the wire fence at the edge of the cane.

Did ah tell you ah was suffering as ah crawled on mah hands and knees unner the barby wire? Tormented as ah got snagged. Tortured as ah ripped a clump of hair from mah skull in the process of getting unsnagged. Blinded by tears of rage as ah tore mahself free. Mortified by a hill of hog-shit and the hand that ah unwittingly plunged into it. Kneeled in it too, got it everywhere. Out of control as ah groped for mah sickle and swung it at whatever stood in mah way, which just happened to be a lot of sugar-cane. Ah recall the singing steel, and the tall virescent stalks – some as high as eight feet or maybe even ten – crashing down about me, crashing down about me, bruising me, scratching me, spiking me – and me, swinging that sickle regardless and thinking, slash slash O yes at last slash slash at last mah arm it feels complete . . .

Ah lay upon mah back staring up at the violent sky, wringing mah blistered hands and shivering.

Ah thought of returning to Doghead and spending this mean and very unchristian eve in mah menagerie coaching mah beasts, but they'd all become so demanding of late. If only they would just – ah mean, God knows, they are not the only ones *waiting*. In any case, there was a kind of a need that had hounded me from the Kingdom with increasing urgency, that stole mah sleep and made mah waking days a downright misery – a need that Doghead could no longer sate, that all the mortification inflicted upon mah flesh could no longer quell. And yet, for all mah efforts, ah simply could not name it.

With these thoughts troubling mah mind ah crawled through the wire fence at the far side of the crop without so much as checking for the presence of any possible persecutors. An act of uncharacteristic recklessness. Of that there was no doubt. It would prove to be one very sorry mistake.

Ah staggered into the yard of the workers' camp, mah captain's jacket torn and smeared with pig-muck, mah sickle still in mah hand and swinging at mah side. Sitting at a trestle table in the middle of the yard were six or so newly arrived workers, shooting the shit over a bottle or three of malt mash.

Ah froze in mah tracks. Ah stared at them and they all stared back at me. Ah recognized their kind at once.

They were 'lifers' – old hands. They had been coming to the valley every ingathering since they were old enough to swing a machete. They were a breed unto themselves, and as far as ah was concerned a bad breed – the baddest.

They sat in a cluster, dressed in foxed singlets, canvas trousers and army boots. The skin on their faces was red and leathery, and so badly weather-beaten that the only thing that distinguished the mean line of their mouths from the thousand other cracks and scars was the soggy butt of a hand-rolled cigarette. They had little empty piss-holes in their heads that served as eyes. They sweated and belched and farted, and evilness and baseness and violence sat like low things in every pock and pore of their bastard fucken faces.

Mah heart seemed to hang between beats, suspended in some queer kind of limbo, retarding mah body action. Ah could smell mah own sweat turning sour with fear and ah wiped drops of it from mah eyes with one braided cuff.

'Run!' ah thought. 'Run!' But ah could not.

'Jeeshus freaking Christ! What the . . .' blurted out one, lifting himself to his feet, and the entire company erupted into laughter, pointing at me and slapping the table, happy as pigs in shit that some sorry bastard like me had come by so that they had their chance to get ugly.

O ah knew that sort of laughter all too well. Ah was well

acquainted with the sort of fun it could inspire. No sirree, there is nothing funny about laughter. Nothing funny at all. Out of all the correction that has been dealt mah way, ah cannot recall a solitary time when laughter has not been the battle-cry.

Ah felt mah hand tighten around the handle of mah death-dealing sickle, thinking, 'Ah don't know what you men are so happy about. You ain't got me yet. In case you haven't noticed, ah have a very big fucking sickle in mah hand and ah plan to lose it in the first face that tries anything,' trying mah hardest to bolster mah confidence by thinking tough, trying to curb the fear, trying to thaw mahself out. But all the thought-threats in the world weren't going to stop those drunken bastards from laughing at me – from mocking me – from plotting against me.

Ah noticed that the one that was standing was different from the others. He was younger and did not laugh. Rather he shook his head slowly from side to side, a strange expression in his eyes ah had never seen before. Pity was there, compassion. Ah have never come across that look again. Ah was petrified by the five who so openly ridiculed me, but not by this man, not this heart-swollen sympathizer. Rather ah was consumed by such a blood-boiling hatred for this miserable son of a bitch that ah was tempted to hang the consequences, leap on him there and then, and rip him all to pieces.

'Trigger Treat,' one joker with a beak like a bird and a bottle of booze in each hand called me. 'Trigger Treat,' he bawled, and they were off again, hooting with laughter and weaving about in their seats. Ah noticed that three of them were now standing, and it worried me that ah had not seen them rise. Someone said something about me looking like ah'd taken more triggs than a St Louis whorehouse – evidently a real cracker, for they launched into another bout of laughter.

'Give the shailor-baw a treat, then,' said a lanky, bald-headed joker guffawing into his handkerchief, and, in an attempt to divert mah attention, he howled like a dog and fell backward off his stool. At that exact moment the beaked one pitched a full fucken bottle of booze right at mah head, yelling, 'Catshit!' But ah saw it coming and simply stepped to one side, letting the bottle sail right past me and explode against a concrete trough that sat beside the trolley-tracks a few paces away.

'You'll have to do better than that if you wanna knock down Euchrid Eucrow,' ah thought, and there was a second when ah almost felt the urge to laugh, so feeble was the throw. Ah could almost have caught the thing in mah bare hands. 'Oh no, you'll have to do better than that!'

Suddenly they were all standing, their faces clenched like angry fists. They were not laughing any more. And ah knew that the time to act was nigh. The time was nigh to move. 'Run!' ah thought. 'Run!' And do you know what? That's exactly what ah did.

Ah did not look back, but ah knew that they were following me for ah could hear their threats roaring at mah hind – their sour breath burning like a brand into mah neck. 'Freak.' 'Sicko.' 'You'll pay, you screwball.' 'That was a fool boddle, punk. You'll pay. You'll wish ya hadda catshit.' You name it, they flung it. Ah was bad news and they were gunna rewrite me if they ever catched ahold of me. Ah plunged on, with nothing in mah mind but to haul ass out of there.

Just when they stopped chasing me ah do not know, but let me tell you this, ah wasn't going to stop and find out. As ah charged out of their work-camp and bounded along Maine, their blistering threats seemed to swell in intensity and their oaths of vengeance grew more and more virulent, more scathingly eloquent, taking on a new horribleness. But this was not all. O no. Not at all. As ah ran, sucking great aching lungfuls of the mad valley air, ah heard the voices slowly but surely multiply, as the original group of cut-throats were joined by other new arrivals – to the valley and to the hunt – so that what followed me was no longer half a dozen cranky old men but a mob, liquid and swelling with each passing second – a malign and clamorous evil shrouded in red dust and dealing death. And was that a hound or two that ah heard?

Ah allowed an image of them to take form in mah mind –

O mah mind, the racket inside of there – of *here* – forget it – a giant centipede or millipede – for all the time the numbers grew – its thrashing appendages armed with hay-rakes, machetes, axe-handles, chains, ropes, rocks, sticks and stones – scurrying closer, yes, gaining ground. Yes, ah could hear it. Mah head thundered with its many-tramping beaters, blood-oaths and death threats, as ah passed the city-limits sign and bowled headlong into town.

And ah ran on. And ah ran on. And ah ran on.

And as ah ran, as ah bounded on, ah remembered what these animals had done to Queenie. Have ah told you about Queenie? No? Did ah tell you what they went and did to Queenie? No. No ah didn't. No ah don't think ah did.

Ah told you about the lame 'bo and Kike – the two evil winos of Glory Flats. Remember? Yes? Well Queenie was a friend of Kike's. Ah forget where he found her.

Ah suspect she crawled out of one of the tin humpies that sit, obscured by heavy wooding, on the other side of the western ridge – ah'm not sure – at least ah don't remember any freak shows passing through town at that time. She was just there in the church one night when ah delivered their dose of moonshine.

Queenie didn't say much but she liked to laugh very loud and then listen to the laughter come bouncing back. 'Laughing Queenie' was the handle Kike, the great giver of names, hung on her. She was one of God's less complicated creatures, finding pleasure in the more simple things. She was at her most contented sitting on the church altar – her 'throne' as Kike put it – in her grimy blue frock, a bottle of White Jesus clasped between her pudgy pink hands. Here she would bounce up and down on her haunches, expelling a loud flat 'Ha!' with each flop of her fat little body. 'Ha! Ha! Ha! Ha!' Piling echo upon echo, rebound upon rebound, until the whole church seemed to vibrate with her merriment. Even the grim bloodless Christ that hung, ghastly in its unredeemed whiteness, above the altar – why, even He appeared to tremble on His rack. Queenie would stop, lift the bottle to her mouth, drink, place the bottle back between her legs, then begin again, her tiny round eyes dull and lifeless in the centre of her face.

Kike would applaud and the ever-sullen bum with the mangled foot would stew in his corner, holding a prayer book over each ear.

Kike used to get lickered up and for a few fingers of White Jesus he would futter Queenie on two pews pushed front to front. The other bum, the one with the scar and the mangled foot, would recite slabs of Leviticus until he was hoarse, then turn beseechingly to Queenie with tears in his eyes and a quarter of a bottle of watered-down shine proffered in his trembling hands.

With childlike enterprise, Queenie collected the coloured labels off liquor bottles, and when the alcohol ran low Kike would hunt for suitable unbroken vessels amongst the trash that covered the church floor. Standing in the annexe with his sleeves rolled up, he would soak the bottles one by one in the stagnant water of the font, carefully peeling off each paper label and arranging them in neat rows on a bench-seat to dry.

Ah was about sixteen at the time, and lured by the beacons of knowledge that beckoned dimly through the fog of mah youthhood ah would climb the steps leading to the pulpit and spy upon the fornicators.

The booze-shrivelled gimp would immerse himself in the gobbling folds of Queenie's raw and porcine loins like one engirdled in a huge pink tyre-tube. From the pulpit ah could see his backside, a hairy white knuckle, thrusting with an increasing urgency – a rhythm that began with cursing Queenie to hell and back, but ended in clonic supplication upon her sprawling breasts. Kike, on the other hand, a giant of a man himself, would hammer away at Queenie from beneath his filthy green greatcoat. Sometimes the only thing that would betray Queenie's presence in congress with Kike would be one numb and dumpling forearm crooked around his steaming neck, two or three liquor labels clutched in its fist.

Late one afternoon on the last day of the harvest – lay-off day for the majority of the workforce – a bunch of workers got together and stomped the bounce out of laughing Queenie's ball.

This is the way Kike put it to me:

'Murdering slime from the camp come whup the fucken custard outa her. Twenny, maybe twenny-five. Queenie ain't got the God-given brains to be afraid. Get shitted off cause she ain't puttin up no struggle. No fight. No fucking fun. Slap her about when she starts with the laugh Ha! ha! ha! ha! Shut up Queenie is all I'm thinkin, shut up. Ha! ha! ha! ha! If only she had've been scared. Kicked or squarked or spat or bit, something other than just that laugh. Ha! ha! ha! ha! "Shut it," they say. "Shut it." All the while they're getting drunker and sicker, sicker and meaner, hammering away at her. Some jerkin off over her laughin in the garbage. Ha! ha! ha! ha! "Fucken shut it, you stinking piece of shit," and I hear her cop a punch that shuts her up for a second or two but that's all. Ha! ha! ha! ha! and then she's off again. Before ya know it, they're puttin the boot in and her body's jerkin all over the floor. No stopping them now. They stomp on her. But hard. "Scummy shit!" Someone breaks a bottle cross her teeth. Torch her hair. Piss it out. "You sloppy bitch. Queenie! Queen of what? Eh? Queen of this!" And someone jams a beer bottle up Queenie's cunt. Another slaps his liquor-bottle label on to Queenie's belly, another slaps one on her forehead, another on her breasts until she looks like an old seaman's trunk, her legs, her body covered in bruises and blood. Queenie's dead. No doubts.'

Kike stopped speaking and hunched over the back of a pew, growling like an animal as he sucked rank air through the cavities of his great cratered beak. He glared at his comrade, the lame 'bo, and cussed.

Reading from the Bible, the raving cripple hobbled up and down the cluttered aisle, and shouted out the text at the figure of Christ Crucified that hung above the altar – oblivious, it seemed, to the disappearance of Christ's head, which now lay lost beneath the shredded blue folds of Queenie's discarded frock.

'. . . Go see now this cursed woman and bury her: for she is a king's
   daughter.
And they went to bury her: but they found no more of her than the
   skull and the feet and the palms of her hands . . .'

The cripple threw back long slugs of moonshine with alarming
insistence, his hobble becoming less and less pronounced, less
and less painful, until the straight line up and down the aisle
began to take on a slightly pacier figure-of-eight course. Kike and
me looked on. Listened.

'. . . In the portion of Jezreel shall dogs eat the flesh of Jezebel:
And the carcass of Jezebel will be as dung upon the face of the
   field . . .'

Kike reached into his coat and produced a piece of blood-
speckled paper upon which were printed bold capitals in blunt
red pencil.
   'Tell me, boy, what ya make outa this? Take it. Look,' whispered Kike, thrusting the paper at me. Ah looked at the page but
did not need to read it. Ah looked back at Kike. Ah shrugged
nervously. Cowered just enough.
   He nodded knowingly. His ugly blistered features almost
organized themselves into a look of genuine sadness. He looked
back to the cripple.
   'Thought so. Ya can't read. Couldn't have been you, then. Just
as I suspected. If you didn't write the message and I didn't write
it then it must have been the preacher . . .'
   The *preacher*? What *preacher*? Mah heart pounded. Scalp shrank.
Nausea.
   'Look at him. He's mad,' Kike continued. 'Used to be the
preacher in this here church. Did ya know that? Abie Poe. Was
a time when the fanatics hailed him as the saviour. Gathered up
cane-fronds, laid them before the hoof of his stallion. Builded
effigies in his image. *In his image!* Saviour? Shit! Was a conman.
Was a shark. Worse. They say he burned a witch up on Hooper's

222

Hill. Never believed it. Do now. He is a low man with some dangerous kinda sick. I pity him but I do not forgive him. Killed Queenie, he did. Good as. This note may as well have been her death warrant. Damn near could have been mine too! Cain't forgive that. No sir. Can get down on his knees until they bleed but I ain't forgiving that.'

Kike looked at me and I looked back at him. Kike wanted to confide in me. Ah wanted to kick his fucken brains in.

'Speak-no-evil,' said Kike, annunciating each word slowly and clearly. 'You ain't been given a proper name yet, Speak-no-evil. I'm gunna start calling you Speak-no-evil. What do you think of that, Speak-no-evil?' Ah wanted to throw up all over him, then say, 'Fine, Kike. Love it. And what do you think of that?' But ah managed to smile back at him, knowing that he wasn't about to get too many opportunities to call me anything, if things continued to fall mah way.

Ah looked at the gimp. The cripple. *Poe!* A chill bit at the nape of mah neck and the skin on mah arms grew horripilant and tight. But ah stayed calm.

Thinking about it now, you know, ah guess ah always knew that the gimp was Poe. Why else would a crippled hobo engender such complete and arrant hatred? Ah'm not the type to go around hating just anyone.

'Just weren't right of him to write that note, Speak-no-evil. Just weren't right. All that hot-gospelling and holy-rolling, that's a trough of hog-slop. Is a fucken phoney and he killed my Queenie. Ain't getting away with that. Don't want you hanging around. Gunna get ugly around here shortly. You better piss off – and bring me back a bottle tonight.'

Kike returned his attention to Poe and ah could hear his booming voice as ah exited the church.

'Sing it, Preacher, and sing it sweet. Is your last sermon. You can tell it to the Devil. Time to meet your maker!'

Ah returned with a bottle later that evening. Kike was already loaded, oscillating between the supine and the sitting position. As ah ventured down the aisle ah saw Kike for what he was – a low animal – a rogue in a lousy green greatcoat – a great grunting grizzly with blood all over its face and hands – a pie-dog of the baddest blood – a flea-bag – a scum-sack – a shit-hill. Ah handed him the bottle and he uncorked it and took a long, lushy guzzle. Then, slamming the bottle down on the oaken pew, and expelling a rancid belch with a little thrust of his body, he roared for no apparent reason. 'Aw fuck. Shit. Blaaah. Aaaach. Shit.' Then, cutting a resounding, flapping fart, he swore again and began to examine his bloody hands. He thrust them toward me theatrically.

'The blood. Won't come off. Wonder if it ever will,' he queried in a stage whisper. Then he wiped his tell-tale ten – his finkers – down the front of his greatcoat. Damp with the chocolate-coloured blood, the spongy felt fabric of the coat seemed to dispense more gore than it was prepared to receive and Kike inspected his sticky scarlet snitchers a second time.

'To the font! We'll wash this stubborn blood away!' he bellowed in a manner of high drama, as if the mere presence of Poe's blood was sufficient to imbue the stewed giant with all the thespian artifice of the preacher.

'Wash it off!' he bawled.

Kike stood suddenly, extravagantly, and slugging the bottle he attempted a cavalier flourish, tangled himself in his greatcoat and crashed to the floor like a felled pine, cushioned by empty bottles, biscuit boxes, rat-soil and rubble. Trussed in his coat, arms pinned to his sides, he looked up at me with tears welling in his eyes and opened his great mouth to reveal a couple of lonely molars and a swollen green glossa. He began laughing. He was clearly out of control, laughing like that. And laughing.

Squatting on the pew, ah peered down at the creature that juddered and jack-knifed at mah feet, a remugient pupa covered in blood.

A smile tugged at the corners of mah mouth and ah opened it wide and bared all mah forty-six teeth to the wigging pupa on the floor. Ah could feel mah own gut-muscles dancing but their spasms were, as usual, short-lived, because in the world of the mute the rewards for hilarity are as beggarly as the causes. Or haven't ah told you?

Ah squatted on the oaken pew, ringent as a granite gargoyle, mah eyes busily meeting his as the gales of laughter levelled to become less extravagant expulsions of left-over mirth – his stupid, blaked face twitching with little pains – a grimace, a wince, a pursing of his blanching lips. Kike was looking a little green. Ah squatted. Ah watched. Ah waited.

Then Kike was not laughing at all. Free from the girdle of twisted felt, his squalid cocoon opening into limp and scumbered wings, the chrysalis flapped unsteadily to its feet then flopped on to the pew, massive booted legs stretched athwart the aisle.

'Speak-no-evil, are you listening?' he said. 'You listening, Speak-no-evil?'

Ah was standing now, so that the balance had shifted again, leaving me still in the advantage should the atmosphere darken or the beast snap or things start turning berserk. Ah looked down at Kike. Ah held the bottle inches away from his reaching hand, so that he was forced to strain and stretch a little in order to take hold of it – just a little – ah didn't want him getting wise just yet.

He slugged again at the bottle, our eyes locked as he drank. His hands were caked in black blood and each knuckle, shaved raw, was crowned with an angry, purulent abrasion. Beads of cold sweat oozed from his fleshy upper lip, and across his furrowed brow, and made little tracks through the claret smears unner his eyes. Sprawled so, on the bench, he looked like a very fucken unfunny clown.

Kike groaned once, long and low.

'Got something ah want to tell ya, Speak-no-evil. Justice was dealt. Queenie rest easy. The balance of the scale is even again. Seen the last of Abie Poe, we have. Was my friend. But listen. Leaving that note at the work-camp was unforgivable – just nod if you agree, baw. Asked him to come clean and when he did not, I beat him. Yep. Beat him right up. Asked him again and

225

again. Refused to confess. Was like . . . was like he really believed he didn't do it.'

Kike started to tear at the collar of his greatcoat in an attempt to loosen it from around his throat. He dabbed at his forehead with his sleeve. 'Can't breathe so well . . . Shit . . . Sweating like a freakin sow . . . Gimme the bottle, will ya, boy . . . Pain growing in the guts . . . where was ah? Right. Standing over him and shaking the fucken note in front of his eyes, I'm saying, "Don't make me kill ya, Poe. Don't . . ." His nose already hanging off his face by a thread, so that I'm really looking down the throat of the buggy bastard. And he damn well dared to look me in the eye and say through a mouthful of teeth, "Kill me, Kike . . . and may the Lord forgive you . . . I don't know what you're talking about." '

Kike gripped his stomach and leaned back against the pew. 'Shit. Head . . . Guts . . . Throat . . . Boy, pass me the bottle . . . Throat . . . tight . . . What, all gone? All empty? Anyway, I yelled at him, "Po-o-o-o-oe! You know what ah'm talking about. The letter. This death warrant! How could you, Poe! Even after ah shared her with you. You saw what they did to Queenie. Don't go with a lie on your lips, Poe. Tell me the truth, Poe. The truth. Or ah swear, ah'll post this fucken letter in your face . . ."

'He opened one dying eye. Just a fraction, then . . . after twenty seconds, maybe thirty . . . he said . . . very soft, very slow, very clear, "No-o-ooo, Kike . . . You've made a terrible mistake, Kike."

'Said, "And so have you, Poe. So long, Preacher, see you at your resurrection." Drove my right fist into his face.'

Kike was taking a lot longer to go unner than ah had estimated he would. Kike was not a very big man – he was a very big *animal*, but ah was not so worried. Ah had put enough poison into the Jesus to deck a woolly mammoth.

Kike tried to stand but lost balance and folded like a deck of cards back against the pew. His voice had become a tremulous croak but ah could detect confusion there, as well as a note of terror, receding and building up respectively.

'. . . don't understand him. Denying everything. When he is

226

clearly the only one who could have done it . . . shit. Feel so goddamn ill all of a sudden . . . yeah, and ah dragged his body outside and put him under . . . the . . . church . . .' and Kike stopped his babbling and wrapped his arms around his belly and rocked.

Then suddenly, bizarrely, he leaped to his legs, crowed like a bird, collapsed on to the pew again and vomited a torrent of blood and bile into his lap. He stared at the marbled egesta, muttering and blowing bubbles. Perhaps that was his way of excusing himself for his behaviour. He did not seem to notice the sound of vehicles climbing Glory Trail, headed for the church.

It was the sound ah had been waiting for. The signal. Time to get serious, ah thought. Time to get serious.

Ah got his attention – he was doubled over, blubbering – by pushing him up into a sitting position so that he rested in the corner of a pew, his head lolling about on its massive neck. Ah put down the bottle and pulled a Bible from mah back pocket. He was watching me through very weird, popping eyes. Ugly, florid blotches had sprung up on his face and neck.

Ah belted him squarely across the face with the Bible. The animal dribbled muck on it. Then as he looked on in disbelief ah flipped nimbly through the foxed pages of the Old Testament. Genesis. Exodus. The wonderful Leviticus. Numbers. Yes, Numbers. Chapter 35. Verses 18 and 19.

Ah took a red pencil from mah bib pocket. Freshly sharpened. Ah flashed a smile at Kike, all teeth, and looking into his eyes ah licked the tip of the pencil.

Again Kike heaved violently, but for all the noise he made whilst doing it it was disappointingly unfruitful – a brief spill of watery blood that ran over his bottom lip and hung in scarlet dribbles from his jaw. He remained propped in the corner of the pew watching me operate. Mouth wide open. Unmoving.

Ah unnerlined the appropriate verses and then in bold capitals, across the top of the passage, ah wrote, and likewise unnerneath the passage, so that the page appeared thus:

CAN YOU READ THIS, KIKE?

18   *Or he that smite him with an hand*
wherewith he may die, and he die,
he is a murderer:
the murderer shall surely be put to death.
HA HA HA HA HA HA HA

SPEAK-NO-EVIL

Ah took his great, beefy hands and wrapped them around the Bible, and Kike let his head drop and stared stupidly at the pages. The blotches on his face and neck had turned a ghastly grape colour. Bloody sputum strings dangled and dropped, punctuating the ominous pages with prophetic aptness.

Ah could hear the vehicles – two, three, four – skidding in the gravel as they pulled up outside the church. Ah heard the crackle of a two-way radio and ah knew the Ukulites had taken seriously the message that ah had pinned to the door of the tabernacle. Ah could hear them breaking down the little slatted gate that let them unner the church. They would find Poe's corpse and know that the rest of mah note too must be correct, and a few minutes later they would storm the church looking for the murderer.

'Come on, Kike. Comprehend. Work it out, you fool. It's all over for you, whoremonger. It's all over for all of you. You and Poe and Queenie. All over,' ah thought.

Finally Kike lifted his great blotched face, his eyes poisoned, spiralling. He blubbered and bawled and boo-hooed and ah swung the empty bottle like a bat, smacking Kike square across the bridge of his nose and taking him out in one.

Ah looked at him there, slumped against the back-board of the pew all covered in muck and not making a sound and ah thought to mahself, 'You are an ass, Kike, you are an ass.' Then ah brought the bottle down again.

Ah removed the Bible from Kike's hands and quickly extracted the incriminating pages, then ah reached into the pocket of his greatcoat and retrieved the first letter ah had written – the one ah had left for the field-workers – the letter inviting the cane-men up to the church. Pocketing them, ah disappeared into the annexe, just as the Sheriff brought in from Davenport and his two deputies began battering down the main doors.

'Use the goddamn handle,' ah thought, as ah slipped out the side entrance and crept down the hill through the tall grass, 'it ain't locked.'

All the way home ah smiled. Ah just could not get rid of it.

All about were charred black fields. Cane, chopped and stacked, awaited transport to the refinery.

Later, after everyone had gone, ah went back and sat inside the church. Ah closed mah eyes and simply basked in the knowledge that ah had served God – without even waiting to be asked. Yes, ah had served mah Lord and that was reward enough in itself. In a world full of profiteers it felt good to give. The meek shall indeed inherit the earth. Ah made a pact there and then to maintain this hallowed premises, this temple of the Lord, and keep it free from all intruders. And as ah sat there, humbled by its vastness and its silence, ah could feel God was there with me, there beside me, all about me, deep within me. In time the seraphs sang, filling the great hall with their music. And they sang for me. And they sang for me.

Two days later the Ukulites burned the church down.

And ah ran on. And ah ran on. And ah ran on.

And ah knew ah fled the very fists that had beat poor Queenie down. And ah ran on.

Ah knew that ah was good as dead were they to catch me. Ah held no illusions as to the extent of the violence they would mete upon me. Ah wondered whether the valley walls would prove sufficient to contain the dispersement of mah many parts. And ah ran on. Some terror driving me. Fear at the wheel.

Hurtling past a strip of green ah saw the muzzle of a small dog or ferret squeezing unner a white picket fence. Ah saw its sleek shape dart on to the road, felt it scuttle past mah heels as it disappeared into a dark area on the other side.

At one point the galloping ground beneath mah feet grew suddenly spongy and ah took a fall of some kind which ah can't remem– . . . of which ah will spare you the details. Suffice to say that ah ended up flat on mah belly, the palms of mah outstretched hands neatly skinned and powdered in red road. Did ah ever tell you about mah dogs? Yes? Did ah ever tell you about mah dogs and what they could do to a hamster? Did ah? Mah dogs could atomize a hamster!

Ah waited to be atomized. To be taken apart. Shredded. Blitzed.

Ah could hear footsteps coming toward me. Mah whole body shook with them. Boom-boom boom-boom boom-boom boom-boom. Ah turned to find the mob had gone. No. Not gone – hidden. Ah turned to find the mob had hidden. Stretched out behind me, emptied of its froth and frenzy, the road receded into the distance like a dusty red tongue.

Something rustled in the hedge to mah right. Ah could see strange, pulsing shadows crouched in ambush. A machete winked from behind a nearby roadside pine. Ah backed off. Ah felt low laughter coming at me from behind. Ah spun around. Leaning on some grain sacks in the tray of a utility, a lean weasel-faced youth sneered and sniggered at me as he whittled a piece of kindling with a large knife. Keeping mah eyes fixed on him, ah started walking backward. Mah foot squelched in its boot. Ah glanced down. The toe of mah boot oozed a little puddle of bright blood. It shimmered in the dust like a jewel. Ah noticed a trail of such jewels scattered behind me.

A toothless hag watched me from her window, then drew back out of view.

Ah looked up and saw the weasel-faced youth thrusting his knife toward me and screwing it. His lips were curled back. He had black teeth and brown foam around his mouth.

'Wha y'loog gnat?' he barked viciously. Ah noticed he was very cock-eyed, very insane.

'Why y'fuggin loog gnat?'

Ah turned to run. A spear of pain shot up mah leg. The

particles in the air blushed. All around. Ah stumbled on, holding mah leg as ah ran.

Ah heard the giggling of many children but ah could not see them. Through the red air.

The wind whispered. Chattered. A million pine needles rained down upon me. Tinkling as they fell.

'What's going on?' ah thought and the ground beneath mah feet turned spongy again and ah think ah went down. Ah remember lying on mah back on the ground and looking up at the awnings of the shop fronts, at the lamp-posts, at the crackling wires, at the street lights, at the tree-tops, at the dusky sky, at the birds, and seeing there the peril intrinsic to all these things.

And then ah was crawling on mah hands and knees. The palms of mah hands stung. Bled. Mah mouth was full of grit. Eyes blurred. Ah could see in the doorway of a building three men wearing false snow-white beards, their weapons hidden in newspapers. A black man with a towel over his arm pushed past them. He was angry. His hair was steel.

'Are y'jes gunna stan dere d'win nuttin?' he said, and he went for me and it was then ah noticed the very fucking big cut-throat razor in his hand. Ah spun mah arms wildly. Mah fists.

Ah ran. Ah looked behind me. The men were on the road now, wiping off their disguises and shaking their fists at me. The black man hadn't accounted for the spongyness of the road and was laying sprawled out in the dust.

To mah right – no, to mah left – a man hiding behind the hedgerow of Memorial Square held a huge pair of shears in his hands. He looked at me and chopped the air menacingly.

Ah saw a lark screaming.

It was only then that it really struck me. Ah was running through the centre of town. A truck lumbered past, blasting its horn. Ah sped up. Ah was running through the centre of town, right down the middle of the main street. Ah turned to see who was pursuing me. The old negro was on his feet and the men were dusting him down, but no one was following.

Run. Don't look back. Run. Don't look back again, ah thought.

There, crossing the road in front of me was . . .
But ah was going too fast. It was too late to stop mahself.
We collided.

Ah didn't want to tell you about this but ah guess ah have to. Yes, ah do. Yes ah guess ah really do. But ah don't want to – it gives me the creeps just to think about it.

Let me take you back to the night before. The night before all this running and fleeing.

Ah had fallen asleep sitting outside on the front steps of the shack – this ah can remember – and ah guess ah had shifted inside at some point through the night as ah awoke the next morning, on mah bed, aching all over, naked, crapulent. Ah swung mah legs over the side, and stared at the little white nightdress ah held in mah hands. Ah fingered the fine cotton fabric, entranced by its whiteness, and stared in disbelief at the embroidered emblem stitched into its bodice. Beth's nightdress.

Ah stood up and mah whole body ached in protest. Ah bent over to pick up a half-empty bottle of White Jesus. Ah glanced in the mirror and froze.

Ah was scared. Ah could have shit pigs.

Mah back and shoulders were covered in thick black bruises, some of them sticky with seeped blood. Heavy bruises that sure weren't there last night when ah dropped off to sleep on the steps.

Ah crawled back to mah bed and gingerly laid mahself down on mah stomach, the nightdress still clutched in mah hand, and positioned thus ah looked at everything about me – all the muck and all the misery and all the rotting filth – and ah folded the bright white nightdress and put it under mah cheek. Ah could smell sweet lavender perfume upon it, feel the softness and the cleanness of the fabric.

Perhaps ah sensed mah destiny in that heavy-hearted instant, for hot tears flowed down mah cheeks as ah lay there on mah stomach, not knowing what to do or what ah had done – how on earth ah had come to have in mah possession Beth's nightdress and how in God's name had ah obtained such ghastly contusions? Endless questions bullied mah memory but ah drew a blank every time. What did ah do last night? Did ah go down into the town? Did ah visit Beth? Ah shuddered at the thought. Were the bruises on mah back self-inflicted? Did ah scrap with one of mah beasts? Were the angry stripes God's work? Satan's? Why did ah harbour such terrible feelings of dread? Of anguish?

And ah lay on the bed, haunted by a thousand such questions made all the more bitter by the presence of the sweet lavender-scented garment. And ah unfolded the nightdress and held it at arm's length in front of me, then allowed it to descend in skirts of virgin light and sacral lavender over mah shamed, mah tearful face.

We collided.

She had not seen me coming as she ambled across the road. Nor ah her, as ah came hurtling down it.

Sky. Ground.

Ah stood, heaving for breath, in the middle of the road.

Ah held a little girl by the tops of her arms. Ah could feel her soft, warm shoulders and the fabric of her smock beneath mah skinned palms. Mah head swam in a sea of rowdy blood.

Ah held mah breath. Ah held mah breath Ah held mah breath Ah held Beth Ah held . . . *Ah held Beth!*

Beth stared up at me and mah mind jabbered.

O mah . . . O mah God . . . O please . . . Please don't scream . . . Please don't cry . . . *Please don't scream!*

But Beth had no intention of screaming, of crying. She simply looked up at me, her large, liquid eyes peering through her parted tresses of gold. Ah could feel her body trembling in mah hands but she was not afraid. Nor was she hurt.

Beth smiled and – and – well, there was no evil in that – no, at least ah didn't notice any and – and then Beth spoke – to me. Ah held her at arm's length but she moved a step closer. She took a deep breath. Two. Her lavender scent seemed to negate the stench of pig-shit, the collected soil of mah day's bungling, that poured from mah person. Did ah tell you that she moved a step closer? Did ah? *She moved a step closer.*

'It is You,' she said. 'It is You. You have returned. O Lord, ah thought You would be angry. Forgive me, Jesus. I am sorry that they beat You last night. They are scared. But I am not. I am so happy that You came. I have so much to tell You now. But You know, don't You? I need tell You nothing. Be careful, my saver. They do not like You. They will try and harm You. Quick! You must go.'

She slipped something into mah jacket pocket. Ah stared back in disbelief. Ah realized ah was still holding her by the shoulders and ah dropped mah hands. Ah looked into her welling eyes. She bit her bottom lip and swallered and a tear rolled from one eye.

'You've got the wrong God, girlie,' ah wanted to say. 'Ah was sleeping off a two-day drunk last night. Ah'm afraid you got your wires crossed, ah'm no . . .'

But mah thought responses were no sooner kindled than they were terminated – hell, they were burked! – throttled by a terrible squawking to mah right. Ah did not need to look around to know that the odium that inspired such an ungracious fray was me, but ah took a look anyway, glancing over mah shoulder as ah adjusted mah sickle for flight and took off.

Thundering over the porch of the house next to Beth's there lunged a seven-foot mastodon in a baby-blue housecoat. She barrelled down the steps toward me, mouthing insanities and swinging a wooden rolling-pin like a battleaxe.

'That's him! That's him!' she boomed. 'Look! He's got the child! He's got the child!'

'No ah haven't! No ah haven't!' ah cried dumbly.

'You want more, eh? You've come back for more? You want me to bash your pervertinizing brains in this time? I ain't afraid of you! Sardus! Sardus! Where the blazes are you?' she squawked. Ah looked back again and the woman had stopped chasing me and was dabbing at Beth's face with a corner of her housecoat. Beth struggled and squirmed.

'What did he do, child? What did the nasty man do to you?

Answer me, child! Did he touch you? Answer me! Where did he touch you?'

Ah ran and ran and did not stop even when ah passed the city-limits sign at the south entrance to the town. No one followed me, but ah had a feeling this incident was not over yet.

At last ah came upon a bridge. Hallis Crossing. It was many years since ah had been there. Each side of the bank was clogged with a thickly knitted briar of wild rose. Ah unsheathed mah sickle and set to work.

The night moved in on Hallis Crossing and ah squatted beneath the bolted beams of the bridge, listening to the shifting of its wood, the shifting of the waters, while the air got serious around me. The moon was a steely prong stabbed into a sky as black and untried as the chambers of a dead nun's heart. The moon was trying to rattle me and it had chosen the right night to do it. There was an indisputable aura of imminent catastrophe in its attitude – the way it was so carelessly perched in its invisible sling, supramundane and to mah eyes top-heavy, this sickle moon, top-heavy and tilting over as if the slightest disturbance would topple it from its heavenly roost and send it crashing down upon me. The reservoir of courage that ah'd had cause to milk so frequently on this day had all but dried up – the last brave drops spent on getting me through the raking brambles of the briar.

Ah had looped mah belt over a bridge beam and lowered mahself down, knowing ah had gone about it in the wrong way at about the same time as ah realized ah could not turn back again. It was too dark and the briar seemed deeper than ah had at first thought. Denser. Thornier. Mah belt wasn't long enough. Or strong enough. Or was it that ah was too heavy, what with mah many burdens, mah mass of troubles, mah great whacking load of woe? Anyway ah'd taken a tumble in the wild roses and found mahself sprawled on the bank of the cloacal rivulet, free of the clawing snagglepatch, but with mah body, face, hands and neck a feast of tiny bubbling welts and scratches. Crawling unner the bridge ah took off mah jacket and trousers and spent some time in silence plucking the angry thorns that had become embedded in their fabric, in mah flesh.

'If there was a thorn for every time that ah have died today,' ah thought, 'a thorn for every time that they have killed me, the world would be one big briar patch.' And ah sighed a sigh so deeply wrought, so full of despair, so full of grief, yes, so fucking bloody sad, that ah was forced to say to mahself, 'Steady up there, Euchrid, steady up. Stay brave. You're safe now. No one can get you here. No one can hurt you here. Chin up. Everything will turn out all right in the end.'

And ah guess the sluice-gates on some other reservoir opened up, and wearily and with many deep and draining sighs ah cried and cried and in time ah fell asleep upon the bank of that filthy little creek. And just before mah dreamtime crowded in ah remember thinking that some very bad moments were yet to be lived. Some good ones too, maybe, but most of all ah remember thinking that there were some very bad moments heading for me, close and coming fast, bad moments demanding to be lived.

Ah dreamed ah was a carpenter. The best carpenter in town. One day ah made a great cross and carried it up a hill all alone. The sun was hot and a warm wind blew, bringing the hue and cry of the townsfolk to mah ears. Ah turned to see many people young and old clambering toward me. Ah hoisted the great cross on to mah back and ran on up the hill.

There ah met a harlot who was digging a hole and when ah asked her what she was trying to unearth she told me nothing ah am burying the sins of the world. Ah looked in the hole and saw only a blood-brushed glove and ah reached in and took it out and she said lie down. Ah lay down on mah cross and she undressed me. She pulled thorns from mah flesh. She covered mah body in lavender saying that she must prepare me and draped mah loins in her own pink nightdress. Still the crowd grew closer. She hammered me on. Then she jammed mah cross in the hole and ah hung there absorbed in mah own tiny pain.

*

The sound of an automobile in low gear, a pick-up, all motor-hum and grinding gravel, accompanied our sudden ascent, cruising through the back alleyways, the crime slums of mah subconsciousness. Ah opened mah eyes. Mah body was wrapped in a binding caul of placental warmth and the pong of fresh shit and the sound of its trickling waters – the sensory devices of mah dreams – continued to dominate mah senses. Lying on mah side on the bank of the creek, ah gazed into the black night. The air was warm and thick and wet, and the creek shifted its load and pumped it into the fields somewhere. Fear came like the droning motors that crept closer. Only when they were nearly upon me – there were two now – and ah could see the sweeping beams of torchlight fanning the foisoned fields, did mah mind alert mah body to the impending danger.

Ah scrambled up the cool damp clay of the bank, sliding and slipping in the muddy earth, and mounting the steep upgrade ah clung to a wood beam support beneath the bridge and listened in silence to the funereal approach. Ah counted four beams of light, two on either side, which meant six men in all, including the two drivers. Their progress was thorough, painful, predatory. Ah crawled between two pylons where ah would be safe from the beams and listened carefully, mah eyes gazing absently at the waters, and for a moment ah thought the moon *had* fallen from its heavenly nest, along with a handful of stars, and landed in the creek.

'It's only the moon's reflection,' ah told mahself, as the wheels of the first pick-up hit the wooden planks of the bridge directly above me. The stars looked as big as gold coins.

'Shit!' ah thought, and ah slipped and skidded back down the bank to the creek – to the moon and the six gold stars. 'That ain't a reflection!' ah thought, and ah scooped up mah captain's jacket and mah sickle that lay beside it. The vehicles had stopped on top of the bridge and ah heard the sound of cranky metal doors grating open and slamming shut.

Ah mounted the slope again, fearful for mah own bright nakedness, and as ah climbed between the pillars ah saw the plunging beams of light prod the briar, the bank, the creek, and ah squeezed into the niche where the unnerstructure of the bridge met the top of the bank. Ah could feel their booted footfall clopping on the boards inches above mah head. Ah tried to take command of mah whistling anhelations but the rising fist of pain tightened about mah throat and mah heart. O mah heart pounded up such a resounding alert in that shallow crawlspace that ah felt it necessary to roll mah jacket and trousers into a thick muff and press it against the left side of mah chest. The clay felt cold and clammy, like dead skin, and ah could hear all around me weird scratchings coming from the inky recesses of collected scum and rotten timber. Ah could see the light of the torches winking through the slatted beams. Fat slugs glistened and groped on the unnerbelly of the bridge, thrown into a state of confusion by mah sudden presence.

Two men stood almost directly over me, shining their torches down at the creek and the bank, one of them leaning out over the railing and trying to probe as much of the darkness unner the bridge as the angle of the beam would allow. But the crawlspace in which ah huddled, naked as a baby, lay well beyond the searching finger of light.

In the darkness ah listened to those above me talk, and with each footfall tiny deposits of sand would spill on to mah body from between the slatted beams.

'Ain't a lot of fucken life left in these here batteraries. Only bord em last fucken week and look at em. Hey! Prong! How's ya batteraries holding?' cried one.

'Wha-a? Is that you, Sal?' called back another man from the other side of the bridge.

'Yeah. Ah said how's ya fucken batteraries holdin out?'

'Batter him? Ah'm gunna bash the little fucker black and blue. If there is one thing ah cain't stand, it's a freakin secko, know what ah mean?' replied Prong, who came clomping across the bridge to stand by Sal.

'Dumb bastard,' hissed Sal, unner his breath.

Again there was a silence, only longer this time. Beams probed.

'Where's Groper and . . . ah dunno . . . what's his name . . .
the youngster?' asked Prong.

'Chisolm or Prism or Jism . . . ah dunno . . . they're down
checkin unner da britch. Let's get going. Ah cain't see a fucken
thing with this here torch. He's probably clear of the fucken
valley by now, anyway. Why don't this Swift character do his
own fucken man-huntin?'

Across the creek ah could see two pale beams flashing through
the briar on either side of the bridge.

'How's your side, Groper?' called a voice.

'What was that?' replied Groper.

'Wha-a-a?'

'Ah said, what was that?'

'Ah said, how's your si– . . . oh forget it, it don't matter any.'

'Yeah, mine too, and ah only bord 'em last week.'

A bottle smashed on the rocks that lined the creek. Ah gasped.

Sal or Prong, one or the other, said sharply, 'Shhhh. Shut up.
Do ya hear that?'

'Hear what?'

'That. Shhh. Listen!'

'Wha-a?'

'That funny breathy sound. Is dat you, Stoat?'

'Wha-a-a?'

'The fucken breathy sound! Christ!'

'No! It ain't me,' said Stoat nervously, 'it certainly ain't me.'

'Shut up! Everybody listen and hold their breaths. Shhh.'

Ah held mah breath.

A screaming, head-splitting, lung-frying, heart-punishing lifetime ensued, and in the interminable ache of its passing when
the atmosphere pounded with deep reds and dark blues, ah
remember thinking to mahself that for all the beating of gums
that went on, nothing much was really said and that maybe, just
maybe, the gab wasn't such a great fucken gift after all and that
it was action that spoke louder than words, *action* ah say, as ah
waited for them to find me and put me to death.

And they did.

Torch beams of naked light felt me out. Little hairless animal. Clomping boots encircled me. Machetes pared the air. Parted the slats. Carved me into long strips of meat. Cleaved mah skull with a dead hit. Hacked me into cubes. Into mince. Into mush. Into soup. And not a peep of protest.

And from the pool of creamed corpse a perfect soul, complete in every way, floated up to be received into that heavenly breast of His into that heavenly breast of His into that heavenly breast of His.

But they did not. No, they did not.

'There he is, crawled into a ball, unner the bridge!' exclaimed Prong or Sal, dropping to his knees with his trembling torch in his hand. With eye glued to the floor of the bridge, he peered at me through a gap in the beams.

'O mah God! He's completely naked, and he's smiling at me weirdly!' gasped Prong or Sal, and kissing the pricked tip of mah sickle ah slogged the steel claw up through the slatted beams and sunk it to the hilt into his great, gawping face, then wrenched the sickle back again, ripping it from his skull like a mask – that silly face – ripping it from his skull like a screaming mask.

Yeah, but me neither. No neither did ah.

'There ain't no fucken breathing sound, chucklehead. Let's get going,' said Sal and they turned and headed for their vehicles.

'The tamperer's there, ah know he is!' protested Chucklehead, but they loaded him into their pick-up and eventually both vehicles were roaring down Maine, toward town.

Maybe it was all the fleeing, all the fearing, all the falls, the earth mauls, bad steering, all the goddamn *feeling* ah had had to do on this dark descent, this day, this night – or perhaps it was the thoroughly obstetric secureness of mah pouch of earth, the pulse and lull of its clay. Or maybe ah needed to dream, to purge all of the rogue thoughts that had been hidden for so long in the backstreets and basements, the alleys and attics of mah subconsciousness. Or could it be ah just hadn't been sleeping much lately – oh but ah had, ah had, hadn't ah? Or perhaps it was none of these reasons and God had just deemed it necessary for me to tarry a little longer in that queer crawlspace, ah dunno, but that is exactly what ah did, crouched and naked and slumbering there.

Never unnerestimate fear. Fear is the boss. Fear is king. Fear is God. It is everywhere and in everything. The peril potential. What do you think? Fear is a good chief but a bad brave. That's mah view. That's the way ah see it. Of all the emotional influences that play upon the senses there is none so all-consuming, so arrantly demanding and so downright insistent as fear. So much so that, as ah lay entombed in earth in that creeping crawlspace beneath the bridge, so afraid – so *in fear* – ah barely noticed the frightful condition mah body was in. Though it had no doubt been remonstrating, mah brain had been so thoroughly ravaged by fear that mah sensory switchboard had jammed. Now, as the motors died in the distance and fear subsided for the moment, pain bullied its way in.

A ferocious cramp gripped mah right leg. Mah left leg was numb and dead. Gripping on to a support beam on the unnerside of the bridge with mah free arm, ah lifted mahself up a few inches and twisted mah body around, knees still drawn up to mah chest, and lowered mahself down upon mah back. Ah screamed as a sizzling pain ripped through the angry stripes across mah back and shoulders and ah hoisted mahself upward, disturbing a handful of slugs that seemed to welcome the warmth of mah body, peeling from the wooden beams and falling cool upon the conflagration of mah flesh.

The pain generated by the great bruised swellings across mah back and shoulders seemed to stimulate parts of mah memory that would have otherwise remained dormant – stark jumbled bursts of recall – baffling – foreign – lost re-runs all triggered by shouts of white pain – terrible snippets of deadtime, ghastly in their vividness and somehow made even more harrowing by their transience, their disjointedness and their inconclusiveness. Deadtime revisited in agony.

Darkness. Creaking floorboards unner mah feet. A slip of moon shining through a wide open window. A flapping curtain.

Ah am near naked, but it is night and there are no lights in this room. But ah know the room. *Ah know the room.* Girl smells. Clean sheets. Soap. Powder. *Her* smells. Then an urgent whisper, trembling and excited. Excited. *Her* voice. An arm's reach away. Come . . . upon . . . me . . . Jesus. O . . . Jesus . . . please . . . come . . . upon . . . me. Boom-boom boom-boom boom-boom boom-boom. Sickle flash. The moon a scarlet slice. Here in the dark. In her room. The breath of her words against the skin of mah face. I . . . am . . . prepared. I . . . am . . . prepared. Clean cotton fabric. Mah body glistening in the moonlight. A brush of lavender across mah cheek. Your little doll . . . little doll . . . is prepared. Blushing blackness. Blushing blackness. Deadtime.

Then an explosion of light. A wall of waxed dolls with hinged jaws. Beth's face wet with tears. And me – and me standing in the centre of the room, shamed in light. And in the doorway – an ogress. Flowery apron. Florid face. Wooden rolling-pin in her fist. Screaming teeth, screaming O my God . . . O my God . . . O my God. Ah spin around. Glimpse Beth wrapping herself in a white sheet, sitting up in the bed. And me, shaking with fear. Ah turn to the window. Go climbing through. The brutal whacks across mah back – with the club, with the pin. Their dull thud. One. Two. Three. Four. Screaming and spinning and rushing ah go, like a wounded dog, through the night. Crawling through the dust and the darkness to mah refuge, to mah Kingdom. And there, in mah room, howling, mad with pain. Ripping apart a kennel with an axe-handle. Dull meat whacks. Pain transferral. Me, howling with pain like the dogs in the dark. A clutch of lavender fabric. Fresh and new and all unbuttoned. Still warm with her. In mah hands –

Ah heard a pitter-patter of slippered feet above me. In the moon-glow the girders of the bridge looked like filed teeth and the moon, it looked like a fang. The pitter-patter of slippered feet grew louder, closer, and with it came a gust of lavender. Could that be Beth on the boards above me? As ah lay in the crawlspace, fast asleep – no, not asleep – *awake*. Could that be Beth on the boards of the bridge above me? As ah lay in the crawlspace, wide awake.

'Jesus,' she said, 'Jesus, are You near me? I think You are. Yes, I can feel You all about me. Oh I just know that You are near.

'I waited for You in my room tonight, but then the cane-men came and I heard one tell Daddy that You were under the bridge, but no one would believe him because of the briar patch. They said the only way You could have got under the bridge was by changing into a rabbit. Did You, Jesus? He said that he heard You breathing and that's how I knew it was true, and I knew that I must come to You. I crawled out of my window just like You did.'

She went quiet for a moment, and all ah could hear was the patter of her cautious steps. Then again she spoke. So frail. So tender. 'I love You, Jesus. You have stopped my loneliness.'

And she fell silent again. And again there was the scuffing of her feet. It was as if she was consulting the silence in order to find me, stopping to listen, then taking another careful step or two, always drawing a little closer – for the silence, to be sure, was imparting some very accurate intelligence, what with mah wheezing, what with mah blooding – until the child was stepping on the rickety boards directly above me, the soles of her slippered feet literally a plank's width from mah straining, throbbing face.

'O Jesus, it is me, Beth. You need not speak. I know You are there. I cannot see You. But I know. Please don't speak. It is safer if You just listen.'

Then ah think she must have squatted down, for, though her voice had dropped to a whisper, ah could hear her words perfectly – ah fancied ah could even feel the sweet heat of her breath through the slatted beams – while mine – mah breaths – why mah breaths wheezed away, growing more and more raucous as ah tried desperately to control them – and, well – ah could have – perhaps – controlled them a little better, if ah had not been so tied up with mah barn-storming heart and all its panicky clamour. God, the noise in there.

'I know that the women are wise women. I know that. They

predicted You would come and choose me to be Your . . . handmaiden. But I do not like them. I am sorry, Jesus. I know that it is wrong, but I cannot help it. I hate them because they hate You and are frightened of You and wish to do You harm. I wish I never had to see them again, any of them. I wish I never had to answer another of their questions. I am sorry that they beat You. I will never forgive them, though I know that too is wrong.

'I know why You have chosen me. Because no one could ever love You as I love You. I am Your little doll. I give myself to You without question.'

Her tiny voice chimed on and on.

'And I know why our friendship must be kept a secret. Or they will kill You like they killed You in the Bible. And then we could not be together. If not for them we would live in this valley together. As best friends. But we must be careful, Jesus. I think I would die if anything happened to You' – she cried ah think, for ah could hear her little sobs as she spoke – 'just close my eyes and die.' And she let fall a heavy tear, and it passed through the slats and exploded upon mah face, just below the right cheek. And as the droplet began to roll, ah caught it with mah tongue. And ah was shocked momentarily by that tear's sweetness, having known them only as bitter things – only bitter things – always bitter things.

'You come to me, Jesus, in my dreams. I am sitting on the steps of the monument, where I was left by God when he stopped the rain, and I hear something behind me and I turn around. The stone angel has come alive and Jesus, it is You, with big white wings and sickle raised above Your head – Your sickle of blood – Your mark. You see! I understand everything. And Your beautiful hair hangs down past Your shoulders, and Your beautiful eyes so full of love. Not a word do You speak, but all Your wounds are bleeding.

'Please, Jesus, don't be angry with me. I am so sorry that they hit You. It hurt me too. First they tell me to love You, then they chase You away. This world is too cruel for us.

244

'What is Your world like? It must be beautiful and quiet. A place of understanding where there are never any questions. Will You take me there? To Your beautiful world?'

Beth fell silent. Ah listened to her footsteps retreat and then come scurrying back. Then urgently, 'Here they come! Please, Jesus, stay there. Don't speak. Listen. Memorial Square. Celebration Eve. I will await You.'

Ah heard the sound of a vehicle – of two vehicles – come screeching to a halt. Then the sound of running feet, heavy, adult.

'Beth! Beth! It's Daddy. Are you hurt?' called Daddy.

And then more hurried footsteps, only heavier, slower. And a weird ticking of wheels.

'Let her go, Sardus Swift,' came a hawking female voice. 'This has gone too far! No! Don't protest, Sardus. If you cannot control the child then we will have to find someone who can. Hilda, put her in the car. She will stay with me tonight.' Ah could hear the company retreating, but the ticking of wheels and the clumping footfall dallied a little and another female voice, deep and supremely stupid, drawled, 'Well, Wilma, now do you believe me? Or do all of Christ's brides wander about half naked in the middle of the night?'

'Shut up, you fool,' replied Wilma Eldridge in a venomous whisper, and her words sent a chill right through me. 'Whether or not you caught someone in the child's room last night is not the point. That has happened. It's out of our hands. What is important, dimwit, is that no one finds out. Now only me and thee know about this incident, which means that if I hear so much as a hint from anybody else then I will know who went and opened her big mouth. Do I make myself clear? And believe me, Hilda, sparks will fly if I do. Understand? Now stop standing there nodding and wheel me to the car.'

Ah shuddered in mah crawlspace as the whining wheels faded – tick tick tick squeak, tick tick tick squeak – and the two conspirators joined the others.

Angry engines, motor sounds. Fading. Fading.

*

You know, sometimes God reminds me of the misunderstood ogre with the heart of gold, who lives in friendless isolation behind his mountain, who is feared and shunned by all who live unner his shadow, but who unbeknownst to anyone performs deeds of great kindness – like blowing a raincloud out of the path of a princess. But the people can only see his bad side, when overcome by frustration and sadness he stomps out a few towns. But if the people would just stop and see his good side and encourage it and be his friend and ask him to come and live with them in the town, then he would stop being frustrated and sad and would have no cause to harm them at all. But, oh no, they wouldn't. They didn't even try. Did you?

For example. Swampland is one big, sound-proofed circle of vegetation. Enter swampland, even only a few paces, and you will come to notice the utter absence of sound. The swampland has its own language – a little groaning, a little creaking, a little gasping for air. But as ah sink into this plashy circle of quickmud, it is important for me to hear the progress of mah executioners, lest ah lose track of time completely and simply fall away. Well ah can hear them! Ah can!

And that is the God-given beauty of it. Listen.

Ah can hear cars. Cars and pick-ups. Ah can hear their horns blaring, their avenging engines revving. Ah, mah executioners. Mah killers. They are converging on mah shack.

Ah can hear their shouts right now, at this very moment, carried on a boreal wind over the swampland – this fortress of trees and tangled vine – and down into its hypaethral capsule of mud – this bogdom – this murky kennel – this coop into which ah am disappearing – melting, melting away.

They are confused by the presence of the great wall that surrounds Doghead – confused by its daunting dimensions and its ferocity.

Bang! Now they are trying to break down the gate. Bang! Now they are ramming it with a vehicle.

Ah hear a c-c-crash. Thanks to God and his big heart.

Two things have happened. Just as ah planned they would.

First off, they have broken down the gate.

Secondly, they have pulled all the wire-mesh fronts off the cages in the process. Ah rigged up a simple device, last night, using a few pieces of rope and some pulleys. Now they have some kinda trouble. Believe me. Now they have some kinda trouble.

Mah dogs! Ah can hear the sinister music of mah dogs. Ah can tell that they are mah dogs and not theirs because no dogs sound like mah dogs. Mah dogs do not bark. No they don't. When mah dogs bark, they whine – a chilling, high-pitched hummance – one long extended note but very loud. When they are hungry, mah dogs, and ah mean blood-hungry, they pull back their lips and bare their mangled teeth and from deep within their knotted bodies comes this weird sound – all at different pitches like some eerie satanic canting.

There is fury in the air. Ah can hear it from here. Evil radar. Mah dogs are sending some very unfriendly transmission. Making bad waves. And it ain't no hamster that they're looking for.

Oh bounty-hunters. These are *mah* dogs. Hobbling from their kennels to meet you.

As the eastern flank of the valley smarted with the new day, the fading night could be seen to crystallize, infused with minute greyish grains of visibility, and it was into that semi-obscurity that ah dragged mah crucified body from beneath the bridge.

Looking back at it, ah marvelled at the neat little funk-hole ah had found, fashioned by the very hand of God, for He had surely poked his little finger into the damp earth, pending mah persecutory flight and subsequent hiding out – hidden behind a wall of thorn and bramble, impervious to all but me – the one who has lived a life of briar and thistle, whose every path was choked with nettle and thorn, he whose very head was crowned in the stuff.

Ah stood by the creek and plucked fat grey slugs from mah naked body, and ah was touched by the way each slug clung to mah skin, holding on for dear life with their big fluted feet and producing a soft smacking sound as ah peeled them off.

'Does a kiss feel like this?' ah thought, as ah placed the slugs carefully on a handkerchief ah had laid out on the ground. And ah thought of Beth and how she had stood on the bridge above me in slippered feet, and ah imagined the breeze pushing the thin fabric of her nightdress against her body. For a moment ah thought of going back to the crawlspace, but dismissed the idea just as quickly, as ah didn't have a lot of time left before the citizens would be out and about – and ah intended to be well and truly inside the confines of Doghead by then.

Ah tied the corners of mah handkerchief together, hooking the weighted pouch of kisses from mah belt buckle, then set off by way of the creek, following it up to the refinery, then round the back of the crops, leaving the creek to meander up the side of the valley. Ah approached Doghead from the east, and instead of walking around to the front gates ah entered mah Kingdom by way of a secret door ah had fashioned in the wall, just in case anyone had staked the place out and was waiting for me to return. You can never be too careful when you're playing for keeps. That was one of the first things God told me.

The secret door was based on a simple horizontal winch system that hoisted a corrugated-iron panel set in a modified window frame – like a guillotine – just enough to crawl through comfortably. Once ah had disconnected the net and the leaping pitchfork – ah told you about the leaping pitchfork, didn't ah? – sure, sure, of course ah did, it's one of mah favourites – so simple, but what terrible potential! – and had crawled through the wall unscathed, and once ah had watched the corrugated panel close behind me and the steel skewers rise up from the ground and all the booby traps had been re-set, and once ah had sauntered down to the still and filled a bottle with the last of the brew, rolling the two empty barrels against the wall for added fortification and scattering the piles of cold ash about the place, yes, once ah had done all that, ah walked blithely over to the old Chevy, leaped up on the bonnet, took a deep and well-deserved slug of the Jesus, kicked mah boots high into the air and banged them back against the battered bumper, did it again, kick bang, kick bang, kick bang, slugged Jesus again, rocked forward, putting mah head between mah knees, fell backward so ah lay on mah back upon the bonnet, kicked up mah legs, banged down on the bumper, rocked forward, fell back, kicked up, banged down, rocked, fell, kicked, banged, rocked and rocked, laughed and rocked and laughed and laughed and drank and rolled and fell and laughed and laughed and laughed and laughed and said, 'Atta boy, Euchrid! You made it. They tried, O how they fucken tried, but they didn't get you. O fucken no. They fucked right up. Yes sirree, they fucked right up!'

And ah stood on the bonnet and climbed on to the roof and, still laughing, ah took another slug at the bottle, then began jumping up and down, hard and loud as ah could, yes, up and down – bang, bang, bang, bang, spinning mahself around and around – saying, shouting, 'That's right, you stinking fucken cunts! Come and get me! Ye-e-e-a-ah! Ye-e-e-a-ah! Beat me down! Beat me down! Ye-e-e-a-ah! Just try and fucken beat me down!' And me thrashing the whole fucken world with mah giant sickle, heads rolling, heads rolling down, rivers of blood, sewers of gore, oceans of the wicked, headless, limbless. Slash! Slash! Mass extermination, mass death, mass bloodshed, by mah hand. Slash! Slash! By mah own hand, slash! slash! at mah own slashing, silver, sickled hand.

And suddenly, from the corner of mah eye, ah saw it – a flash of scarlet smeared down the back wall of the shack, and the sight of it damn near knocked me over. Someone had infiltrated mah sanctuary, mah Kingdom, mah refuge, and left a hideous sign of their trespass!

Ah climbed down off the roof of the Chevy, mah eyes riveted to the wall, took another slug from the bottle, corked it and walked bravely forward.

It took some seconds before ah realized what it was.

'They have chosen to violate mah property, and there is simply nothing ah can do about it,' ah thought. 'Nothing.'

And a multitude of chattering voices, imps and gnomes and trolls gnawing at mah brains, needled me with their solutions. A solution.

Ah scooped up a hammer all covered in blood and ah gripped the handle tightly in mah fist.

'They come and mock openly without fear of reproach. Soon they will tire of it all and stop with their toying and simply put an end to me. They will come here – three, four, ten, twenny, ah don't know, but they will come and kill me. If God had not willed it that ah spent last evening unner a bridge instead of here, then it could have been me they nailed to the wall,' ah reasoned.

And ah took the hammer and prised the three six-inch nails out of the crucified she-bitch and let the stiffened decollated carcass drop heavily to the ground, rolling on its back in the blood-hardened dust. Its front legs – arms – had been splayed outward unnaturally, while its hinds had been broken at the thigh and lay in the dust at impossible angles like the hands of a clock. Ah did not find its head until later that evening, bludgeoned to paste and alive with ants at the bottom of the incinerator.

By that time there was no turning back. Some major decisions had been made. Some serious instructions had been received. Ah had no choice but to comply.

To be? Hmmm. To not be? To be not any more? Ah'm not asking you a question – ah sink therefore ah am! Yes? Am. Am not. Am not to be? Ah mean, what would your advice have been? What measures would you have taken if you were in mah boots, ah wonder? For me such eschatalogical deliberations are a grievous waste of time. But all the same it's funny how the value of seconds rockets the moment you decide to sell out. Don't you think so? Hello? Still, ah haven't traded in all mah coupons. Ah still have a few last grubby moments left to be. Mah arms and legs and torso and genitals and hands and feet – they are all warmly gone, never to be seen in their earthly form again. Never to be seen. Never to be. In short, ah am nearly not. And while this limits mah range of options, severely, there is still the odd decision left to make – like to sink, or not to rise? To blink or not to – one moment – miasma – burning mah eyes – gotta close

them for a while – shit, damn – and the pressure on mah chest –
one moment – one moment, please –

*Euchrid stood in the yard, mouth agape, stupefied, breathing in short,
shallow gasps. The headless dog lay in the dust at his feet. He looked like
a trained circus chimpanzee with his captain's jacket, his question-mark
stance – a performing ape in some gag involving a bloody hammer and
a stuffed dog. He nudged the dead weight lightly with his foot, then,
rocking a little, leaned back and, turning his eyes to the sky, bared his
teeth and hissed like an animal.*

Ah stormed around the yard, ma– . . . angry as hell, gnashing
mah teeth and swinging the hammer at the thousand imagined
faces that hovered there before mah eyes, smashing the skulls of
mah tormentors like eggshells – all the gloaters that sought to
stand in mah way. Ah broke their fucken idiot faces to bits. But
it gave me no relief. Even as ah lay flat out in the dust and closed
mah streaming eyes and looked on like some higher being at all
the spilling thought-vengeance that mah head played host to, ah
found no cause for comfort, found no cause for any comfort
there at all.

And after a time, the boiling sea of blood and all the lopped
and all the hacked-up humanity that swam within it drained from
mah head, and from it rose a pillar of chaogenous calculus, cold
and hard. And some serious weighing up of terms ensued. Yes,
there, supine beneath a bold and brazen sun, ah struggled with
some pretty eternal, some pretty adult problems. Listen.

*Then, swinging the hammer wildly, Euchrid ran about the yard,
ducking under the skins and pelts, running to the great wall of junk
and listening, ear pressed up to mute tin, dumb plank, dead brick.*

Ah cast mah mind back to that – to *this* dark place, where nothing
grows that isn't twisted, where nothing exists that doesn't twist
– mah heartland – the swampland – mah dim sanctuary. Ah
thought of mah bridal chamber where mah guardian angel was

so long ago invoked – the temple of mah tokens, mah treasures, mah solitary pleasures. There, in those darksome quarters, ah had passed away one thousand hours, secure in the absence of man, away from the mock and the savage, safe from the beat-downs. There ah had indulged in harmless congress with mah invocations, mah fetishisms, in peace.

Then Euchrid began pounding the wall with his hammer, stopped, heard something, and ran across to the other side of the yard, booting a jaw-bone as he went. Pressing his ear against the wall, he listened for any outside sound, began pounding the wall again with his hammer, chopping the air with his teeth.

But they sought me out. They did. Into the swampland they came, trespassing without hesitation. They came to violate. They came to rape. They came to sully mah last shred of self. They went and smashed mah grotto down. They scattered mah tokens like unwanted things. They scared away mah supernal bride. The cunts.

And Euchrid was off and running again, past the leash-pole and the training wires, to listen again at another part of the wall. Pitchforks, pointed sticks, pieces of brick and sheets of tin all trembled at perilous angles above, all the booby traps perilously trembling.

Ah had never been able to find, in that holy shelter, the same state of transport again. Instead ah grew spines. *Doghead.* God's work. For in violating mah sanctuary, they had violated God as well. He was not pleased, ah can tell you that.

Euchrid staggered back from the wall a few paces and clapped his hands over his ears, then turning he fled into the shack, the slam of the front door resounding over the stillness.

And, although ah built a fortress and enclosed mah humble shelter within its great wall, still they came, and still they will continue to come, on and on, to lay their snares and to set their traps until ah am thoroughly dead and even then they will jig on mah grave, dig me up and kill me some more.

Euchrid burst through the front door and on to the porch, the shotgun cradled in his arms. The shotgun was wrapped in newspaper, and the paper was stained with large brown spots as though the gun itself had bled into its wrap. He stood on the porch, his legs apart. Jaw clenched, he spat into the yard, then marched briskly down the steps and strode across to the great wall, ripping away the paper as he went. He pointed the gun at the spot where he had last stood and brought his eye up to the sight. The sun had climbed higher into the sky, and all about him shadows pooled as he stood aiming. There was no sound, within the Kingdom or without. Euchrid lowered the gun and walked across the yard, past the leash-pole and the training wires, to the other part of the wall where he had stood listening. And again he raised the shotgun and pointed it at the wall, and again he lowered it and did not shoot.

And still ah went on thinking. How will ah die? How will ah go? Ah cannot destroy all of them, so what will ah do? Shall ah just wait for them to kill me? To crucify me too?

Euchrid looked at the shotgun, turning it in his hands. Tears rolled down his cheeks. He had scared himself.

Or is there a better way? A nobler way?

He bowed his head and walked inside, still turning the shotgun in his hands. The door slammed behind him. Final.

Ah walked up the steps and opened the front door of the shack. The door slammed behind me. Kind of final.

And . . . and inside . . . and inside . . . you know, it's hard for me to admit this, to come right out and say it, but ah will, ah will . . . inside mah shack, there in front of mah subjects – O

for shame, for shame at mah lack of spunk, mah lack of pluck –
and me, their terrible master! Yes, there with all mah dark-eyed
subjects playing audience, ah took some certain steps to end it
all. Yes, *end it all*. To defer mah celestial mission *permanently* and
for all time, and in doing so deny mahself mah seat in Paradise,
mah place in the Kingdom of God. And ah can barely remember
even doing it.

Ah entered the shack. Right. Ah remember that. The slam of
the door. But what happened then was lived by some other part
of me, some part that isn't telling, for the next thing ah recall
ah'm down on mah knees with the shotgun clamped between
the jaws of a pig-trap and both its barrels jammed in mah mouth.
Ah knelt there a while, peering down the length of the shotgun.
Ah noticed a taut line of twine attached to both triggers and
running the three or four feet to the doorway, where it was tied
neatly around the doorknob. Ah guess ah was waiting for a visitor
to come and kill me. An intruder! Yes! For ah was convinced
they would come. Ah had heard them there, behind the wall. Ah
had. 'So let them come,' ah thought. 'Let them come. What's
good enough for mah deadtime is good enough for mah living-
time too. Come on,' ah thought. 'Ah'm waiting,' ah thought.

And ah waited. Ah did. There, on mah knees. One. Two.
Three hours, until mah skull split, teeth ached, jaws cramped.
Yet still ah waited, sucking death, for someone, *anyone*.

And they came. They did. Only not through the front door.

They – it – *she* was just there, and very gradually, very won-
drously revealed.

First ah became aware of a faint flimmering of light behind
me and to mah right. So stealthily did it encroach upon mah
awareness that ah could not pinpoint the very instant of realiz-
ation. But first it was the light, that is sure. A silver-blue effulgence
unmistakably supernatural in its nature. But if it were not the
light, if it were not that, then it was the glow of shifting wings
and the rank gusted air that stormed suddenly and whipped up
the floor trash – the paper, the shavings, the gauze strips, the
feathers, the moulted fur. And if it were not any of these things,

then it was the voice, yes, the voice that betrayed the identity of mah erumpent, mah shuffling, mah extravagant caller.

'Remember, Euchrid, there *is* a sin unto death,' came a voice, and gingerly ah slid the barrel out of mah mouth and turned mah face toward it. Could it be? Could it be . . .

Mah angel. Mah long-lost guardian angel. Mah straight and guiding hand. And O how wonderful, how awesome was her blaze! Ah climbed to mah feet and stood before her. Stiff, ah stretched, arms raxed outward, and ah beheld mah winged theophany. Glory! Glory!

'You have not yet been summoned. Withhold yourself, for the time of your calling is ripe. There is corrupt fruit to be plucked. Do His work, justly and goodly, and you will be thuswise received,' she said, sort of chiming. And ah noticed that sometimes mah angel seemed to be clad in clinging veils of web, while other times she wore nothing but her teasing pinions, opening them wide when she spoke so as to reveal to me all the luminary delights of her body. Then, lowering her crown of golden locks, she would draw silent, wrapping her wings about herself like a sleeping bat or a blue flame, when ah gathered she tuned in on some Godly advice – instruction, warning, or whatever.

And ah inclined mah head and closed mah eyes and listened, and slowly came the pulse of His voice, the double-beat, the low chant and its portentous climb – the time is nigh the time is nigh the time is nigh, it said – and ah wondered as ah deciphered the chant, nigh for what? And word by word, chant by chant, instruction by instruction – go down to the town go down to the town go down to the town – God spelled it out for me. And in time ah learned the business of mah existence, plain and simple – dressed in your best dressed in your best dressed in your best dressed in your best. And with His most precious portent God illuminated the grinding darkness that had whelmed me all mah life, and ah saw the way in which *mah* life – *mah* cog – slotted neatly into another smaller cog from which an axle turned that sprung a mechanism which, in turn, ignited a tinder attached to a long wick that fizzed and spluttered down to a pyramid of red sticks – till death us do part till death us do part till death us do part – *Boom!!* Till death *Boom!* Till death *Boom!* Till death . . .

KILL BETH BOOM!

And so ah began the preparations.

'Screeeeeeeeeeeeeeeeeeeeeeeeeeeeee . . .'

Ah ground the sickle's screaming lip into the whirring whetstone, pausing to catch mah breath and to sprinkle a little water around. Then leaning into the spin ah resumed grinding, pumping at the treadle furiously and feeling a trifle uneasy that the sickle had kept screaming all through the breather, irrespective of the simple laws of logic. Sparks spat at mah guiding hand. The winch belt whirred up its own rolling rhythm, and ah sat huddled over the bucking contraption as the entire machine whirred and creaked and shogged, until the sickle grinned evil in mah fist, screaming-keen and sharp enough to skin shit.

All sun and no wind and the air hazed in the heat. Ah slashed mah way across the yard to the great gates of Doghead and mah mind jabbered and rhymed, as it so often did. God surged through me as ah razored the space before me – the blistering, the stifling, the still, still breath kill Beth kill Beth kill Beth.

Ah climbed up the gate and looped four lengths of rope to the four iron hooks that ah had screwed along the top of the gate earlier. Then ah followed the lines inside, checking as ah went the forked posts that kept the ropes aloft and tapping the ropes occasionally with the flat of mah sickle for tautness, making sure the steel eye-hooks held fast in the doorframe. And lastly, kneeling by mah panting tea-chests, ah checked each rope was securely fastened to its kennel's wire screen.

Each cage was a wrestling knot of expectancy. Ah had instructed mah beasts earlier on their pending release, their mission of death. Ah had explained to them that the laurels of Glory lay in the spilling of blood, and they had drooled hate as ah clued them in on the enemy. And as ah briefed them on the rudimentary aspects of unarmed combat – go for the throat, bark a lot – they sharpened their fangs on the wire screens and low growls rose deep in their throats. 'Kill for your King and die for your God. You will find Glory in the spilling of blood,' ah told them, and it was then that the fearless brutes began their blood-curdling whining, their freedom song, their serenade of sadness for all of brute creation, yoked or harnessed or bridled or locked in bestial dungeons or scumbered tea-chests filled with straw.

Ah know that you did well, mah hobbling death-squad, ah know that you did well. To die with the name of the King on your lips, what greater honour could there be? O glory-bitches of Doghead, ah cannot hear your music any more. How was ah to know that they would come with guns? May the cage of bestial paradise be opened to you. Your King is well pleased. He is.

That was yesterday, you unnerstand. O yes, past time is rushing, fast approaching, racing and racing toward me. But let it come. Ah'm ready for it. Ain't afraid of it. Ain't afraid to die.

Anyway, later that day – yesterday – mah chanters were working mah thoughts, sending them to me in irritating sing-song couplets – get some rope – string and twine – wool and wool – fencing wire – electrical cords – fishing line – gather them up – all you can find – tie them together – in a long line – ain't much time – ain't much time – fucken brains! Idiot rhyme . . . it's enough to make you lose your . . . Shit! Fuck! Shit! Shit! Shut up. Shut up. *Shut up!* And in frustration ah booted a tea-chest that sat in the corner and out of it spewed just that – lengths of rope, balls of wool and string, ribbons and belts and a couple of pairs of old bracers, strips of sheet, old bandages, even a kite tail, so ah figgered ah had more than likely been collecting this stuff for some time. They were already tied end to end. So ah coiled up what was to serve as a lifeli– . . . a deathline – and headed for the swampland. Reaching its edge, ah tied one end of the line to the vine-burked bole of a tree that stood on the outer perimeter. Then, using the compass from Captain Quickborn's chest, ah proceeded in a south-south-easterly direction, uncoiling the line as ah went.

Ah thrashed at the denser sections of vegetation with mah sickle and ah thrilled at the ease with which it pared all that sought to obstruct mah path – which was not a great deal actually, for it seemed that a pathway of sorts had already been fashioned, and for a while ah was pleased to have struck a natural contour in the umbrage that so conveniently maintained a south-south-easterly slant. But soon ah became aware of the damaged foliage and the trampled unnergrowth, suggesting an animal of some kind had made the track. Putting mah powers of observation to the test, ah surmised that the beast was large and travelling at a furious rate as most of the twigs and vines were broke clean off. In time the answer dawned on me and ah felt a surge of relief at having solved the riddle.

Ah followed the pathway right to the inner perimeter of the swampland, to the edge of the bog, and secured the other end of the line to the trunk of a tree there, thinking that it was sure as hell funny the way the line of belts and wire and string and rope happened to be exactly the length required to make a direct line from the outside of the swampland straight into its heart. Anyway now ah could get within from without in the shortest possible time by just following the line, hand over hand. And just as ah was about to leave ah turned, crouched, and sighted one eye along the deathline – and anyway, two things happened at approximately the same time.

First off, a niggling little voice inside mah head said, 'That fucken skew-bald, saw-boned antique came galloping through here over six years ago. No spooked-out flea-bitten nag cut up this path!'

Ah bent down and picked up a severed twist of vine and examined the cut. It was whistle-clean. A little green. Even a touch sap-damp.

'This track has been forged in the last few days,' ah thought, and ah threw the cutting into the air and slashed it in half with the razored hook of mah sickle before it hit the ground. Ah was confused and frustrated, angry at mah stupidity and feeling as though there were influences at work beyond mah control, working silently and insidiously.

'Something else did this,' ah thought, checking the path for further clues, 'some other animal. Some different beast.' Then it dawned on me. Yes it did. 'A wild fucking boar! A razor pig! That's it! A swamp hog with a really sharp tusk!'

Ah turned quickly, making to leave this place before mah mind had the chance to contest the wild-boar theory. And it was then the other thing happened.

The outer-ring of the swampland appeared as a series of dark cringing silhouettes, distorted by occasional shouts of daylight, and so it was not until ah was nearly upon her that her silhouette took shape and broke forth into form. The perimeter's harsh light scattered shadows, and mah head swam and crackled, set alive by her brightness. Flanked by two logwood boles, green with creeping death, the ghost of Cosey Mo appeared unto me.

She reached out and bid me come unto her.

Ah could hear the tendons hiss beneath her skin. Ah felt tears upon mah cheeks, upon mah chin. Ah tasted them. Ah could not tell from whom they'd come. Her breasts pulsed with the stridor of a mad heart. Her fingers traced a ticking vein. She lowered me within the network of exposed roots, showed me the slickness there. She passed her mouth along the cobbled heap of mah spine, whispered words against the crooks of mah arms, drew shallow throats of air. She placed the lacquered tips of her fingers against the numb cartilage of mah throat, and, encouraged by the faint vibrations there, ah made a bid to speak. And ah do believe a word then passed mah lips, but with all the yabbering echoing in mah skull the word was lost for ever. One word and the spell was broken and the ghost began to fade. Her body blended with the dimming surrounds, and despite the intensity of mah embrace, somehow she slipped from it, called back to where ah now go.

Ah felt cold and dirty and sick down amongst the knuckled interclutchment of tree roots, but ah made no effort to rise and collect up mah clothes, all of which ah . . . all of which she had removed in the frenzy, and which now lay draped about the place. Craning, ah searched for mah sickle. Ah found it in mah left hand. Mah right – mah kill-hand – crackled with the waxen leavings of ectoplasm and ah wiped it on a clump of knotweed. Ah gripped the sickle now with both hands. Ah stared up at the virescent mesh – the garlands of creeper and vine. The canopy seemed to be in a continuous state of flux, swollen and alive. Ah felt as ah had when ah was a mere boy, hidden beneath the bed covers, naked and utterly shamed, striking matches and . . . ah squeezed the sickle tighter and mah knuckles glowed bloodless and white. The air grew fumid, nauseous. Ah began to shiver, to shudder involuntarily. Something was contaminating mah insides – bad juices, sulphur leaks, bitter acids, bile. Mah breath soured. The great logwoods, centuries old, groaned and creaked. The insidious creepers hissed, shifted. Mah hands tingled, sweated copiously, and ah could feel it trickle down mah wrists and drip on to mah belly. Ah watched it pool there, blood-red and warm. Mah stomach heaved in sudden disgust and ah vomited across mah left arm. Ah gasped like a fish. Ah sweated red everywhere.

Ah spent last night – *the* last night – perched in mah turret, looking out over the valley, watching the creeping night swallow up the township as one by one the house lights died.

Strange was mah mood or mah shifting of moods. It was like mah heart had begun to turn slowly in its cage.

Climbing the steps to the turret, ah felt exhausted and more than a little edgy, having hauled six of the larger trip-snares across the marshes, floating them on two tyre tubes and lugging them into the swampland. There the ghost of mah father had appeared. He had flitted from tree to tree, keeping his distance as if he were afraid of me. He called instructions to me, which were only just audible because of the space he insisted on maintaining between us, but ah made them out to be, '*Murder her!*' and '*Stab at her!*' alternately. Mah initial response was to ignore him and so ah had set the traps and sought to leave that place of ghosts and God.

Ah had thought of turning back and confronting him, and ah even did take a few steps toward him in order to breach the gap, but in doing so ah perceived more clearly the nature of the old man's bark and ah changed mah mind and fled, leaving the tyre-tube raft behind me and scrambling across the marshfields, the turn of his words burning in mah ears.

'*Murderer! Saboteur!*' Each syllable charged with venom and echoing through mah head, through mah bowels, as ah climbed into the turret.

'*Mur-der-rer! Sa-bo-teur!*'

Ah reached into the pocket of mah jacket in search of a handkerchief to wipe mah brow. Ah found there a child's little white glove and ah laid it out flat so that it covered the wounds on mah right hand. Ah inspected it. Ah held it close to the spirit lamp. It was clearly Beth's glove, and it seemed to me to be the whitest thing in the whole world.

Ah remembered a dream ah had had. Of a glove. Of Beth. Ah squeezed three grimy fingers into the glove, and just before closing mah eyes ah glimpsed a slick, taut sky of the deepest blue, the moon a bloodless, flesh-coloured gash in its infinite expanse.

And mah heart turned, awash on warm waters then tossed on the shores of disgust. Ah opened mah eyes and looked again at the glove and all the whiteness seemed to have gone, smeared like everything else ah could see, everything else ah fucken touched, and ah noticed a rich crimson spot appear in the very centre of the glove, then grow in size and intensity, until ah had to cup mah own hand lest the pooling blood spill over. Ah bound mah hand in a handkerchief.

The glove. The blood. The moon. All signs not gone unheeded.

Ah flung the messy glove over the wall.

Ah looked down at the town and a cold stake of hate brought mah heart to a standstill as ah thought of the devilry Beth had done there. Thought of the devilry Beth done there. Thought of the devilry Beth done there.

And so passed the night, like that.

*

Down below – in the valley – all hell and ferocious vaultings of fire raged, sweeping through the cane-fields at a tremendous rate. A gusting south-westerly blew. Roaring walls of flame hissed and crackled, fouling the firmament with voluted bloats of evil black-green smoke.

Ah saw the valley as a great lake of dark oily blood, and me, sickle gleaming between mah teeth, taking elegant swooping dives into the claret, describing scarlet arcs through the steaming ether.

It was morning. Late morning. Celebration Day. The 'burn-off' had begun.

One crow, stranger. Two crows, danger. Three crows, a summons.

A gang of four black hecklers perched at equal distance along the sole dead bough of the gallows-tree. *Four* bad black birds!? Four? *Double-danger! Double-danger!!*

Mah beasts paced, prowled in their cages.

This is the day! This is the last day!

Ah stretched mah arms outward and then upward, and as mah body fell prey to an excruciatingly delicious muscular cramp, ah allowed mah arms to flop to mah sides, mah body folding forward into breathless relief. Ah love cramps usually, but this one left me exhausted. Ah felt spent. Ah felt weak and sick and dirty.

Gradually the day's business dawned on me and no longer did ah feel just exhausted and weak and spent and sick and dirty, but ah felt pretty doubtful as well, doubtful that mah reserves of courage were sufficient for me to unnertake such a terrific task. Ah mean, Christ knows, ah was no more capable of killing Beth than ah was of killing one of mah own flesh and blood – unless ah be fuelled with a little of His strength and determination, of course.

So, ah climbed down from mah turret – never had those steps been such a slow and serious obstacle – and began to limp and ache mah way through the shack.

Did ah tell you that mah beasts paced, prowled in their cages? And did ah tell you how they all fell silent when ah entered their

262

quarters, and all about me ah saw dog-eyes wink derisively, fangs and flews snickering, how ah could smell the cold mockery of those brutes fill the sunless room? A blood-shitting anger coursed through me – a blood-shitting anger and a fearful shame – and ah threw mahself at one particularly smug kennel, kicking it all over the room and throwing it and striking it with mah bandaged fists and jumping up and down on it until the tea-chest split wide open and a swarm of blowflies rose from the opening like a dirty brown cloud. Smirk gone, the dog cowered at the bottom of the cage, covered in slimy straw and scared stiff, making no attempt to escape, even to move.

Ah walked a tense circle around the room offering the remaining beasts the chance to ridicule me, but not a peep sounded from their kennels and hutches and coops and cages. Nor could ah see the laughing eyes or the jeering dog-teeth any more, and to tell you the truth, ah let out a sigh of relief as ah stepped on to the porch, glad to be out of there, the silence being a little too silent, a little *too* respectful.

Ah threw mahself down the porch steps and fell to mah knees in the middle of the yard, wringing mah hands and beating at the sky and wailing and reeling in the red dust and petitioning the Almighty with perfervid prayer.

Ah left Doghead a little before midday, covered in red dirt and still damp with the morning dews. Mah cheeks were raw and drawn and salt-stung. Mah wounds throbbed beneath the gauze bandages and ah hoped to hell they wouldn't open up and become a problem. As if the palm wounds weren't severe enough impediment, ah had badly barked mah knuckles while meting out dog-pain that morning and ah could feel them weeping and seeping and sticking to the bandages even as ah strode down the track toward Maine – toward town – *toward her* –

Rolling eructations of black smoke rose from the fields in thick, fat coils. They moved across the colourless sky and gathered together in the valley's south-west corner like a herd of fretting buffalo. Fields yet unlit, heavy with the crop, rustled excitedly as they awaited the fiery lustration that would purge them of trash, whilst walls of flame romped hell-like through others, the scorching fire dying by way of its own paroxysm as suddenly as it had leaped alive, leaving the sky filled with wind-whipped cinders, sparks and flakes of black ash. Those crops already put to fire stood in silence, black and smouldering. Men coated in soot jockeyed around the perimeters of the crops, shouting oaths and orders into cupped hands. Groups of moon-faced children stood in craning clusters on the side of the main road, hypnotized by the fire, by its fastness, by its effervescent fury. Already the children were smudged and smeared by the very air that engulfed them. Trucks and trolleys moved slowly back and forth.

So entranced were they by the fires sweeping the fields, none of the townsfolk noticed Euchrid, dressed in a filthy over-sized naval jacket, sickle slung through his belt, as he hobbled down Maine. His eyes shivered and his sick, cachetic complexion was smeared in muck and blood. Hanks of greasy hair stuck to his face. Both hands were swathed in dirty gauze wraps. As he walked he hunched over nervously, peering through his hair, suspicious of everything – of every sound, every shadow, as he scrambled along the roadside ditch behind the clusters of children watching the burning fields.

God put blinkers on them. He did. He blinded them to mah progress – or rather *we* blinded them, such was the pure force of mah determination, the sheer power of my intention. Yes, and ah *strode* down that road.

He passed under the city-limits sign, crawling along the roadside ditch as it grew shallower, arriving at last at the gas station. The streets were nearly completely empty. The womenfolk who usually filled them around this time were busily preparing for the banquet, either cooking in their kitchens or helping set up the Town Hall, where everyone would eat before spilling into Memorial Square for the singing and dancing and fireworks.

Euchrid slipped up the bank and squatted between two petrol pumps. He surveyed the street before him, and finding it empty he crossed and disappeared into a wedge of shadow, coffin-shaped, thrown by the hedgerow. Every six or so feet a picket broke up the hedgerow, making a small gap in the shadow so that the blocks of shade gave the impression of many coffins, lids open, arranged end to end, all down one side of Maine. And Euchrid hopped from one to the other, casket to casket, like an illusionist involved in a macabre folly of deception.

The wind was forcing all the smoke from Hell down over the town and the visibility was a touch on the caliginous side as you might well imagine – yes? – well, anyway, the more ah ventured into town the more caliginous it became. Ah mean it was nothing compared to the great all-engulfing fogs that would come rolling over the sides of the valley in the winter months, but, even so, the very nature of the air now had the power to transform the ordinary, the commonplace, into something else altogether – something queer, unearthly, eerie, ah found. Everything was a little dim, a little obscure, and this was at once a bane and a blessing, for whereas they couldn't see me, ah couldn't see them all that clearly either.

Still, ah crept along, doing mah best to maintain mah confidence – to ignore the tricks of the air, of the light, of the shade, of the smoke, of mah eyes, of mah ears, of mah nose, of mah mind, of mah mind and of mah mind.

Clutched shadows made suggestive humping motions behind things, but faded from sight before ah could disentangle their thrusting forms. Ah saw a glistening arm gripping a machete covered in blood and flies appear from a belch of smoke. Ah ducked, but it was gone. Ah heard the whistle of a blade slashing dim air, and ah thought ah felt the same air fanning mah cheek. Ah heard the hum of flies, coming, converging, growing. Ah crept on, keeping low. Ah passed an ancient cast-iron horse trough full of scummy water. Ah parted the skin of slime with the tips of mah fingers and peered in. At the reflection. Mah head appeared like it was being ambushed by tiny black flies. Mah face, mah hair, mah head, mah eyes, mah mouth, mah mind, all infested by tiny black flies, and then the water was disturbed by a very fast silverfish on the rise. For some reason, ah recalled the time ah found the corpse of a skinned puppy on our junk-pile – its four little paws had been tied together with copper wire – ah was six years old. Ah scrambled over the steps of the Town Hall undetected. Ah could hear the women nattering as they worked. 'They sound like flies,' ah thought, 'and ah guess that's what they are.' Ah crawled unner the hedgerow that formed a fence around Memorial Square.

Ah peered through to the other side, surveying the grounds, the monument, the playground, but there was no one there, no one there at all. And ah guess ah drifted off for a bit, as ah waited there, unner the hedgerow.

Beth entered the Memorial Gardens by the wrought-iron gate, opening and closing it behind her like she was entering a vast marble hall, and she gazed up at the smoke-filled sky with a kind of awestruck intensity, as though it were a fabulous ceiling that stretched above her. As she made her way across the Square, birds twittered nervously, but to Beth's ears the sounds came rather as songs of confirmation, fortifying her belief that this day, above all others, would hold the key of understanding, and that the thousand baffling questions that HE alone could resolve would be answered. For Beth, everything about her – the sun, the flowers, the trees, the wind, the birds – all seemed to augment this belief, that on this day HE WOULD COME – to make her see, yes, and make her know.

For how long had Beth been subjected to endless, convoluted explanations of her 'divine pendency', of her 'preparation', of her 'numinous destiny'? How often had she heard the women speak in low voices of 'the tokens of virginity' or 'the odour of sanctity' – words that loomed monstrously in her mind, that took bestial forms and haunted her sleep?

Now, sitting on the monument steps, dressed in a gleaming white cotton smock, a chaplet of pale violets woven through her curls, with the great marble angel, girded and male, hovering over her like a thought, Beth appeared dwarfed by her own grandiose imaginings. She clutched to her breast a crude cross made from two broken wood slats and she murmured a song beneath her breath.

It was late afternoon and the townsfolk had already begun to break bread in the Town Hall, and Beth knew that her time alone in the Square was limited, and that soon the people, having eaten their fill, would be spilling from the Hall into the Square to continue the night's festivities.

But Beth waited patiently, there upon the steps, content in the belief that He would come.

And on the other side of the gardens, down by the Town Hall, under the hedgerow, Euchrid lay upon his back with his eyes rolled back in his head. The collar of his naval jacket was meshed in spittle strings and his tongue hung from his mouth coated in red dust.

Ah woke to a child singing and scrambled to mah feet. Ah felt weird standing there. Ah felt – ah felt strong. Yes. Ah felt full of – of motive. *Motive.* Yes! Ah felt strong and very fucking full of motive. Ready to go. Ready to move. Ready to rip. Yes. Ready to rip.

And ah removed mah boots and slid them unner the hedgerow.

'There is a sleepy river I know
Down that sleep river we go.'

Beth grew silent. She squeezed the wooden cross to her breast and closed her eyes and she sat, just so, on the monument steps, head inclined slightly as if listening for something.

A full minute passed.

And then she drew a short breath and, trembling, smiled.

Shoeless, ah crossed the Square to the monument. Beth had fallen asleep it seemed and ah congratulated mahself on such a stroke of luck as ah mounted the four stone steps on the other side of the great marble angel and unslung mah sickle. Ah sidled around the statue until ah stood behind her, towering over her.

Ah raised mah sickle high into the air, tightening mah fist around the handle.

*

*At last Beth opened her eyes and the smile was in them too, but there
was something else in those green eyes, something akin to wonderment,
expectant and reverential. And, with her thin fingers clasped around
the rough little cross, the child turned, arching backward and as she
did so a billow of purple smoke rolled down from the fields and engulfed
the tableau of flesh and stone.*

*Beth gazed up. She saw Euchrid. She saw the angel, chiselled from
marble. She perceived the uncanny echo in their attitude, of pose, of
purpose. She saw one, winged, bone-white and suffused with grace,
and she saw its fleshy manifestation, impennous and wretched and
covered in muck. And she saw his wounds, his long hair, his naked
feet, his palpitant breast. And she saw a faint, new evening moon slung
in the sky and a syzygy of sickles, upraised high, and Beth lifted one
trembling hand to her mouth. And, staring up at Euchrid's mad face,
she spoke.*

And Beth woke up at that point and swung around. She fixed me
with her eyes and then she spoke.

'At last, Jesus, You have come.'

And it was as if those words sprang a trigger inside of me,
because mah heart just burst. And such was the rush of blood to
mah head that ah started to reel on mah heels, spinning wildly,
and ah could feel the blood pouring from mah nose, smell it,
taste it, feel all mah wounds opening up, hear the chanters going,
going, feel the nerve running from mah hand – mah sickle hand
– so that it began to shiver and shake and ah stumbled and ah
steadied mahself and ah put mah sickle inside her.

Ah had placed mah boots on the crushed and eaten body of a
lark and they were teeming with a family of tiny red ants, so ah
left them there beside the hedgerow, and wearing nothing on
mah feet but the dust from the road ah took off down Maine,
heading north.

Back inside Doghead silence prevailed. Everyone was lost for
words, it seemed. Ah had demonstrated the effectiveness of direct

action and suddenly words seemed futile – idle confabulation, mere procrastination.

Mah Kingdom was one very fucking hushed arena, that is true, but it was far from being asleep. Expectancy and anticipation charged the air with muted urgency, like everyone was holding their breath, and walking across the yard ah could smell the electricity in the atmosphere, taste it. The booby traps trembled with restrained energy. All about me things pended release. Pitchforks, skewers, snares, saw-teeth, nets, all seemed ready to leap, impale, plunge, slash, stab, rake or drop. Ah made a quick check of them and then climbed up into mah turret.

Ah manned the scope.

The air was warm and windless. The fields had ceased smouldering and although most of the smoke had drifted from the valley the sky appeared tainted and the underbellies of the clouds discoloured.

Pungent wafts of rot drifted up through the trap-door, and ah pinched mah nose lest ah gag, taking the air orally, and reluctantly. Ah wondered how the beasts could stand it, living like a lot of pigs.

Ah foked the scope on the Town Hall, and just as ah had expected the townsfolk were still engaged in their feastings. But ah calculated that it would not be too much longer before the great oaken doors would swing open and the enemy would saunter down the front steps and into Memorial Square.

Ah pointed the scope at the Memorial Gardens, drawing it down toward the blurred white shape that ah recognized as the monument. Ah screwed it into focus, dragging the structure of stone neatly into mah one super-eye, sizing up the scene in its entirety before zooming in for a more detailed appraisal. In this moment of clarity ah was struck by the effect of the new addition to the tableau and the sight of the angel and the child, and by the sublime relationship set up between the two, as if the one depended upon the other, like good and evil, Heaven and Hell, and indeed, life and death. Each illuminated the other by virtue

269

of its essential difference. And ah pondered that idea for a moment as ah studied the monument – the very embodiment of this notion – the flesh and the stone – the erect and the super-incumbent – the upraised sickle and the sickle brought down – the pooling shadows and the puddling blood – the Heaven-sent and the Hell-bound – the caducity of flesh and the endurance of stone – the frailty of one and the other's enduring might and, y'know – well, ah don't really know how to say this, but – well, ah mean, *that thought* – yes, that idea seemed to me, at the time, like one very fucking bright and beautiful thing to think – yes, it did – and what with the living proof of the simple beauty of it there before me, ah found mahself getting hot in the face and kind of puffed up and ah bit mah lip and ah found mahself choking back the tears, and saying to mahself, 'Stay brave, Euchrid. This is not the time to come apart.' Saying, 'Unner no circumstances will ah cry. Unner no circumstances will ah . . .' And ah sobbed but once, then embarked on such an unbridled bout of weeping that ah thought mah heart would explode, so fucking God-swollen up with – not sadness – O no, not that, no – the tears ah so furiously wept were tears of – of – of *pride*. Yes. *Pride*. And you know, it is mah guess that this is the unique feeling enjoyed by those who exist only to achieve *Greatness*, to achieve greatness despite the odds, even if they must pursue it to the grave. This day ah had proved mah rightful existence beyond the petty dictates of ordinary men, and ah wept proud waters, tears of greatness, rivers of salt and glory.

Up jumped mah heart! For now the gardens were swarming with people! All about the monument, yes, all about her, all about and all around and all over the fucken place they gnashed their teeth and raged and wailed and beat their breasts, and ah saw a man, sharp and dark, his face all twisted up and frenzied, lift Beth's limp little body from the steps and draw the sickle from her body.

Ah knew that it would be only a matter of minutes before someone recognized mah trademark, mah sickle. And indeed even as ah looked a figure swung around, and stretching out its

arm dramatically pointed its finger straight at me, at mah eye –
and all the mob turning, all, and all the mob looking up at
me and screaming for blood, all, all screaming at me for blood,
and ah said, and ah said it's time, and ah said it's time to move,
ah said, *it's time for me to move.*

*And even as Euchrid climbed from his turret and scrambled through
the garbage and filth that covered the shack floor, a dozen rattling
utilities and bucking pick-ups careered down Maine toward him. In
each vehicle men crouched and bounced and grimaced into the gritty
rush of speeding air. In each hand was an implement held as a weapon.*

Ah bade mah Kingdom farewell and the silence in there told me
mah subjects were fit to tangle – ready to rumble.

And suddenly there was peace in the valley no more.

Suddenly the air was hijacked by pirate violence – every sound
amplified and infused with threat. All the infernal static – all their
shrieks and shouts and oaths, the roaring, the gunning of motors,
the rush of their coming, of their coming *in outrage* – rang terrible
in the air. Terrible. Even the clamour of mah retreat was like
thunder-drums. Mah breaths were rushing, ringing clouts to the
ear. Mah heartbeats – why, mah heartbeats were outrageous.

*Having crawled through a hole in the wall, Euchrid paused a moment,
looked once to the vehicles that came charging along Maine, then
once again took flight. Bootless, he tramped through the marshlands,
following a vague trail already coursed. Bulrushes knocked at his knees
and he left them rocking in his wake, inverted pendulums anchored in
their reeky, paludal bottoms.*

*Reaching the outer boundary of the swampland, Euchrid turned and
took one last look at the wall of red dust that moved steadily toward
the shack. He removed his jacket and hung it from a tree. From the
same tree he untied a length of rope and followed the line of wire,
string, strips of sheet and chain into the trembling spissitude of the
swampland, reeling in the line as he went.*

*

But the moment ah breached the threshold of the swampland, the queerest absence of sound prevailed and mah flight became dreamlike, rhythmical, painless. Ah felt as though the line that ah followed, hand over hand, was, in fact, attached to me – that it was a part of me, and that *ah mahself* was being reeled in – that *ah mahself* was being called home.

Arriving at the gates of Doghead, Sardus Swift leaped, from the front seat of a pick-up, Beth's smock bundled under one arm, the murder weapon in his hand. He raised the blood-glazed sickle above his head, and, in a voice shrill with rage, commanded Euchrid to come forth. Already sweat-soaked cane-men were attaching tow-ropes to the gates. An order was given to stand clear, followed by an angry gunning of engines, whereupon the great gates of Doghead were torn from their hinges.

The mob stormed the yard, their farm tools poised awkwardly over shoulders and above heads, pitchforks and long-handled hay-rakes held straight out in front like lances. They charged into the space defined by the bizarre wall of reconstructed junk.

Even from the yard the stink of death should have been intolerable, but the rage that consumed them was a blind kind of rage, and so strong was their collective anger that the queer contraptions, the rigging, the obsessionals, the booby stakes, the flags, the poles – all the flights of fetish knocked together to construct the absurd kingdom of steel and plank and rope and nail and bone and skin and blood – inspired no horror, no outrage, nor even wonder in the hearts of these men – just as the foul stench that wafted from the shack went unrecognized as the mob clambered up the porch steps and charged headlong inside.

The bright fingers of their torches probed the dark interior. The turbid air clung to their faces like warm wet skin and all about them was revealed an appalling vision of bestial and human filth, of gangrenous crawling carnage, of death piled upon death.

And it was only then, inside, that the sickness became apparent, and rage shrank back and grew clammy and cold. The men swatted wildly about their faces and panicked at lumps of flyblown meat hung from the ceiling, tripping on piles of soiled bedding and screaming at the death, screaming at the death and the rats screaming back. And the men fled the shack, blundering across the porch and lurching over the rail to disgorge their festal supper across the clumps of sun-shrivelled periwinkles that grew below.

But the screaming was for inside. Outside no one spoke. And from the shack came the work-song of the flies – a relentless whine, high and strange.

Though no order was given, petrol canisters were opened and splashed about the shack, and in silence the men stood together in the yard as they watched the shack become a vast crematorium before their eyes, witnessing the sky seared by hungry flames a second time that day.

Two men came running through the gates, shouting.

'We found his trail!'

'He's in the swampland!'

And the crowd all turned. And the crowd all cried out.

Ah eased through the inner boundary of the hypertrophia, into the clearing – the girdle of unvegetated terra firma, no more than four paces wide at any point, that encompasses the circle of quickmud. Ah was bereft of all robing and in a state of nature and mah body was covered with a legion of new welts and wounds, nettles, spines and thorns and blotches of ivy irritation.

Yet the pain is perfect, for the warm mud is so completely soothing to mah crucified flesh, that that which passes out of life is relieved of its suffering, whilst that which remains within merely hurts.

Death is the poultice to the pain of Life – that's mah news to the world.

And ah stood there before the bog, sweating salt into mah wounds and consciously suffering the pricks of mortality, that mah death be that much sweeter – and it is! *It is!*

In town, in Memorial Square, women clad in black prostrated themselves, while others reeled about on bended knee, gnashing their teeth and execrating the heavens. Others stood chanting, frozen, as if hypno-tized, and others still simply ran in blind circles, beating their breasts with stones.

The glass in the prophet's sepulchre had been shattered and his white robe shredded and strewn about the grounds. Three women slogged at the marble monument with mallets.

In time ah began to circle slowly the awesome muck, taking step over painful step, observing the way of the quag and noticing subtle undulations and shifts of tension upon its surface – sullen, soundless contractions, a slow building swell, then a sudden retraction – indeed, a clench – and ah saw the ringed swamp as a sinister, annular muscle, and this threw me into a state of fear – of doubt.

Walking a complete circle around the bog, ah drew to a halt, inclined mah head and folded mah fingers together, as in prayer.

Ah prayed.

And then – and then ah knew exactly what to do.

Full of God, ah stepped bravely out and gently lay mahself down in the very centre of the circle, in the mire's eye. Upon mah side, knees pulled up to mah chest, head tucked in, ah was secure, sainted, unborn.

The clamorous mass that bulldozed its way across the marshlands appeared in the uncertain light of dusk to resemble a giant black beetle with many thrashing, tramping beaters going, returning to its sinister nest. But once the crowd had entered into the swampland itself, it was hard to imagine that it had ever existed, so thoroughly was it absorbed into the darksome terrain. It was only the crushed and trampled rushes, and the three carrion crows that circled beak to heel above, that betrayed there ever having been any trespass at all.

You know, as ah go below – and really ah am so nearly almost gone – all that remains is mah head, and perhaps the very crest of mah hump – ah can hear them coming, yes ah think ah can. All the trees about me, why, their heads are veiled in fog, inclined toward me – inclined toward me like ah am a source of light, a luminary. O could it be that ah am glowing, even now?

And once inside the confines of the swampland, the mob beat and hacked a blind trail – blinder now, for their rage had by no means tempered and their road to revenge had become a bright and blinding one – but no matter, for the bog brought them miraculously on, drawing them toward its threshold.

Is it you, Death? Is that you, Death, there behind me?

Crashing into the clearing they come, from all sides, heaving and panting from fear and from rage and from blindness. They had come for his head and this, of course, is all they will get – but time is against them. They must work fast.

Look there, up above me. See the heavenly hemisphere? Notice the way it curves around me, like ah am the middle pin! And the trees, see how they too lean toward me!

And now. Look! Up there. Great grape-coloured storm clouds moving single-file across the empyrean plains. O ah know, ah know, they are the souls of the dead marching out to greet me. See? Look! The spooked nag! Hear its beating hooves.

A series of leaden nimbuses cross the dome, gathering at its northern extremity then sealing off the clearing as cloud piles upon cloud.

From above, the clearing looks like a cattle brand, seared into the hide of the world. Makeshift weapons point at the central pin, at the one they hate, like so many broken spokes.

A bolt of lightning leaps from the sky like the finger of God, to point at the circle of men and charge them all with a stuttering blue light.

The heavens bark and the mob in turn look toward the turbulent skies to read the heavens and to absorb their significance. One word is written across every gaping upturned face – rain – the return of rain, the return of too much rain.

*

And lo! Ah can see Mule. Ah can! Watch how proudly he high-steps across the heavens. Now there's your dignity in death, sir! There's your just reward! Spine straight, coat brushed, head high – O long-suffering life, there's your fucking prize! And there, look, coming up behind, mah loyal subjects, mah beasts! See the parade of innocents, winged brute creation, marching across the firmament to await the advent of their King. See them all falling into their ranks.

For some a mere glance at the sky served to alert them to the oncoming threat, and no sooner had they looked up than they were looking down again, their fury rekindled – for ah brought the rain, ah *brought the rain – for it was, after all,* HE *who brought the rain.*

O now ah know, now ah know what's happening.

Here she is descending. The shifts of breeze tell me. The blue effluxion, the flutter of wings. O mah winged protector! Mah guardian angel! Is it you? Is it you, come to carry me through the gates? Can you tell me? O can you tell me? Can you tell me what's happening?

They pour gasoline from canisters.

O weeping angel, do you cry?

Euchrid strains his dripping chin upward.

Will they sound the trumpets? Roll the drum?

The empty canisters crash about him.

Ah, here they are! Death's lights!

Epilogue

Dark was the night and the township of Ukulore cringed beneath a merciless rain.

Doc Morrow battled to save a life, while a group of five women waited anxiously in his office for reports of his progress.

The door opened and an ashen-faced Philo Holfe entered, his tired eyes cast downward.

'Well?' demanded Wilma Eldridge.

'He may have to choose,' replied Philo Holfe.

'He has had his instructions,' said the cripple, turning toward the window to contemplate the downpour outside. 'There is no choice.'

Inside the surgery the doctor battled to save a life – to save two lives. It was Beth's life for which the doctor so earnestly fought – her life, and another's.

'She is a strong child,' said Hilda Baxter. 'Look at what she has already survived.'

'But she has never really recovered from the accident,' said Widow Roth.

'Accident! By God, it was no accident,' barked Wilma Eldridge.

'Just like her father was no accident – or have you convinced yourself that he *fell* into the swamp?'

'Can you blame Sardus for that, Wilma? He thought that Beth had died.'

'We each have our cross to bear. Our lives are a test,' replied Wilma Eldridge without mercy.

But the doctor could not save both lives, nor was there any choice. Emerging from his surgery, a man at low ebb, wan and grey and barely able to support the weight of the bundle that he cradled in his arms, he entered the office.

'The child lives. It is a boy.' And holding out the bundle he added blankly, 'The mother died in labour.'

'He is born,' said Wilma Eldridge, her arms outstretched to receive the infant. 'As the prophet predicted, He is born.'

And with the babe in her arms and the rest of the women huddling around, the cripple folded back the swaddling rug with one finger. A thunderbolt leaped from the teeming night sky and the craning sisters ruckled and clucked at the tiny infant face that stared up at them with shivering, pale blue eyes.